Black Apple

By

Lawrence Bell

ISBN: 9798673238431

PublishNation

www.publishnation.co.uk

Special thanks to Mr Colin McMorris for his advice and his diligence. And above all, for his friendship.

Author image by Ania Pankiewicz Photography (www.aniapankiewicz.co.uk)

Chapter 1

In the United States of America on the early morning of Tuesday, September 11th, 2001, four passenger aircraft were simultaneously hijacked by terrorists.

Two of those planes were then flown into the North and the South Towers of the World Trade Center complex in Lower Manhattan, in New York City. A third plane then crashed into the Pentagon, the United States Department of Defence, in Arlington, Virginia.

The fourth plane was originally flown towards Washington DC, presumably intended to be used to attack the White House. But it prematurely crashed in Shanksville, Pennsylvania, after the passengers took the brave and heroic decision to try to thwart the hijacker's attempts.

The plane then crashed and all onboard were killed.

Everyone onboard each of the four hijacked planes was killed. No one survived.

At the World Trade Center Complex, and after burning for almost an hour, the South Tower collapsed. And approximately forty five minutes later, the North Tower also collapsed.

The attacks caused the deaths of 2,996 innocent people, including the lives of 343 dedicated fire fighters.

More than 90 different countries lost a number of their citizens, irrespective of their nationality or religion. Dozens of innocent Muslims were also killed in those September 11th attacks.

The youngest victim of the attack was a child, just two years old, the eldest victim was aged eighty five. It was also reported that at least eleven pregnancies were lost.

Like the ripples in a pond, thousands of lives were affected that day, along with thousands of families. There were children who lost their parents, and there were parents who lost their precious children, no matter what their age was, and along with all the would-be parents who would never have the promise of children of their own.

So many lives, all so cruelly extinguished.

That one irrevocable act of shame, that one disgrace to humanity, was brought about by the so-called evil preachers of hate.

And those terrorists, those, the misguided who were all so fundamentally culpable, all of them indoctrinated and lied to by the dishonourable and the so very self-righteous.

Yes, those preachers of hate, living their own selfish lives with no regard for anyone else, blind to the good, and to man's true ability and our capacity to help others.

To all you evil men, so devoid of any regard or respect for your fellow man and to man's true capability. To all of you, at some point, you may have to explain your actions to your God...

Thousands of lives were ended that day, and with it there were a thousand different and very personal stories.

Here, perhaps, are a few of the possibilities.

Chapter 2

'Why is it that love can break a person's heart?

Why can being in love bring with it all the misery and the heartache that can crush someone's every fibre and make them turn away and weep with despair.

The loss of another, that one person loved, in truth, is more than just the loss of a friendship. To never again experience something as simple as that other person's touch, and with it the end of the most intimate of conversations, a man and a woman, two people together.

And a love lost, and a pain so unbearable. It is enough to bring even the strongest to their knees, ever confused and upset, distressed, and gasping for breath. To be left behind with all the memories of better times, and still be there, begging for more.'

The place and the date...Barcelona, Spain...Mid-year, 1999.

Adam Tyler had spent the last two years, living and working in Spain.

Adam lived in a stylish third-floor apartment, located on the Carrer Rosell, in the well respected Eixample District of central Barcelona.

From his very elegant balcony, Adam would regularly sit in the early morning sunshine, sipping a first cup of bitter black coffee, as he looked directly across to the 'La Sagrada Familia', the uniquely famous church which Antoni Gaudi began to build in 1883 and is still unfinished to this day. A truly magnificent obsession, it was possibly Antoni Gaudi's own personal addiction.

Adam Tyler was in his his late twenties, and he was tall and amiably good looking enough to be considered 'reasonably' quite handsome. Adam had been transferred to Barcelona by the Santander Bank in London where he'd worked for the previous three years.

3

Adam Tyler was sharp, very sharp, and he was clever. And he could also speak fluent Spanish, something that had always been somewhat of an asset to him. And when the Santander Bank had asked him to consider the possibility of taking a post in Barcelona, Adam had jumped at the chance. It was a promotion, definitely, and it paid well. And Adam Tyler was nobody's fool. He knew that in the world of banking, once you were offered an opportunity and turned it down, you would never be asked again. Simply put, you were either on the way up, or down, and 'down' usually meant that you wouldn't be employed for much longer and that your career in banking was basically in the trash can.

However, that would not be a problem for Adam. He had no real ties. He'd lived in a flat in London, which he rented, and his family lived in Devon and he saw them occasionally, but there was nothing that actually tied him there either. And there was always the telephone, of course.

He'd had girlfriends, but they'd somehow breezed in and out of his life and never bothered to overstay their welcome, something that Adam had found vaguely disconcerting but had managed to put to the back of his mind. For Adam Tyler, career came first. There would be plenty of time for women and wives later, but there was still a somewhat nagging realization that as the years quickly ticked by, he'd hardly had one serious relationship with anyone.

It seemed that he'd forever met most of his girlfriends at drink-fuelled parties or on late evenings in some bar or at a pub. Young women, who were drawn to Adam by his good looks, his dark hair and his athletic build, and also the possibility of his very promising career at the Bank. However, as with the alcohol, the effect somehow wore off, if not a little too quickly. The problem being that Adam would always put his work first, and his girlfriends second. Something that they all too quickly realized, it was almost a callousness.

There had however, been one girl, there's always one. And she was Miss Joanne Berkley.

Adam had met her in his final year at Winchester University. He had been taking degrees in Business and Finance Studies and Spanish language, whilst Joanne had been studying Art and

4

History, she was in her second year. By chance, or a twist of fate, Adam had first met her as he'd been walking through the University grounds on one sunny afternoon. It had been a beautiful summer's day and Adam had become bored and rather annoyed with his study group and some of the people in it, and he'd decided to go for a walk before he ended up having an argument with one or two of the more pretentious students in his class. Adam was becoming somewhat exasperated with the antics of some in his group, those fellow students who were only at University because their rich and affluent parents needed to do something with their offspring for a couple years, before those same 'children of privilege' could then go off on their obligatory 'gap year', the essential twelve months of travel and partying, and/or possibly even longer. And all because they evidently, 'so' deserved it.

The problem for Adam, was that he actually wanted to get some work done because he really needed to obtain his degree. And trying to study with people whose main input into the group was the recurring topic of 'where' they were going that weekend, and where they'd 'been', and with it of course, the all too predictable 'relationship' update. It all drove Adam mad, and it was an irritation that slowed the group and resulted in a loss of direction. And on that particular afternoon, Adam had thrown up his arms in despair and had slammed out of the room, leaving some of his fellow students with raised eyebrows and shrugs of total incomprehension.

And that was how he'd come across Miss Joanne Berkley.

As he walked through the University's beautiful grounds, he'd come to the inevitable conclusion that he would have to study alone, and then he thought about some of the more serious students in his group and he considered that maybe he should talk to them and that they could form some sort of smaller splinter group. These were the students who, like him, needed to obtain their degree. And so with that in mind, Adam's mood lightened slightly, there were still possibilities, and as he continued to stroll through the university grounds, he began to appreciate his surroundings. The sun was shining and it felt good to be outdoors for a change. Something that he'd had little chance to do of late.

Miss Joanne Berkley was sitting in the shade of a large oak tree. In front of her was a small easel, and Joanne was drawing a picture, not of her present surroundings, but from an old colour photograph that was pinned onto the edge of her canvas. She was drawing using pastels, and at the side of her on a small folding table was an oblong tin containing fifty or so multicoloured pastel pencils, each one placed in its own particular colour and shade group.

Adam was walking along in no particular direction, and as he strolled towards a cluster of shaded trees he suddenly realized that he would not be on his own. His actual intention had been to quietly sit down there and to take off his jacket and prop himself against a tree and think things through, and then maybe have a short nap in the warm afternoon sun. But no, the privacy he was looking for had already been invaded, a rather self-seeking attitude, until his curiosity then got the better of him. He stopped and he stood there for a moment, watching a young girl, another student presumably, as she carefully pencilled in coloured lines which she then diffused by rubbing the colours gently with her forefinger. It was all quite fascinating. Adam knew nothing at all about art or painting, the last thing he could ever remember about drawing was at primary school with crayons. And then he recollected his smudged attempts at watercolours as a teenager at his local grammar school, and the ever dissatisfied art teacher who would shake his head in despair as he crumpled Adam's worthless masterpiece into a ball and once again dispatched it to the wastepaper bin.

Adam stood there, and he looked at the girl. He was standing directly behind her and all he could see was her long, light brown hair which fell over her shoulders. There were streaks of blonde in her hair, it was really quite beautiful.

And in a moment of curiosity and uncertainty, he suddenly blurted out the word...'Hello'.

His timing was not good.

Joanne Berkely was at that moment applying a thin line of cobalt blue to her drawing, but Adam's uninvited interruption completely startled her and she almost gouged a line in her canvas and with it managed to snap off the end of her pencil. She immediately spun around and glared at him.

'Oh damn it...thank you very much,' she exclaimed.

Adam immediately held up his hands as some form of explanation, along with an excuse.

'Oh, I'm really sorry, I didn't mean too...' he tried.

But his words had already fallen on deaf ears. Joanne Berkley had quickly turned back to her drawing. She put the broken pencil on her table and was using a small cloth and an eraser rubber to try to remove the rough and unwanted stripe of deep blue colour.

And thankfully it was working. Adam just stood there in silence, and he watched as the surplus jagged colour slowly disappeared.

After a couple of minutes, Joanne sighed.

'There, it's done,' she said, almost to herself.

'I...'am' really sorry,' Adam said to her, and he immediately felt that he was interrupting her once again. But this time Joanne turned to him and then she smiled.

'No harm done,' she replied, 'you just startled me, that's all. I thought I was here on my own.' And then she looked at him curiously.

'How long have you been standing there?' she asked.

But Adam just stood there looking at her. He said nothing for a moment, he was slightly taken aback. Miss Joanne Berkley was actually very beautiful.

She stared back at him. 'Excuse me...Hello?'

Her words suddenly broke the spell, and though he was slightly flustered, Adam managed to quickly divert his growing embarrassment.

'I...I was just looking at your drawing. It's really very good. I hope I've not spoiled it. I am really sorry.' And then he gave her his little 'I'm guilty' smile, the smile that he'd always used since being a small boy. And it worked. Joanne Berkley again smiled back at him.

'It's okay, it's fixed now,' she said, and she relaxed somewhat and turned back to her work.

Adam looked at her drawing. It was the portrait of an elderly lady. The woman in the portrait had silver grey hair and a soft complexion and the most enchanting deep blue eyes. She wore a very dark dress, almost black, and around her neck was a

7

stunning necklace, and pinned to her dress was a matching brooch. The necklace and brooch were inlaid with blue sapphires, almost the same colour as the lady's eyes. Adam then noticed the old and slightly worn photograph that was pinned to the top corner of the canvas.

'I thought that you were out here painting the view,' he said.

Joanne turned around once more.

'No, actually I was drawing...'

But Adam interrupted her...'Your grandmother,' he replied.

She stopped for a moment and looked up at him, slightly bemused.

'And how did you know that?'

Adam stared down at her.

'Because you have the same very beautiful blue eyes,' he said to her.

It was an obvious compliment, but a compliment that worked.

Joanne Berkley laughed, she was actually quite charmed. However, she was nobody's fool, well certainly not to a young Adam Tyler anyway. But it was a start. And she looked at him and suddenly realized that the young man who was disturbing her artwork was actually quite good looking, in a youthful sort of way. But it was his observation that slightly intrigued her. He'd seen her drawing and he'd seen the photograph of her grandmother, but in that first instant he had also noticed the blue of her own eyes. And she liked that.

They chatted for several minutes, and then Adam excused himself, with the pretext that he 'didn't want to interrupt her any longer'.

That left Joanne on her own once more, and she continued with her drawing. But somehow her mind was now elsewhere, and she suddenly realized that she was still smiling.

The next day, Joanne again returned to her retreat in the shade of the oak trees. It was another sunny day and she once again set up her easel and continued to draw her grandmother's portrait. She liked it there, nestled between the trees, it was peaceful and quiet and away from the bustle of the University. Joanne had always found it preferable to draw or paint on her own. When she worked alongside her fellow students, she'd realized just how

8

easy it was to become drawn into the different conversations with her friends within her art class. Joanne was popular, she had many friends, and there was always the regular gossip. However, all that chatter could also become a distraction. But here on her own she could concentrate and get on with her work.

Two or three hours passed quickly, and by then Joanne had completely lost track of the time.

Suddenly, she realized that someone was walking towards her, a young man appeared, he was about twenty yards away when she spotted him over the top of her easel.

He was grinning as he walked towards her. It was, of course, Adam Tyler.

'Oh, hello,' she said to him.

'Hi,' he replied, and then a bit sheepishly, 'I thought you'd be here.'

Joanne frowned at him and smiled at the same time. Only women can do that.

Adam then continued, 'I learned my lesson yesterday, never to surprise you. It can be detrimental to your work,' and he laughed.

Joanne looked up at him and she chuckled.

'So you've learned that lesson then?'

'I certainly have,' he replied, 'please consider me severely reprimanded.'

He looked at her, and yes, she was really very pretty. In fact, he'd spent the most of the previous evening thinking about her, and the best part of the morning.

'I've brought you some lunch as a peace offering,' he said, 'I hope you like tuna sandwiches?'

'Oh right,' she replied, ' I do have a flask of coffee and some biscuits, I usually just snack.'

'Ah well, today we can feast like kings and queens,' and he laughed again, 'and I've brought a flask of coffee too.'

'Oh, so its 'we' is it. It's not just for me?' she taunted him.

Adam shrugged, he was still smiling, but now it was time for the truth.

'Well, actually I'm having a bit of a problem with my study group at the moment, in fact, they're all driving me mad, and I need a bit of space and I need to rethink things. That's why I came here yesterday. I just wanted a bit time on my own.'

'And then you ended up with me?' Joanne laughed.

'Yes well, you certainly took my mind off things. I'd just stormed out of my group.'

Joanne put down her pencil and reached for her bag, which contained the flask and the biscuits.

'Okay, come on then,' she said to him, 'I'm about due for a break.'

Adam sat down on the grass and he took out the sandwiches and his own flask. And they talked. Joanne told him about her own problems with the people in her own art class and hence the need to be there on her own. And straightaway they had a common bond.

They ate, and they talked. It was relaxed conversation, easy and interesting for both of them and without any awkward silences. The best part of an hour passed and most of the food and the rest of the coffee were consumed. Adam finally stood up.

'I'd better let you get on with it,' 'I've probably wasted enough of your time.'

'No, it's been nice,' and she smiled.

'Do you want to do the same tomorrow?' he suddenly asked her, 'it'll be corned beef sandwiches tomorrow.'

Joanne burst out laughing.

'Yes, okay. That would be nice. You do really know how to tempt a lady.'

'Of course I do,' he replied, and he picked up his bag, 'I'll see you tomorrow then.'

As he walked away, Adam grinned to himself. It was a start.

And Joanne watched him go. She didn't know where all of this was going, but she had a fair idea.

The next day Adam returned, along with the promised corn beef sandwiches and another flask of coffee. Joanne was pleased to see him, and there was no awkwardness between them, none at all. This time Joanne sat on the grass at the side of him and then she produced a small box of cakes from out of her bag.

Adam laughed, 'this is turning out be a bit of a picnic,' and they both laughed.

At one point, as Adam was talking to her, Joanne's hair fell across her eye and she instinctively, or more by habit, shook her head sideways to move it out of the way. But Adam just leant forward, and as he continued to speak to her, he gently pushed her hair to one side.

And there it was, their first touch, so simple. Joanne said nothing, she just looked at him.

And at that moment Adam Tyler stopped talking. He looked into those deep sapphire blue eyes and he took a deep breath.

'Miss Joanne Berkley,' he said to her, 'you are so stunningly beautiful.'

Joanne looked at him, it was the moment, and they both knew it. And Adam leant over to her and they kissed. Their first kiss, the deal done.

From there they became a 'couple'. And Adam's life took a subtle twist. He stopped taking life so seriously. Sure enough, he had to finish his degree, but he stopped being so critical about everything. He returned to his study group and became quite happy to again, work alongside those fellow students who at one time completely infuriated him. He simply carried on with his studies, knowing that he would be spending yet another wonderful night with the beautiful Miss Joanne Berkley.

And all was going well. On some nights, Adam stayed at her flat, and on others, Joanne stayed over at his. Yes, all was going swimmingly well. Adam had even thought about asking her to move in with him. After all, it was on the cards. But after them being blissfully happy for the best part of three months, Joanne Berkley dropped the bombshell.

Joanne rang him up in the middle of the afternoon, she sounded quite elated.

'I need to talk to you,' she'd said eagerly, 'I need to talk to you about something.'

Adam, on hearing her, totally misread the situation.

'And I need to talk to you too,' he replied, and he'd laughed. He thought that Joanne was in fact going to ask him to move in with her, or whatever. Because wherever they lived, it wouldn't actually matter. Just as long as they were both together.

So they arranged to meet in one of the local pubs at tea time.

11

The 'White Bull' was a rustic old pub which sold good beer cheaply, along with fairly decent food at the 'right price' for the many penniless students who regularly frequented the place.

Joanne and Adam met up there at five o' clock, and Adam went straight to the bar whilst Joanne grabbed an empty table in the corner. He ordered his usual pint of beer and a glass of decent white wine for Joanne, and he then went over to their table and sat down. Joanne was full of smiles.

'Go on then, what is it?' he said to her, knowing what was coming. Adam was inwardly quite happy, this was going to save him the possibly awkward task of asking her if they could live together.

But no, not today.

'I'm going to Australia, Adam,' she suddenly blurted out.

He looked at her for a moment. What she had just said to him didn't sound quite right. And for a brief moment, he just didn't understand.

'What' he asked her again, thinking that he'd not heard her correctly?

'I'm going to Australia,' she said again, and again with an excited smile.

Adam just stared at her.

'What do you mean, you're going to Australia...When?'

'Probably in about two week's time,' she replied enthusiastically.

'What do you mean? Are you going on holiday?'

'No silly, I'm going to go and work over there.'

'Work..?' Adam said to her, 'and how long for?'

Joanne looked at him strangely for a moment.

'How should I know? A few years I suppose, if all goes well. And if it all goes really well I might emigrate over there, it's a great lifestyle. I'll be based in Sydney.'

'Stop for a moment, Joanne', he said to her, 'just explain to me what's going on?'

And in front of his very amazed eyes, she started to babble excitedly.

'I got a phone call this morning from Steve. He's in Australia, in Sydney. And well, the Advertising Company that he works for are looking for a talented artist to work in their graphics department. Steve...'God bless him'...mentioned my name and recommended me as an outstanding young talent, and you wouldn't believe the money they're willing to pay me, it's phenomenal. Steve says that he'll help me to find an apartment and that I can stay at his place until I find somewhere. It'll be wonderful.'

Adam was utterly stunned.

'And who is this...this 'Steve', he then asked?

'Oh, he's my old boyfriend. Have I never mentioned him before? He's a darling really, we've always sort of kept in touch. You know what I mean?'

But no, Adam didn't know what she meant. Not one bit.

'And what about your degree, and what about University?'

Joanne just shrugged. 'What about it? University and a degree is just a good way of getting a job. And even with my degree, I'd have to start at the bottom of the ladder somewhere. This way I can leapfrog my way to the top. And if I can make a success of it the sky's the limit. I'll be working for an International Advertising Agency. And if I can make a name for myself there, well, who knows? They have offices all over the world, I could work anywhere. In fact, I could work for anyone. The big companies are always on the lookout for talent.'

Adam just stared at her, somewhat in disbelief. He suddenly felt that he didn't know the girl sitting in front of him anymore. It was a though he was talking to a stranger, not 'his' Joanne.

And at that point, the whole question of him asking her to move in with him seemed like a lost cause, a sad mistake.

And then he asked her the one question. It was desperate, and it was pathetic, or so it seemed.

'But what about 'us', Joanne?' he asked her.

Joanne looked at him strangely.

'What do you mean, Adam,' she replied?

'Me and you...together. You must know that I love you?'

Joanne just stared at him. And now she was looking at him as though he was someone that she didn't fully understand, either.

'Me and you?' she said suddenly. But actually, it was more of a question.

She looked at him across the table.

'What did you think this was, Adam,' she continued? 'We've both had a great time, but that was it, a summer romance at University, that's all it's been. It's just been a 'fling', Adam, and a bit of fun, but that's all it was ever going to be. I thought you knew that.'

Adam just sat there. He felt humiliated and he felt stupid. How could he have been such an idiot, and how on earth could he have got this all so wrong?

And like thousands of men before him, who'd found themselves in the same awkwardly dismal situation, there was only one remaining thing to do. It was a last attempt, a final grasp at trying to retain some form of personal dignity.

He slowly stood up and then he looked down at her. She was still looking at him strangely.

'Goodbye, Joanne,' he said to her.

And with that, he turned around and quietly walked out of the pub.

Adam finally arrived back at his flat, still somewhat bewildered. He sat down on the end of his bed, the same bed that he and Joanne had shared and had so many tender and wonderful moments. And then he realized that they would never share this bed ever again, and that he would never be with her ever again. And his flat suddenly seemed a lonelier place, and at that moment he felt the sudden pang of deep despair. He'd lost her. And as he sat there, his eyes began to blink. The hopelessness of it all, and there wasn't a damn thing he could do about it. And then suddenly, a single, stupid tear ran down his cheek.

It had all been a lesson learned, and though it had all happened a few years ago, it was a lesson that Adam Tyler would never forget. Time is a great healer, and Adam made the decision that he would never be fooled again. However, only time would tell.

Adam Tyler was enjoying Barcelona. Living there had opened new doors for him and with it the opportunity to live a completely different lifestyle. The people of Barcelona lived life to the full and also lived to a completely different timescale. Everyone seemed to be more relaxed and were somehow that

14

little bit happier in the workplace, certainly a lot happier than Adam's fellow colleagues in London, who had to put themselves through the never ending daily grind,

Adam strolled to work every morning in brilliant sunshine, and he would stop off at his favourite cafe bar, and depending on his mood, he would drink a bottle of beer or sometimes a 'cafe con leche' with a shot of brandy and a slice or two of wonderfully toasted Spanish bread. As he ate, Adam would usually view the day's news on the cafe's aging television and reflect that back in London, if he'd gone for a drink every morning before going into work at the bank, eyebrows would have been raised and he would quite possibly be branded as some kind of alcoholic. But in Barcelona, nobody gave a damn. Lunchtimes too, could be pretty extensive. And after finishing work, most 'Barcelonese' would head for one of the many of the bars and enjoy a glass of good Rioja and a plate of Tapas before making their way home. Dining out of an evening was also another matter. Only tourists would dare to enter a Barcelona restaurant before nine o' clock, much to the restaurateur's disgust. But for the general populace, the general habit was to dine later, starting at around ten or eleven, at least.

Yes, Adam Tyler was a happy man, and for him, life was good.

Adam worked at a branch of the Santander Bank, situated on the Avenue del Bogatell, where he handled business loans and personal mortgages. His fluency in both English and Spanish was particularly useful, especially when dealing with the English or American clients.

It is estimated that over seventy five percent of Barcelona's total population speak 'Catalan', a language peculiar to the region, and so, and on a recommendation, Adam had straightaway enrolled himself into a local Catalan Language School where he fairly quickly managed to take command of the dialect. He was actually very good with languages, a fact that the Bank's Manager, a Mr Jorge Baroja, was more than impressed with.

Adam Tyler had become a very valuable member of Mr Baroja's highly efficient team, and along with that, Adam was getting referrals from other English speaking customers too, and that was all extra business for the bank, which was actually doing quite well. And all of this was something that Head Office in Madrid had certainly taken notice of and had congratulated Mr Baroja in the form of a sizeable annual bonus.

Pleasantly located along the Avenue del Bogatell, the Santander Bank was particularly well placed, well certainly for Adam. He could easily walk to work in the pleasant morning sunshine. And just across the road from the bank was the Barcelona Palace of Parliament de Catalunya, which was situated in the beautiful grounds of the Parc de Ciutadella. And depending on his mood, Adam would regularly sit in the park grounds and enjoy an uninterrupted and easy lunch as he mulled through his papers.

On other occasions, he would wander down to the nearby beach to the well known golden sands of the Platja del Boatell, where he would regularly sit at the 'Via Moana' restaurant and take a glass of cool white wine, along with a plate of cold meats and some fresh Spanish bread, whilst gazing out to the sea. It was always very relaxing and it gave Adam time to contemplate the rest of the day's upcoming business.

Adam actually preferred to eat alone, and it was a habit that he had become quite comfortable with. And if truth be known, he'd actually not made many friends during his time in Barcelona. The last twelve months had easily flown by and Adam had been kept quite busy.

In fact, his only regular associations were with a small circle of people who he worked with within the bank. Or occasionally, he would ask a client to have lunch with him, usually to discuss some business or their affairs at the bank. Adam would always take them to his very favourite restaurant, just a short walk down to the harbour. A trip to the 'Restaurant Hispano' was not only a delight, it was where you could feast on the finest seafood in Barcelona.

Strangely however, on one particular afternoon, Adam was having lunch at the 'Hispano' with one of his colleagues from the bank. He was Carlos Villena, a bright young man who was one

16

of the more 'informative' personnel at work. And halfway through their plates of rich Paella, Adam decided to broach a possibly difficult subject.

On the previous day, Adam had been called into Mr Baroja's office. The bank manger had sat and spoken to Adam for the best part of an hour and they'd discussed the progress of some of the business loans that Adam was about to advance. Some of those loans were quite sizeable, however, Mr Jorge Baroja wasn't particularly worried. He had complete faith in Adam Tyler, although he did like to keep his eye on the ball, especially since he had to justify some of those loans to the Bank's directors back in Madrid.

The meeting was not unusual, it was actually quite a regular thing. Adam Tyler was a busy man, increasingly so, and both men were quite comfortable in each other's company.

As their meeting came to a close, Jorge Baroja suddenly opened the top drawer of his desk and produced a bottle of good Spanish Brandy and a couple of glasses. Adam, for once, was quite surprised.

'Now that business is over,' said Jorge Baroja, 'I would like to talk to you about something'.

He then poured a reasonable amount of brandy into each of the glasses and offered one to Adam. Both men took a sip of their drinks and then Mr Baroja sat back in his chair.

'Adam,' he said amiably, 'you are doing well, you are doing a good job and I am more than pleased with your progress.'

Adam nodded.

'Thank you, Mr Baroja,' he replied, quite respectfully.

Jorge Baroja smiled. He liked Adam Tyler.

'Adam, you work very hard, I do know that.'

Adam again nodded.

'But maybe too hard, sometimes,' Jorge Baroja continued.

Adam was slightly surprised at that comment, but he said nothing.

'Young man, you know what they say about 'all work and no play.'

Adam smiled, and then simply shrugged.

'I'm happy at what I do, Mr Baroja.'

'Yes, yes, I know that. However, let me give you a bit of advice, Adam. You do need to socialize a little bit more, especially with your fellow associates who work here at the bank.'

For a moment, Adam didn't quite understand the significance of his manager's advice.

Jorge Baroja continued, 'It has been noticed that you are only friendly with 'certain' people in the bank.' He then raised his eyebrows somewhat, 'and I have to tell you Adam, that you are becoming to be known as a bit of a 'cold fish.'

Adam was quite taken aback by this, he'd simply never realized. But before he could reply, Jorge Baroja continued to speak to him.

'I however, do know that you're not a 'cold fish', I've known you for over twelve months now, Adam, and I've gotten to know you fairly well.' Jorge Baroja then took a deep breath, 'but you do need to socialize a bit more. You need to get out with your workmates in the evenings and meet people, other people. Having lunch alone in the park or down at the beach is not conducive to making friends. I want you to build a team here, Adam, you can't do everything yourself. In the future you will need to communicate more and pass on your enthusiasm.'

Adam just sat there for a moment and he wondered 'how on earth' did his manager know exactly where he'd been having his lunches?

At that point, Jorge Baroja smiled at him.

'Adam, I want to offer you a promotion, to be the head of commercial banking, here at the bank.'

Suddenly, Adam Tyler realized what he was being presented with. Yes it was a promotion, a huge promotion. And suddenly all of his hard work was finally paying off. He was on his way to the top. There was no doubt about it.

Adam immediately stood up, and he reached across the desk to shake his manager's hand.

'Thank you, Mr Baroja,' he said earnestly, 'thank you very much for your faith in me. And I 'will' take everything you've said onboard, I'll build a good team here, believe me.'

Jorge Baroja smiled back at his protégé. His mission had been accomplished, and with ease.

'Oh yes, and just one more thing,' Jorge Baroja continued, 'My daughter will be getting married next month, and I'd like to invite you to the wedding.'

On hearing this, Adam was quite surprised. This was a personal invite. This was an act of friendship.

Jorge Baroja smiled. 'I'd really like you to be there, Adam. But please, keep this between us, not all of the staff here are invited. I'll send you an invitation of course, but also, have a word with young Carlos Villena. He'll be there too. You see, his father and I are old friends.'

When Adam had left the office, Jorge Baroja sat back in his sumptuous leather chair and congratulated himself. Everything had gone to plan. He now had Adam Tyler's complete loyalty, at least for the next few years anyway. And Jorge Baroja was nobody's fool. He'd realized Adam Tyler's talent and he knew a rising star when he saw one. Baroja would let Adam run the commercial side of the bank for a couple of years, and then he would talk to Adam about taking over completely and becoming the Bank's Manager. Jorge Baroja had planned well. He certainly didn't want Adam Tyler getting itchy feet and moving on to fields afresh. In a couple of year's time, Jorge Baroja would be at an age to retire. And hopefully, and with Adam Tyler's help of course, he could retire with a huge bonus and a large accumulated pension.

And so, that very next day, Adam had invited Carlos Villena to go to lunch with him at the Restaurant Hispano, down by the harbour. Carlos Villena had been impressed, not only by Adam's choice of restaurant, but also by the sudden show of a greater friendship. In truth, he and Adam had always got on quite well at the bank and they did have regular meetings. But never lunch, and to be taken to the 'Hispano' would certainly be a lunch to remember.

And with that, and as they ate the succulent paella, a house speciality, they both chatted away, mostly about the bank, and also on the quality of the food that they were eating. And it was then that Adam decided that it was time to ask Carlos Villena for bit of advice.

'Actually, Carlos, I need to talk to you about something,' he said.

Carlos Villena looked up from his food, he'd noticed the change in the tone of Adam's voice and for a moment he was slightly concerned. This could be bad news.

Adam smiled at him. 'No, it's nothing to worry about, Carlos, really.'

Carlos Villena looked relieved.

'Actually, Mr Baroja has asked me to have a word with you in private.'

Carlos Villena suddenly reverted to looking worried again.

Adam laughed. 'No really, this is nothing to do with the bank, or your work. It's more of a social thing.'

Carlos Villena again looked visibly relieved, and then he tried to look optimistic.

'Yes, what is it Adam, is there a problem?' he asked. It was in Carlos Villena's nature to seemingly worry about most things really.

Adam took a deep breath.

'Mr Baroja's daughter is apparently getting married next month. I've been invited to the wedding. Mr Baroja spoke to me yesterday about it. He also informed me that you would be attending too and he asked me to speak to you.'

Carlos Villena sat back in his chair, he looked somewhat surprised. And then he smiled.

'My god, Adam, he must think very well of you.'

It was now Adam's turn to look surprised.

'Why's that?' he asked.

Carlos Villena reached for his glass of white wine, and he shook his head, still smiling.

'Let me tell you something, Jorge Baroja is a very private man, especially when it comes to his family. He and my father are old friends.'

'I believe so,' Adam replied.

Carlos Villena again shook his head. 'You surprise me that he even spoke about it.'

'Well he did, Carlos, and he asked me to speak to you. You see, I've never been to a Spanish wedding before and I'd like to know the protocol.'

Carlos nodded, and then he laughed.

'My father always jokes about Mr Baroja's daughter 'even' getting married. He's such a private person, especially with his family. My father always wondered how she'd managed to get out of the house to actually meet someone.'

Adam laughed at that. 'I didn't know,' he replied.

'His daughter is 'Maria', said Carlos, 'she's a lovely girl. She's marrying some guy, he's an accountant, I think. 'Antonio...' something or other, I can't remember his last name. I met him once, but he seemed okay.'

Adam shrugged. 'Well, anyway, I've been invited. And there's some other good news too.'

'Have you won the lottery? Carlos Villena laughed.

'No, I'm getting a promotion. I'm going to be made the Head of Commercial Banking.'

Carlos looked at Adam for a moment, just a moment too long. And then he relaxed and smiled again.

'Nice one,' said Carlos, '...and welcome to the family,' and then he laughed again.

But Adam saw it, and he wondered if there was a hint of jealousy there. And so he decided to tactfully change the subject.

'So, what do I wear for the wedding?' Adam asked him.

Carlos Villena gave it a moment's thought.

'Dress very smartly, Adam. That's what I shall be doing. I'll be wearing my sharpest suit on the day. Dress to impress, and that in turn will impress Jorge Boroja. It's a sign of respect, and he will notice it. Some people may turn up more casually dressed, but no, not me. And anyway, there will be lots of beautiful young 'senoritas' there too, and we will definitely need to impress the ladies.' Carlos grinned, 'and you never know, Adam, we may get lucky.'

Adam grinned back at his new friend.

'You know, Carlos, I'd never thought of that,' he replied.

'Well I think about it all the time,' said Carlos, 'We should work as a team, Adam. Those young ladies couldn't possibly resist two good looking guys like us.'

Now it was Adam's turn to laugh.

'You know something, Carlos, you're right. 'All work and no play' isn't good.'

And with that, he raised his glass and gave a toast.

'Here's to the ladies,' he said out loud.

Their glasses clinked together and both men laughed. Adam looked across the table at Carlos Villena. Carlos Villena was actually quite good fun.

The following weekend, Adam Tyler went shopping. He went to the Hugo Boss Store at the Passeig de Gracia in central Barcelona. Once there, he was shown an array of different suits in an assortment of colours, by an enthusiastic assist, a slightly over friendly young man. But Adam finally opted for a beautiful pale grey silk suit which fitted him perfectly. The suit was sharply cut, but the material was lightweight and had a slight sheen, and it would be perfect to wear on a hot summer's day, especially at a wedding. The assistant was slightly overjoyed too, Adam Tyler had just picked one of the most expensive suits in the store. Whilst he was there, Adam also bought a crisp new white shirt and the assistant then came up trumps with a red tie that had a pale grey pattern running through it which matched the suit exactly. Not one to skimp, Adam then purchased a pair of dark brown Sebago loafers, which also complemented his outfit perfectly. He then made his way back home and duly hung his new suit in the wardrobe. He had another quick look at the shoes. They were really very smart.

On the following Monday afternoon, Carlos Villena asked Adam if he wanted go for a drink later, along with a few tapas at a local bar. Adam agreed, and after work as they sat enjoying a glass of wine and the food, they spoke about the upcoming wedding, and Adam happened to mention the new suit that he'd bought from the Hugo Boss store for the wedding. For a moment, Carlos suddenly looked a bit perturbed.

'I have a pale grey suit that I purchased from Hugo Boss, and that I was going to wear', and then he laughed, 'oh dear god, I hope they're not the same. We'll look like a couple of twins!'

'No, we'll look like a couple of idiots.' Adam replied, and he suddenly realized that they may have a problem.

Carlos Villena looked at him, 'Hey, I'll tell you what, after we've finished here, why don't we call in at your apartment and let me look at your new suit, and then at least we'll both know?'

An hour later they arrived at Adam's apartment. Carlos Villena was immediately impressed. Adam offered Carlos a glass of wine, but not before he showed Carlos his new suit.

Carlos picked up the jacket and examined the material closely.

'It's beautiful material,' he remarked, as he examined the jacket closely, 'in fact, I'm a bit jealous, my suits a similar colour but not as nice.'

Adam laughed, and then he went to the fridge and took out a bottle of chilled white wine.

'So I'll have the advantage with the ladies then, that'll make a change,' he replied, trying to be somewhat diplomatic.

But Carlos was having none of it. 'No you won't my friend,' and he grinned, 'I have a beautiful pale blue suit that I'll wear instead. In any case, the ladies prefer blue to grey. And I'm still going to blow you out of the water my friend, and no problem.'

They both laughed at that assumption, and then they went to sit on the balcony to enjoy the last rays of the early evening sun. They joked and then discussed work and after the best part of an hour, Carlos finally left.

Adam poured himself another glass of wine and then went back to sit on his balcony. He thought about Carlos Villena for a moment. They were actually becoming quite good friends, and the thought of them both attending the wedding should make the day somewhat more enjoyable. At least there would be one person there that he knew and who he could talk to.

The following weekend, Adam's curiosity got the better of him. With a couple of weeks to go before the wedding, he decided to unwrap his new shirt and hang it in the wardrobe along with his suit. But first of all it would need pressing to take out the new creases. He took his steam iron and an old ironing board out of a cupboard and then went to work. Once done, he put the shirt on. It was perfect, made from 100% pure white cotton, it felt crisp and clean.

He then decided to try on the whole outfit, just to make sure that everything matched. He put on the suit pants and the new shoes, and then the red tie. And finally, he put on the jacket and stood back to look at himself in his full length mirror. And he liked what he saw. He looked good, very good. And at the back of his mind he remembered what Carlos Villena had said to him about dressing to impress the young 'senoritas', and that too made him smile and it gave him something to think about. Who knows? His Spanish was excellent, so speaking to any young lady would certainly not be a problem for him at all. And then for a brief moment, an image of Miss Joanne Berkeley suddenly flashed through his mind. He dismissed it immediately, but still considered it a bit strange, he'd not thought about her for months and months, or had he?

Adam went over to his window and looked out across Barcelona. There in front of him stood the magnificent 'La Sagrada Familia', along with a host of other very beautiful buildings. He stared out at the view, he felt good. Barcelona was a truly beautiful city.

And then for no reason at all really, Adam put his hand into his jacket pocket. And suddenly he felt something, some paper. His immediate thought was that it could be the envelope containing the spare suit buttons for his suit, or even some form of wrapping paper. But when he took his hand out of his pocket and looked, he was holding a folded receipt. He looked at it, and it was a a receipt from a restaurant. Adam stared at it, it was a bill, and it was from somewhere called the 'Angelique Bar-Restaurant'. The bill seemed to be for food and drinks for two people. He then turned the receipt over and there was some writing scribbled on the back. It read...'Dominique', and there was a phone number written below it. Adam just stared down at the piece of paper, and then he suddenly realized the truth of it. His 'so called' brand new suit had already been worn by someone else, and on some previous occasion. Adam was astounded, and then he was immediately annoyed, and quite rightly. This suit had cost him a small fortune, and to him it had been an investment, but suddenly, it now felt second hand, and almost soiled. He stood there for a moment and took a deep breath. What could he do? He could take the suit back to the store, of course. But then what? He would have to find another suit, but the wedding was taking place in a couple of weeks and Adam was really busy at work and he hadn't got the time, or the enthusiasm to start shopping again. He went back to the mirror and stared at himself. And then, damn it, he really did like the suit. However, he still found it all very irritating. He looked again at the receipt in his hand and at the telephone number written there. He was slightly angry now, and in a rush of frustration he reached for his mobile phone, and began to dial the number on the receipt in front of him.

Adam didn't actually know what he was going to say, or even who he would be speaking to. Would it be a man, or would it be this 'Dominique', whoever she was? The phone started to ring, several times in fact, and then Adam thought about what he was about to say...?

'How long had the previous owner had the suit? And how many times had he worn it, and obviously, what was the reason for him taking it back to the store?'

He suddenly felt justified in his actions, and then, someone picked up the phone on the other end of the line. There was a silence, and a few long seconds passed by, but Adam realized that there was someone there, listening. Slightly irritated, and momentarily forgetting that he was not back in England, he blurted out the words...'Hello, is there someone there on the line, please?'

There was another few seconds of silence, and then a woman spoke, also in English.

'Hello, who is this please?' she asked.

Adam heard her voice, it was English spoken with a Spanish lilt. He decided to carry on the conversation in his native tongue, it might just give him the edge.

'Hello,' he said again, 'You don't actually know me, and this is rather awkward, and strange, but is there a gentleman there that I can speak to. It's about a suit that he bought, and has then returned to the Hugo Boss store at the Passeig de Gracia, here in Barcelona?'

Again, there was a short silence, and then.

'A suit...what is this about please?' came the reply.

Adam took a deep breath, he would have to do better and he would have to try to explain.

'Okay,' he said, 'you don't know me, but my name is Adam Tyler, I'm English.'

'Yes, I can tell that,' came another sharper reply, and Adam felt a little bit foolish. And along with that he was also beginning

25

to lose his initial anger. In fact, he was beginning to wish that he'd never picked up the phone, let alone the damn suit.

'Let me explain please,' he tried again. 'I bought a suit last weekend from the Hugo Boss store in the Passeig de Gracia. And today I've put the suit on, and in the pocket there's a receipt for a meal at a restaurant, and written on the back of the bill there is this telephone number and the name, 'Dominique'.

Another short silence, and then...

'Yes, that me, I'm Dominique. My name is Dominique Cassens'

Adam took a deep breath.

'Okay 'Dominique', well, I bought the suit from Hugo Boss and it was quite expensive. And now I find that it's obviously been worn by someone else and I'm a bit mystified, and actually, I'm rather annoyed with the store.'

'What colour is the suit?' she asked suddenly.

Adam was now feeling a little exasperated, but he replied.

'It's pale grey, it's a lovely suit actually, and that's why I can't understand...'

But she cut him off.

'And what restaurant was it...on the bill?' she asked quickly.

Adam looked again at the other side of the receipt and he read it out loud, 'It's somewhere called the 'Angelique Bar-Restaurant'.

'When, what's the date?

Adam checked the receipt, 'About a month ago.'

'And for how many?' she asked.

'What?'

'For how many? How many people dined there? She was becoming quite insistent.

Adam examined the bill again.

'It looks like it was a meal and drinks for two.'

The line went silent for a moment.

'Where do you live?' she said suddenly. 'Give me your address, please.'

Adam was at a loss for a moment, and then suddenly, he was guarded.

'And why on earth should I give you my address?' he said.

There was another brief silence.

'Because I need to see that suit,' she replied, 'and I need to see the handwriting on that bill.'

'And why's that?' Adam asked.

Adam could hear her breathing on the other end of the line, and then she answered his question.

'Because I think that I bought that suit,' she replied.

Adam was slightly confused.

'I don't really understand all of this,' he said to her.

The woman on the end of the phone, 'Miss 'Dominique Cassens', spoke again, but this time more slowly.

'I'm afraid I'm having a slight problem. You see. I have a fiancé,' and then she paused for a moment, 'or should I say, I 'had' a fiancé. I've not seen him now for a few weeks. It's hard to explain over the phone, but he's disappeared and I've had a few things stolen from me, and I also think that he's been seeing someone else. It's happened before. But this time I just need to know the truth, that's all. Please, if I could just see the suit, I would know, and I would also recognize his handwriting.'

Adam felt rightly apprehensive. 'I don't really want to get involved,' he tried to explain, but Miss Dominique Cassens was quite determined.

'Please help me,' she insisted, 'I've had money stolen from me and I think that I need to notify the police. It would only take a couple of minutes, please.'

There was something in her words...'the money stolen', and 'the police', that brought about something of the honest banker in Adam. He almost felt as though he was duty bound. He'd had to deal with fraud and personal theft before and he knew all about the problems that it caused, and also all of the headaches. And so, and against his better judgement, he relented. He gave her his address and she promised that she would be there within the hour.

Forty, slightly long minutes later, and then the doorbell to his apartment finally rang, during which time, Adam had several misgivings over his judgement, but he realized that it was all too late. He had rather naively given this woman his address and she was already on her way.

On hearing the doorbell chime, Adam walked down the short hallway to his apartment door and he opened it, and then he stared, and then he blinked, twice.

She just stood there. And Adam Tyler looked at her, and fell silent.

Miss Dominique Cassens was five foot four inches of true Spanish beauty. And for a moment, neither of them spoke. And then she gave a hesitant smile and held out here hand.

'Hello,' she said quietly, 'I'm Dominique Cassens.'

Adam stared back at her, he was slightly dumbfounded. Dominique Cassens had shoulder length, almost black curled hair which fell loosely around her face. Her skin was the same beautiful, soft brown colour as the 'cafe con leche' that he drank and enjoyed every morning. Adam was more than slightly taken aback, she was undoubtedly 'someone and something' that he'd not expected. He rather nervously shook her hand and then managed to say 'Hello,' as he looked at her small upturned nose and her almost perfectly shaped red lips, she wore the reddest of lipsticks and it suited her. And then he suddenly realized that he was behaving like an idiot.

'You...You'd better come in,' he said hurriedly. 'Oh, and I'm Adam Tyler.'

'Yes, you did tell me that on the phone,' she promptly replied.

Not the best of starts.

She stared back at him, and then she shook her head wearily.

'I'm sorry, Mr Tyler. I'm being quite rude. I am really sorry, but it's been a very difficult time for me.'

'Do please come in,' Adam said again, and with that, Miss Dominique Cassens stepped into his apartment, and into his life.

Once inside, Dominique Cassens looked around Adam's apartment and then she turned to him.

'It's a lovely apartment, Mr Tyler, quite beautiful.'

'Come through,' he said to her, 'I'll show you the view from the balcony.'

He guided her through his living room and onto the balcony, and there in all of its glory was the wonderful view of the splendid church, 'La Sagrada Familia'.

'My god, what a wonderful sight,' she said to him.

'Yes,' Adam replied. 'Gaudi was such a genius, his works embody this city.'

'Yes,' she agreed, 'I love Gaudi's park, the Parc Guell. Have you ever been there?'

Adam smiled at her. 'Yes, plenty of times, it's beautiful.'

Dominique continued, 'I love it there, I like to sit and watch the people wander by. It's such a lovely place, so relaxing.'

Adam took a deep breath, he could smell Dominique Cassen's perfume and he suddenly realized that he was staring at her.

'Would you like some coffee?' he said, rather awkwardly.

She turned to him and smiled. 'Yes please, that would be lovely, thank you.'

'Okay then,' he said to her, 'sit yourself down here and enjoy the view, I won't be long.'

And with that he almost dashed into his kitchen and filled the kettle. He grabbed his faithful old percolator and began to charge it with some of his best ground coffee. And as the kettle began to boil he took a tray and found some milk and some sugar and then he washed a couple of his nicer cups and saucers. He poured the boiling water into the percolator and then let it go to work, and suddenly the apartment began to fill with the aroma of freshly brewed coffee. Once it was done, Adam calmly walked back onto the balcony with the tray of coffee and effortlessly placed the tray in front of her.

'There you go,' he said, and then he poured the coffee.

They chatted for several more minutes, and then Adam turned to the more serious topic, the reason for Dominique Cassens actually being there.

He finished his coffee and hesitantly put the cup back down on the tray.

'I'll go and get the suit. You can take a look at it.'

He then stood up and returned a couple of minutes later with the suit, still on its hanger.

Dominique Cassens took one look at it, and then she sighed and shook her head.

'That's the one,' she said to Adam, 'it's the same suit.' And she sat back in her chair and sighed.

Adam said nothing, but then she looked up at him.

'Can I see the receipt, please?

29

Adam went back into his apartment and picked up the receipt which was still by the side of his telephone. He then went back onto the balcony and passed it to her. Dominique read it quickly, and then put it down on the table in front of her.

'Yes, that's his writing...the bastard,' she said angrily.

At that moment, Adam felt at a bit of a loss, so he tactfully asked her if she would like another cup of coffee.

Dominique Cassens took a deep breath.

'Yes, thank you,' she replied. But she wasn't looking at Adam, she was still staring at the receipt in front of her.

When Adam returned with the pot of replenished coffee, Dominique's mood seemed to be a little more relaxed.

'Are you okay,' he asked?

She shook her head, but then actually smiled.

'I'm really sorry,' she said to him, 'I'm a fool, I should have known.'

'Do you want to talk about it?' Adam asked her.

She gave a small, bitter laugh.

'There's not a lot to say really. I met him, he's 'Rafael Molina', and I met him about two years ago, and he's led me a merry dance ever since. I should have left him a year ago, he was already having another affair then, but you know how it is,' and then she shrugged her shoulders. 'The man's a charmer, and a complete liar. I caught him having an affair a year ago, but he begged for my forgiveness and then asked me to marry him. And I fell for it. He's a complete wastrel, he never has any money. In fact, I've always seemed to pay for everything, he never has a proper job and he never pays me back. That's why I bought him the suit. He was supposed to be going for an important interview, at some property company somewhere. It was going to be his 'big chance', but he needed a good suit for the interview. He said that he had to 'impress'. Well I fell for that one didn't I. We went to the Hugo Boss store and I think he picked out the most expensive suit in there, and I of course, paid for it. He said it would be an 'investment'. Some investment! He must have taken it back to the store straight away, and then had the money reimbursed. But this has been going on for a while. He's kept disappearing for a few days and never returning my phone calls. Then my credit cards and bank cards were lost, or should I say 'stolen', obviously by him, and then money was spent on the cards and cash was taken from my account.'

She shook her head, 'I've been an idiot.'

Adam looked at her. 'Hey, we've all been fools for love, you're not the first or the last.'

And with that said, he stood up, it was time for more coffee. He returned with fresh coffee, but this time he brought with it a bottle of Fundador Spanish Brandy.

Dominique looked at the bottle, and then she smiled. 'Thank you,' she replied.

It was Adam's turn to shrug. 'There's nothing like a drop of brandy in your coffee to brighten up the day.'

And for the first time that afternoon, Dominique actually laughed as he then proceeded to pour the drinks.

'Where do you work, Dominique,' he asked her?

'I'm a secretary at a mail order company,' she replied, 'we sell clothes mostly. It keeps me busy, I work till all hours. And where do you work...Adam?' And she said his name for the first time, and Adam took notice.

'I work for the Santander Bank here in Barcelona, on the Avenue del Bogatell.'

Then suddenly, he had a thought. 'Do you bank with the Santander, Dominique? Maybe I could chase up the stolen money from your account or at least get some details for the police?'

She stared at him for a moment and then slowly smiled, 'I'm sorry,' and then she laughed, 'I'm sorry, Adam, but I'm with 'La Caixa' Bank, I always have been.'

Adam gave a false scowl.

'Oh, so you're banking with 'the enemy' are you?' he said to her, 'La Caixa' are the opposition,' and then he too laughed and he looked back at her. 'Never mind, I'll let you off,' he said, still grinning.

'Well, they've always been very good to me,' she replied.

Adam just shook his head, as he poured more coffee, and more brandy.

The afternoon passed by and the two of them became friendlier and somewhat bolder. And in truth, Adam Tyler was becoming somewhat entranced by this woman. She was so stunningly beautiful and an easily good conversationalist. And as he looked at her, he realized what he'd been missing in his life And if only?

'Well, that sorts out my questions about the suit,' Adam remarked

'Yes,' Dominique replied, 'and when I think about it, he almost certainly never had any job to go to either. It was probably just another ruse to get more money from me.'

She scowled, 'I've been a fool, Adam, I know I have. But at least now I know.'

She sat back and then sighed. 'If he ever comes crawling back, it's over...never again.'

And those words, and that statement, suddenly made Adam Tyler feel pretty good. And then a thought occurred to him.

'Dominique, why would he write down your phone number on a receipt, especially if he was entertaining someone else?'

She stared at him for a moment.

'My phone,' she then said, 'my phone, it went missing. Yes, I thought I'd lost it, but now I realize that Rafael probably stole it and sold it. It was about a month ago and it was quite an expensive phone, so I just went out and bought another one, just a cheap one. I've still got it.'

'Obviously the phone that I rang you on?' he said to her.

She nodded to him. 'Yes, that's right. I do vaguely remember phoning him to tell him my new number. He must have written it down on that same receipt, the bastard.'

Adam shrugged. 'He's not a very nice man, Dominique.'

She just looked at him. 'No, he's not,' she said.

Adam stood up and went to get more coffee. And then he turned to her.

'Are you hungry,' he asked?

'Why?' she replied, and Adam suddenly felt slightly embarrassed.

'No, I just wondered,' he said quickly, 'I've not eaten. I'm starving actually. And there's a nice bar just down the road the makes really good tapas. I just wondered if you were hungry too.'

32

Dominique looked at her watch to check the time, and Adam inwardly cursed his own incompetence. He was being so obvious and so very naive. This woman had just come out of a bad relationship and here he was, trying to hit on her. What a fool.

'I can't stay out late,' she suddenly replied, 'I actually have to work tomorrow, we have a large order that's got to be rushed through, and I stupidly volunteered to go in early.'

Then she looked up at him, and there was a look of regret.

'Well, I had nothing else to do, Adam.'

It was a simple statement. And Dominique just sat there, expressionless and sad. And at that moment, Adam Tyler felt like going over to her and taking her in his arms and hugging all the pain and the heartache out of her. But no, he would wait. And at the back of his mind, he remembered Miss Joanne Berkley

'Don't be fooled again, Adam,' he reminded himself.

It took them around fifteen minutes to get to the 'Bar Mont' on the Carrer de la Diputacio. It was one of Adam's favourite haunts. The beer was always cold, they served really good house wine, and the food was exquisite. And at that hour, they managed to find a decent table, the bar was only half full as the afternoon revellers were already beginning to leave and before the ever popular bar-restaurant prepared for the tirade of regular evening customers.

Bar Mont, was quite well known for being a 'food heaven' and had an ardent and very appreciative clientele.

As they entered the bar, heads turned. And the men looked twice at Dominique when they saw her. Eyebrows were raised, even from the busy waiters and the bar staff. She was without doubt, strikingly beautiful. And Adam felt a swell of pride, and lucky to be in the company of such a stunningly pretty woman.

He ordered the wine, a fairly robust Rioja which they both enjoyed. And Dominique left it to him to order the food, Adam spoke to an attentive waiter whom he already knew.

Mixed tapas were to be the order of the day. and Adam left the choices to the waiter.

Dominique looked at him, quite surprised.

'What, no menu?' she said to him.

But Adam just laughed. 'Don't worry, 'he said to her, 'everything here, is good.'

And it was. They ate tiny sobrasada and cheese dumplings, along with meatballs made from prawns and pork. Then they tried the Tacos, which were filled with sliced artichokes, subtly flavoured with butter and sweet balsamic vinegar, a beautiful dish. Eventually they were served with small dishes of sliced Tuna fish, along with the most heavenly smoked sardines. Adam had ordered a bottle of pink Cava, to complement their fish. They talked about almost everything, with one obvious exception, not one mention of Mr Rafael Molina. He had already become 'persona non-grata'.

'I'll order some coffee,' said Adam. 'Would you like some dessert?'

Dominique laughed. 'I'm already so full,' she replied, 'however, I'm a real sucker for Tiramisu,' and she giggled.

'Well, they don't always have Tiramisu, I do know that. But would you like to try my own recommendation?'

'Yes of course, anything you say,' she replied with a smile. 'You're the expert.'

He waved to the waiter who came straight over to their table.

'Can I have two coffees, please? And for dessert, we'll have the Carrot Cake.'

As the waiter left, Adam turned to Dominique who once again had started to giggle.

'What's so funny now?' he asked her.

'I don't think I've ever tried 'Carrot Cake' and she began to laugh, 'it sounds ridiculous.'

'Oh, you woman of little faith, just wait until you've tried it before passing judgement.'

The waiter arrived carrying a tray with the coffees and the desserts.

Dominique took her spoon and scooped up a piece of the cake, along with some cream and then she tasted it. Then she stopped, and she looked up.

'Oh my goodness, this is just wonderful. I've never tasted anything like it. It's gorgeous.'

'I told you,' said Adam, and then they both laughed, just for the fun of it.

They talked, and then ordered more coffee. But at last, Dominique looked at her watch.

'I'm really sorry, Adam,' she said to him, 'but I do really have to go, I have to get up early for work tomorrow.'

'I'll go and pay the bill, and I'll also order you a taxi, Dominique. Hey, I've never even asked you. Where do you live?

Dominique suddenly blinked.

'I live the other side of Las Rambles, in El Raval.'

Adam tried to remain expressionless, but that had caught him somewhat unawares.

Las Ramblas was the long street that divided the area of Barcelona which led all the way down to the busy harbour. The 'other side' of Las Ramblas... 'El Raval', was the known rougher quarter of Barcelona. The El Raval District was the noted residential area for many of the city's Arabic and African population. One did not wander lightly into the El Raval District, especially after midnight.

And Dominique caught the look of concern in Adam's eyes.

'I have my own apartment, and I've lived there for five years. I do know how people regard the area but my apartment is quite nice and I do have good neighbours, I know most of them and it's pretty safe,' and then she sighed, 'I know I should have left there years ago, but Rafael Molina put paid to that. He always spent our money, but the rent's cheap and I can survive there on my own, especially now.'

Adam could only shrug. This was none of his business, really.

'I'll come with you in the taxi,' he said to her, 'just to make sure that you're okay.'

But no, she insisted that everything would be alright and that there wasn't a problem. And then she looked at her watch again and Adam took the obvious hint.

He paid the bill and ordered the taxi. And as they stood there outside the Bar Mont, their conversation cooled, along with the night air. There was maybe some expectation for both of them. But Adam didn't want rejection. He'd had a great night with this beautiful woman and he wanted it to finish well. The taxi quickly arrived and before she got into it, she turned to Adam to thank him for the meal and all that he'd done for her. She felt better for it.

They both stood there awkwardly, almost in expectation. But nothing happened. And then suddenly, Dominique took his hand and simply shook it. That was all. She then thanked him again and got into the taxi, which immediately sped away. And that left Adam alone on the pavement, wondering what had just happened. He looked up at the darkening sky, and then he cursed himself.

'Adam Tyler, you are one stupid man,' he said out loud, and then, 'you stupid, stupid bastard.'

And so, he walked back to his apartment in somewhat of a bad mood. He considered that he'd failed badly, very badly, especially for a smart young banker who dealt with very important people every day. Once he got back to his apartment, he poured himself an even larger glass of brandy and he went to sit outside on his balcony. Still there, was the empty chair which Dominique Cassens had sat on only hours before, and he remembered their conversation and he thought about her smouldering good looks. Adam cursed himself again. He looked out to the famous spires of the 'La Sagrada Familia', which were beautifully lit up in the night sky. Then he drank his brandy in one go, and then he went back into his apartment to make some more coffee. Whilst his percolator boiled, he went into his living room and picked up his suit, he was going to put it back into his wardrobe. By the side of the suit was the receipt from the now infamous 'Angelique Bar-Restaurant', the receipt with Dominique Cassens telephone number written on it. Adam poured his coffee and went back onto his balcony. As he sat there, he examined the receipt once more. And then he reached into his pocket and took out his mobile phone. He stared at the receipt again and at the phone number, and he sighed to himself. It was now or never. He had to see this wonderful woman again, there was no doubt about it.

And so he dialled the number.

The phone rang four times before being picked up.

'Hello,' came the reply.

'Hi, it's me, its Adam. I was just checking that you got home okay,' he lied.

'Oh hi,' Dominique replied cheerfully. 'Yes, I've just got in, and yes I'm okay. Thanks for phoning. And thanks for a great night out, I'm sorry I had to leave early.'

Adam listened. It all sounded quite positive. She wasn't offended at him contacting her again, far from it, or so it seemed.

'I just wondered,' he asked cautiously. 'Would you like to do it again, go out I mean?'

There was a short silence, and then Dominique Cassens laughed.

'Of course I would, Adam. I've really enjoyed myself today. It's the first time that I've laughed and relaxed so much in a very long time. Yes of course I will. When do you want to go out?'

All of this left Adam rather overwhelmed. He'd finally had a success. And at last he'd got himself a date, and what a date. She was so very beautiful.

'Tomorrow,' he said quickly, 'we'll go out tomorrow night. Is that okay?

Dominique laughed again.

'Adam Tyler, are you trying to whisk me off my feet?'

'I certainly am, Miss Cassens, there's no doubt about it.' And he heard her giggle down the end of the phone, and then she spoke to him.

'I'll come around to your apartment at around nine o' clock tomorrow evening, it'll be easier that way. And also, I'll be able to stay out late this time, I'll have a word at work. They owe me some extra time off.'

Adam smiled, all was going exceptionally well.

'Alright then,' he said to her, 'I'll see you tomorrow.'

'Yes, you will, she replied, '...and Adam...thank you.'

Chapter 3

The next day when Adam awoke, he immediately found himself thinking about Dominique Cassens. She was without doubt, so very beautiful. And as he lay there he imagined her face, and he remembered their conversations. And as the sun's early morning rays shone through his bedroom window and flooded the warm golden light into the room, Adam slowly stretched in his bed and he smiled to himself. Tonight, he would see her again.

He spent the most of the day relaxing in his apartment, and watching the clock. It was Sunday, which was always a most appreciated and relaxing day for Adam. Occasionally, he would go into work on a Saturday morning, the bank was closed, but left on his own he could usually get a good amount of work done and then be prepared for Monday's business. However, Adam never worked on a Sunday, never, it was almost sacred to him. On Sundays he would usually get up around nine o'clock and then begin to prepare his coffee, and as it slowly percolated, he would stroll across the road to the kiosk opposite his apartment building to pick up the morning newspapers. He would always buy copies of the 'El Pais', Spain's most popular newspaper, and then of course, The Sunday Times.

On returning to his apartment, he would prepare the coffee and then sit on his balcony for the next couple of hours, reading his papers from page to page.

Adam rarely bothered to make breakfast on Sunday mornings. He much preferred to drink several cups of good coffee and digest the newspapers instead.

By the time midday arrived, Adam would, more often than not, feel his appetite return and it was his general preference to go and have a long leisurely lunch, somewhere nice. He enjoyed the walk to a decent restaurant and he loved to stroll around Barcelona on Sundays, it was such a diverse city. Sometimes he would simply make his way down to the harbour and have an ice cold beer or a chilled glass of the local Cava, before finding somewhere to dine.

And so, on that particular Sunday, and after the newspapers and the coffee, Adam once again made his way down to the harbour, this time to the L'Eixample District, to the Sicilia and the

'La Higuara' bar-restaurant. Once there, Adam ordered his favourite gin and tonic, gin being the speciality of the house. At the 'La Higuara', not only did they stock a huge array of different types and different flavours of gins, they also served some of the finest tapas in the city.

Adam sat outside the bar in the bright sunshine and enjoyed his drink, along with a couple of plates of tapas, squid in chilli, and some tiny mixed sweet peppers, smothered with layers of finely grated manchego cheese, all were doused in the finest Spanish olive oil.

The food was enough for Adam, after all, he would be dining out again later. And with that in mind, his thoughts turned once again to Miss Dominique Cassens, her beautiful face, and with a body to match. Adam Tyler was no fool, he'd observed her perfect shape. He'd watched her as she moved so easily, so comfortable with herself, almost feline. And as he sat there he thought about her dark colouring and her perfect skin. Oh dear lord.

Adam quickly finished his drink and then paid his bill. He needed to go for a walk to clear his thoughts. But actually, there was only one thought on his mind, and he knew it.

And maybe...just maybe.

He left the bar and then he walked down to the harbour, as was his regular habit, and he strolled past all the moored boats, it was a leisurely pastime. And as usual, Adam wondered just how the owners did ever manage to accumulate so much money, as to be able to afford these rich man's 'toys'. As a banker, he'd dealt with many very wealthy people in this city, but he'd seldom ever spoken to any of them about the possibility of a 'boat purchase'. And as he walked along, he smiled ruefully. It was the way of the world, all over the world.

Eventually, Adam made his way back to his apartment. He opened a cold bottle of white wine and then he sat on his balcony and drank slowly as he enjoyed the heat of the day, along with his thoughts of Dominique. After a gradually sipped second glass he began to yawn, it was far too hot out there. And so he went back into his apartment and into his bedroom, where he lay on his bed. He looked up at the ceiling. His thoughts still lingered, he would see Dominique that evening. And yes, maybe, just maybe.

And then he closed his eyes and he slept.

Adam awoke a couple of hours later, somewhat refreshed. He glanced at his wristwatch, it was just after five thirty, and so he stretched in his bed and relaxed. He had plenty of time. His thoughts once again returned to Miss Dominique Cassens and the promise of the night ahead. And after several minutes he realized that more sleep was improbable and he got up and went into the kitchen to make some coffee. As the percolator began to boil, he went through to his balcony and looked out across the city. The sun was beginning to turn and the bright sunshine that reflected the light off the buildings was beginning to turn a deeper yellow. For Adam, it was the autumn of the day, it was something that he always enjoyed. The harsh mid afternoon sun was finally beginning to wane as the ever present heat became somewhat more bearable. He returned several minutes later with his coffee and he sat down at his small table as he contemplated the view. He had plans, and with that, he picked up his mobile phone and dialled a contact number. The phone rang a couple of times and was almost immediately answered.

'Els Quatre Gats', said a voice on the end of the line.

Adam replied in Spanish.

'I'd like to make a reservation for tonight, at around ten o' clock please, a table for two, and in the gallery please.'

The reservation was made without any problems. And Adam sat back in his chair as he sipped his coffee. The restaurant was a good choice.

The 'Els Quatre Gats' Restaurant, translated as 'The Four Cats', is one of Barcelona's more famous establishments.

40

Originally opened in 1897, the restaurant had several owners, but unfortunately managed to go bankrupt just as many times and was closed down in 1903. Nevertheless, in 1978 the restaurant was restored to its former glory and was reopened to the public. Its main claim to fame however, was that as a young man, Picasso and his group of young modernist painters, used to regularly frequent the restaurant. In fact, Picasso actually held his first solo exhibition there in the main room.

All of this added to the ambience, something the new owners exploited very successfully to promote the place. Add to that, some of the most exquisite food, and the 'Quatre Gats' soon became the legendary restaurant that it is today.

At around seven thirty, Adam began to get himself ready. He went over to his wardrobe and chose a pair of pale grey slacks and a smart white shirt. He placed them on his bed along with a medium blue jacket and a pair of dark brown 'Chelsea' style boots.

He then went to shave and also shower, there was no rush, he could take his time.

Once done, he liberally applied a good amount of aftershave, his best aftershave, and then he dressed.

Adam stood back and looked at himself in the full length mirror that was attached to his bedroom wall. He nodded, and yes, he felt pretty good. And then he looked at his watch again. It was eight-thirty. He went through to the kitchen and took a cold bottle of beer from the fridge and then went to sit on his balcony.

At ten minutes to nine, his doorbell rang. Adam sat up with a jolt. It had to be Dominique. He'd been deep in thought, not expecting her to be early. Most of the women in his life had always been fashionably late, and so Adam's mind had turned to work and the business of the bank. And now suddenly, she was here. He went to the door and opened it.

Dominique Cassens stood there smiling at him. She was wearing a sharply fitted white dress that had a restrained floral pattern running through it. The cut of the dress wrapped itself

41

around her perfect shape, her dark curly hair fell over her shoulders and she wore that same deep red lipstick.

Yes, she was beautiful. She was perfect.

Adam just stared at her, and Dominique laughed and immediately stepped forwards and threw her arms around him and kissed him on the cheek.

'Good evening, Adam,' she said and she stepped back and looked at him. 'You do look very smart tonight,' and she laughed.

'And you are very beautiful,' he said to her.

'I know,' she replied, and she burst out laughing, they both did.

She walked into his apartment as though she'd been there a hundred times and naturally made her way towards the balcony.

'White wine?' Adam asked.

'Oh, yes please,' she replied.

Adam brought the bottle of wine and two glasses to the table, and as he poured the wine he couldn't help himself. He leant down and kissed her neck, and as he did he smelt her wonderful perfume. And she let him.

He slowly exhaled.

'Dominique...'

'Yes?'

'You smell like peaches, it's lovely.'

She giggled, 'Do I really, well thank you, Mr Tyler. I'll take that as a compliment.'

Adam poured the wine, and they sat, and they talked.

The best part of an hour very quickly passed by, and Adam glanced at his watch and realized that he would have to phone for a taxi.

'Where are we going?' Dominique asked.

'Quatre Gats,' Adam replied.

'Really?'

'Yes...have you been there before?'

'No, never. But it's supposed to be really good. One of the girls from work went there a few weeks ago with her husband and she told us all about it. The food was fabulous, apparently.'

Adam rang the taxi firm and was told that they were on their way. He and Dominique finished their wine and then went downstairs and out onto the road as the taxi turned the corner and picked them up. Ten minutes later, they pulled up in front of the restaurant. Adam paid the driver, and then he led Dominique into the renowned 'Els Quatre Gats'.

The restaurant itself is split into two separate rooms, a smaller room just through the entrance and then a larger, divided main dining area to the rear. As they walked though the entrance, Dominique stopped to look for a table, it was really quite busy. But Adam took her arm.

'No, no, we're going through there, into the main room.' and he pointed towards the large, glass panelled double doors at the end of the smaller restaurant.

'This part always reminds me of a cafe,' he commented, 'it's for the more casual dining. I think it's where they put the tourists,' and he laughed.

A waiter then approached them and Adam immediately spoke to him in Spanish.

'We're in the main dining room,' he informed the waiter, 'we have a table booked in the gallery.'

The waiter smiled and then led them through.

Once they were in the main restaurant, Adam spoke to the Maitre-de, who quickly glanced at Dominique, and then led them both to the stairs up to the gallery, from where they could look down to the main restaurant below. The restaurant itself was very busy, but some of the noise actually settled as people, mostly the men, took notice of Dominique. Adam saw it, he saw the look in their eyes and it made him feel good, very good. She was a thing of beauty.

In the lower dining area, two musicians played soft Spanish ballads, there was a guitarist and a pianist, and the music was subtle and unobtrusive.

They were seated, and Adam immediately ordered a bottle of good wine.

The Maitre-de nodded in appreciation.

'An excellent choice, sir, it is a beautiful Rioja.'

Dominique smiled as he left.

'Why, Mr Adam Tyler,' she giggled, 'you're quite the expert.'

'Yes, I am,' Adam laughed, 'and tonight you and I are going to have only the best.'

Dominique smiled at him, and then she reached over and took hold of his hand. She was suddenly serious.

'Adam, thank you. I really mean it. You are a breath of fresh air, I'm lucky to have met you.'

And then she took hold of his hand and kissed it. It was almost submissive.

Adam looked back at her, and then he turned her hand and kissed it too, almost as a reply, the deal done, sealed.

'No, I'm the lucky one, Dominique,' he said to her, 'I really am.'

The spell was broken by the waiter, who arrived at their table with the bottle of wine and two glasses, and with two large menus tucked under his arm. He rather awkwardly placed the wine and the glasses on the table and then offered Adam and Dominique their menus.

The wine was opened and efficiently poured and then the waiter disappeared.

They toasted one another, and the evening ahead, and Dominique commented on the quality of the Rioja.

'Nice choice, Mr Tyler,' and they both smiled at one another.

They then looked at the menus. But after a couple of minutes Dominique shook her head and placed her menu back down on the table.

'What's wrong? Adam asked her, 'don't tell me you're not hungry?'

'No, no. It's nothing like that. It's just that there's so much choice, I don't know what to order.' She smiled back at him.

'You choose, Adam. You choose something for us, like you did last night. It was wonderful.'

Adam looked at her across the table, but in his mind, it was she who was wonderful.

The waiter arrived and Adam ordered the food as he casually perused the menu. Part of it was all an act of course. He'd dined here before and he knew what was good, and even better, he knew what was excellent.

'We'll have the Iberico ham with potato croquettes, and some of your salt cod fritters in Romesco sauce with 'patatas bravas'. For our main course we'll have the lobster paella. Oh yes, and

44

bring us some Catalan crystal bread and the tomatoes in Arbequina olive oil, please.

The waiter wrote down their order and nodded professionally. 'Gracias Senor,' he added, as he turned and quickly headed back towards the kitchens.

Dominique began to laugh.

'Adam, I don't know if I can eat all this food. I don't have a large appetite, I hope you're hungry.'

'Don't worry,' he said to her, 'we've got all night. And anyway, there's no rush, is there?'

Dominique had already told him that she wasn't working the next day. Hopefully, everything was going to plan.

'No, there's no rush,' she replied, 'and you're right Adam, we've got all night.'

They drank more wine. And as their food began to arrive, Adam ordered a bottle of chilled white Cava. The waiter returned with the Cava and expertly removed the cork from the bottle, almost managing to eliminate the infamous 'pop'. He carefully poured it, chilled and delicious, into two fluted glasses and then placed the bottle into an ice bucket.

Downstairs, the duo played some unobtrusive music, it was undemanding and easy on the ear and it allowed the diners to continue to talk to one another.

From the gallery, Dominique looked down at the restaurant floor.

'It's really nice up here,' she said to Adam, 'it's more private.'

As Adam agreed, there was applause from the downstairs dining area. A large family party, who were celebrating an eightieth birthday, had started to applaud as the elderly gentleman had stood up to address his guests. At that point, the musicians stopped playing and it seemed that everyone in the restaurant stopped eating. It was a sign of respect.

The silver haired gentleman coughed slightly as he faced his audience and spoke.

'My family, and my friends. I thank you for coming here today to celebrate my birthday. To my family, most of you I have known from the moment that you were born, and to my friends, I have known you for all the years that mattered. I have had a

45

wonderful life because of all of you. And with God's grace, I hope to continue for the many years to come.'

And with that, he lifted a glass of red wine and gave a toast to everyone....'Salud!'

There was more applause from everyone.

And at that moment he turned to the duo and nodded, and then the two musicians started to play the Catalan National Anthem...the 'Els Segadors'.

In translation 'Els Segadors' means 'The Reapers', and it is the celebrated anthem of all proud Catalonians. The tempo of the music suddenly changed as the pianist began to pound out the notes, and then the silver haired man took a deep breath and began to sing...

"Catalonia, triumphant, shall again be rich and bountiful.
Drive away these people, who are so conceited and so arrogant."

And at the end of that first verse, everyone in the restaurant then joined in on the chorus. They all sang together...

"Strike with your sickle!
Strike with your sickle, defenders of the land.
Strike with your sickle!"

The man continued, stoically singing the next two verses, and at the end of each verse everyone again sang the chorus...

"Strike with your sickle, strike with your sickle..."

And finally, at the end of the last chorus, everyone stood up and cheered and applauded. Even the busy waiters stopped to cheer. Adam and Dominique and the rest of the diners up in the gallery also stood up and applauded. It was a proud moment, a proud moment for Catalan.

Eventually, everyone sat down again and continued to dine, but the atmosphere in the restaurant was now palpable. There was an unconditional feeling of goodwill to everything Catalan, to Catalan and their fellow countrymen.

Adam stared across the table at Dominique, she was smiling and happy, and so proud. She looked vivacious and so very vibrant, and Adam Tyler was absolutely smitten by her.

And at that moment he realized the truth of it, he was in love.

'That was wonderful, Adam,' she said suddenly. And that interrupted his line of thought and he had to agree with her as they sat down at their table again. Adam picked up his glass and gave the toast...'To Catalonia...and to Spain.'

Dominique raised her glass. 'Yes, to Catalonia and Spain, but mostly to Catalonia.' And she winked at him and they both laughed.

Adam already knew that the Catalans valued their own independence, above everything else.

They both ate, and they talked, they talked about everything.

For their dessert, Adam ordered lemon and almond infused olive oil cake with lemon ice cream and fresh double cream, along with some coffee and some good brandy. As the waiter departed to the kitchen with their order, Dominique laughed about the amount of food they had both consumed. Several minutes later two waiters arrived back at their table. One was carrying their desserts, the other carrying a tray with the coffees and the brandies.

The food was again delicious. On tasting it, Dominique just raised her eyes and uttered the words...'Oh dear god...this is wonderful'.

After they'd eaten, the bowls were pushed aside and they sipped their coffees and the brandy. Dominique suddenly leant forward and took hold of Adam's hand, it was a moment of intimacy as she looked at him.

'Adam,' she began, 'Adam, I love this. I love being with you, I really do. I feel that I can talk to you all night and I can tell you anything, anything and everything. You don't know what all of this means to me. I never realized...' and then she paused for a moment, 'I never knew, you see, I've never had this before. I feel so comfortable with you.'

Finally, it was an admission, for both of them.

Adam took hold of her hands and stared directly at her.

'Dominique Cassens, I really care about you. Are we going to make something of this?'

Her eyes widened and she nodded. 'Yes, we are Adam, we definitely are' and then she smiled at him. 'Who would have ever believed that this could happen, and all over a silly suit?'

Adam raised his glass. 'Well, here's to Mr Hugo Boss,' he replied.

And she smiled at him again, and then took another slow sip of her brandy.

'Let's go home, Adam,' she said to him.

Adam paid the bill and the waiter then ordered them a taxi, and they left the restaurant arm in arm. Within fifteen minutes they were back at Adam's apartment on the Carrer Rosell. Adam unlocked the door and let Dominique enter as he switched on the lights.

He asked her if she wanted a glass of wine on the balcony, or some coffee, or even a brandy. But Dominique just stood there and looked at him. And then she took hold of his hand.

'No Adam,' she replied, 'I don't want a drink.'

And with that she led him into his bedroom. Once there, Adam took hold of her, he kissed her and they embraced, but then she pulled back. And for a brief instant, Adam didn't understand.

'Please Adam, please wait for a moment,' she said quietly.

She stood back, and unzipped the back of her white fitted dress and then slipped the dress off over her shoulders and then slid out of it. Underneath, she wore deep red, matching frilled underwear. Dominique looked directly at him, and then she unclasped her bra and then finally stepped out of her panties. She stood there in front of him, totally naked, and so very beautiful. And then she spoke.

'I'm yours, Adam Tyler, totally yours. Do what you want with me. But I'm yours to love.'

Adam stared at her, he was overwhelmed. She was so perfect, her shape, her skin, and her face, the face that he loved. There was nothing more to say. He went over to her and they again embraced and kissed, and then he took her to his bed.

The next morning, Adam awoke early and rang the bank to arrange an unofficial day off. Dominique got up at around ten o' clock and made them both some coffee and took it back to their bed. Two hours later they got up and showered together, and then Adam went out to buy his newspapers, as Dominique made them omelettes for a late breakfast.

They sat on the balcony and ate and talked and read the papers. Everything was easy.

In the afternoon they went out for a very late lunch and then went back to Adam's apartment and made love one once again. At around nine o' clock, Adam rang for a taxi and Dominique made her way home, back to her apartment in the El Raval District.

And that was the start of their relationship, and their new romance, together.

For Adam, life suddenly took a different twist. She was constantly in his thoughts, it was almost an addiction. And they began to see each other on most nights, and after dining and bed, Dominique would take the taxi home, sometimes in the early hours, because she always had to work the following day. The weekends however were different, the weekends were fabulous.

Almost straightaway, Adam spoke to Carlos Villena about his new relationship, and it was Carlos who recommended that Adam should invite Dominique to the upcoming wedding, the wedding of the daughter of Mr Baroja, the bank's manager. Carlos Villena told Adam that to be at a wedding with a beautiful woman on his arm would certainly gain Adam a lot of admiration and respect. Carlos had laughed and commented that it would now be he, who would suddenly be the most eligible man there, and that the women now would flock to him of course, now that Adam was 'out of the running..'

From there, Adam in turn had spoken to Mr Baroja about the possibility of inviting Dominique to the family wedding. And Mr Baroja, ever agreeable, was only too happy to include Adam's new partner to the family's celebrations. Mr Baroja was in fact quite pleased to see that his young protégé was suddenly somewhat settled. If Adam Tyler was in a settled relationship, then he wouldn't be so easily tempted to wander off to fields afresh.

So everyone was happy.

The wedding took place two weeks later. It was a Saturday.

The wedding service took place at the Temple of the Sacred Heart of Jesus, a stunningly beautiful Roman Catholic Church and Basilica, which is located on the summit of Mount Tibidabo on the outskirts of Barcelona. The views from there, down to the city and the harbour were spectacular.

The church was filled with guests, the groom was handsome and the bride looked beautiful, of course. It was a success. And for Jorge Baroja, it was a proud day.

After quite a lengthy service, the wedding party then proceeded to the reception at the

'Hotel Juan Carlos', a most prestigious and esteemed five-star establishment, where an impressive reception was planned to take place. It was a beautiful sunny afternoon, and as the guests arrived they were guided through to the extensive gardens where they were immediately served with glasses of chilled champagne. Friends, relations and old acquaintances all met up and greeted one another, talking about happy times, rekindling memories of the past, and laughing about old age, aches and pains, and the children and the grandchildren. And all the reminiscences and recollections, some forgotten, some not.

And then of course there were the new and younger generation. Young men talking about business and bragging about money and cars, and their wives stood in groups with the other wives, all expensively clothed, conceited, and talking about everything and nothing. Describing their smart houses and their children's accomplishments, along with the latest in fashion and the most fashionable places to dine.

Adam and Dominique followed the usual protocol and arrived at the reception correctly late, or at least, later than the immediate family. It was an accepted tradition that the family should all meet and rightfully get together before the other invited guests. It was the etiquette.

Dominique had arrived at Adam's apartment earlier that day, her head wrapped in a towel and carrying a bag full of assortments, along with an outfit hidden in a cover. She immediately disappeared into the bathroom and Adam was only allowed to pass her a glass of chilled white wine through a barely opened door. Adam dressed, and then he waited on the balcony. The only sound he could hear was that of a hairdryer. An hour later Dominique walked out of the bathroom.

Adam stared at her, and then he gulped. She looked stunningly beautiful. Wearing a red silk flared dress and a matching smart fitted jacket, her shoes and handbag also matched perfectly. Her dark hair was perfectly curled and her makeup immaculate.

She stood there and looked at him. 'What do you think?' she asked.

Adam walked over to her. 'I think I'm the luckiest man on the planet,' he replied. And then he reached over to kiss her, but she pulled back.

'No, no. I've just done my makeup. You'll have to wait until later.' And then she laughed at him as he shook his head.

They made their way to the Church by taxi, and Adam spoke to her about Jorge Baroja and also Carlos Villena.

Adam grinned. 'I'll have to steer you away from young Mr Carlos Villena, he fancies himself as a bit of a ladies' man. In fact, he truly does think that he is god's gift to all women.'

Dominique laughed. 'He sounds like a bit of a character.'

'Yes he is, or he thinks he is. Actually he's okay, we're good friends. But when he sees you I might have to pour cold water over him.'

Dominique giggled. 'Listen, I'm with you. You're my man and just remember that.'

Adam smiled, yes, life was good.

When they finally arrived, they'd both sat at the back of the church. Adam looked around and finally spotted Carlos Villena further down the church. He was sitting in a row with a couple of younger men and some middle aged women. Adam looked for someone who would possibly be Carlos's father, but he couldn't see anyone. However, Mr Villena Snr was apparently a close family friend of Jorge Baroja and so he may have been sitting nearer the front of the church. Suddenly, Carlos turned around and he spotted Adam, or he probably spotted Dominique, and then Adam. His eyes widened and he nodded to Adam and smiled.

Adam turned to Dominique. 'See, he's noticed you already, I told you what he was like.'

But Dominique just shook her head. 'Don't be silly,' she replied.

After the wedding, and once they'd arrived at the reception, Carlos immediately came over. Adam introduced him to Dominique but for once, Carlos was actually quite restrained, which surprised Adam. Maybe Carlos Villena was a slightly shyer person than he actually portrayed himself.

Other men, and their wives, had certainly taken notice of Dominique. Adam saw the men admiring her. For the women, it was a different sort of observation.

Later, when Dominique had disappeared to the Ladies room, Carlos made his way over to Adam and commented that the 'new lady' in Adam's life was certainly a beauty, but that was all, and Adam suspected that his friend was possibly slightly jealous. Adam had then asked Carlos about his father and that he would like to meet him. But apparently Mr Villena Snr had been taken ill, and because of that, Carlos's father and mother had not been able to attend the wedding. Carlos then quickly changed the subject, and that led Adam to wonder about the severity of Mr Villena's illness. He decided not to pursue the subject.

Dominique returned, and the three of them made some small talk about the wedding and then Carlos excused himself.

'My god, I don't believe it,' Adam commented, 'he's not the ladies man he portrays himself to be.'

'Maybe he's just a little shy,' said Dominique.

But Adam just laughed. 'Shy, no, he's the most conceited man I know.' And then Adam looked around, only to see Carlos chatting away to three young ladies, in a very animated fashion. They were all laughing as Carlos related some humorous story or other to them and he had their full attention.

Adam nudged Dominique and nodded in his friend's direction.

'See, I told you. He's at it again.'

For a brief moment, Dominique stared across at Carlos, and then she just laughed.

'You're only jealous,' she said. 'And anyway, you're spoken for, Mr Adam Tyler.'

As the afternoon and then the evening progressed, Adam manoeuvred himself, along with Dominique, around some of the guests that he knew or vaguely knew, and then he had conversations with some of the older members of the family, who were noticeably more sociable and somewhat more appreciative. Eventually, Adam got to introduce Dominique to Jorge Baroja himself.

Mr Baroja's eyes brightened when he saw Dominique.

'Young lady,' he said to her, 'you must look after this young man. He is my rising star and an asset to the bank. I don't know what I'd do without him. I want you to take good care of him.'

Praise indeed from Jorge Baroja, who after several glasses of champagne and good wine had mellowed somewhat. They talked about the wedding and Adam praised the bride and the groom, and commented about the service and the stunning church set on Mount Tibidabo.

Jorge Baroja took to compliments with a good heart. He was a happy and proud man.

And then Adam asked him, 'It was a shame that Carlos Villena's father couldn't make it. I know he's an old family friend of yours, I believe he's been taken ill?'

For a moment, Jorge Baroja said nothing. And then he shrugged, it was a strange gesture.

'We can only hope that he gets better soon then,' he replied. And then someone caught his attention and he excused himself.

Adam thought that the comment was slightly strange, but the wine was flowing and Dominique began to say something to him, and the night moved on.

Towards the end of the evening, Dominique disappeared to the Ladies Room and Adam struck up a conversation with someone at the bar, a man he didn't know and had never met before, but they merrily discussed the merits of living in

53

Barcelona, and then the man began to talk about football and Adam suddenly realized that he needed to escape. Football had never been his passion. He looked around for Dominique, as an excuse to get away, and then he saw her making her way towards him. The man beside him suddenly stopped talking when he saw her, but she walked straight up to Adam and grabbed his arm and kissed him. It was all very vital, and passionate, and the man just stared at them both.

'I want to leave, right now,' she suddenly demanded.

Adam looked at her, quite surprised. Her eyes were very wide and bright. And she suddenly laughed out loud and leant over and whispered in his ear.

'I want to go dancing. I want to go out and go dancing and get drunk.'

Adam stared at her, she had a wild look in her eyes and then he realized that she was maybe already too drunk. But this was strange, and she hadn't seemed that tipsy before. But booze was booze, and the alcohol affects everyone in different ways.

'Come on, Adam, please,' she complained, now somewhat more loudly, 'I want to go...now!'

And a few heads around the bar turned, and Adam realized that it was now probably a good time to leave.

He turned back to the man to excuse himself. But the man just smiled and shook his head knowingly, as Adam took hold of Dominique's arm and led her away from the bar.

Once they were in the foyer, Adam enquired about a taxi and he was informed that there were already a row of taxis waiting outside to take the invited guests home, and that Mr Baroja had seen to everything.

Dominique was suddenly becoming quite animated and she insisted that they should go to some club. But when Adam refused she became quite adamant and somewhat argumentative. He took her outside to save any embarrassment, and he lied as he explained to her that he had to work the next day and that it was already late and also that she'd already had enough to drink. But she just laughed.

'Had enough to drink?' she said to him, 'I haven't even started.'

'I don't care, Dominique. We're not going to a club.'

She looked at him, eyes wide. She was alive, very alive.

'But I want to drink vodka, Adam,' she insisted, 'Lots of vodka.' And she laughed again.

He stared at her. 'But you don't drink vodka.'

She giggled. 'Oh yes I do.' And then she leant forward and put her arms around him.

'Okay then, let's go home, Adam, 'let's go home and drink vodka. And then I'll make love to you.'

Adam continued to stare at Dominique, he'd never seen her like this. And with a slightly forced laugh he told her that he didn't have any vodka at home, he never drank it.

'But I have,' she replied, 'we'll go back to my place. No problem.' And she kissed him again.

It was an offer he couldn't refuse. He too, had drunk enough champagne and good wine all through the afternoon and the evening, and he too was becoming fluidly pliable. So they tumbled into a waiting taxi and headed off to Dominique's apartment in the El Raval District.

Ten minutes later they arrived at the 'Carrer Sant Pacia', one of the many narrow roads that cut through the 'El Raval'. Dominique told the driver where to stop and she and Adam both got out of the taxi, which then quickly drove away. It wasn't an area to loiter in. Dominique took hold of Adam's arm and led him down a narrower and badly lit darker street. There was a strange orange glow about the place which reflected from the lights of the nearby road.

'Be careful, Adam' she giggled, 'the road here's not very good.'

Then she suddenly stopped outside a plain, high fronted building and she smiled at him. Reaching into her bag for a key, she stepped forward and unlocked an old and very solid, worn green painted door. Dominique opened it and again laughed as she then took hold of Adam's hand and led him inside.

It was dark, but Dominique obviously knew the building and she clicked on a light switch from somewhere on the wall. The room was illuminated by a small bare light bulb that hung from the ceiling by a thin cord. Adam blinked, as he realized that they were both standing in a small square hallway that led to some stairs.

Dominique leant forward and kissed him, and then she ran her hand down the front of his pants and Adam gasped. She laughed, and then he laughed. And then she started to fumble with his zip.

'Make love to me here, right now, here in the hallway,' she said to him. And for a moment Adam almost complied, but then he pulled back and grinned at her.

'You crazy woman, you really are drunk, Dominique.'

But she just laughed, and then they both laughed at the madness of it all.

They made their way, rather unsteadily, up three flights of stairs and across a small landing, to where Dominique unlocked the door to her flat, and still laughing they both went inside.

Once again, Dominique switched on the lights and Adam followed her inside and closed the door behind him.

'Sit down somewhere, I'll get the vodka,' she said to him, and then she disappeared into her kitchen.

Adam glanced around for somewhere to sit, there were only two options really, a very upright and quite faded yellow moquette armchair, which did look rather uncomfortable, and a large brown leather sofa. The sofa was draped in some sort of multicoloured woollen fabric, and was laden with an assortment of cushions, all of various shapes and sizes, and also in a multitude of different colours. Adam chose the sofa, obviously. He sat down and looked around. Directly in front of him was a sizeable coffee table. It was constructed from a dark wood, but the legs were made from some kind of brazed silver metal and had a twisted shape to them. And then Adam realized that the table was of an Arabic design. He looked around the room, the lighting was very subtle, but the walls and the mantelpiece were full of small framed paintings and plaques, and plates, all Spanish or North African in nature. It was a strange, eclectic mix, but somehow it all worked.

Suddenly, Dominique came out of the kitchen. She was holding a litre bottle of vodka in one hand and two glasses in the other, which she then put onto the table in front of him. Adam looked at her. Her eyes were wide and alive, and she immediately spoke.

'I've got some lemon and ice and some cola. Wait for me, I want to pour.'

And with that she disappeared into the kitchen again.

He called after her, 'I don't usually drink vodka.'

'You will...' she replied, and then she laughed.

A minute or so later, she returned. She was carrying a tray, and on it was a filled ice bucket, a bowl of sliced lemons and four bottles of very chilled cola. However, this time she wasn't wearing her dress. Dominique put the tray down in front of him and then stood back, she was just in her red underwear and she wiggled her hips.

'You like..?' she giggled.

He stared up at her. She was incredible.

'Yes, I like, I really like,' he said.

She sat down beside him and then flung her arms around him, kissing his face and his neck, and then she suddenly leant over and bit his ear. The bite was quite hard and it actually hurt and Adam pulled way.

'Ouch...hey, steady,' he said to her.

But Dominique just sat there and she stared at him, almost in glee. And then she put her fingers in her mouth, as if to mimic some kind of 'naughty girl' attitude.

'I want to bite you, I want to bite you all over' she said, and her eyes were bright. And then her attention suddenly changed and she looked across to the bottles on the table.

'Come on, Adam, let's get drunk.'

'I think you're already drunk, Dominique,' he said to her.

'No, no, Adam,' she replied, '...I mean 'really' drunk.'

The two glasses were quite large tumblers, and Dominique half filled them with the vodka and then added some ice and lemon and then topped them up with the cola.

'Come on,' she said to him, 'let's drink these quickly,' and she passed him his glass. 'Cheers darling.' And with that she picked up her own glass and in one go almost emptied it.

Adam stared at her, he'd never seen her like this. Her eyes were so bright. She was so wild and alive. And somehow, different.

Then she took hold of Adam's glass and began to pour the vodka into his mouth, he almost choked, and Dominique just laughed.

'Come on, Adam, quickly.' And she made him drink the vodka again, and then all of it.

Adam sat back as he felt the sudden rush of strong alcohol hitting his stomach.

Dominique took their glasses and once more refilled them.

'God, that's strong.' he said to her. And he could feel the vodka running into his veins.

Dominique turned, and smiled at him. And as she looked at him, she slowly unclipped her bra and casually dropped it to the floor. Then she took the bottle and poured some of the Vodka into her cupped hand and then she proceeded to rub the clear liquid onto her breasts and over her nipples.

'Would you like to taste it 'neat', she said to him slowly, 'come on, Adam...lick me.'

He couldn't resist.

It turned out to be a night of absolute drunkenness and the most raucous sex. They'd almost finished off another bottle of vodka when Dominique dragged him off into her bedroom. By that time they were naked as they'd both continued to play their game of pouring neat vodka onto each other's body and licking it off. They were both crazily drunk. Then they'd ended up in Dominique's bedroom and they had the most indecent sex and made love.

Nothing mattered any more.

Adam awoke the next day, it was around lunch time. His head throbbed and his stomach was in turmoil. He opened his eyes and lay there for the next ten minutes, basically wondering where he was and trying his best to remember what had happened. Slowly, it all came back to him and he turned to look at Dominique. She had her naked back to him and all he could see was her head of curls on the pillow. In the end he managed to roll himself over and swing his legs out of bed. Adam sat there, almost wheezing. His mouth was extremely dry because he was dehydrated, and as he sat up his head began to spin. Twice he tried to stand up, but had to sit back down again before he realized the obvious.

He was still drunk.

Finally, he managed to stand, but had to steady himself by grabbing hold of Dominique's dressing table. Then he lurched across the bedroom, but had to place both of his hands against the wall to support himself and try to remain upright. Adam shook his head, his mouth felt like sandpaper and he desperately needed to drink some water. He cautiously made his way through the living room and went into the kitchen where he found some glasses in one of the cupboards, his hand shook slightly as he held one and then he went to sink and filled the glass with cold water. He drank the full glass in one go. The water felt so very soothing as it poured into his mouth, and over his extremely dried tongue and throat. But when the cold liquid hit his stomach, Adam began to spasm. He then staggered, as best he could, to the bathroom, where he spent the next ten minutes violently retching and vomiting into the toilet bowl.

Afterwards, Adam could only lean against the bathroom sink, again to steady himself, but then he made his way back into the kitchen to drink some more water. He sat himself down on a small wooden chair and put his head in his hands as he rested on the bare kitchen table. He felt dreadful. He considered making some coffee, maybe for both of them, but then he realized that his stomach couldn't handle it. In fact, he wondered if he was even capable of making coffee. And then his thoughts turned to Dominique and he wondered how she was feeling. And as he sat there, Adam remembered some of their evening's antics. Their lovemaking and their sex had been unbelievable, some things he'd never experienced with anyone else before. There had been no shame, and there were no boundaries, none at all.

Sitting there in his still drunken state, Adam almost managed to smile.

He eventually stood up. He drank another glass of water and then he slowly made his way back to Dominique's bedroom. As he walked through the living room he looked across to the table where they'd been drinking that previous evening. It was strewn with empty bottles, vodka and wine bottles and some upturned glasses, all littered with little pieces of sliced lemon. There was a plate that someone had eaten off, but Adam couldn't remember. His clothes and the remains of Dominique's underwear were strewn over the sofa and on the floor, and it was only then that Adam realized that he was still naked. He shrugged, he was past caring. It was a little too late for coyness.

He went into the bedroom and knelt at the side of Dominique. He began to slowly rub her shoulder as he tried to wake her. But she was completely out of it. Adam knew that he needed to go home. He knew he had to go home and sleep it off. The next morning he had some important business meetings at the bank and he realized that he couldn't arrive in this state. He wondered if he should just leave, but then he felt a pang of guilt. What sort of person would just leave her on her own? No, that wouldn't do, not one bit. He loved this woman.

Adam thought again about the previous night, she had suddenly become so bright and so animated, he'd somehow never seen her like that before. She had almost dragged him away from the wedding. Adam looked around, there was another empty wine bottle on the floor and some more glasses and the almost empty bottle of vodka, and he remembered even more. He took a deep breath. Yes, what a night.

He leant over her and spoke...'Dominique.' But he couldn't waken her. And so he slowly began to shake her as once more he spoke into her ear..'Dominique.'

Suddenly, she awoke, almost violently, and as she opened her eyes she spun around and stared up at him. There was a look in her eyes, it was almost a mixture of anger and fear, and then there was confusion. She just stared up at him, it was as though she didn't even recognize him.

Adam stared back at her, he was slightly concerned.

'Are you okay, Dominique?' he said to her.

She didn't say a word. Dominique just looked up at him, it was as though she was looking at a stranger for the first time.

'Dominique, it's me, Adam,' he said to her.

She said nothing, and then suddenly she started to blink as her mind began to work.

And then her eyes widened and she spoke.

'Adam, Adam it's you. Oh, thank god...'

He didn't understand. 'Who did you think it was?' he said to her.

She shook her head, 'No...no, you don't understand,' and then suddenly, 'I think I'm still drunk, Adam. I just didn't know where I was.'

'We're at your place?' he said to her again.

But she just lay back and rubbed her face, and then she closed her eyes.

'Do you need some water, or coffee?' he asked her.

'I need to go back to sleep, Adam, I don't feel well.'

'No wonder,' he said to her.

She heard him but didn't reply. And then she rolled over with her back towards him. There was obviously nothing more to be said. Adam just stood there. For a moment, she hadn't known him. It was as though he had been a stranger to her, a complete stranger.

He shrugged. It was probably the alcohol of course. It had to be. He didn't feel too well himself, either.

So he made the decision, he needed to go home, there was nothing he could do there. She needed to sleep it off. They both did.

So Adam went back into the living room and found his clothes and dressed himself. Then he took his phone out of his pocket and rang a taxi. He remembered the road, the 'Carrer Sant Pacia' in the El Raval district. Before he left he took a quick look into Dominique's bedroom. She hadn't moved. She was asleep.

Adam quietly left her apartment and then carefully made his way down the flights of stairs and out of the building. The bright afternoon sunshine dazzled him as he realized that somehow, somewhere, he'd lost his sunglasses. And then his head began to pound in the midday heat.

He walked down the narrow street that led onto the Carrer Sant Pacia. And then he stood there and waited for his taxi to arrive. Adam felt ill and was not taking much notice of anything as he rubbed his eyes. But slowly, he looked up, he needed to see if his taxi was on its way.

And that was when he saw it. There were people looking at him. Mostly men, in small groups, some of them standing on the different street corners, Arabs, and Africans, and Eastern Europeans, Armenians or Turks, and all dark skinned and even darker eyes, and all talking amongst themselves and glancing over at him. And suddenly, and for the first time ever in his time in Barcelona, Adam Tyler didn't feel safe.

And then from nowhere, his taxi arrived.

Just as it was about to stop, two Arab men began to walk across the road towards him, but when Adam quickly got into the taxi, the two men simply turned and walked away. And it made Adam wonder, why?

On his way back to his apartment on the Carrer Rosell, and back to the safety of the Eixample District, Adam began to wonder about Dominique's own safety. The El Ravel was a rough district, he'd always known that, but never realized. And then he remembered her telling him that she'd lived there for quite a few years and that she had good neighbours, she knew most of them and that she felt pretty safe.

Maybe he was over thinking things, maybe.

Once he was back in his apartment, Adam made some coffee. He managed to drink only half of it and then he dragged himself off to his bed. He then slept for a solid ten hours and it was almost approaching eleven o' clock in the evening when he finally awoke. He straightaway rang Dominique, the phone rang a dozen times but there was no answer. He surmised that she was probably still sleeping, and so he ended the call. By then he was ravenously hungry, and he went into the kitchen and made himself a plate of bacon and eggs, along with thick chunks of bread, laced with butter. It was a strange time to have breakfast, but he took his plate of food and a large mug of fresh coffee out onto his balcony and then he ate in the still warm heat of the night under the reflection of the bright city lights of Barcelona. As he ate, Adam stared across the city and to the approximate direction of the El Ravel District. Somewhere over there was the woman he loved. He wondered once again about her safety. And as he sat there on that warm summer evening, so safe and secure, he suddenly shuddered.

The next morning, a Monday, Adam awoke somewhat refreshed. The first thing he did was to ring Dominique, but there was still no answer. Maybe she had got up and gone to work, or maybe she was still asleep. Adam made some coffee and had a light breakfast and then he showered and changed and went off to work.

Once there, back at the bank, it was business as usual. Adam made his way to his office, he had the usual paperwork to sort out and then a business appointment at around 11-30. He had some ongoing talks with a builder who wanted a loan to build a new block of apartments. Adam had dealt with the same builder before, and on similar projects. The builder was a decent man with an equally decent business. So the meeting would be no more than a formality really.

At around ten o'clock, Adam decided to go and speak to Jorge Baroja. It was good manners to speak to his boss and thank him for his generosity over the weekend. Adam left his office and took a lift to the next floor to Mr Baroja's office. Once there, he spoke to Mr Baroja's secretary, a Miss Montero, a long serving lady in her late fifties who sometimes considered her role as being Mr Baroja's personal guard dog. To speak to Mr Baroja without an appointment could be difficult. However, Miss Montero had always had a bit of a soft spot for Adam, and she also knew that Mr Baroja trusted Adam explicitly. So there was never usually a problem.

'Is he available?' Adam said to her, with his usual show of boyish charm. It usually worked, and it did again.

Miss Montero looked up at him and smiled. 'Yes he is, I'll just give him a buzz.'

She pressed the intercom button, 'Mr Tyler to see you, Mr Baroja.'

'Yes, okay,' came the reply.

Miss Montero nodded towards the door, and then she added, 'He's in a good mood.'

Adam grinned at her as he tapped on Jorge Baroja's office door and entered.

He was greeted with a smile. Jorge Baroja was sitting at his desk, as usual, and surrounded by mounds of paperwork, again as usual.

Adam walked over to Jorge Baroja and immediately shook his hand.

'Congratulations, sir, he said, 'the wedding was wonderful. A complete success, it was absolutely fabulous.'

Mr Baroja grinned, 'I'm glad you enjoyed yourself, Adam. It was a great day for my family.'

'You did them proud, sir,' Adam replied, 'you really did. The wedding service itself and then the reception afterwards, everyone enjoyed themselves, they really did.

Jorge Baroja smiled, he was a happy man. And a proud man.

'Thank you, Adam, it was good to have you there.'

And then Jorge Baroja laughed, 'and what about you and your beautiful young lady?' he asked, 'she certainly turned a few heads.'

Now it was Adam's turn to grin, and then he just shrugged.

'What can I say, Mr Baroja, I'm a very lucky man.'

'You certainly are, she's a beauty.'

And then Jorge Baroja looked at Adam, somewhat inquisitively.

'Could this be 'the one' for you, Adam. Could this young lady be the next 'Mrs Tyler?' And then he laughed.

Adam just stood there, rather dumbfounded. It was something he'd never really thought about. And Jorge Baroja's suggestion had been like a bolt from the blue. But why not?

Adam sighed. 'Do you know something Mr Baroja? We've never even spoke about it, we've only been going out together for a short while. It's early days yet, I suppose.'

'Well young man,' said Jorge Baroja, 'don't lose that one. I have been married to my wife for over forty years, and let me tell you something. It is true when people say, 'Behind every successful man there's always a good woman'.

Adam laughed, slightly embarrassed. 'Well apparently, I am now seriously spoken for, Mr Baroja. At least that's what she keeps telling me.'

Jorge Baroja smiled as Adam continued, 'So I suppose I'll have to leave the ladies of Barcelona to the likes of young Carlos Villena. He certainly is a ladies' man, I don't know what happened to him after the wedding?'

And at that moment, Jorge Baroja suddenly stopped smiling.

'Ah,' he said, 'Our Mr Villena. I actually need to have a word with you about him.'

'Why, what's wrong?' Adam asked. He was genuinely concerned.

Jorge Baroja picked up his pen and then began to tap it on his desk. It was an old habit.

'He's getting more than a bit scrappy, Adam. Not only in his timekeeping, but also his workload. He seems to have gone off the boil somewhat. I've seen it before of course, with different employees. But it won't do, and as you know, I run a very efficient team here, I always have.'

Adam nodded, but said nothing.

'Did you know that he's not turned in 'again', this morning, Adam?'

Adam did not, and he shook his head, but he heard the word 'again', and he wondered?

Mr Baroja continued, 'he's becoming rather erratic, he comes in late and has started to leave early. I know everything that happens in this bank, you do know that?'

Adam did, and the one reason that Jorge Baroja knew everything that was going on in his bank was in a long way due to his secretary, Miss Montero. Miss Montero had for years, taken it upon herself to listen to all the office gossip, dissect it, and then pass on the appropriate information to her boss.

'I've looked at his workload too,' Baroja again continued, 'he's not pulling his weight.'

Jorge Baroja stopped tapping his pen on the desk and he looked at Adam.

'Could you take him on one side and have a word with him, Adam? I know his family and I don't want any more upset.'

'I'll speak to him, sir,' said Adam, efficiently.

Jorge Baroja nodded, and Adam knew that their meeting had come to an end. He thanked Mr Baroja once more and left.

As he walked down the corridor towards the lift, Adam considered the position. If Jorge Baroja had to eventually sack Carlos Villena, it would be an embarrassment for both their families. They were apparently all old friends. And when Mr Baroja had said 'I don't want any 'more' upset,' Adam could only conclude that he was talking about Mr Villena's apparent illness.

Adam grabbed a coffee from the office vending machine and then he went back to his own office. The coffee was barely drinkable, but it was liquid and it was hot.

As he sat there, he thought about his conversation with his boss. And then the comment about, 'could Dominique be the next Mrs Tyler? Adam thought about it. He loved her, of course he did. He was besotted by her. But it was early days, very early days, and the weekend had shown him that there were things about Dominique Cassens that he certainly didn't know. He took a deep breath, and then for some strange reason he suddenly thought about Joanne Berkley. Yes, Miss Joanne Berkley, and he'd loved her too, or he thought he had. And he remembered his promise to himself...'that he would never be fooled again.'

And then he sighed. Dominique was not Joanne Berkley. Dominique loved him, and he knew that. And he smiled to himself. Yes, marriage was a thought, and a possibility. He would never find anyone more beautiful, and he remembered Jorge Baroja's advice, that 'behind every successful man there's always a good woman'. Could Dominique be that one woman? Yes probably. And Adam smiled, again he would have to give it some serious thought.

Adam's 11-30 appointment went well and his business with the builder was concluded after a very pleasant hour. Both men shook hands on a deal which satisfied both parties. After that, Adam could then go somewhere for lunch. He tidied up his desk and filed a few relevant papers, and then stepped out of his office. As he walked down the corridor he considered where he was actually going to dine, there were several possibilities, but at that moment he suddenly saw Carlos Villena coming down the corridor towards him. Carlos grinned and waved as Adam checked his wristwatch. It was nearly one o' clock, and Carlos Villena was only just arriving at work. Adam sighed, he knew what he had to do, and any thoughts of a lengthy and peaceful lunch were abruptly cancelled.

'How are you, buddy?' Carlos asked. And Adam could immediately smell the stale alcohol. Carlos Villena had been drinking. His eyes were slightly reddened and his clothes were somewhat dishevelled.

'Did you have a good weekend?' Carlos then asked.

Adam took hold of Carlos's arm. 'Come with me, now,' he said.

'Why, what's wrong?' said Carlos.

But Adam said nothing, he just led Carlos down the corridor and back to his own office. On the way there they stopped at the coffee machine and Adam pressed a few buttons and got them both a cup of coffee. He made sure that one of them was black and strong, for Carlos of course. They went into his office and Adam offered his friend a chair. Carlos sat himself down, he looked comically quizzical.

'Drink your coffee,' said Adam, and he watched as Carlos picked up his cup and took a sip. His hand was slightly tremulous.

Adam went around his desk and sat down.

Carlos just looked at him. 'What's wrong, Adam?' he asked again.

'You're in trouble,' Adam replied.

Carlos Villena stared at him.

'Why am I in trouble, what the hell's wrong?'

'Jorge Baroja, that's what's wrong.'

Carlos sighed, shrugged, and then sat back in his chair.

'Go on, what have I done now?' he asked, almost too casually.

'Jesus, man,' Adam replied, 'well, look at the state of you. You're still half drunk, and you're only just turning into work.'

'I was at the wedding,' Carlos immediately stated, 'We were all celebrating, it was the Baroja's wedding, for god's sake. What's his problem?'

'Well for a start, it's now Monday and everyone else has managed to make it back into work, including Mr Baroja himself. And, he's been watching you're timekeeping, apparently you've developed a habit of coming in late and then leaving early. He's not happy with you, Carlos, and he's asked me to have a word with you.'

'Fuck him,' said Carlos, in a sudden outburst of anger. He took another quick drink of his coffee and then almost slammed the cup back down on the desk.

'Fuck Baroja,' he continued. 'I've worked my heart out at this bank, and for what? Little or no reward, that's what.'

'Hey my friend, you've got a very good job here,' Adam said to him.

Carlos looked at him, and suddenly it seemed to be a look of resentment.

'You, you don't know anything. I was forced into this bloody job when I left school. Baroja and my father, they thought it

67

would be a good idea. Dear god, sometimes it drives me mad being stuck here.'

Carlos Villena was angry, and for some reason his anger seemed to be directed at Adam.

There was an impenetrable silence, and for a brief moment neither of them spoke.

And then Carlos slumped back in his chair, his anger dissipated. He just shook his head and sighed, and then he again reached out for his coffee.

'I'm sorry Adam,' he said. 'You're right, and it's not your fault.'

Adam looked across his desk to his friend. 'It's okay, Carlos. It's just the booze talking, I know that. Actually, I've had a pretty heavy weekend myself.'

Carlos again shook his head.

'No, I need to sort myself out,' he replied.

'Actually, it's a bit more serious than that.'

Carlos Villena stared at him, 'Why, what else is there?'

'Apparently, you're not pulling your weight. Mr Baroja has been looking into your workload and he's not happy with the results.'

'But I work hard,' Carlos tried to explain.

'Not according to Mr Baroja,' Adam replied.

There was suddenly another flash of anger in Carlos Villena's eyes, and Adam saw it. He raised his hands.

'Hey Carlos. Don't shoot the messenger here. And think about it this way, Mr Baroja's asked me to have a word with you. If things were really serious, he would have had you marched into his office.'

Carlos sat back in the chair, he rubbed his face and nodded. And with it, the Carlos Villena that Adam knew so well, always slightly nervous and worried about work, suddenly returned.

'What have I got to do, Adam, to make things right,' he asked.

'You need to get your head down and do some serious work. And you need to be here early and put in the hours. You do know that.'

Carlos nodded.

'I'll have a word with Mr Baroja,' Adam said, 'I'll give him some bullshit story. I'll tell him that you've been having some personal problems with one of 'your' women. He'll understand that.'

'Thanks Adam,' Carlos replied, and he actually managed to smile, and then he stood up. There was nothing more to say.

However, Adam continued. 'Don't worry. You're father is a good friend of Mr Baroja's. And friendships always count, you'll be okay.'

But Carlos just looked back him. 'Really, is that what you think?' he said, and he shook his head. And with that, he walked out of the office.

As Adam watched Carlos leave, he considered his friends last statement. It seemed to be a rather odd thing to say.

Chapter 4

For Adam Tyler, the next six weeks were just about perfect.
His relationship with Dominique had fallen back into their usual comfortable regime. There was none of the vodka fuelled 'madness', in fact, they never even really spoke about it. Dominique had been somewhat embarrassed by her behaviour and had apologized, and Adam had told her not to bother because the sex had been unbelievable, and they'd both laughed it off and had gotten on with their lives. Their habit was that Dominique would stay the weekends. She would come over on the Friday evening after finishing work and she would leave again on the Sunday evening or on a Monday morning to go back to work. It all depended on their mood, or where they had dined. And that suited Adam, he preferred it that they stayed at his apartment. He wasn't keen on the thought of returning to the 'El Ravel' District. And anyway, Dominique had never offered. It was another thing that they had decided not to talk about.

Carlos Villena too, had got himself back to normal. He was putting in the hours again and was always busy. Their lunches together had gone a little 'vague', but Adam suspected that his friend had maybe been a little embarrassed by it all. Anyway, his 'pep talk' had seemed to have worked and Adam was a little relieved, and pleased. Yes, all was well.

There had only been one minor event, not a problem really, and if truth be known, it had suited Adam.

Two weeks after the Baroja wedding, Dominique had arrived at Adams apartment, and she was fuming with anger. It turned out that she had become overdrawn at her bank and on inspection, it seemed that the bank had charged her a ridiculous amount of interest.

Adam had looked at her bank statement and the accompanying letter, which had informed her of the charges. She was overdrawn by several hundred Euros.

'How on earth am I supposed to get out of debt when those bastards are charging me that amount of interest?' she complained.

And it was true. Adam had looked at the charges, and they were indeed excessive.

'I thought you said that 'La Caixa' Bank' always looked after you?' he asked.

'Well, apparently not anymore.' And she'd scowled at him.

'Calm down,' he'd said to her. 'I'll get a bottle of wine out of the fridge, go and sit on the balcony.'

He went to the fridge and picked out a decent bottle of white wine, and then along with two glasses, he went out onto the balcony. Dominique was sitting there, again looking at her bank statement and tapping her finger on the table top in a very agitated manner. Adam tried hard not to smile. He sat down and poured the wine.

'Here you go,' he said to her.

'It's not fair,' she said suddenly, out loud.

Adam just sat there.

'I am being robbed, aren't I?' she asked him.

'Yes, you are,' he replied, and he smiled.

Dominique didn't. This wasn't the sympathetic reply that she was looking for. She picked up her glass and turned away from him. She sat there, still agitated, as she looked out across the city.

Adam smiled. Miss Dominique Cassens wasn't speaking to him. Miss Dominique Cassens was sulking. And Adam grinned as he realized that it was all about to become 'his fault', simply because she was a woman and he was a man. And it was always the man's fault, obviously. He would have to do something about it of course, so he decided to act seriously.

'We have to do something about this, Dominique, he'd said, 'this is ridiculous.'

She turned to him and did some sort of tiny sideways movement with her head. It was her acceptance that he was finally saying something positive.

'I've been thinking,' he said to her, ' I can sort this problem.'

She looked at him.

Adam continued. 'We'll open you an account at my bank. It's not a problem, I could go in tomorrow or on Monday and open

71

you an account with us. And I can act as your personal reference, it won't be a problem at all.'

She frowned. 'But I've no money to open an account, Adam. I'm overdrawn for god's sake.'

It was time for him to smile. 'Yes, I've been thinking about that. Well, I'll open a new account for you and I'll get you preferential rates, and then I'll transfer a thousand Euros into your account from my account. Then you can go to 'La Caixa' Bank' and with that money you can close your account there. Tell them to 'stuff themeselves', and then have your wages paid directly into your new account at our bank. It's that simple.'

Dominique stared at him for a moment, rather passively.

'I don't want your money, Adam. I'm not a charity.'

Adam smiled at her, he'd expected this.

'It's not a gift,' he said, 'it's a loan, that's all. Once you get back on your feet financially, you can pay me back a bit at a time. It's not a problem, really it isn't.'

Dominique sighed. 'It's just that I've got a little bit behind with my rent, and I've been spending too much money on new clothes.'

Adam nodded. He could understand that. He'd taken her to a host of really good restaurants and she always looked fabulous. That was why she'd been spending money on clothes, obviously. And he felt a slight pang of guilt, part of all this could actually be his fault. And after all, he was always so proud of her when they walked into somewhere and all heads turned.

'Don't worry,' he said to her, 'I love you...you know that.'

She smiled at him, and for Adam it was like the sun shining back at him. She leant forward and kissed him.

'Thank you, Adam,' she said, 'I've been really worried,'

She picked up the bottle of wine and refilled their glasses.

'And when we've finished this bottle of wine, Mr Tyler, I'm going to take you to bed and reward you for your generosity.'

Adam laughed. 'Oh thank you, Miss Cassens,' he replied. 'Our bank always prides itself in giving our customers a really good service.'

Later, as they lay together in bed, Adam came to a decision. It was something that had been at the back of his mind ever since he'd spoken to Jorge Baroja, after the wedding.

'Have you ever thought about moving in with me?' he asked her.

She turned to him and frowned, 'In here...with you?'

'Yes, of course 'in here'...and 'with me.' Who else?'

She looked at him, 'I've never given it much thought.'

'Well, I've been thinking about everything,' Adam continued, 'It seems a bit silly for you to be paying all that rent when you could live here for nothing, and then you could maybe work fewer hours. Or you could even find a different job and maybe work part-time instead?'

For a moment, Dominique said nothing, and then she spoke. 'You seem to have thought everything out, Adam?'

He looked at her curiously, 'Is there a problem?'

Dominique took a deep breath. 'Well, yes and no,' she replied. 'Part of me would love to move in with you and be with you all the time. But you see, I do value my independence. I've just come out of a long term relationship and we've not been together all that long really, and what if we did fall out over something? I'd be homeless.'

Adam smiled, 'We're not going to fall out over anything. I love you, you know that.'

'Yes, and I love you too. But I'm enjoying my life at the moment, for the first time in a long while, and I don't want to spoil it.'

Adam was about to say something, but she cut him off. 'And I do really quite enjoy my work, Adam. I have some good friends there.'

Adam shrugged. 'It was just a thought, that's all.'

She leant over and kissed him. 'And I appreciate what you're saying, but let's just carry on the way we are for a while. And at some point, I will move in with you, when I'm ready. It's a promise.'

And that was it. A promise was enough.

Adam went into the bank on Monday and opened the new account for Dominique. He sorted out the references and did all the paperwork. It was all fairly effortless, and then he transferred a thousand Euros from his own account into her account. Along with that, Adam also arranged that she could have an overdraft facility of up to a thousand Euros before incurring any charges, and any charges that were incurred would be dealt with at a preferential rate. It was one of the perks of his job.

Once it was all organized, Adam handed the appropriate documentation to Dominique and basically left her to it. Her finances were nothing to do with him, and in truth, he wasn't interested one bit in her ever paying him back.

For the next two or three weeks, life was easy. Life was good.

Adam and Dominique enjoyed each other's company, they wined and dined, and they did all the simple things that couples do. Going to a movie or a restaurant, and then making their way back home to Adam's apartment. On other nights they would just stay in and eat and watch TV. They only ever drank wine or the odd bottle of beer. Adam never bought vodka, and Dominique had never again asked for it, thankfully.

And then, on one particular Saturday night, they'd decided to go out for a meal. They went to the 'Can Valles', a fairly local restaurant on the Carrer d'Arago on the other side of the L'Eixample district heading for Sant Antoni. It was a restaurant that Adam had never actually been to but had been recommended to him by one of his business clients. A table was booked for ten o' clock and they'd arrived on time by taxi, thanks to the prowess of their driver, whose knowledge of Barcelona's countless backstreets and the possible shortcuts was beyond profound. As they entered, they were met by the maître d', who showed them to their table. The menus arrived, along with a bottle of chilled Cava. As the drinks were being poured, Dominique smiled and giggled.

'I'm ready for this, Adam,' she suddenly announced, 'let's have a really good night'.

'We always have a good night, don't we?' he replied. And he smiled too.

And with that, Dominique picked up her glass of Cava and almost drank all of it in one go. Adam looked at her.

'Come on Adam,' she said to him, 'let's have some fun.'

Adam did as he was told, and drank, and as soon as he put his glass down, Dominique straightaway refilled both their glasses and then she drank again.

Adam looked at her. 'Hey, we've got to eat first, you know'.

And Dominique laughed, 'Yes I know, but I'm thirsty,' and she pouted at him, almost like a spoilt child. And Adam just shook his head as he turned back to the menu.

They ordered tuna in balsamic and olive oil, and then sizzling beef with grilled vegetables. And as the waiter took the order, Dominique looked up at him and asked for another bottle of Cava. The waiter nodded, and then disappeared back to the kitchens.

'So we're on the 'second' bottle of Cava?' Adam enquired, 'I was going to order a good bottle of Rioja, as usual'.

But Dominique just laughed at him. 'Oh come on Adam, its Saturday night and I want a good time. Let's celebrate'.

'Celebrate what?'

Dominique giggled as she again picked up her glass.

'I'll think of something,' and she giggled and she drank, 'and if I can't think of anything, I'll make it a night that you'll certainly remember, once we get back to your flat. And now cheers, Mr Adam Tyler,' and she raised her glass to him.

That bit of information put Adam into a much better frame of mind, and he too raised his glass and drank, just as the waiter arrived with another bottle of Cava, to replace the first.

They ate, and they drank. The food was delicious, as Adam expected. And Dominique was on form, on very good form in fact. After the bottles of Cava, Adam ordered a bottle of decent, Rioja Blanc, and then somehow, they followed on with two bottles of the red. They talked, and Dominique was quite animated and they both laughed. They were happy, and they were both becoming slightly drunk. At the end of their meal, Adam asked Dominique if she wanted some coffee. But she'd scoffed at the idea.

She laughed, 'I want more than coffee'.

'Brandy coffee?' Adam suggested.

But Dominique smiled at him, and then she reached over and as she took hold of his hand, she looked at him.

'Can we have a change, Adam? Can I have some vodka, please?'

Adam looked back at her.

75

'Really?'

'Yes please' and she giggled. 'You know how it makes me feel.'

And that reminder, and of all the possibilities of the evening ahead, and also the fact that he was slightly intoxicated himself, had Adam quickly looking around for their waiter.

They drank large vodkas with cola, and then as Dominique went to the toilet, she asked Adam to order another round of drinks. He of course complied.

The drinks arrived just as Dominique came back to the table. She smiled, and then giggled, and then burst out laughing. Adam looked at her, so vibrant and so alive, so very, very alive, in fact.

'What's so funny?' he asked her, but she just shook her head.

He glanced at her. 'You look different, somehow'.

She laughed again, 'Its makeup...and the vodka,' she giggled. And she raised her glass and they both drank. Her eyes suddenly gleaming with excitement. It was probably the vodka.

Adam continued to talk, but then Dominique suddenly interrupted him.

'Adam, I want to go dancing. Take me dancing, please Adam'.

He stared at her for a moment.

'I thought we were going home,' he said to her, 'I thought we were finished here.'

'Yes I know, but it is Saturday night and it's not that late, and you never, ever, take me dancing, Adam.'

And then she took hold of his hand, again.

'Please Adam, just for an hour, and then we'll go home. I promise.'

'But I don't know any clubs,' he said. It was an obvious excuse.

'Yes, but I do,' she replied, and then she laughed out loud, again.

And because of the drink, Adam capitulated. So he paid the bill and ordered a taxi.

They'd just finished drinking their vodkas when the taxi arrived, and so they left the restaurant arm in arm and rather giddily walked over to their awaiting car. As they opened the taxi's rear door, the driver turned around and asked them, 'Where to, my friends?'

Dominique leant forwards. 'Club Le Souk', she replied. The driver nodded.

And then they both climbed into the back and the taxi sped off immediately.

Less than ten minutes later, and they were driving through the rather disreputable El Raval District. Adam realized this, but said nothing, as Dominique chatted away excitably. In fact, she'd never stopped talking since they'd left the restaurant. They finally arrived.

The taxi stopped outside a garishly lit building, the club obviously.

'Club Le Souk' was a decent sized, smart white painted building. It had a large front veranda with long wide steps leading up to it. Above the entrance was a blue neon sign, lit up with the name of the club in the flowing writing of an Arabic style. People were milling about outside and on the veranda and Adam noticed that the men seemed to be mostly Arab and African, and there were several Spanish girls there too, all very pretty, in tight fitting dresses and perfect make up, and all so scintillatingly beautiful.

Adam began to pay the taxi driver as they both got out of the car, and Dominique went over and spoke to some of the girls, who seemed to know her, and they all chattered and laughed.

As Adam approached they all looked at him and smiled. Dominique said something to them and carelessly giggled, and then she took hold of Adam's arm and they went into the club.

'You know them?' Adam asked her.

'They're just neighbours,' she replied casually as she looked around. And then she spotted the doorman.

'Jonah...' she practically shouted out loud.

Jonah was a tall and very well built African man. Muscular, and dressed in a sharp black suit and matching tailored shirt, and he looked every inch the part.

Dominique skipped up the steps and onto the veranda, she went straight over to him and flung her arms around him and laughed. Adam just stood there at the bottom of the steps, feeling rather out of place and slightly embarrassed. Dominique continued to talk to Jonah and then she suddenly looked around at Adam. She stared at him for a moment, and then smiled, and then she turned back to Jonah and continued her conversation, now seemingly more serious. Adam watched them both, and then Dominique turned back to him again and gestured for Adam to come up onto the veranda. Jonah glanced at Adam for a moment, and then he took a mobile phone from his inside pocket and began to dial. As Adam approached them, Dominique started to hurriedly speak to Jonah again, who in turn spoke to someone on the other end of the phone. And suddenly Adam realized that this was a three way conversation. However, what amazed him even more, was that they were all speaking in Arabic.

Jonah nodded to Dominique, and then he turned off his phone and put it back in his pocket. Dominique smiled, and then she said something to Jonah , again in Arabic. Then she turned and took Adam by the arm and led him into the club. Jonah said nothing, there was not even a hint of acknowledgement.

'What was all that about?' Adam suddenly asked her.

'Oh, I needed to check with the owner, I've got us into the club for free,' Dominique replied.

'I didn't know you spoke Arabic? Adam suddenly continued, but Dominique just shrugged.

'Everyone around here knows a smattering of Arabic, it's nothing unusual.' And she quickly dismissed the subject as she waved and called out to some women who she seemed to know. Adam glanced around, apparently they'd got into the club for free, but no one else seemed to be paying either, and in fact, there seemed to be nowhere 'to' actually pay. And as he looked around, he failed to notice Dominique looking up at the small video camera that was attached to the ceiling. And neither did he see her smile at the camera, and then nod.

Upstairs in his office, the owner of the club looked at the monitor and he smiled.

'Ah, Dominique,' he said to himself.

There were another two similar monitors on his desk, and from there in his office he could switch from camera to camera and see everything that was going on inside or even outside his premises. He could check on the entrance and the bar, the dance floor, and even the toilets. He knew everything that was happening and what everyone was doing. And if he saw anything that he didn't particularly like, he could quickly contact Jonah, who would sort out any problem, along with the other four or five of his security men who casually wandered around the club, virtually unnoticed. The owner liked to keep his security very low key, only to be used whenever absolutely necessary.

They both walked into the club, and Adam found himself being pulled in the direction of the bar, Dominique was quite insistent. The music was loud and the club was very busy, but Dominique just laughed and her head swayed to the music.

'Come on, Adam,' she shouted, 'let's have some fun.'

Adam in turn tried to reply, but she wasn't really listening. She was just waving and calling out to the people that she knew.

They got to the bar, which was full of people, all trying to get served.

'God, Dominique,' Adam had to shout, 'it's mayhem in here, we're never going to get a drink. Do you really want to stay?

She shot him a glance. It was partly annoyance, but there was something else there in her expression. And then she suddenly threw her arms up in frustration. She turned back to the bar and to one of the bartenders who was busily making some concoction or other.

'Luis..!' she shouted out loud. Luis immediately looked up. He was a tall, thin faced man with gelled back dark hair. He could have been Spanish, or maybe Turkish. It was hard to tell. He stared back at Dominique, and there was a look of recognition.

'Luis...Dos vodkas grandes,' she called out. 'Two large vodkas.'

Luis nodded. She would apparently, be served next.

There were three Arab men in front of her, waiting to be served, and they turned to Dominique to complain about her obvious rudeness. But one of them immediately recognized her. Adam heard him say 'Dominique' as he broke into Arabic. Dominique just shrugged her shoulders and laughed. And the man turned to his to friends and spoke to them, and they just smiled and looked at Dominique in a way that Adam didn't particularly like.

79

Dominique giggled and began to speak to them in Arabic, and then the men laughed too. One of them stared over her shoulder at Adam, and then he looked away.

Dominique turned back to Adam.

'Give me some money,' she almost demanded.

'How much do you want?' he asked, and then he felt slightly stupid.

'Just give me some money, Adam. And give me enough. I need to pay the bartender and give him a good tip, or we'll be waiting here all night to get served.'

Adam took out his wallet and gave her half of the money that he had in there. Luis, the bartender, quickly arrived with their drinks and Dominique peeled off some notes and handed them to him. She also shook her head at him as a sign that she didn't want any change.

'Cheers, Adam,' she said as she passed him his drink. But Adam just stared at her. He was becoming annoyed. They'd both had a lot to drink and the alcohol was beginning to work the wrong way. And Dominique saw it. And she suddenly changed, and softened.

'I only want to have some fun, Adam,' she said to him, and she looked around. A couple who had been sitting against the opposite wall on two tall bar stools were just about to leave.

'Come on, we'll sit over here. It's quieter.'

They quickly went to sit on the vacant stools and Dominique continued to chatter away relentlessly. She also continued to drink, her glass was soon almost empty. And then suddenly, she stopped and looked at him.

'What's wrong with you, Adam?' she asked.

'I don't like it here,' he replied.

'Why not?'

'I don't know. I just don't like it.'

Dominique stared at him for a moment.

'I'll get us some more drinks,' she said, as she slid quickly of the stool and went back to the bar. But Adam didn't want any more booze, and called after her, but his voice was lost in the noise and the pounding music.

Dominique got served almost immediately, of course she did, as she once again handed over the money to 'Luis'. She made her way back to Adam, now once again smiling and moving rhythmically to the dance music. She handed him his drink and then kissed him on the cheek.

'I'll make it up to you tonight when we get back home, you'll see.' And she giggled.

And only that thought, finally made Adam grin, and the alcohol kept working and he shook his head, almost carelessly.

Dominique suddenly looked at her watch, and then she looked around.

'I'll just go to the bathroom,' she said, and she put her glass down and kissed him quickly on the cheek again and then disappeared to wherever the bathrooms were.

Adam sat there, and he began to look around the club. 'Club Le Souk', was definitely a base for an Arabic and Middle Eastern audience. The carpets there were all deep red with golden coloured Arabic patterns around the edges. And all the fittings in the club, the doors, the chandeliers and light fittings, and everything metal around the bar were all made to look like gold in the subdued lighting. Although in fact, everything was highly polished brass. But the effect certainly worked. The music, also so rhythmically Arabic, pulsated throughout the club, and on the dance floor people gyrated and swayed to the addiction of it.

So easy, and so compelling.

And at that moment, Adam realized that he was out of place, and possibly out of his depth. And again he felt slightly uneasy and he looked around for Dominique. Where on earth was she, she'd now been away for more than fifteen minutes, and Adam was suddenly concerned. However, the club was busy and maybe the toilets were too. And after all, women were well known for reapplying their make up while they were in there, so god only knows.

Several minutes passed, and finally Dominique returned. But it was a different Dominique.

She appeared out of the blue and then roughly grabbed hold of Adams arm. She was laughing and moving her body to the music. Then she let go of him and stood back and began to dance in front of him with her arms high in the air. Her eyes flashed wildly and she couldn't stop laughing. She was drunk, and for Adam, it was time for them to leave.

81

'Come on Dominique, it's time for us to leave.' he said quickly. Once outside he would phone a taxi.

But she just stared at him hypnotically and she grinned as her head weaved from side to side to the music.

'Come on Dominique, please, let's go,' he asked her again.

'No, no, no, Adam. I want to dance, I want to dance all night,' she said to him and she laughed loudly.

Adam stood up and he reached for her arm. But she didn't want that and she pushed him away. And her wild eyes stared at him and she laughed again, but now she was laughing 'at him' as she continued to dance. And suddenly Adam became angry, and this time he grabbed her arm firmly and pulled her close to him. But Dominique just stared at him.

'I've told you, I want to leave,' he said in a low voice. But Dominique just continued to stare back at him, wildly.

And then he noticed something. He looked at her, and around her nostrils he could see some sort of white shadow, traces of white. It was white powder. And then Adam realized straightaway what it was. It was cocaine.

And he suddenly realized that Dominique wasn't drunk, far from it. He held her arm firmly.

'What have you taken, Dominique?' he asked her.

But she ignored him and then began to move her head from side to side, again to the music.

Adam shook her, to try and get some sense into her.

'Dominique, what have you taken? Its cocaine isn't it, I know its cocaine,' and his voice got louder.

Upstairs in his office, the owner of the club sat down and watched them on his monitor.

All of this amused him somewhat, and he knew what was happening, and what could happen. Because he had just been downstairs and had met up with Dominique, and it was him who had just given her the cocaine. And now he would sit back and watch what happened.

Yes, he was amused.

Dominique didn't like being manhandled.

82

'What's your problem, Adam?' she almost slurred, and she wrenched herself free. And then suddenly she began to laugh again.

'Oh, come on, Adam. I want to dance,' and she started to sway to the music once more.

'I don't want to 'bloody' dance, Dominique,' he almost had to shout over the music, 'why are you taking that stuff, where did you get it from?'

But Dominique only heard...'I don't want to bloody dance...' And she just shrugged.

'Please yourself then, Adam,' she said to him, and with that she turned around and began to dance her way onto the packed dance floor.

And Adam just stood there, somewhat stunned, and somewhat helpless.

Dominique gyrated onto the dance floor and began to sway to the music along with the rest of the people there. Her arms were raised above her head as her body moved from side to side to the incessant beat. The music took hold of her.

At that moment, two of the Arab men who had been at the bar earlier moved closer to her. Dominique didn't notice them at first because her eyes were partially closed, the effect of the music, the cocaine, and the alcohol all combined. Then one of the men took hold of her waist and began to move with her and she opened her eyes and saw him, and then laughed and shook her head to the music as they began to dance together. The second man moved behind her, and he took hold of her hips and began to dance with her too. Dominique turned to him and she began to giggle and laugh and began to move her hips provocatively. He moved closer. Then he began to run his hands up and down her legs and onto her bottom, and Dominique continued to laugh and dance. And then the man took hold of the bottom of her dress and started to lift it, and he rolled it up over her underwear so that her bottom was now visible through her negligee. And he started to grope her buttocks intimately, and Dominique continued to dance. The man dancing in front of her then began to run his hands up from her waist and up to her breasts, and then he started to caress her, and Dominique moaned and then leant forwards and put her arms around his neck and she started to kiss him as the rhythmic music played on.

Upstairs in his office, the owner of the club smiled as he watched it all on his monitors. He'd seen it all before and he knew, he knew exactly where this was going to end. And he reached over and picked up his phone and pressed a button.

Adam stood there horrified, he could not believe what he was seeing and what was happening in front of him. And then all of his emotions exploded. He charged over towards the dance floor. He was full of alcohol and he was ready to fight, he didn't care if there were two of them. He didn't care about anything, except Dominique.

But as he reached the dance floor, two 'middle eastern' looking men stepped out in front of him to block his way. Adam tried to push them out of the way but they grabbed hold of his arms to stop him. Adam began to fight back, when suddenly, a huge muscular arm gripped him around his neck, so hard that it virtually paralysed him. He felt as though his neck was being squeezed in a vice and he was left powerless as he struggled to breathe or even move.

It was Jonah, the huge doorman who gripped Adam's neck, and then he nodded to his two security assistants and they grabbed hold of Adam's legs and then they carried him towards the exit. They dumped him unceremoniously outside on the veranda and as Adam lay there dazed, the two security men went back into the club. Adam lay there for a few minutes, aware that the doorman, Jonah, was still standing over him. And as he lay there he suddenly thought about Dominique. She and Jonah were friends, surely he could explain to him what was happening to her inside the club. He rolled over and he finally managed to stand up, and then he turned to Jonah to try to explain.

But the huge black man just raised his hand and he slapped Adam across the face so hard that it knocked Adam off the veranda and onto the pavement. For a moment he almost lost consciousness. Jonah then stepped down off the veranda and he kicked Adam in the chest. Adam groaned and he rolled into a ball, fearing that the next kick would be to his face. But Jonah

84

just walked around him and kicked him in the back twice, and just as hard. Adam groaned again, he was in absolute agony. Jonah then reached down and grabbed Adam by the throat, so as to get his full attention. Adam couldn't speak, and the huge black man just stared down at him.

'Don't ever come back here. Come back, and I'll kill you, do you understand?' he said

Adam was shaken and upset, and fearful, but he managed to nod back.

Then Jonah simply stood up and walked back into the club.

Adam lay there for a couple of minutes, and in that short time a hundred thoughts ran through his head. Dominique was still in there, and she'd become someone that he didn't know, he didn't know at all. And he couldn't understand what was happening, he was in a daze. But the one thing he did realize was that he wasn't safe there. He had to get away, get away from the 'El Raval', before even worse could happen to him

Adam managed to stand up, and he rather unsteadily began to walk away. He had to get back to the 'Las Ramblas' and to the centre of the city. He made his way, carefully avoiding anyone who came anywhere near him, anyone who could rob him or maybe just beat him up, simply for the fun of it. Then luckily, he finally managed to flag down a lone taxi who took him home and back to the safety of the Eixample District.

Adam staggered into his apartment and he collapsed onto his settee. He lay there for half an hour, his thoughts continually running through his head, over and over, and again and again...

'Where was Dominique, what had happened to her, and the cocaine, and was she being raped by those Arab men, and why did everyone in that club seem to know her. And why was she behaving like a prostitute? Was she a prostitute..?'

And then it dawned on him, the reality of it all.

Of course she was.

Finally, he slept for a few hours. When he awoke his body ached, but he got himself up and then made some very strong coffee. After that he went into his bathroom and turned on the shower. He stood there as the hot water worked on his sore face and his aching body. The slap to his face wouldn't leave any bruises, but there were deep red marks across his chest and across his back that would. And as he stood there, his thoughts returned to Dominique.

Truth be known, he knew very little about her private life. She'd never really spoken about her work, and then when he thought about it, did she work? Adam didn't actually know where she worked other than it was some factory somewhere. But was she really a prostitute, it was something that Adam didn't want to readily think about or even admit to himself. He loved her. He did love her, didn't he? He was certainly infatuated with her, and he knew he was, she was his one and only weakness. But she took drugs, and that was another hidden secret, and how had he missed that? She had been very clever, too clever

But now he knew that he had to find everything out, and he knew that he had to know the truth. And the truth would be in her bank account. There would be details of her wages and who paid them. And there would be other details too. Adam was a banker and for him, looking into someone's personal bank account was like looking into their diary. What was paid in, how it was paid in, and by whom. And then there was the withdrawals, those regular standing orders and direct debits always told the story of how someone ran their life. But more importantly were the cash withdrawals, they were the figures that told you everything about someone's lifestyle, especially if they were regularly buying and taking drugs.

Adam came out of the shower. He got dressed into some comfortable clothes and then made himself some more coffee. He'd made up his mind. It was Sunday and the bank was closed. He would go there and he would go through Dominique's bank account. He had access to the bank, his senior position allowed that, he could and did go there whenever he wanted.

An hour later he arrived at the bank, and he let himself in as usual, he had the keys and the alarm's security codes. On his way there he'd tried to reconsider everything that had happened. They were almost excuses really. Maybe the cocaine thing had been a 'one off', maybe he'd been mistaken, or had someone spiked her drink, and he immediately thought about the barman 'Luis' at the club. Could he have something to do with it? And then he had feelings of immense guilt. What had happened to Dominique last night with those two men? Would they have taken advantage of her? She could have been raped. And at the thought of that he felt sick. What was he going to do? Was she hurt? Could he forgive her? And in his heart he knew he could, he would have to. He just couldn't let her go. He couldn't lose her.

Adam locked the doors to the bank behind him, and made his way to his office. He always felt the loneliness of the bank when it was closed and empty of people. And today even more so, as he walked along its echoing corridors.

Once he'd entered his own office, Adam immediately turned on his computer and logged in. As the computer's screen flickered into life, Adam opened one of the drawers in his desk and pulled out a thick pile of paperwork. He quickly rummaged through the accumulated sheets of paper until he found what he was looking for. Just a single sheet of paper, and written on it were Dominique's account number and details. When he'd originally opened the account for her, he'd scribbled down her banking information, in truth, just in case she had ever lost her own bank details, or if she'd ever been short of money again, because he would have transferred some more of his own money to her.

He took the sheet of paper and began to copy her account number into his computer, and then he used his own password to 'okay' everything. The computer screen flashed for a moment and then the account came up immediately. Adam read the name 'Miss Dominique Cassens' with the appropriate account number underneath. And then he began to scroll down the column of figures below. And then he stopped. Adam stared at the figures, and for a moment he didn't understand. And then he continued.

In front of him, the computer showed that Miss Dominique Cassens had a balance of over seven hundred and fifty thousand Euros in her bank account.

Somehow, Miss Dominique Cassens, unbelievably, had a bank balance of almost three quarters of a million Euros.

Adam sat there in disbelief. How was this? And he just stared at the computer screen and the figures that it was showing him.

Adam was more than just confused. How on earth had Dominique accumulated all of this money? Certainly not working at a Mail order company. And once again, Adam scrolled down her accounts to check her payments, and he straightaway saw the cash deposits and the amounts of between five to ten thousand Euros, paid in almost daily, and sometimes even twice a day.

Adam was astounded, and as he sat there he wondered what the hell was going on. And he knew that whatever it was, it must obviously be something that was highly illegal.

And then Adam suddenly realized something. He'd opened this account for her. And he had opened it with no references at all or checks. He'd simply used his position to open her a bank account and he'd 'okayed' everything too. And also, he'd opened an account for someone he was romantically involved with, openly involved as far as the bank was concerned. And now this?

Adam sat there and he put his head in his hands. What was he going to do, and how had this happened? In the space of less than a day his life had been turned upside down.

One minute he'd been happy and in love and been content, and now 'his Dominique' was gone, he didn't even know who she was anymore, and he could also be implicated in some sort of financial scam. Along with this he'd also just been into her bank account, something which was traceable and also meant that he could now be party to what was going on. Adam cursed himself. He sat there for several minutes, and then he came to a decision. He had to find Dominique. He would have to go to her apartment and speak to her to find out what was going on. And if she wasn't there, he would have to wait for her to arrive home, from god only knows where she'd finally ended up.

Adam locked the bank after setting the alarm's security codes, once again all traceable to him. He shook his head at that knowledge, and then he rang for a taxi. It was now past nine o'clock in the morning and Barcelona was beginning to awake. The taxi did eventually arrive and Adam directed the weary driver to Dominique's address at the 'Carrer Sant Pacia' in 'El Raval'.

Ten minutes later they reached their destination. Adam paid the driver and then went into the apartment building. He made his way up the stairs, and with it a hundred repeated memories swirling around in his mind. Adam made his way down the small landing and knocked on Dominique's door. There was no answer. He stood there for a few minutes and then he knocked again, this time a little harder and slightly more insistent, and but again there was no answer. And then in a moment of impulsiveness, he reached for the door handle and turned it, and the door opened. Adam stood there, suddenly apprehensive. What was going to happen if he entered? Dominique was obviously in there, she must be asleep, or unconscious. But would she be alone? And at that moment, Adams pulse began to race a little bit faster.

He took a deep breath and walked into the apartment, whatever happened now, he was committed. He entered the living room and was met by the story of the evening. There were empty vodka bottles on the floor, along with some wine bottles. But the story of the night lay there on top of the coffee table, faded lines of white powder, the remains of several lines of cocaine. It said it all.

Adam looked down at the whole event, still with feelings of despair. He knew that Dominique was in bed, and with whom? But he knew he had to find out, this whole business had to be finished. He had to know what was going on. He went to her bedroom, the door was open and he walked straight in. There was enough light in the room to tell him what he needed to know. Dominique lay there in bed, she was alone, but had not been alone. The bed had been slept in by two people. It was all so obvious. And Adam felt the sudden pain of anger and jealousy, and all of the upset caused by the lies and the deceit. He looked down at her. Her makeup and her lipstick almost rubbed away. Her eyes were smudged and swollen, her lips were swollen too. And Adam shuddered at the obvious understanding of it all. He leant over and shook her, but there was no response, and so he shook her again, this time harder, but there was still no movement, the drugs and the alcohol had taken their toll.

Adam sighed. What was he going to do? He had to talk to her about all the money in her account, there was no other way. And he made the decision. He would stay there with her until she finally regained consciousness. He couldn't leave this, or her, because something illegal was going on and it could implicate him.

Adam stared down at her, and there was a pang of sorrow. This woman, and now it was over. He knew it was. He'd loved her, he still did love her, but not this Dominique. Not the used and drugged and unconscious woman who lay there in her bed.

Adam thought about the cocaine, and Dominique had been his addiction, he knew she was.

Once again, he'd made the mistake. The mistake of thinking that infatuation was love.

Adam went back into the living room, he opened the curtains and the morning sunshine flooded into the room and highlighted the devastation in there. Adam shook his head and went into the kitchen to make some coffee. He would have to stay there and wait, and eventually try to get some coffee into Dominique. There was no milk in a depressingly empty fridge, so he poured himself a mug of strong, black coffee and then returned to the living room and sat down on Dominique's large leather couch. He moved a couple of empty glasses and placed his mug amidst the remains of the cocaine. It was almost surreal.

Twelve hours ago, he'd been a different man, and she had been a different woman, and for him, it had been a different world.

And as he sat there contemplating all of this, he suddenly heard a noise. Adam quickly looked up. It was the door handle to the apartment. Someone had arrived, someone was returning to the apartment. And Adam sat there, transfixed. What was going to happen now?

And then the door slowly opened, and a man walked straight into the apartment. He was carrying two bottles of vodka and he was somewhat dishevelled and his eyes were bloodshot and red. He looked across and he straight away saw Adam. Both men just stared at one another with some astonishment. But then the man suddenly seemed to relax and he shrugged his shoulders.

'Finally,' he said to Adam, 'Well, this was always going to happen, I suppose.'

But Adam just stared back in disbelief, as he tried to grasp the situation. Because he knew the man standing there in the doorway in front of him.

It was Carlos Villena.

'What...!' They were only words that Adam could even say. He was astounded.

Carlos Villena casually closed the door with the back of his foot. And then he walked over and put the two bottles of vodka down on the coffee table. He looked at Adam.

'You look like you need a drink' he said.

Adam was speechless. He stared up at Carlos Villena. The man still seemed half drunk, half drugged. The bleariness in his eyes said it all.

'Oh Adam, Adam...don't look so surprised,' he continued. And he went over to the cupboard and took out two glasses. And then he opened a kitchen drawer and took out a long, sharp carving knife.

With his knee, Carlos Villena pushed the faded yellow moquette armchair across the floor, until it was facing Adam, and then he sat himself down. He put the two glasses down in the centre of the coffee table, and then slowly and intentionally, he placed the knife down in front of him.

Adam just stared at the carving knife in wonder and disbelief.

'I know you are not a violent man, Adam,' said Carlos Villena, 'but we need to talk, and I will have to explain things to you, things that may make you angry. So you need to know, that I will protect myself. Do you understand me now, Adam?'

But Adam said nothing.

Carlos Villena smiled, and he reached over for a bottle of vodka and began to unscrew the cap.

'Drink?' he asked.

'I don't think so,' Adam replied, somewhat warily.

Carlos Villena just shrugged as he filled one of the glasses with the vodka. Then he sat back in the chair and took a sip.

'So Adam, where do I start?' he continued. 'You do realize that Dominique is a prostitute? She's a prostitute, and she belongs to me?'

'Belongs to you?' Adam couldn't believe what he was hearing.

'Yes, Adam,' Carlos Villena replied. 'She belongs to me.'

Adam started, 'Last night in a club, she was with two other men...'

'Yes, yes,' Carlos Villena interrupted, 'I know all that, I saw it all.'

'You were there?

Carlos Villena smiled at him. 'Adam, of course I was there...I own the 'Club Le Souk'.

Adam stared back. 'You own a club?'

'I own a lot of things, Adam. You see, I have my own little empire. And last night I saw you arrive, I have the club monitored, I can see everything from my office upstairs. To tell you the truth, I wasn't expecting you, but that stupid little bitch needed her drugs and she can't let it go. So that's why you ended up at my club.'

'You supply her with cocaine?'

'The cocaine, and all the men,' Carlos Villena replied as he took another drink from his glass. 'When she left you last night to go to the toilet, she actually came up to my office for her powder. Those two men had already asked Jonah if she was available, and so I sold her on for the night.'

Adam was suddenly angry, but Carlos Villena glanced at the knife, and Adam saw the movement in his eyes.

'I'm actually quite sorry, Adam,' he continued, 'I know you've become quite infatuated with our 'little' Dominique, but it's just a business you see.'

'I don't understand..' Adam blurted out, almost involuntarily. But in his mind, a thought was already beginning to form. All of this must be linked to the amount of money in Dominique's bank account.

Carlos Villena laughed and shook his head. He drank the rest of his vodka and put the glass back down on the table, and then he picked up the knife. Adam was suddenly wary, and he moved slightly on the settee, quickly wondering how he could defend himself.

Carlos Villena laughed again. 'Adam, Adam...please, calm down.' And he took the knife and began to scrape the remains of the lines of cocaine together until the powder formed into a neat little pile, and with that he scraped the powder off the edge of the table and into the palm of his hand.

Adam just watched him. And he suddenly realized why Carlos Villena was permanently late for work. He also realized that he'd never really known the man, and it had all been an act. The man in front of him, wearing crumpled and dishevelled clothes and unkempt hair, and those bloodshot eyes.

Carlos Villena raised his hand up to his nose and he snorted the powder into his right nostril. He sat back in his chair for a moment and shook his head. And then he looked up. And it was as though a curtain had been lifted. Carlos Villena was suddenly alive and smiling. Even his eyes became brighter and alert. The drugs were working. And he laughed out loud and reached for the bottle of vodka and filled his glass once again.

'Are you sure you don't want a drink?' he persisted.

But Adam didn't reply, he just shook his head.

'You may do, once you know exactly what's happening, Adam.' Carlos Villena replied, and he sat back and took a drink from his glass. He was smiling now and comfortable, almost invigorated. He was also becoming quite talkative. And then he looked across at Adam.

'Let me tell you a story, Adam, he said. 'Let me tell you all about our 'little' Dominique...'

'I first spotted her when she was twelve or thirteen years old. She was always such a pretty little thing, always with so much promise. Back in those days I used to go down into the 'El Raval' regularly. I would go there to drink and buy some weed and the occasional woman. They were great times, and being Spanish and not a 'Gringo' like you, I could fit in there quite easily and I made friends. From there I started to buy weed and sell it on to my own friends, and then eventually to 'friends of friends' and from there it all just grew. There will always be a demand, and the buyer always needs a regular supplier, and I became that supplier. From there, the cocaine became an obvious addition to my business. I'd seen Dominique hanging about on street corners, she was always up to no good and I made it my business to find out about her. It turned out that her mother had been a prostitute when she'd been younger, but her looks had turned against her and she'd taken to the cocaine too, and then eventually on to heroin.

Dominique's father was Moroccan, and that's where her dazzling looks come from, and that's why she's always had that

93

'bit extra'. Her father came over from Morocco and moved in with her mother and became her 'pimp'. When she lost her looks and was demanding more and more cocaine, he dumped her and left, leaving them penniless and living off whatever Dominique could steal. I started to talk to Dominique and I began to give her jobs. She would pick up the drugs and also deliver to some of the rougher places, the places where it wasn't safe for me to carry around any sort of cash. She would pilfer some of the drugs or the money, of course, but I kept my eye on her. I got to know her mother too, an ugly little woman who hardly left the house. I told her mother what was going on and that I would give her some drugs and a little cash if Dominique worked for me. The old woman was only too happy to agree, she was an addict by then and this was an easy way out. By the time Dominique was fourteen she was sharing my bed, she was a delicious little thing. Even at that age she was good, and she would do anything that I asked her to do, anything at all. But after a couple of years I became bored, and by then she was about sixteen or seventeen and I could see how men looked at her. So I made her 'my' business. By then she was already taking cocaine and she would also screw anybody behind my back, as long as they paid her. So there you go. Eventually her mother overdosed on the heroin that I'd supplied her with, so that was one problem less. And so I then moved Dominique into this apartment, and that worked too. It was a good base for her, and I could also 'use' her whenever I wanted. She really is good at sex, Adam, isn't she?'

And Carlos Villena grinned.

'You should thank me for that, Adam. You really should.'

For a moment, Adam didn't speak. He just sat there breathing heavily, thinking about the story that he'd just been told. And then something finally struck him.

'So what happened to 'Rafael Molina', her supposed fiancé? Adam then asked, 'I gather he wasn't the villain that Dominique portrayed. Did he get ripped off too?'

Catlos Villena looked at Adam for a moment, and the he burst out into almost hysterical laugher.

'Adam, you are so stupid, you bloody fool. There was never any 'Rafael Molina', we simply made it up.'

'But there was the receipt from a restaurant, the receipt that he'd left it in my suit pocket.'

Carlos Villena just shook his head as he drank more vodka, He was becoming quite animated and he grinned at Adam.

'I put the receipt in your pocket, Adam. It was me. The day you invited me back to your place to look at your pretty, little, 'Hugo Boss' suit. While you were in the fridge getting the wine, I simply slipped the receipt into your pocket. That's why I made such a fuss about the suit.

I knew you'd be upset when you thought that someone else had worn it. You English, you're all such bloody snobs. And I knew that you couldn't resist ringing the number, and when she arrived at your apartment, I also knew that you wouldn't resist little Dominique either. It was all so obvious.'

Adam was annoyed that he'd been so easily tricked, and he had been. He'd been made a complete fool of, by a woman who he'd mistakenly thought he loved. But what hurt him even more, was that he'd thought that Dominique loved him too. And that was the something that really hurt him.

His mind began to tick, there was an obvious reason for all this deceit, and it culminated in the amount of money in Dominique's bank account. It was obviously drug money.

'Why me?' Adam suddenly asked. 'Why me, what do you need me for?' He needed to keep Carlos Villena talking, because he needed to find out exactly what was happening.

And then suddenly, there was some sort of noise, and Dominique walked into the living room. Both men turned to look at her, she was completely naked. She was slightly dazed and for a moment somewhat unsteady. She looked around and then she saw the two bottles of vodka on the coffee table. Carlos Villena watched with some amusement as she immediately grabbed one of the bottles.

'Dominique, look...Adam's here,' he said to her and he pointed his finger to Adam.

Dominique squinted as she stared across at Adam.

'Who?' she asked.

'Adam, he's you're boyfriend, remember?' Carlos Villena replied, grinning.

Dominique blinked, and she stared at Adam again. Then she shook her head.

'Oh. Okay,' she muttered. But she didn't even recognize Adam, and both men knew it.

Then she smiled to herself, it was nothing more than a stupid grin really. She was drunk and drugged and she was naked. But she didn't care, she was oblivious to absolutely everything.

She turned to Carlos Villena.

'I'm keeping this,' she said to him, as she waved the bottle.'

'Okay,' he replied.

And then Dominique leant over him and she began to kiss his cheek and his neck.

'And don't be long,' she said to him and then she stood up and began to make her way back to her bedroom. She stopped for a moment, rather unsteadily, and she waved the bottle at him once more.

'Don't be long,' she said again.

Adam just stared at her. She was supposed to be 'his' woman, and he loved her. And now this. She didn't even recognize him. It had been a lie, all of it, just one great big lie, and he was suddenly angry. It was jealously of course, but he couldn't help himself. And his anger suddenly got the better of him.

'So this is all about the fucking money, is it?' he blurted out. And then, 'So this is all about the three quarters of a million Euros that you've got stashed away in her bank account.'

Carlos Villena stopped for a moment, and he took stock.

'So you know about that then,' he replied. 'Clever boy. When did you find out?'

'This morning,' Adam almost snarled.

'Oh, so you've been to the bank this morning have you?' And Carlos Villena smiled to himself. He knew that all of this implicated Adam Tyler. On finding any discrepancy, Adam should have straightaway rung his Bank manager, Jorge Boroja, and then the police would also have to be informed. But no, Adam was sitting here in front of him, so obviously no such thing had happened. And that made Adam Tyler somewhat complicit.

Very complicit, considering.

But at that moment, Adam didn't see it.

Carlos Villena looked at Adam, and then he poured himself another vodka.

'I'm going to tell you another little story Adam, it may amuse you, and it may not. But there you go.' And he took a deep breath.

'You Adam Tyler, are partially to blame for your problems. You are the problem, and now here we have the result."

Adam stared back at Carlos Villena. 'I don't understand,' he replied.

'Well, Adam. Everything was going to plan until you arrived at the bank. Adam 'bloody' Tyler, the 'golden boy'.

Adam could now see and hear the effect the vodka was taking.

But Carlos Villena continued, 'You see, I had everything planned. I was supposed to be the 'golden boy'. That was supposed to be 'me'. I never even wanted to go into banking, but it was my father who talked me into it as a 'steady profession'. He and that 'bastard', Jorge Baroja had been lifelong friends and they'd obviously discussed my future. And it was almost a certainty that I should have been the next 'Head of Commercial Banking'. But no, you came along and Baroja suddenly informs us that he's going to promise the job to you. He and my father fell out over it, that's why he didn't go to the Baroja wedding. They'll never speak again. It was going to be so simple. I would run the commercial banking and I would launder the money through several hidden accounts. But more than that, the drug cartels all need somewhere to hide their money legally, and I was going to be the conduit for that money. There's millions involved, millions and millions of Euros. I would have been a millionaire within a couple of years. But then you come along and I'm suddenly passed over. Or so it seemed. But no, not now.'

Adam was suddenly alert. 'What do you mean by that?' he asked cautiously.

Carlos Villena took another drink.

'You're implicated, Adam, and I'm not. You see, you opened a bank account for 'your girlfriend', the girlfriend who Jorge Baroja and other members of the staff have actually met.

And now in her bank account there are three quarters of a million Euros. You've obviously got access to her account because you already know about the money, and that will be flagged to you. You've found out about the money and you should have contacted Jorge Baroja immediately, but you didn't, you came here instead. And if the bank and the authorities were to ever look into Dominique's account, they would see that the regular deposits of between five and ten thousand Euros were made by you, Adam, and you alone.

Adam stared back at Carlos Villena. 'What do you mean, 'deposited by me?' he demanded.

'It's quite simple. I deposited the money in your name. Even Dominique doesn't know how much is in there, thank god.' And at that, Carlos Villena laughed to himself.

Adam was stunned. 'You'll not get away with it.' But it was useless threat.

'Actually, I will Adam. I have no visible association with Miss Dominique Cassens. In fact, I only met her briefly at the Baroja wedding and we hardly spoke.'

Adam suddenly remembered Carlos Villena's apparent shyness at the wedding. All a lie, and all a planned deceit.

'In fact, she came to me at the wedding for her cocaine. And thats why you got dragged back here for your wild night of sex. She told me all about it, and I had to make her behave after that, because I needed you. But the 'icing on the cake', Adam, is that I've covered my tracks to this eventuality, just in case this day did arrive. You see, I've written a report on you, and all of your supposed dealings. And in that report I've written about my suspicions, when I inadvertently discovered that you'd opened a bank account in your girlfriend's name. All the cash deposits made by you, have been historically noted along with an accurate account of what I believe has been going on. That information is filed on the bank's computer and I could print it off or email it straight to Jorge Baroja or anyone else at the bank. You see, I could even send it directly to head office. You would be implicated of course, and arrested. There would be an enquiry and the possibility of prison. You would be ruined, Adam. And I would become the 'golden boy' again. No doubt about it. And I would quickly become the next commercial manager, even Jorge Baroja would be under scrutiny because of his deemed incompetence. All of this going on right under his nose, and by one of his staff, not only that, the supposedly top member of his team. If he wasn't sacked, they would certainly have retire him earlier than planned.'

Adam eyed Carlos Villena, the once shy and culpable, and likeable, was now arrogant and aloof, and drunk.

'So why don't you, Carlos? Adam asked, 'Why don't you file your little report and have me arrested. As you say, and possibly quite rightly, you could end up being the manager.'

But Carlos Villena just smiled.

'You are a very clever man, Adam, but not as clever as you think. You see, if there was a scandal at the bank, and then an enquiry, they would see how easy it was to open an account and be able to launder money. The security there is actually pretty lax and new systems would then have to be employed to counteract this sort of thing. And for me, that would be a disaster, if absolutely everything was going to be scrutinised. No, that wouldn't do at all.'

And at that, Carlos Villena grinned.

'Actually, Adam, I have a different plan. In truth, I don't want the position anymore. I would find it rather boring, having to turn up at the bank every single day, and all that paperwork and the reports, and the decisions too, Oh dear me, no. No, I have a better plan, well better for me, and for you too, actually.'

Adam frowned, and he wondered where all of this was leading.

'We will carry on as normal, Adam. And congratulations!'

And with that, Carlos Villena laughed as he raised his glass as a toast.

'Yes my friend,' he continued, 'we will carry on as normal and it will be business as usual, and no 'ripples in the pond', as they say. I'm going to take a back seat and you're going to cover me and make me look very efficient. I'm going to sit back and let you run everything.'

Adam took a deep breath, and he suddenly realized what was happening to him. He was being used and he was going to be further used. He said nothing, he needed time and he needed to think, because he was now caught in a trap.

But Carlos Villena continued. 'It will be good for both of us Adam, believe me. Together we can both launder the drug money. And in a couple of year's time, when Jorge Baroja finally retires, which he certainly will, I have no doubt at all that you will then take over at the bank. And then we can deal with the cartels. We can launder the drug cartel's money for them and make ourselves millions. In five years time I'll see to it that you and I are both very, very rich men. And then we'll bow out. We could both resign or retire, and then disappear and live our lives in luxury. It's so simple.'

Carlos Villena was now fairly drunk, but he still had his wits about him, Adam realized that.

'I...I'll have to think about it, Carlos,' he said warily. But Carlos Villena just looked back at him, and he was no longer smiling.

'So...I see, Adam,' he said, suddenly in a harder tone. 'So now you're trying to be clever. You're trying to be cleverer than me and you think that you can outsmart me. Well you can't, because I have everything figured out. You're a clown, Adam Tyler, and I have you in the palm of my hand, you arrogant bastard.'

He was becoming angry now and Adam once again began to worry about the knife.

Carlos Villena took another swig of his vodka.

'And now Adam, I want you to leave, you can go. Go on, leave.'

Adam immediately stood up and was heading for the door. At last, an escape of sorts.

But as he reached the door, Carlos Villena turned around and called after him.

'Adam, tomorrow we start afresh, or I'll have that report on Jorge Baroja's desk by nine o' clock in the morning. Do you understand me?

Adam could do nothing but lower his head and he replied, 'Yes, I understand.'

Carlos Villena then stood up, rather unsteadily and then he grinned.

'Okay then, you can go now, because I need to go to bed and fuck your little girlfriend, again.'

Adam left the apartment, he walked down those familiar steps and out of the front door and into the bright sunshine. He stopped and then he looked up to the 3rd floor and he wondered what was happening in there at this moment to Dominique. And then he felt disgusted with himself for being so pitiful. He had to realize what had happened and why, and what was happening now. He was being used, and he had to get all if this through his own thick skull. 'His' Dominique was no longer his. And she was no more than some prostitute.

Unbelievably, it was still mid morning, and at that time and mainly because it was Sunday, the El Raval was still fairly quiet and therefore relatively safe. And so he decided to walk. He could easily walk back to Las Rambla and from there he would get a taxi.

In fact, he didn't. Adam was so deep in his own thoughts that he walked all the way back to his apartment on the Carrer Rosell. Once he got there, he made a pot of coffee and then went to sit out on his balcony. As he sipped his coffee, he suddenly looked around and then he looked back into his empty apartment. Over the last months he'd had the happiest times of his life there. He'd made plans for them both, and he would have married her, yes he would. And they would have had children together and had a wonderful life. So many wonderful dreams, and a future for them both, yes together. But now suddenly, it was all over, as though it had been ripped from his arms, his life had taken on an ugly twist which he found hard to understand. And now he was stepping onto dangerous ground, and the last twenty four hours had turned his life around, or it could. Adam sat there, staring into space. He was trapped, surely he was.

Adam sat there for over an hour, mulling things over in his mind, over and over again.

He'd lost her. He loved her, but he'd lost her. And part of him couldn't understand why.

And then something occurred to him, and something clicked in his mind.

And finally, something happened.

Adam Tyler became angry.

He'd been tricked, and he'd been used and he'd been lied to. And by whom? Well the answer was quite simple really. He'd been deceived by a drug dealer and a prostitute. And where would all this lead too? It would end up being a disaster for Adam, and he realized that all the evidence would point to him and not Carlos Villena. And not even to Dominique either, because she could simply deny any knowledge of the account. There were no signed papers, Adam had simply approved everything. And that was just one possibility, either that, or Dominique Cassens would simply disappear.

So no, Adam wasn't going to become embroiled in something that could send him to prison. And then he realized something even worse. Carlos Villena had spoken about laundering money for the drug cartels and Adam would be party to absolutely everything.

Knowledge was a dangerous game. It could even end with him being murdered.

Adam Tyler made a decision, he needed a plan.

An hour later he looked at his watch, he would now have to wait. Maybe, just maybe, there was a chance that he could work things out.

Adam waited until seven o'clock that evening, and then he picked up his phone and dialled a number.

Chapter 5

It was one o' clock in the afternoon in New York. It had been a dull sort of day and there had already been a few sporadic bouts of drizzle and rain earlier that morning. But the clouds were finally beginning to thin and a few rays of delicate sunshine had started to reflect on the myriad of concrete and glass buildings that have made New York City the financial hub of America.

Paul Maynard was sitting at his desk attempting to eat a pastrami salad sandwich, whilst drinking from a flimsy plastic cup, now half full of lukewarm and very tasteless black coffee. He was trying to concentrate on the computer screen in front of him, however, he was having some difficulty in trying to complete the three or four activities all at once, as he repeatedly clicked the mouse to continually move from page to page on the display if front of him.

And hence, the rapidly cooling coffee.

Watching the Dow index, the ever changing, and at that moment, the rather erratic stock market, the various money markets and the other financial markets all around the world was no mean feat. Not only watching them, but also trying to understand them and stay one step ahead, was akin to chasing a very frightened rabbit around a very large field. However, sometimes you could get lucky.

Having previously moved from England, Paul Maynard, was now an investment manager at the highly renowned and respected 'First Global Bank'. Actually, he was one of the managers, he worked in a large office that was also crammed full of investment managers. The First Global Bank was situated over both floors 92 and 93 in the North Tower of the World Trade Center, and Paul worked on floor 93.

Paul Maynard didn't usually 'do' lunch. Competition there was great, and it was his habit to grab his lunch on the way to work. Most mornings, he would usually call in to 'Katz's Deli' on the Lower East Side, where he seemed to buy the same pastrami salad sandwich almost every day. The coffee came out of a vending machine that was strategically placed in a corner of the corridor next to the toilets. The pastrami salad sandwich was always good, the coffee was not. The only exception to the rule was possibly on Fridays. And depending on how Paul Maynard's week had progressed, or if sometimes the stock market was suffering from the Friday afternoon blues, Paul could be tempted to 'close the shop' for an hour or so and follow his fellow managers to the latest trendy bar or restaurant where he and his co-conspirators would just basically continue to discuss their work and the latest financial trends.

And he was not alone. Half of his office followed the same routine. Some went out to lunch, others didn't. And there was an argument for either case. Hovering over your computer during the lunchtime break kept you up to the minute on everything that was happening around the world, however, the gossip picked up over a lunch could be invaluable too.

It was the toss of the dice really.

Working at First Global was hard and tough, and the hours were long. Starting at nine in the morning, it was up to you when you left, as long as it was after five o' clock, of course. Sometimes the offices were still busy at seven or eight o'clock and if the financial markets were on a roll, or sometimes in a sharp decline, some of the managers would still be there until way after midnight. In essence, the job was manic, but the rewards were excellent. And if you worked hard and were successful, you got paid, and paid very well. Yes, it was stressful employment with ridiculously long hours, but Paul Maynard absolutely loved it.

The office door swung open as three of the other managers returned from their lunch. Paul looked up and immediately recognized one of them, it was his friend, Reza Mastoor. Reza walked into the office and immediately acknowledged Paul and he grinned. The two other managers worked on the other side of the office, one whose last name was 'Becker', the other was Richard 'something' or other. Paul couldn't remember his last name but it didn't particularly matter. Reza Mastoor, who was Egyptian by birth, shared the cubicle opposite Paul's. They'd both worked together for more than four years and got on in a sort of reasonable way. Reza, whose sense of humour was recognized throughout the office, was quite a successful fund manager himself, he had a sharp eye and an even sharper ear.

And as he sat himself down, Paul called to him over their divide.

'How was your lunch?'

'How was your pastrami?' Reza laughed in Paul's direction.

Paul smiled. 'So come on,' he asked. 'Any gossip?'

'I'm not telling you,' Reza replied, and he laughed again. And then a ball of scrunched up paper was thrown over the divide and landed on Paul's desk. This was a regular stunt, Reza had the habit of throwing bits of paper over at Paul, which normally bounced off his head.

Paul picked it up and threw it back.

'Your aim's off,' he called back. But Reza just laughed at him.

Paul stood up and peered over the divide.

'Come on then, anything happening?'

Reza, who was already typing something, didn't even look up from his screen.

'No, my friend, not really, only the usual office shit. Oh, and Tony Becker's getting a divorce, the poor bastard.'

'Jeez,' Paul replied, 'how much is that going to cost him?'

'Thousands,' Reza replied, ' probably hundreds of thousands, he'll be paying her off for years.'

'Bloody hell,' said Paul, 'divorce in England is bad enough, but over here in the States it's a lifetime's curse.'

'Yes,' Reza replied, 'they should do what we do in Egypt. We just throw our women down a well,' and he laughed.

'Hey,' said Paul, 'You're married to an American woman, pal. If anything happened between you two, you'd have to disappear back to Egypt.'

'Not much chance of that, my friend. You see, my wife loves me. And unfortunately, there aren't any wells in New York, not that I'm aware of anyway.'

Paul laughed, 'Well okay, you'd have to chuck her into the bay then.'

And at that moment, his mobile phone rang.

Paul took his phone out of his pocket, he sat back down again and pressed the reply button.

'Hello,' he asked.

'Is that you Pauly?' It was a man's voice.

There were only two people who had ever occasionally called Paul Maynard...'Pauly'.

One was an old girlfriend who he hadn't seen or spoken to for over a year, or maybe two years now. The other was his very good friend from his University days back in England, Adam Tyler. And it wasn't the old girlfriend, thank god.

Paul Maynard smiled as he spoke into the phone, He'd not heard from Adam for quite a few months.

'Hey, bloody hell, Adam. How are you?'

There was a moments silence from long distance, across the other side of the world.

'Hey Pauly, how are you doing?' finally came the reply.

'I'm okay...I'm okay. You still in Barcelona?'

'Yes I'm still here.'

'How are things going over there?'

'Yeah, not bad, I've done nearly three years over here now. Yeah, and I'm still with the same bank.'

Paul Maynard and Adam Tyler had spent their time together at Winchester University and had first met when they shared a dormitory together in their first year there. Though they were both on different courses they had become good friends and good 'drinking buddies' as they made good use of the student bar there and the local pubs. Paul Maynard had proved himself a particularly true friend when he'd had to prop Adam up after the disastrous break up with Miss Joanne Berkley.

After that, Adam had once visited New York to see Paul when he'd just got the job at the First Global Bank, and they'd both enjoyed a pretty wild week there.

'So, you're still with the Santander?' said Paul.

'Yeah, I'm still here,' Adam replied, and then. 'Actually, that's what I'm ringing you about.'

Paul's ears pricked up. 'Yes, go on.'

'Well. I know we've talked in the past. And I know you've always said that I should come over there and work in the States.'

'Yes,' said Paul, 'you should. You'd do well over here, and the money's very good, and so are the career opportunities.'

'Can I ask you something, Paul? Is there anything going at your place, at First Global?'

'I would think so,' Paul immediately replied, 'there's always room for a man of your fabulous talents,' and then he laughed. 'Why...do you fancy a change?

There was a moment's silence. 'Yes, I think I do,' Adam replied. 'I need a change of scene. I've enjoyed Barcelona, but I don't think that I want to spend the rest of my life here. Actually, I'm now the Head of Commercial Banking here, and there's every chance that I could take over at the bank when the manager retires.'

Paul whistled. 'Wow, the Head of Commercial Banking. That's a hell of a promotion at your age. You must be doing something right.'

'Yes, I know. But I don't know if I want to stay here for evermore'.

'Okay,' said Paul, 'I can understand that. Listen, I'll have a word around and put out a few feelers. But email me your 'resume' so that I have it available. I'm almost sure that there will be a job for you here, but hey, there are loads of jobs and banks and financial institutions in New York. At the moment there's a lot of demand within the industry.'

And then Paul had an idea. 'Do you know what you should do? You should come over here. Everything happens very quickly in this city and you should be on hand. If an opportunity does come up and then you have to get all the way over here for an interview, the job could be gone by the time you get here. Why don't you take a break, Adam? Use some of your holidays and come over here to New York. You can stay with me again, it'll be like the good old days. I'll show you around and we could hit a few of the bars. It'll be 'good times' all over again.'

Adam listened to his friend's advice. And he saw the sense in it, and it fitted in with his plans. He had to finish things. And he couldn't stay in Spain anymore.

'Give me a couple of days,' he replied, 'I'll be on my way. I'll call you.'

The next morning, a Monday, Adam went to work as usual. But before going to his own office, he went to see Carlos Villena.

He looked through the glazed-over glass of the office door but couldn't see anyone and when he opened the door, the office was empty. He went to his own office and turned on his computer and started to read some of the incoming emails, but he kept looking up at the clock on the office wall in front of him. At exactly fifteen minutes past nine o' clock, he stood up again and went back to see if Carlos Villena had finally arrived.

This time Carlos was there. Adam knocked on the door and walked in. Carlos Villena looked up and stared at Adam. He was now seemingly back to normal, wearing a smart suit, his eyes no longer bloodshot, and he was no longer drunk, drugged or dishevelled.

'Ah, Adam,' he said, unsmiling. 'And how are you today?'

'I'm okay,' Adam replied coldly.

'And what we discussed yesterday. Do we continue as normal?'

'Do I have any choice?' Adam again replied.

Carlos Villena shrugged. 'Not really.'

And with that, Adam turned around and walked out of the office.

Adam spent the next few days thinking and writing and planning. This time, he had to get things right.

Finally, on the Friday morning, Adam had made an appointment to speak to Jorge Baroja at twelve o'clock, just an hour before lunch. He'd arrived on time and had the usual quick chat to Mr Baroja's ever faithful secretary, Miss Montero. She in turn spoke to Mr Baroja on the intercom and she nodded to Adam to go through.

Adam walked into the office. Under his arm he had two large brown envelopes and an unbound folder, which was full of papers. Jorge Baroja looked up at Adam and smiled.

'Ah, nice to see you, Adam. Come in, come in and sit yourself down.'

And Adam's heart sank, it was as though he had to give some bad news to his father.

Adam sat down and he put the folder and the envelopes down in front of him, and then he looked across the desk at Jorge Baroja, who was still smiling expectantly.

'Now then, what is it, my boy? Mr Baroja asked.

Adam coughed. 'I have some bad news, Mr Baroja, very bad, in fact. And it involves money laundering here at the bank, and it involves me, and it involves Mr Carlos Villena.'

And with that, Adam began to tell the whole sorry story. Jorge Baroja stopped smiling.

Adam told Mr Baroja absolutely everything that had happened. About how he'd been set up with Dominique Cassens, a prostitute, and how he'd been tricked into inadvertently opening a bank account for her which now contained three quarters of a million Euros of laundered drug money, and her collusion with Carlos Villena. He also informed Mr Baroja about Carlos Villena's double life as a drug dealer and as the owner of the 'Club Le Souk' night club from where he distributed the drugs. From there, he told Jorge Baroja about the blackmail, it was Carlos Villena who had deposited the drug money into the account, but under Adam's name. So on paper, there was no proof. Adam had opened the account, and it was he who had deposited the original money in there too. There was no evidence at all that led to Carlos Villena, all he had to do was to deny everything.

Adam then went on to tell Mr Baroja about Carlos Villena's future plans and his dealing with the drug cartel's millions, which he was also planning to launder through the bank.

Jorge Baroja just sat there listening, almost glass-eyed.

Adam then told him about the events of the weekend and what had happened, and that he wasn't prepared to be blackmailed or to be forced into going down that illegal route.

He then pushed the folder across the desk in front of Jorge Baroja.

Adam continued. 'In there, I've written the whole story, just as I've told you. It's basically word for word. And also in there are all the statements from Miss Dominique Cassens private account. You will see the pay-in dates and the corresponding amounts, all seemingly paid in by me. It's all been very cleverly done. Carlos Villena has seen to that. He's told me that he has a report on file in which he raises his suspicions and totally incriminates me.

And of course, legally, I haven't a foot to stand on, other than coming to you, Mr Baroja, if of course you believe me.'

Adam then slid the other two envelopes over to Mr Baroja.

'And what are these, Adam?' he asked.

One is a hand written letter by me, sir. It totally admonishes you from any knowledge of what's been going on, by the unscrupulous and calculating acts of one of the bank's employees. The other letter is my immediate resignation from the bank, sir. All of this is an obvious embarrassment to the bank and other than what's written in my report, there is nothing else that I can actually tell you. It's better that I left. I plan to fly back to England on Sunday afternoon, I have a five o' clock flight booked back to London. From there I will have to make other plans and then try to rebuild my life. This has all been a huge mistake, in fact, it's been a disaster.'

Jorge Baroja raised an eyebrow as he stared across his desk at Adam Tyler, his protégé in the making.

'You realize, Adam, that I will have to contact head office immediately, and in doing that, head office may wish to inform the police, who may need to question you?'

'Yes sir, I do.'

Jorge Baroja grunted. 'I always knew that Villena was a lying little bastard. His father and I fell out over him, over a promotion. I had to tell his father that his precious son was lucky to have a job here at the bank, let alone a damn promotion. And that was that, and because of that he didn't come to the wedding.'

'I believe so, sir,' Adam replied.

'Adam, I will try to support you over this. I think that you are telling me the truth. However, the police may find it differently.'

'I understand, sir.' Adam again replied.

Jorge Baroja just stared across at Adam for a moment.

'You had better go, Adam.' They were his final words.

'Thank you, sir,' said Adam, and he stood up and walked out of the office and out of the bank.

Once he'd left the bank, Adam took a taxi back to his apartment on the Carrer Rosell He had the taxi wait for him whilst he went to get the two full suitcases that he'd already packed the night before. The cases were loaded into the back of the taxi, but before he left, Adam crossed the road and pushed an envelope into the letter box there. It was to be delivered first class to Mr Jorge Baroja, at his home address. The letter would arrive there the next day. Adam then skipped back across the road and climbed into the taxi.

'Take me to the airport, please,' he said to the driver.

Three hours later, Adam's flight to New York took off on time.

The next morning, Jorge Baroja opened his mail. Even though it was a Saturday, today he would have to go into the bank. He'd rung head office the day before, somewhat later in the afternoon, and explained what had been going on. All hell had broken loose and the auditors were to be sent in the very next day, and then the police would also have to be involved.

He finally opened the hand written letter that had been posted to him by Adam Tyler.

Jorge Baroja read that letter, in which Adam apologized profusely and admitted that he'd lied about going to London on the Sunday flight and that he'd already flown out of Spain later that same afternoon. He thanked Jorge Baroja for everything he'd done for him, and he again apologized. Jorge Baroja looked down at the letter, and he slowly began to smile.

His final words to Adam had been...'You had better go, Adam.' And he'd meant it. And thank god, Adam had taken his advice, either that or he'd already booked the flight, it didn't really matter.

'Good man,' he said, under his breath.

The next day, Jorge Baroja would go and speak to his estranged friend, Gabriel Villena Snr. He would shake hands with his old friend and then tell him all about his son's activities. Whether they would still remain good friends after that conversation, would be Gabriel Villena's decision. However, Jorge Baroja knew that his friend was unquestionably, a man of principle. But, whatever the outcome, the police would be involved, Jorge Baroja would see to that. And if nothing could be proved at the bank, at least the police would have been informed about the goings on at the 'Club Le Souk' and would undoubtedly close it down.

111

Hopefully, they would also be able to implicate Carlos Villena with the drug trafficking there.

But no matter what, come Monday morning, Jorge Baroja intended to review Carlos Villena's very inefficient work rate, along with his poor timekeeping. It was all on record of course.

And from there, he would see to it that Carlos Villena was sacked, and for security reasons, obviously, he would be sacked immediately. And it was also bank protocol that Carlos Villena would have to straightaway clear his desk, and then be escorted from the building.

But then Jorge Baroja scratched his head for a moment. There was just one more little problem, something that he'd never even given much thought to. What on earth was he going to do about the three quarters of a million Euros that still sat in Dominique Cassen's account?

He just shrugged his shoulders. He would have the account frozen. It would then become another problem for another day, or whatever.

Adam Tyler landed at New York City's JFK Airport at around seven o' clock in the evening. He had to adjust his head and his watch as he realized the six hour time difference. Anyway, he'd escaped and arrived. He went through customs without a hitch and then collected his luggage. From there he made his way to the arrivals lounge, and through the crowds of people, there was Paul Maynard, he just stood there smiling with his arms outstretched. Both men met and hugged one another.

'Good to see you, mate,' Paul exclaimed.

'And bloody good to see you to pal, bloody good,' Adam replied.

Paul picked up one of Adam's cases and then directed him out of the airport and into a waiting taxicab.

'We'll dump your gear at my place,' said Paul, 'and then I'll take you for a beer.'

'That sounds great,' Adam replied. And at that moment, he felt that a great weight had been lifted from him. On his flight over, Adam had time to think things over.

112

Dominique Cassens was upmost in his mind. He'd loved her, or he thought he had. But she was never the woman that he thought she was, and it had all been a lie from start to finish. And now she was gone and out of his life forever. It was over. And Adam had made a decision and a promise to himself during that flight. That he wouldn't return to Spain and he wasn't going back to England either. He was going to stay in America. He would find a job, one way or another he would find a job, even if he had to start at the bottom again. He was determined to make a go of it, whatever the odds. It would become his one unwavering goal.

As their New York cab driver dodged and weaved through the traffic, both men chatted easily, they'd always been the best of friends.

'So come on then?' Paul asked '...really, why the sudden change of plans.'

But Adam just shook his head and smiled, 'I'll tell you everything, once we get that beer.'

The taxi headed for Manhattan and across to the Lower East Side, and then to Paul's apartment on 2nd Avenue. They put the taxi on hold while they went up to Paul's second floor apartment, where they dumped Adam's cases and then went straight out again.

They ended up in 'The Ten Bells, a comfortable bar on Broome Street. Paul ordered a couple of ice cold beers and then they sat down at a corner table. Their conversation continued until finally, Adam said, 'Okay then, here's all the shit.'

And he then proceeded to tell Paul the whole sordid story.

When he'd finished, Paul just sat there, astonished.

'My god,' he said, 'no wonder you left in a hurry, I would have done the same.'

'Would you?' Adam asked his friend.

'Of course I would, no doubt about it. No, Adam, you had to get out of there. You could have ended up with a criminal record and that would finish your career. Hell, you could have ended up in prison.'

'I know,' Adam replied.

Paul looked at him. 'Hey buddy, mud sticks. And if you got a job anywhere and they found out that you've been involved with drugs and money laundering, you'd be sacked immediately. I mean, let's face it, you're hardly likely to put it on your resume are you? And once you've been sacked from one place, your history would follow you. You'd become unemployable. No, you did the right thing, believe me.'

Adam nodded and then he shook his head, 'Bloody women, they'll be my downfall.' And then he laughed, 'I needed that drink, I'd better get the beers in.'

When he returned from the bar, they both raised their glasses and gave a toast to 'Bachelorhood', and then they laughed.

'Okay then,' said Paul, 'well now we've got all that out of the way, I might just have some good news for you.'

Adam looked up as he sipped his beer. 'I could do with some, what is it?'

Paul grinned at him, 'I've got you a job interview,'

Adam immediately stopped drinking.

'What?'

'Yes, mate, I did a bit of asking around the bank. I told you, there are always job opportunities at our place and they're desperately looking for talent. And yes, so, you've got an interview on Wednesday at eleven o' clock with the Head of Finance, a guy called Norman Roth. He's a good guy, very sharp. His department do a lot of business financing, you know, you're sort of thing. I had a chat with him and mentioned you that you were 'Head of Commercial Banking' at Santander over in Barcelona, and that you'd got itchy feet and were looking to come to New York. He was interested, very interested really. I told him that you were coming over for a sort of 'working' visit. The next day I gave him your 'resume', he was impressed. And so I arranged an interview for you, he said that Wednesday would be fine and it would give you a couple of days to settle in and find your bearings, that sort of thing. So there you go, first job interview, pal.'

Adam sat back in his chair and grinned.

'You're a star, you really are, Paul.'

'Hey, it would be great if you worked at our place.'

Adam laughed, 'It would be bloody marvellous, absolutely brilliant. Hey, and on that note, and I know this may be a bit premature, but I'm going to buy us a bottle of cheap champagne.'

And with that, he stood up and made his way back to the bar.

Wednesday arrived, and so did eleven o'clock, and Paul met up with the Head of Finance, Norman Roth. The interview went well, very well. It was quite a relaxed affair really and Adam and Mr Roth spoke quite freely. In fact, Adam actually mentioned to Mr Roth that another of the reasons that he wanted a change of space was that he and his long term girlfriend had broken off their relationship. It was a sort of 'white lie' and it was really, partly the truth. Norman Roth was sympathetic. He then went on to tell Adam about a position that was available and what it entailed, and what he expected in return. Adam was quite happy with everything.

It seemed to be much of what he was doing back in Barcelona. Companies or individuals would approach the bank for loans, mostly for either commercial purchase or business expansion. First Global's practice was to then work 'hand in hand' with the customer. It was a form of security for the bank, it let them see just where their money was being spent, and the bank also offered advice and direction to the customer. A useful plus, was that it was sometimes more financially efficient to take on loans on a 'stage payment' basis, which left the customer only paying interest on the amount of money borrowed at the 'actual time'. It was a sort of 'drawdown' system, as opposed to borrowing the whole amount all at once.

This was particularly advantageous if the loan was to be used in something like a large construction project, a project that may last over one or two years, or even longer.

After an hour, Norman Roth offered Adam the job, and then they discussed the salary and the bonuses and all the benefits. It was all pretty lucrative. And finally, both men shook hands on the deal as Norman Roth welcomed Adam 'on board'. There was only one dark moment, and that was when Norman Roth mentioned that he would of course, need a reference from Santander, back in Barcelona. It was First Global's policy, obviously.

'Get them to email it to my office, it'll be much simpler,' he continued.

115

At that point, Adam managed to maintain a calm smile, along with a casual reply.

'Yes, no problem', he replied, ' the manager there is Mr Jorge Baroja. Over the years he's become a good friend, more of a father figure really. He understands that I want to move on and he knows that I've come to New York for a reason. I'll have to contact him anyway, to offer my resignation.'

'And how do you think he'll react?' Norman Roth asked.

'Oh, I think he'll be okay with it, there'll be a tinge of sadness I suppose, I've had happy times there, he was a good man to work for.' And then a thought suddenly struck Adam.'

'The moment I resign, my position at the bank will be terminated immediately, it's Santander's banking policy, for security reasons,.

"Of course,' Norman Roth replied, 'we have the same policy here at First Global, I think it's the same procedure with most banks these days, and a lot of other businesses too, it's a possible 'conflict of interests'.

Adam nodded in agreement, but at the back of his mind he realized that it could be a problem. What if Jorge Baroja had taken Adam's immediate exit as an insult? He could only hope that his letter had smoothed things over and explained everything. Hopefully.

'So when do you want to start?' Norman Roth suddenly asked.

The question broke Adam's concentration.

'On Monday, Mr Roth,' he replied immediately.

'Monday. Are you sure?' Norman Roth was quite surprised. 'Don't you need to go back to Barcelona?

Adam shrugged. 'No not really. I can't see the point. I won't be going back to the bank, obviously. And I've packed up all my stuff at my apartment and told them there that I might be leaving. I'll contact them and have them send my stuff over here by carrier. I'm staying at Paul Maynard's at the moment but I'll get my own place.'

'Good man,' and Norman Roth smiled. He was glad to see that Adam was keen. 'Okay then, I'll take you down to the ninety second floor, that's where you'll be working.'

They went downstairs and Norman Roth introduced Adam to some of the team there that he would be working with. They seemed a friendly lot. After that they went back outside to the corridor. Norman Roth shook Adam's hand.

'I've got to go to a business lunch now, but I really hope you're going to enjoy working here, Adam. So okay then, I'll see you on Monday.'

Adam smiled, 'No, you'll see me tomorrow, Mr Roth, and on Friday. I need to get in here and find my feet. It's no use me sat back at Paul's apartment twiddling my thumbs. In fact, I'm going to nip upstairs to Paul's office and give him the good news. I think I'll have to treat him to lunch too.'

'Okay then,' said Norman Roth. He was glad to see Adam's enthusiasm, it was promising.

As he started to walk towards the elevator, he turned back to Adam.

'Oh, and don't forget to ask Santander for the reference,' and he shrugged, 'just bank policy.'

Adam skipped up the stairs and went into Paul Maynard's office. It was still busy. He looked around and spotted Paul and went over to his desk.

'I've got it, mate. I've got the job.'

Paul laughed, and he stood up and shook Adam's hand.

'Nice one, pal. I knew you could do it, that's great news.'

It was Adam's turn to shrug, 'Hey, what can I say,' and he laughed too.

'Any problems, at all? Paul asked him.

'Just one, but I'll tell you about it later. Anyway, okay, I want to buy you lunch. Do you know anywhere good?'

And then unexpectedly, a voice spoke out from behind the office divide.

'You'll have to drag him out of this office, my friend. Mr 'Pastrami salad' there doesn't 'do' lunches, he's frightened that he would have to buy a round of drinks.'

And from behind the divide a dark haired man suddenly stood up and laughed.

Paul Maynard shook his head and sighed mockingly.

'Adam, this is Reza Mastoor. He's the office clown. He's from Egypt and he thinks he's funny. I keep telling him that what's funny in Egypt, isn't funny over here, but he won't listen.'

Reza Mastoor just laughed. 'Hey, let me tell you something about 'Mr Pastrami' here, he eats the same pastrami salad sandwich every single day. He must be Katz's Deli's best customer. I'm surprised they've not given you a medal or an award of some kind. Hey, maybe they'll put your picture up in the shop when you're dead.' And again he laughed. Even Adam couldn't help but grin.

Paul turned to Adam. 'Hey, don't egg him on,' and then he turned back to Reza, 'You're pitiful man, you're just pitiful.' And then he grinned, 'I guess I'm just a creature of habit.'

Adam went over to the divide and shook Reza Mastoor's hand.

'Hi, Reza, I'm Adam Tyler, an old friend of Paul's. I've just managed to get a job here. I'll be working downstairs at Commercial.

'Yes, Paul's told me all about you, and congratulations by the way, nice one. And hey, did you just mention 'lunch'? Me and my friend, Tony...Tony Becker, we're just on our way out for lunch, Why don't you join us? We'll celebrate your coming to work here at First Global. Tony's a nice guy, you'll like him.'

Paul Maynard raised his arms in mock amusement. 'You see how he just invites himself? The man has no morals at all. I don't know why I put up with him.'

'Because I make you look plausible, you 'stick in the mud,' Reza replied. 'Anyway, are we doing lunch or what?'

Adam turned to his friend. 'Come on, Paul. Let's do it. It'll be nice to meet these people.'

Reza Mastoor didn't even wait for Paul to reply.

'Okay that's great then, I'll go over and get Tony.' And with that he pushed back his chair and made his way to the other side of the office.

Once he was out of the earshot, Paul turned to Adam.

'Okay then, before he gets back, what's the 'one' problem?

'It's Norman Roth, he wants a reference from Santander, back in Barcelona. The bank's policy apparently, I suppose I should have expected it really, it's company policy at most places.'

Paul Maynard was suddenly serious. 'Do you think your Mr Baroja will do it?'

Adam shrugged, 'I don't know. If he refuses, I may be looking for another job quickly. We'll just have to see.'

The four of them got together and Adam was introduced to Tony Becker, a tall slim man with gingery red hair, who sported a similarly coloured moustache that seriously belonged to the 1970's. Reza Mastoor made his usual joke about 'Tony being an aging porn star', Paul groaned, and then they all made their way to 'The Trinity', restaurant on Broadway, near to Wall Street. They were seated almost straight away. Adam sat down, with Tony Becker to his left and Paul to his right, and with Reza Mastoor directly opposite. The four of them got on well, easy conversations, helped along by Reza Mastoor's humorous quips. It was a recipe for friendship, and a friendship that would last.

At one point, Tony Becker spoke to Adam about the forthcoming divorce that he was about to suffer.

'What went wrong?' Adam asked.

'Oh, the usual crap. We weren't getting along. I suppose the pressure of work, really. And I wasn't coming home half the time. You see, I live outside New York City in the suburbs and the commute here every day, and getting back home again in the evening is a complete nightmare. So I rent a small apartment. Sometimes I go home, sometimes I don't. But work's kept me that busy of late, that it's just been easier to stay here in the city, and then it rolled into the weekends. Sometimes I never went home at all. Reza does the same, his family lives in the suburbs and he has a place here in the city too, Don't you Reza?'

Reza Mastoor had been half listening. 'Yes, I do. But I only try to stay here on alternative nights, if possible. And also, my wife isn't a bitch.'

Tony Becker just shook his head and then he turned back to Adam.

'We sort of drifted, and she has her own job too, Margaret, she's a teacher. And we were supposed to be trying for kids, but that's never happened either. And now she says that she needs her 'own space'. But no, that's a lie, I think she's probably having an affair.'

Reza Mastoor interrupted their conversation. '

119

'I've told him, when they say they need their own space, what they really mean is that they need a space, but with you not in it.'

Paul Maynard raised his hands up in mock derision.

'See what I told you, Adam, the man has no morals.'

But Tony Becker just laughed. 'Actually, you're probably on the mark there, Reza. Anyway, I'll be spending even more time in the city now, because the bitch has kicked me out.'

Reza Mastoor laughed gleefully. 'Hey, that's okay, really. We can all go out drinking every night. We'll be like the 'Four Musketeers.'

Paul Maynard put his head in his hands, and groaned.

The following afternoon, Adam left the bank early and went back to Paul's apartment. He'd given it some thought, and he took out his laptop and began to send an email to Jorge Baroja's office at the Santander Bank in Barcelona. In the email he once again expressed his apologies for leaving Barcelona so abruptly, and unannounced. He informed Jorge Baroja that he was now in New York and that he had got a job with the First Global Bank. However, First Global required a reference as part of his contract. He asked Jorge Baroja if he could send a reference to the Bank, and if not, he completely understood. And he again apologized.

He then added to the email, Norman Roth's email address and he pressed 'Send'.

And then he waited.

It was mid morning in Barcelona when the email arrived at Jorge Baroja's office and popped up on Miss Montero's computer screen. The secretary examined it and immediately printed off a copy then took it into Jorge Baroja's office. She smiled at her boss.

'Your boy's sent you a message. Apparently, he's in New York.'

And with that, she placed the printed copy on the desk in front of him. Jorge Baroja quickly read the email and then he looked up at her. Miss Montero smiled back at him.

'I always liked Mr Tyler,' she commented, 'He worked very hard for the bank, and he was honest.' And with that said, Miss Montero left the office and closed the door behind her.

Jorge Baroja thought about it for a moment. His ever faithful secretary was right, of course she was. She was always right.

Jorge Baroja turned to his computer, and then proceeded to write a glowing reference for his former employee, Mr Adam Tyler. Once that was done, he emailed the document to the address given for Norman Roth's office at the First Global Bank in New York City.

Jorge Baroja then wrote another email, this time directly to Adam Tyler.

'Dear Adam, I hope you are well. I have, as requested, sent a positive reference for you, to Mr Norman Roth at First Global. It was no problem at all. We at the bank hold you in our highest esteem, as ever. On a personal note, things have been rather lively over the last week since you left. The bank's auditors were called in, along with the police, and everything has been scrutinised.

I gave both the auditors and the police copies of your letters and I informed them that in my view you were quite innocent and were set up. When I was asked why you fled the country, I told them that I didn't blame you, in fact I even advised you to go, if you do remember?

The police arrested Mr Carlos Villena, but that slippery eel had covered his tracks well. He simply denied everything and acted as though he was completely innocent in all of this, and also that he was astonished at the accusations. Eventually, nothing could be proved. The police straight away raided his club. But once again he'd outwitted everyone, there was nothing to connect him to the club at all, any of the documents appertaining to the ownership of the club were under some assumed name that the police could not trace. However, they did discover a huge amount of drugs there, which were then confiscated, and the club was closed down immediately.

I have taken it upon myself to sack Mr Carlos Villena, his position at the bank had become untenable, but we used his very inefficient work rate, along with his record of poor timekeeping as justification. I also went to speak to his father, as you know, our friendship had become somewhat distanced. We sat down and I told him the truth about his son and what had happened. He respected my view and we shook hands. I was later informed that Gabriel Villena had thrown his son out of the house. I was also informed that Carlos Villena has now left Barcelona, the line of thought being that he still owed the drugs cartel a huge amount of money for the confiscated drugs. At this point, Adam, I would like to thank you for your service to the bank, and I wish you well in your new employment at First Global.

It has been a real pleasure, Adam.

Yours, very sincerely...Jorge Baroja.'

Jorge Baroja re-read his email, and he sighed. And then he pressed 'send'.

Back in New York, and after an indeterminable wait, Adam Tyler finally heard his laptop 'ping'.

'This is the moment,' he thought to himself, 'this is my future, or possibly not.' And then he read the email from his old boss. A couple of minutes later he sighed with relief and sat back in his chair.

'Thank god for that,' he said out loud, 'and thank you, Mr Baroja.'

And then he wondered about Carlos Villena and Dominique. He would never know.

Several months passed quickly by. During which time Adam found an apartment of his own, also on the Lower East Side. For Adam it made sense, it was easy to commute to work, and it was in the same district as Paul Maynard, his best friend. But above all, Adam really liked the area. It was fairly laid back and there were plenty of good bars and decent eateries. And all in all, he was pretty well catered for. And he'd made good friends too, Reza Mastoor's promise of them being the 'four musketeers, had in part come true. They finally broke Paul Maynard's 'pastrami' habit and the four of them regularly had lunch together. Paul had to admit that when he returned to work after lunch, he was 'a better man'.

'All work and no play', as they say.

And after work, and in the evenings too, they would all continue to socialize. Tony Becker lived in the city permanently

122

now, as did Paul and Adam. And Reza Mastoor seemed to be the instigator of everything, constantly dragging them off to some new bar or other, when and if he stayed over, instead of going home to his wife and family, back in the suburbs.

At First Global, everything was going well, very well. Adam had hit the ground running, and was as committed as ever. And it showed. He put his own work practices into place and formed a young and very keen team around him. And it showed, there was a 'breath of fresh air' in the workplace and everyone seemed to look to Adam Tyler for inspiration.

Norman Roth had seen it too, and Adam was quickly becoming his right hand man and someone who he could depend on. Yes, things were going well.

And then on one Wednesday afternoon, Norman Roth called Adam into his office.

'Hi buddy, come in a sit yourself down,' Norman Roth had said, It was always very casual, it had been from the start really, and Adam appreciated that.

'Okay then,' said Norman Roth, 'here's the play. We are about to acquire a new account, a huge account actually,' and Norman Roth smiled, and Adam appreciated that too.

Nice one,' he replied, that's good news. Who is it?'

Norman Roth sat back in his chair and gave a confident smile. 'We've hooked 'Cantor Fitzsimons.'

Adam Tyler's eyes widened and he actually sat up in his chair.

'You are joking. Really? How on earth have we managed that?

Norman Roth smiled, like the cat that got the cream.

'A combination of things, really. They were with the Federal American Bank, have been for years, but they've had a few spats with them lately and apparently it's all become personal. Cantor Fitzsimons reckon that the bank is being run by the 'fuddy-duddy' brigade. And Cantor Fitzsimons want to expand into a lot of different areas, not just advertising, and they feel that the old brigade at Federal American are holding them back, and their own management team are beginning to feel 'stifled'. The other plus, is that they're moving their head office.'

'Where too? Adam asked. He was finding all of this rather exciting,

Norman Roth grinned. 'You're not going to believe this, Adam. You just couldn't write it.'

Adam was exasperated. 'Well come on then, where?'

Norman Roth pointed to the ceiling.

'You mean 'here'? Adam asked him.

'Two floors up.' Norman Roth replied. 'They're taking over the whole of floor 95.'

'You're kidding me.'

'Nope, two floors up, and 'in house'. They move in at the end of the month.'

Adam sat back in his chair. 'Wow!'

Cantor Fitzsimons were the 'legendary' advertising agency, formed in the early 1980's by the advertising genius, Berni Speegle.

There was actually never a Cantor, or a Fitzsimons either. It was said that Berni Speegle simply didn't want to put his name to anything, just in case something went wrong.

And the reason for their success? It was quite simple really. They were cleverer than the rest, and they were smarter. Under Berni Speegle's direction and leadership, his group spearheaded some of the most memorable advertising campaigns of the eighties and nineties. Cantor Fitzsimons had the art of making everything look 'cool'. It was their trademark style. And Cantor Fitzsimons had the ability to make a product desirable, and that's what the public wanted. This all very quickly became apparent, and it wasn't long before a host of different companies were queuing up at their door. Berni Speegle kept his Agency one step in front of the others by constantly employing bright young talent who were full of new and inventive ideas, and who knew that at Cantor Fitzsimons they would be given the freedom to follow their own creativity. It was a first class company and a good place to work.

Norman Roth looked across his desk at Adam.

'Cantor Fitzsimons want to expand, Adam. They want to expand into publishing, and they want to do it quickly. They've

124

studied the market and they've been looking at Vogue Magazine and Harpers Bazaar, the two market leaders, and at Cantor Fitzsimons they think they can do something better. They consider that both those magazines are becoming rather staid and a little too obvious. In short, boring. Both those magazines have had the same layout for years and they've gotten a little too comfortable. They are the market leaders simply because there's nothing else on the market. However, their advertising revenues are phenomenal, merely because there are no other high end magazines where companies can showcase their products, there are simply no alternatives. Cantor Fitzsimons have seen the weakness in the market. And this is just the start. They are also looking into other areas of publishing too, such as Men's fashion, Automotive, and Food and Drink.'

Adam was amazed. But Cantor Fitzsimons had done their homework and were possibly correct. Everywhere you looked there were lots of glossy magazines, in every reception area, bars, cafes and even in the dentists, and in a lot of cases people just flicked through them whilst they waited for 'whatever'. But rarely did anything in them really catch your attention.

Norman Roth continued. 'This is big, Adam. This is going to be huge.'

Adam nodded. 'Yes, it is. Or it could be.'

'Yes, I know what you mean,' Norman Roth replied. 'And that's why we've got to get this one right. And that's why I want you onboard, Adam. This is our new baby, and I want it fly.'

'But why us, why have they come to us?' Adam asked.

'Because they know how we work, and they know how we run things here. We work quickly and we work hand in hand with our customers. We offer our financial expertise, and if a project is seen to be viable, we will fund it and fund it to the hilt. We also oversee the financing, and that stops the customer getting into trouble, and along with that we will find the most viable way to finance any new project and we monitor everything, to make sure that the costs don't become a problem. Prevention is better than cure. And that's why Cantor Fitzsimons have come to us. Fast and immediate decisions with a no-nonsense approach, and I think that's the nature of the advertising business too, it's an ever changing industry that can never sit on its laurels, it's always on the move.'

'So where do we go from here?' Adam asked.

I've arranged for a meeting with Cantor Fitzsimons a week from now, next Tuesday, they want us to have the meeting upstairs in their new offices, but there's a lot of work going on up there so alternatively, it could be here at the Bank. It will be a 'get to know you' sort of exercise. The company executives will be here, and that includes Berni Speegle, hopefully. Well, he's still the Company's CEO. Along with that will be the editors, and the design staff, the project managers, in fact, a whole caboodle of people who have any input at all. We want to listen to their views and ideas, and get a 'feel' for the company. And they need to meet us too, if we're all going to work together. We need to get off on an even playing field here, and good communications are the first step. That's the principal anyway. It'll be a two tier affair, afterwards we'll discuss the more exact figures and projections with the company hierarchy.'

'It's sounds really good,' said Adam, 'this is a really exciting project. What an opportunity.'

Norman Roth smiled, he could see Adam's enthusiasm. He knew he'd picked the right man for the job.

'Okay. So, Adam, I want you to get up to spec with Cantor Fitzsimons. I want you to find out everything you can about them so that we know just where we stand. They've already told us that they're willing to work with us on an 'open door' policy, they want full transparency. We can have anything we want, accounts, figures, assets, investments. In fact, the whole caboose. And that's good, it shows we're off to good start, and I like that.

'Okay,' Adam replied, 'I'll make a start. I'll have to make a few changes to my calendar but there's nothing there that my team can't handle.' And with that he stood up. 'Okay then, I'll keep in touch. I'll send you a running report on my findings, along with anything that I think you need to know.'

'Okay, Adam. Nice one. And this goes without saying, you've got to keep all of this to yourself. Believe me, the Federal American Bank don't even know that they're losing the Cantor Fitzsimon account yet. So complete secrecy, okay. Nobody must know?'

Adam nodded. Yes, I understand. Don't worry.'

Once Adam had left his office, Norman Roth sat back in his chair. He thought about their conversation, and Adam Tyler had been right. This was going to be a very exciting opportunity. And done right, it could be huge. There was money to be made.

Friday morning, and the last day of the week finally arrived at the First Global Bank, but unfortunately, Paul Maynard did not.

Adam woke up that morning to find the red light flashing on his answer phone. There was a message, or possibly messages. He pressed the play button and heard a rather ill sounding Paul Maynard on the end of the line. He looked at the screen on his answer phone to see that the recording had been made at five o' clock that morning.

'Hi Adam, it's me. I don't feel so good. I think I've picked up some sort of bug. Don't wait for me today, I'm not coming in to work. Okay buddy, I'll phone you.'

Adam put the phone down and went to make some coffee. He and Paul usually met up and went to work together, but apparently not today. In fact, Adam hadn't seen much of Paul, Reza or Tony Becker for most of the week. He'd been busy with the Cantor Fitzsimons project and he'd missed the lunches and the nights out. Reza Mastoor had rung him a few times and moaned about his absence.

'Hey, we're supposed to be the four musketeers,' he quipped, 'it's not the same without you, and now we have to put up with Paul on our own.'

But Adam had just laughed and told him that he was working on 'something new, and no, he couldn't discuss it.'

At about ten o' clock that same morning, Adam's phone rang. He picked it up. 'Hello?'

'Hi pal, it's Reza. What's happened to 'our boy?'

Adam sighed. 'Oh hi, Reza. Yes, he got a bug, flu probably. He left me a message on my phone this morning at about five o' clock. Actually, he sounded pretty rough. I'll call around to his place tomorrow and see how he is.'

'Oh right.' Reza sounded a bit disheartened. 'Are you up for lunch today, it is Friday, we've not seen you all week.'

'Sorry mate, I'm still busy. I can't make it.'

'Oh, alright then,' said Reza. 'What about tonight after work, are we having a few drinks?'

'I don't think so, Reza. I've got a lot on. I'm probably going to have to work all weekend too, from home.'

'Awe, bloody hell, man. Don't do this to me. Don't leave me on my own with Tony Becker, all he ever talks about his divorce and that bloody ex wife of his who's bleeding him dry. Come on matey, don't leave me on my own, please. Just come out for an hour or two, please, Adam, that bastards driving me mad.'

Adam laughed, somehow Reza Mastoor made everything sound comical.

'Come on, Adam,' he continued, 'please come for a drink. After an hour alone with Tony Becker, I'll be looking to 'top' myself.'

Adam burst out laughing and then he shook his head.

'Okay. Okay, Reza. I'll come out for a couple of hours.'

'Nice one,' Reza said to him, 'we'll come down for you at around five o' clock.'

Reza Mastoor put the phone down and smiled.

'Gotcha,' he said to himself.

At five o' clock, Adam's phone rang once again. And again it was Reza Mastoor.

'Hi pal, we're just finishing off up here, we'll be down in ten minutes, okay?'

Adam sighed, 'Okay, Reza, ten minutes.' And then he put the phone down. He could have done without all of this and it struck him that he should never have agreed to meet up with them. He'd a lot of work still to do. And then Adam remembered one of his own little rules. He emailed all the reports that he'd been writing, over to his own computer, back at his apartment. Adam never liked to go out of an evening, carrying important papers or an expensive laptop computer. After all, this was New York.

He did this, and just as he'd stored away all of his papers and was reaching for his jacket, Reza Mastoor and Tony Becker walked into the office. They were both in deep discussion as to where they should go for their first drink and then where to go afterwards. Reza looked up. 'Hey Adam, you choose.'

'Choose what?'

'Where we should go for a drink? I want to go over to Tribeca, but this cheap bastard wants to go and slum it in Chinatown, I ask you, who drinks in Chinatown? You go to Chinatown to eat, not drink. Anyway, the bars there are crap.'

'Hey, I know some really good bars in Chinatown,' Tony Becker argued.

Reza laughed, 'Yes of course you do, Tony. And that's why you can't get a woman, along with that stupid moustache. You're completely clueless.'

'Oh yeah,' Becker continued, 'and what would you know, you Egyptian idiot.'

But Reza just laughed at him. 'Oh, so now you're a racist. How low can you go, Mr Becker, and hey, you can be my witness here, Adam. I'm going to report him.'

Adam shook his head, and then he pulled a coin from his pocket.

'Heads or Tails?' he asked.

'Heads' Reza called out immediately.

Tony Becker just shrugged, there was only one other choice. Adam spun the coin, caught it, and then placed it on the back of his hand. He looked, and then nodded in Reza Mastoor's direction. Reza laughed and almost danced a jig.

'Damn you,' replied a slightly disgruntled Tony Becker.

Their first call was the 'Patriot Saloon Bar' on Chambers St. The place was fairly packed, but it was Friday of course, so everywhere would be pretty full. Since it had been Reza's choice, he went to the bar and bought a large pitcher of beer, whilst Adam and Tony managed to luckily grab a table, where the occupants were just leaving. The beer was cold and it tasted good, and the three of them began to relax and enjoy themselves. The conversation flowed, along with another couple of pitchers of beer. From there, they made their way to 'Tiny's Upstairs Bar'. They went up a flight of stairs to enter the warm and wonderfully cosy drinking establishment, all red brick walls and a wood burning fireplace in the corner. They had more beers along with some shots of bourbon. Adam was becoming relaxed. He'd had a hard week and had missed regular meals, and he'd also been working late into the night once he'd got back to his apartment.

But he was doing okay. Every night when he'd finished a report, he printed everything off and added it to his file. He didn't want to lose any his hard work, just in case his computer crashed. It was all invaluable information.

Reza Mastoor suddenly looked at his watch, it was just past seven o' clock.

'Okay you guys,' he said, 'I've gotta go.'

'Already?' Adam exclaimed.

'Yeah, I've got to get home to the 'Wifey' and the kids.'

'Stay and have another,' said Adam. He was feeling slightly mellow now, especially after the bourbon.'

Reza Mastoor laughed, 'and this from the man we had to almost drag from his office? No, my two bachelor friends. There's a train at seven thirty and I've got to be on it. I'll have to grab a cab to make it to the station.'

And with that, he stood up and then rather dramatically, 'bid them farewell'.

That left Adam and Tony on their own.

'To hell with it,' said Adam, 'I'll get us some more drinks, I like it here, it's comfortable.'

And with that, he stood up and made his way back to the bar. Tony Becker watched him, and he smiled.

Adam returned several minutes later with another pitcher of beer and two glasses of bourbon.

'We're still on bourbon then?' Tony laughed.

'We sure are,' Adam replied. He was relaxed now and enjoying himself. And it was beginning to show.

'Well,' he continued, 'I've worked damn hard this week, bloody hard, I've never stopped. And you know what they say about 'all work and no play...' Adam remembered somebody once giving him that advice, but for the life of him, he couldn't remember who.

'Yes, we do know,' said Tony Becker, 'Bloody hell, man. We've not seen you all week. Where have you been?'

'Mostly stuck in my office. I've had a lot on, something big. I've been working all hours, even when I got home. Sometimes I've been working until midnight.'

'New project?' Tony asked.

'Yeah, brand new, it's huge. Really, really huge.'

'And what's it all about?' Tony enquired.

Adam took a deep breath, he was getting slightly drunk, but he wasn't totally intoxicated.

'To tell you the truth, Tony. I'm not allowed to say. I'm sworn to secrecy, you see.'

But Tony Becker just raised his arms in gesture.

'Hey Adam...Buddy, no problem, honestly. I know how these things work and it's nothing to do with me. I don't want to know, okay. Hey, we all work for the same Bank. We're all one team, you know.' And with that said, he patted Adam firmly on the back.

'Yeah sure,' Adam replied, 'and hey, Tony, thanks buddy.'

Tony Becker just shrugged and smiled, and then he changed the subject. He began to talk about his ex wife and his divorce, of course.

They continued to drink. And then Tony stood up and announced that he was going to the bathroom.

'I'll get us some drinks while I'm there,' he said to Adam, and Adam nodded.

'And I'll take these empty glasses back to the bar,' he continued, 'or they'll get knocked over.'

'Yeah. Good idea,' Adam replied.

After depositing the empty glasses on the bar, Tony Becker made his way to the bathrooms. Once in there he went into one of the closets and closed the door. Whilst he stood there urinating into the bowl, he thought things over...'Mr Adam Tyler wasn't handling his booze very well tonight, not well at all.'

And with that, he reached into his inside jacket pocket and took out a small yellow pill. He examined it and made a decision And then he snapped it into two.

'Better not overdo it,' he thought to himself.

It was an ecstasy tablet.

After washing his hands, Tony Becker returned to the bar. First of all he asked for a tray, and the busy bar staff willingly handed him one. It was a busy Friday night and they didn't have the time or the inclination to fight their way through the busy bar with a tray full of drinks, no matter how big the tip was.

Once he had the tray, Tony ordered a pitcher of cold beer and two fresh glasses to go with it. Once the beer and the glasses arrived, Tony suddenly decided to order two glasses of bourbon. He pointed to a specific bottle that was on one of the higher shelves. The young lady who was serving him did her best not to show her annoyance, but hey, she needed the tips. And as she went off to find the small stepladder that they used for just such occasions, Tony reached into his pocket for the broken tablet and he crushed it into one of the glasses. He then filled both the glasses with the beer from the pitcher. The two glasses of bourbon arrived and Tony tipped the young lady handsomely for her troubles. The money seemed to immediately bring back the smile to her pretty face.

Tony carried the drinks back to their table and he straight away passed a glass of bourbon to Adam and then he sat down and picked up his own glass.

'Cheers buddy,' he said as he raised his glass. 'Here's to First Global, and here's to us, the four musketeers,' and he laughed.

They drank the bourbon quickly. And as Adam put his glass down, Tony passed him his beer.

And Adam belched.

Tony Becker then changed the subject and returned to the topic of his cheating ex wife, who had now moved her boyfriend into Tony's old house. The boyfriend was another teacher, a work colleague, of course, and Tony reckoned that their affair must have been going on for years, obviously, all the time that he was working his guts out at the bank, trying to pay off all their bills. And what a cheating bitch she had turned out to be...etc, etc.

It took about half an hour for the tell tale signs to become apparent, as Adam never stopped talking. After an hour, Adam Tyler was bombed. Tony Becker had actually stopped drinking, but Adam had failed to notice as he drank most of the remaining pitcher of beer, and then another, followed by several shots of cheaper bourbon. Finally, Tony manhandled him out of the bar and down the stairs while he apologized to everyone in the way, for his friend's behaviour. Friday night was now in full swing and most of the crowd simply laughed as they tried their best to get in a similar condition.

Tony flagged down a sympathetic yellow taxicab, and he pushed Adam onto the back seat and they headed for the Lower East Side. They arrived outside Adam's apartment block and Tony paid the rather bemused driver, who laughed at the apparent drunken state that the pair of them appeared to be in, and so Tony played along as he pulled Adam out of the taxi. Tony Becker had been to Adam's apartment a couple of times before for drinks, and so he knew exactly where Adam Tyler lived. He got Adam into the lift and upstairs to the apartment. Then he fumbled through Adam's pockets until he found the right key on a key ring, he opened the door and then dragged Adam inside and rolled him onto the settee.

By this time, Adam was totally out of it. He was unconscious.

Tony Becker quickly looked around the apartment, and he soon spotted Adam's laptop on the top of a desk. He went over to it and switched it on. The screen flickered into life, and then demanded a password.

'Damn you,' he said under his breath. And then he tried several possible passwords, he quickly typed on the keyboar everything from first names to dates, and even the name 'Barcelona.'

If only he'd known that all he had to enter was the word 'Spain.' But there you go.

In the end he started to look through the different drawers in the desk, just to see if he could find any sort clue written down in a book, or on a slip of paper. And it was in the second drawer on the right hand side of the desk that he discovered the file...and Bingo!

Tony Becker sat down and began to read the report. The more he read, the more enthralled he became. And once he understood the basics of what was happening, he only had to skip through the rest of the file, he didn't need to know the intricate details. In fact, he didn't even bother to finish it. He closed the file and looked at it. This was gold, absolute gold. Not the file itself, but the information it contained.

He quickly put the file back in the drawer and closed down the computer. Then he stood up and checked that everything was as he found it. He went through Adam's kitchen cupboards until he found a full bottle of Scotch. He poured some into a glass and placed it on the coffee table in front of the still unconscious Adam

Tyler. Then he poured some of the liquid over the top of the coffee table to resemble spillage. He went back into the kitchen and poured half the scotch down the sink, and then placed the opened half full bottle back on the coffee table, directly in front of Adam. He thought for a moment, and then he tipped the glass on its side. It sort of lent credence to the evening.

As a finishing touch, he dropped Adam's door key on the floor in between the coffee table and the settee. He also left the lights on, another nice touch.

Tony Becker looked around, everything was okay. And with that he left.

The next morning he waited until ten o' clock. And then he rang Adam and left a message on the answer phone. He knew that Adam would still be completely out of it.

'Hi,' the message began. 'It's Tony,' he spoke slowly and groaned. 'What the bloody hell happened, bud. I'm absolutely dying here, I've got the hangover from hell. Listen, I'm never drinking bourbon again.' And then he gave a short pause. '...And what the hell happened to you? Where did you go, you just disappeared. One minute you were there, and the next minute you were gone. We were in a bar somewhere, god only knows where, and you just disappeared.' Another pause, 'Listen, I'm going back to bed. I'm ill. I'll phone you.'

And with that, he put down the phone.

But he wouldn't phone Adam, he'd wait until they met up at work, possibly for lunch.

Tony Becker walked into the bank on the Monday morning. He turned on his computer and was ready to work. He was about to buy all the Cantor Fitzsimons Stock that he could get his hands on. Strangely, he also bought huge amounts of First Global Banking Stock too.

Tony Becker knew when he was on a winner. Of course he knew.

Chapter 6

After being drugged by Tony Becker, Adam Tyler woke up around twenty four hours later. He lay on the couch for several minutes trying to recollect his thoughts, he had to close his eyes and squint, because the room's lighting made his head throb even more. Eventually, and with a lot of effort, he rolled onto his side, and it was at that point that he noticed the half bottle of scotch and the upturned glass beside it. Adam groaned.

He finally managed to sit up, but then had to steady himself as his head began to spin. He sat there for another several minutes, still trying to understand what was going on and why he was there on his settee with half a bottle of scotch. And then some sort of reasoning finally entered his head. It was obvious wasn't it, really? He'd been drunk. More than that, he must have been completely smashed.

Eventually he managed to stand up, he staggered into his kitchen and filled a large glass with water and drank the whole lot to try to slake his thirst. He was suffering from major dehydration. He clicked on his 'ever ready' coffee percolator and listened to it gurgle into action as he leant against the kitchen sink. For the life of him he couldn't remember what had happened to him, and just how he'd managed to get himself in such a state. He felt absolutely terrible.

He managed to make himself a mug of thick black coffee, which he had to pick up with both hands because he was suffering from the shakes. As he sipped the strong coffee, he tried to work things out in his mind. Who was he out with? Oh yes, Reza and Tony Becker. He thought about it for a moment. Yes, but Reza went home. He had a train to catch. So that left himself and Tony. Adam began to remember the drinking and some blurred conversation about Tony's cheating ex-wife and his divorce. And he remembered the pitchers of beer, and then the bourbon. My god, how much had they drank? And how had he got home? And for some reason, he'd obviously carried on drinking. By now, Adam was feeling somewhat embarrassed and stupid. Why had he got himself in such a state, and then he gave himself his own, only excuse, that it was because he'd been 'working' so hard. That must have been it, it was the only reason he could give himself that was vaguely justifiable.

He walked back into his living room and picked up the half bottle of scotch and the glass and then went back into the kitchen and poured the scotch down the sink.

'Never again,' he said to himself out loud. He was still not well at all and he knew that the only remedy would be bed and sleep. As he managed to haphazardly walk across his living room to his bedroom, he suddenly noticed the red light flashing on his answer phone. He went over to the phone and picked it up, and listened to Tony Becker's strained message. He put the phone down and shook his head. Well at least he wasn't on his own. It sounded like Tony was in the same state too. Adam thought about it for a moment, and what Tony meant about Adam 'just disappearing'.

And Adam again wondered just how he'd managed to get himself back home.

He slept for another twelve hours. Adam finally awoke at around ten o' clock in the morning. He got up and slowly plodded into the kitchen for more coffee. Then he sat on the settee trying to remember everything, and it was only when he clicked on the TV to listen to the News that he realized that it was Sunday. Adam stared at the TV, he couldn't believe it. He'd managed somehow, to lose the best part of two days.

He sat there rubbing his eyes, still trying to remember, but everything was now even hazier.

And then he remembered Tony Becker's message on his answer phone. Adam stood up and went over to the phone. He pressed a button and listened to Tony's message again. Tony did actually sound out of sorts, he must have got himself into a similar state. Adam pressed the return button to call Tony, he heard the phone ringing, but there was no reply.

Adam rang Tony Becker again during the day, several times in fact. But there was no answer.

No problem, he'd see Tony the next day at the bank. They'd probably have lunch.

Adam and Paul Maynard went to work together on the Monday morning, as usual really. Paul asked Adam about his weekend and Adam just shook his head.

'Don't even ask,' Adam had replied.

But after a little prompting, well, continual prompting really, Adam owned up and told Paul everything that had happened, or to be more to the truth, all that he could actually remember.

Paul just shook his head.

'I told you, that bloody Reza Mastoor, it's always his fault. He thinks everything's a joke.'

Adam shrugged. 'Actually, he left early after a few drinks. He had a train to catch, he wasn't staying at his apartment, he was going home for the weekend.'

It was Paul Maynard's turn too shrug.

'Oh, right. Well that's strange, I've never known Tony Becker to be a heavy drinker. Mind you, he is having financial problems with that 'cheating piece of work' that he was once married to.'

'Tell me about it,' Adam replied, 'he was going on about her.' And then he thought about it.

'To tell you the truth, that's actually the last thing I remember. Jesus, I must have been canned.'

Paul just laughed, 'You'll never learn. Come the weekend you'll be back at it again.'

But Paul shook his head.' I'll tell you one thing, I won't be drinking straight shots of bourbon again. I've never been so drunk in my life.'

And then he remembered that one wild night, the night he'd spent with Miss Dominique Cassens, lying with her in bed, drinking straight vodka.

Adam closed his eyes for a moment and he sighed. Why could he not get her out of his head? And then he changed the topic of conversation and began to talk to Paul about work.

At twelve o' clock, it was early really, but Adam decided to go upstairs too see if anyone was up for lunch. He didn't phone anyone, because really he wanted to speak to Tony Becker alone and find out just what had happened on the Friday night. He wanted to talk to Tony alone, and though he wasn't bothered

137

about Paul finding out, he didn't really want Reza Mastoor to know anything.

Reza was not only a bit of a comedian, he was also the office gossip, and was well known for emailing any embarrassing information to all of his other work colleagues.

Adam walked into the office. Paul saw him and just nodded, he was busy on the phone. Reza Mastoor looked up too, he was busy doing some paperwork.

'Hey buddy,' he said to Adam, 'you okay?'

'Yeah, no problem,' Adam replied vaguely. 'Is Tony about, I'm trying to sort some lunch out?'

Reza pointed to the other side of the office.

'He'll be at his desk over there. Don't know if he'll be up for lunch though. I've already spoken to him, he reckons he's very busy. I've rung him twice and then he told me to 'bugger off.'

Reza then laughed at his own hilarity, as usual.

'I'll go and have a word,' Adam replied, 'I'll see what he's up to.'

'Good luck, pal' said Reza, and he turned back to his work.

Adam walked around the office and made his way through the cubicles to Tony Becker's desk. But Tony wasn't there.

In fact, for Tony Becker it had a very lucrative morning. And a morning that would eventually become even more lucrative by the middle of the afternoon.

Tony had spent all of his morning using the bank's money, along with various investors' money, to buy every Cantor Fitzsimons share that he could get hold of. Along with that, he'd also bought huge amounts of First Global Bank stock too. Tony Becker had laughed to himself. Buying the banks own stock with it[s own money was something that he considered as an act of genius. But Tony Becker already knew that he was a genius. All that money, and it was all his to play with, it was brilliant. It made Tony feel giddy. It was like gambling really. And Tony Becker just loved to gamble, oh yes.

And the recipient of Tony Becker's investment acumen? Well, Tony handled the portfolios of a lot of people, really. Mainly the bank's customers, but also quite a number of private investors too, along with the big Investment Houses, who then paid the bank a commission for Tony's services.

And Tony Becker was good at his job. People liked Tony, they trusted him.

And Tony, in turn, had made it his own business to go out and meet each and every one of his clients. They trusted him with their money, and Tony felt it only right that he met them personally. Trust needed to be earned, and it had worked. Over the years, those same investors had given Tony Becker a 'free reign' to handle the money in their investment accounts as he seemed fit. And why? Because Tony Becker had always given them a return on their money.

There had been good years and there had been reasonable years, but there had never been bad years, Tony had seen to that. And so, his customers had always seen a return on their investments. And greed, and success, always makes people happy. And because of that, Tony Becker could freely play with the bank's money and with his investor's money. And all was well, as long as he showed a profit. In the Banking World, you only drew attention to yourself when you were losing money.

The bank dealt with thousands and thousands of investors. And the bank employed hundreds of Investment Managers to handle those investments. Tony Becker being one of them. Everyone worked hand in hand. In the end, money had to be made, it was that simple.

It was almost a religion.

But Tony Becker had discovered a little niche, a little loophole that was all his very own.

The real recipient of all those investments, eventually went to 'Woodvale Investments'.

And simply put, Woodvale Investments belonged to Tony Becker. Woodvale Investments was actually based solely in a private account in the Fidelity Trust National Bank in the Cayman Islands, the tax haven for the rich and the famous, and the inscrutable.

In a moment which he considered his own genius, Tony Becker had 'invented' Woodvale Investments as a client. Tony had okayed the company and the accounts, and he'd okayed the necessary trading licences and the appropriate assurances that were all part and parcel of the financial industry.

He was an Investment Manager, and who 'on earth' was ever going to question him over a potentially beneficial customer such as the Woodvale Investment Company, really?

No, it was never going to happen, unless of course, something went badly wrong. And Tony Becker would make sure that nothing ever did.

Tony started to make money by using other people's money, along with the bank's money, and when he bought any investments, be it stocks or shares, he would use other people's money or the banks money to buy for Woodvale Investments too. When he sold, and he invariably made a profit, he would transfer his own profits into Woodvale Investments and return the original money to its source. And nobody every asked any questions, as long as 'the source' got some of the profits too. Along with that, Woodvale Investments only paid a very nominal commission fee to the bank for Mr Becker's services, in truth, it was virtually nothing. Tony Becker had seen to that too. After all, Woodvale Investments were a very good customer.

From there, Tony came up with the idea of using Woodvale Investments as a vehicle to invest money for his clients. Tony recommended 'Woodvale' and had given his personal assurances as to the reputation of the company. And once again, those same clients saw a regular return on their money, and so everyone was happy..

There had of course been the occasional problem. If an investment lost money, Tony Becker took it upon himself to prop up any clients losses by using the cash in Woodvale Investments. In doing so, no one ever asked any questions. Again, questions and explanations were only asked when people lost money. But there were good times, and there were better times.

Tony Becker didn't see this as theft. No, not really. He was simply using other people's money to make his own. And to a point he was right.

Illegal, yes. But theft, no...not theft.

So after a very, very busy morning, and a hell of a lot of coffee, Tony Becker had suddenly realized that he needed to take a trip to the lavatory, and urgently. Without more ado, he quickly ended his phone call and immediately headed off to the loo.

And whilst he was in there, Adam Tyler had arrived. Adam made his way across the large office over to Tony's desk, but Tony wasn't there.

He looked around, but there was no Tony. Tony Becker's desk was just as he'd left it, stacks of papers, full of figures. Even his computer was still switched on. Adam glanced at the screen, and that too was filled with figures, along with some company called 'Woodvale Investments'. Adam turned away, he'd never dealt with that side of banking and he didn't really understand it. Then he caught the girl's attention who was sat in the next cubicle, and he asked her if she knew Tony's whereabouts.

At that moment, Tony Becker walked back into the office. Reza Mastoor immediately spotted him and called out,

'Adam Tyler's looking for you.'

'Oh right, where is he?' Tony asked.

At that moment, Reza's phone began to ring. He picked it up immediately and began to speak to someone, but at the same time, he pointed to the other side of the office, over to Tony's desk.

Tony Becker looked across this office, and he stood there and watched in horror as Adam Tyler appeared to be looking down at Tony's computer. Then Adam began to speak to Mandy, the girl on the next desk. Tony Becker took a deep breath, and then walked as quickly as he could back to his desk. In a moment of panic, he tried to remember what was on his screen? Hoping against hope that there was nothing at all appertaining to Cantor Fitzsimons, please god...no.

As he approached his desk, Adam Tyler still had his back to him as he spoke to the lovely, Mandy. Tony quickly glanced at his screen. It read 'Woodvale Investments, and was full of past share dealings, but there was no mention anywhere about Cantor Fitzsimons, thank god. But even Adam Tyler seeing that, was all too incriminating. Woodvale Investments was a definite secret.

At that point, Mandy spotted Tony Becker over Adam's shoulder.

'Ah, he's here now,' she said to Adam, as she gave him her most agreeable smile. After all, Adam Tyler was a good looking man, and for Mandy, there was maybe always the chance of a possibility?

Adam turned around to greet Tony .

'Hi buddy,' he said, 'you okay?' he asked.

'Yeah, yeah,' Tony replied slightly vaguely, as he reached down and clicked off the computer's monitor. And with that done, he looked up at Adam and then quickly smiled.

'And how are you pal, some night eh?'

'Yes, it certainly was. I just need something, Tony,' and then he silently mouthed the words, 'in private.'

Tony Becker realized what Adam wanted to talk about, and away from the prying ears of Mandy, who at that moment was pretending to work, but was actually listening in to every word of their conversation. The woman had the hearing of a bat, but Tony already knew that.

'Yeah, come on, we'll get some coffee from the machine' he replied, and he turned to go back to the corridor. As they walked away from Tony's desk, Adam glanced down for a second, at the computer's monitor, now switched off, and he inwardly smiled to himself. He'd noticed Tony's moment of unease when he'd quickly turned it off. 'Dear me', these investment people were a secretive lot, they certainly didn't like anyone knowing anything about their business.

They walked to the corridor, and as they passed his desk, Reza, who was still on the phone, gave them both 'the finger' sign as he grinned at them both.

Once out of the office they stopped.

'And how are you now?' Tony Becker asked immediately.

Adam put his hand over his head, 'Jeez, Tony. What the hell happened?'

Tony just laughed. 'What happened? I'll tell you what happened. We got steamrollered, that's what happened. Don't you remember?'

Adam had to smile, 'No I bloody well don't. In fact, I don't remember much after Reza left us. I know we had some beers and those bloody bourbon shots, but after that I don't remember a damn thing. I woke up in my apartment with half a bottle of scotch. Christ, I've never been as ill in my life.'

Tony Becker shook his head. 'Me too, I've been rough for two days. My weekend's been a blur.'

'Tell me about it,' Adam replied. 'I've basically slept for forty eight hours. What happened to us?'

Tony Becker took a deep breath, he was ready for this, it was all prepared.

'Well, we did another couple of bars, same thing, pitchers of beer along with loads of bourbon shots. And then it was you who decided that we 'had' to go down to the Lower East Side, because you knew some brilliant bars down there. We got into a cab, and I don't know just where he dropped us off, because when he drove away, you hadn't a bloody clue where we were.' Tony laughed as he said this. 'So we just staggered into the nearest bar and carried on.'

'Which bar was it, Tony? Adam asked him, still trying to make sense of it all.

But Tony just shrugged. 'How the hell should I know, I was past caring by then. Man, we were smashed. We ended up in another couple of bars, I remember we had to leave one of them because you were beginning to have an argument with some guy.'

'I did? Oh Jesus, no.'

'Yep, you did,' Tony laughed, 'and so we went to another bar and we carried on drinking and suddenly you disappeared.'

'I did?'

'Yep, you staggered off to the toilet and never came back. I actually went in there looking for you, but you weren't there. You'd disappeared. Gone. After that things are a bit hazy. I remember asking the bartender to phone me a cab and I gave him some cash, god only knows how much? And then I remember falling into the back seat and heading home, but that's it. Everything else is a blur. I woke up in bed the next day. Don't remember coming home at all.

God, I've been rough. I'm never drinking bourbon again.'

'Tell me about it,' Adam replied, and then he recounted his own exploits, well, what he could remember. Tony listened, and shook his head appropriately.

'We're not fit to be let out, pal,' and he laughed, and then, 'just a word, Adam. You've haven't mentioned any of this to Reza, have you?'

143

'No, have I hell. Paul knows we got drunk, but no, I haven't mentioned it to Reza, I know what he's like.'

'Thank god for that. That bastard would be emailing messages all over the bloody building.'

'Yes, I realize that,' said Adam, 'anyway, let's put it down to experience, and forget it".

Tony nodded and grinned, and 'Yes', he thought to himself, 'you forget it, indeed.'

'So,' Adam then continued, 'you up for lunch?'

But Tony Becker just shook his head.

'Sorry buddy, I can't make it today, I'm really busy. I've got an important deadline to meet.'

Adam shrugged, 'Okay then. To tell you the truth, I've got a pretty full week myself.'

But of course, Tony Becker already knew all about Adam's 'week'.

And with that, nothing more was said.

They both wandered back into the office and Tony Becker returned to his desk. Adam went over to Paul and Reza.

'Are you two up for lunch?' he asked them.

Reza grinned and nodded, but Paul Maynard had to think about it. Until Reza threw a ball of scrunched up paper over the divide, which once again hit Paul on the head.

'Come on, big boy,' Reza laughed, 'put the pastrami on hold for once.'

Paul looked at Adam and just shook his head.

'I swear, I'm going to kill this Egyptian twerp one day.' And then he sighed and stood up. 'Okay then, come on, let's go and eat.'

Half an hour later, they were eating shrimp at 'Barney's', one of their regular haunts.

Reza Mastoor was on form as usual, he'd hardly stopped talking since the three of them had left the office.

'So,' he said to Adam, as he dipped another peeled prawn into the strong garlic dip, the house speciality at Barneys. 'So how did you go on, on Friday, you and Tony.'

Adam just shrugged,

'Yes, It was okay.'

Paul Maynard quickly glanced at his friend, but said nothing.

'Where did you get to?' Reza again asked. He was fishing for gossip.

'Well, we spent most of the night at 'Tiny's', then we wandered further down the road and had a nightcap at some bar or other, I can't remember the name of the place. After that, I took a cab home. Tony did the same.

'Oh,' said Reza, seemingly slightly disappointed.

Adam continued. 'Well you know how Tony is. After you've had an hour or so listening to him go on about his divorce, it's definitely time to leave.'

Reza laughed. 'Tell me about it, I get it every day.'

Reza Mastoor and Tony Becker were actually long time acquaintances, though not close friends. Their families had never met and they'd never shared weekends together or anything remotely like that. But they'd first started working at First Global within a month of each other, several years ago. As 'new boys' they'd struck up their working friendship, simply because everyone else in the office seemed to be too busy. Though Reza always considered that it was because of his ethnicity, he'd had the same thing happen to him at College.

People were pleasantly distant. And that was why Reza Mastoor approached everything with a sense of humour. He knew that if you could make people laugh and smile, then they would relax a little and lower their guard.

'So you had a good night then'? Reza continued.

'Yeah, it was okay.'

And then Paul Maynard stepped in and tactfully changed the subject.

'This shrimps delicious,' he interrupted, ' I love this place, it's always really good food in here.'

And the conversation then changed.

At three o'clock that same afternoon, word finally broke about Cantor Fitzsimons.

Within an hour, rumour became fact, as Cantor Fitzsimons and First Global Bank stock went through the roof.

The first Adam knew about it was when he got a rather terse phone call from Norman Roth's office. Mr Roth needed to speak to Adam 'straight away.' It was not a request.

145

Adam picked up on the 'tone'. He stopped what he was doing and immediately went to see his boss. He was shown into Norman Roth's office and the door was quickly closed behind him by a very perceptive secretary.

'Sit down, Adam,' said Norman Roth. Again, it was not a request.

Adam was a bit perturbed. This was not their usual manner when dealing with anything.

'Words got out about Cantor Fitzsimons and First Global. Every man and his dog knows, and knows everything.'

Adam just sat there, slightly open mouthed.

'What's happened?,' he then asked. A silly question, really.

'That's what I'm asking you, Adam. What's happened?'

For a moment Adam didn't understand. And then the penny dropped.

'Nobody knew,' Roth continued. 'Nobody knew about this except the top three brass at Cantor Fitzsimons, and then that leaves me and you, Adam. So what's going on?'

Adam just shook his head, and then he wondered where all of this was heading.

Norman Roth stared at him for a moment.

'We've got the meeting with them tomorrow. The staff who will be there, think that the meeting is all about moving office premises. We were supposed to be working with them in an advisory capacity. At some point in the future, they would eventually realize what was going on, but the financing of the actual company has nothing to do with them.'

Adam just sat there. He realized what he was being asked. If only five people knew about this so-called secret merger, then he was the weak link.

'Tell me, Adam,' Norman Roth asked. 'And tell me the truth please. Have you spoken to anyone, anyone at all?'

Adam looked across the desk at his boss.

'No, I have not,' he said empathically, 'I haven't spoken to anyone about it, as instructed by you.'

Norman Roth just looked at him.

Adam knew he had to defend himself. This could cost him his job, along with his career.

'Why would I?' he continued. 'What would I get out of it by blabbing about the merger?'

Norman Roth tapped his finger on the desk, he was quite agitated.

'Well', Adam,' he said,' there's the chance to make a lot of money, for starters.'

'What do you mean, I don't understand?'

'It's called 'insider trading', Adam. You use your knowledge to an advantage, a great deal of money can be made by buying blocks of shares. It happens all the time. People 'in the know' buy shares in a company that's about to fly, or vice versa and shares can get dumped. It can even break those companies. And now it's happened here today.

Adam suddenly became defensive.

'Well I haven't got a great deal of money to buy any 'blocks' of shares. I bank here at First Global, you can check my accounts.'

Bur Norman Roth wasn't interested about Adam Tyler's personal accounts. That could all be traced, obviously. And anyway, money could be hidden in an assortment of different ways, especially if you'd colluded with another party.

'What about your three friends upstairs?' Roth asked. "They're all investment managers, and in theory they would know what was involved. I know you all socialize together. Are you sure that you've not spoken about it to any of them?'

But Adam just shook his head.

'My actual best friend is Paul Maynard. We were at university together and we've been friends for years, and even he doesn't know about this. You told me not to talk to anyone, and I haven't. To tell you the truth, when the four of us are out, we hardly ever talk about the bank.' And at that point, Adam did actually wonder just how Norman Roth knew about his social life.

But Norman Roth said nothing.

'Just how did the news break? Adam asked.

Norman Roth continued to tap his desk, and then he sighed.

'Someone or some company has been buying large blocks of Cantor Fitzsimons and First Global stock all morning. By lunchtime, the stock market finally took notice and the rumours started, and so did the buying, and by mid afternoon it turned into a free for all. Over at Federal American Bank they got the 'heads up' and straightaway contacted Cantor Fitzsimons, they're no fools, they'd quickly figured out what was going on. Apparently all hell broke loose and they called an emergency meeting. Federal American has always been at odds with First Global. We don't like one another. Anyway, the first thing I know about all of this is when I get phone calls from Cantor Fitzsimons, it was Berni Speegle and his two head honchos, they're in a complete panic over there. Apparently, Federal American has decided to pull back all of their loans to Cantor Fitzsomons, and immediately. Their reasoning being that if Cantor Fitzsimons was leaving them, well then, they wanted their money back. And they can do that".

Adam ran his hand over his head.

'Oh hell. And that could bring the company to its knees?'

'Exactly,' Norman Roth replied.

'So what happens now?' Adam asked.

Norman Roth took a deep breath.

'I've told them that we'll cover their loans, or should I say, 'First Global' is going to cover the loans. What else could I do? They accused us of breaking their confidence. Apparently, news is even out about them going into publishing. Maybe it is one of their staff, maybe someone's been talking to one of their staff. I don't know, but who else would know about them leaving Federal American?'

Adam took a deep breath.

'Maybe it's because they're moving into their new offices here and somebody's opened their mouth about the publishing venture? I understand how this looks,' he replied. 'But I swear to you. Nothing at all came from me. I am totally loyal to this bank, and that's the truth.'

Norman Roth looked directly at Adam, before he finally spoke.

'Okay, I believe you, and I believe what your telling me,' and then he leant forward. 'But be warned, Adam. If I ever find out anything that points to you, then I'll ruin you. You'll never work in the banking industry again and I'll bring charges against you, via the bank, and do my best to have you thrown into prison.'

It was a threat and Adam knew it, but he was defiant.

'In that case, sir, I truly have nothing to worry about. Because I know that this is nothing to do with me. And that's a fact.'

Little did he know, or even realize, the error of his words.

Norman Roth finally nodded.

'Okay, Adam. I believe you. But now we've got to salvage all of this fiasco. This is not the way we wanted to start off, without doubt.'

'Well we've got the meeting with them tomorrow. Is that still on?' Adam asked.

'Yes it is, and after that I'm going to have a private meeting with Berni Speegle and his two directors. I just hope I can carry this off. Either that or everything goes kaput, and for all of us.'

'Why's that?' Adam felt that he was missing something here.

'Why? Because it's me who has put my head on the line here,' said Roth. 'It's me who's offered to cover the Cantor Fitzsimons loans. It was me who came up with that little decision, and in,' ...and at that point Norman Roth checked his watch, '...and in half an hour I've got to sit in front of the Directors of this bank and explain to them what I've done, or what I've promised to do. If it goes wrong and they won't allow the loans to go through, I'll probably get sacked for overstretching my authority, and then Cantor Fitzsimons could go bankrupt. Unless of course, they can try to get back in with Federal American and are prepared to kiss some serious butt. Though when I spoke to Berni Speegle, he did tell me that they'd had a terrific row with the guys at Federal and that one the bank's directors had slammed the phone down after promising to 'break them'. So things aren't that good over there either.'

'Oh hell, I didn't realize it was that bad,' Adam replied.

'Well, yes it is. Or it could be.'

'Tell me,' Adam decided to ask, 'do we know who's been buying all these shares?'

Norman Roth shook his head.

'No we don't. But we will, believe me. I'll find out who it is. I'll make it my purpose to find out. If we've got a weak link here at the bank, I need to know who it is. If it's happened once it can happen again, and eventually it could harm the banks credibility. I will find out, Adam. Money always leaves a trace, especially large amounts of money. I'll put the 'feelers' out, somebody will know something. They always do".

Adam realized that Norman Roth had just issued a veiled threat. But since there was nothing for him to hide, Adam decided to dismiss it.

'I think we should carry on as though this doesn't affect us, Mr Roth. I realize how it affects you, and also you're standing with the heads of Cantor Fitzsimons. However, we've got to stick with the business in hand. We're meeting their people tomorrow and we have to get off to a positive start. It's the only way. We've got to move on and look upon this as just an obstacle, it's a hiccup, but certainly not the end. Cantor Fitzsimons are still the same company, and we are still the First Global Bank. We can do this.'

Norman Roth looked at Adam, And he suddenly realized that he should given this young man the benefit of the doubt. And in his heart he also realized that Adam Tyler hadn't betrayed his trust, or the bank's trust either.

'You're right, Adam,' he replied, 'of course you're right. We need to swing this thing. And we need to get everything up and running, because that's our job, damn it.'

Adam nodded, he finally felt as though they'd made some sort of headway.

'Okay then,' Norman Roth continued. 'You carry on and I'll see you at the meeting tomorrow. I've got to go now and speak to the bank's directors. Just one thing though, Adam, I will email you later and let you know the outcome of the meeting. We both need to know just where we stand when we all meet up tomorrow morning.'

And that was it. Adam stood up and reached out to shake Norman Roth's hand.

'Thank you for your confidence, sir,' he said.

Norman Roth shrugged, and gave a hopeful smile.

'Wish me luck,' he replied.

Norman Roth didn't need luck.

Adam got back to his apartment at around seven o' clock. He'd stayed on at the office, writing some final reports. When he finally arrived home, he clicked on his faithful old percolator and made himself a mug full of good coffee. Whilst the percolator was gurgling away to its own particular tune, Adam went to get changed into some more comfortable clothes.

In the end, he went over to his desk and put the mug of coffee down in front of him, and then he reached over to his computer and clicked it on The screen flashed as it came to life, and once it had finally settled down, Adam checked his emails. There were more than a dozen, including the reports that he'd sent to himself from his office. But at that moment there was only one that he was looking for, and there it was.

'Message from...Roth, Norman.'

It read...'Hi Adam Tyler. Meeting finished an hour ago. Everything a success. The Board agreed the loans, no problem. They are actually happier that the loans be 'in house' rather than with Federal American. In fact, they would have insisted on it. Anyway, I have spoken to Berni Speegle and the heads of Cantor Fitzsimons and they're ecstatic, so panic over.

We start tomorrow on an even playing field again, and that's good. It will hopefully be all smiles, and we must be positive.

As you advised, and thank you...yours, Norman Roth.'

Adam sat back and sighed, and then he relaxed slightly. It was over, thank god. The problem was solved. He'd done a lot of work over the last week, a hell of a lot of work and he certainly didn't want to see it all go up in smoke. He skirted through his other emails, but there was nothing of any importance there. He then switched on the printer, and clicked onto his emails for the reports that he'd written earlier. There was plenty of paper in the printer, and so that wasn't a problem. He would print off his reports, because he needed everything to be ready and at hand for the meeting tomorrow.

And with that, he opened the second drawer on the right hand side of his desk, the drawer where he always kept his private file.

For Tony Becker, it had been a very eventful day. Eventful, and very, very profitable.

From his client base, and from the largest to even the smaller investor, Tony had dipped into virtually all of their accounts and

151

transferred a small fortune into Woodvale Investments. From there he had gone to town in buying both Cantor Fitzsimons and First Global Stock.

In the middle of the afternoon the stock market rumbled to what was going on and questions were beginning to be asked. Natural greed then took over as the 'vulture' instinct of the stock market kicked in. As those share prices shot through the ceiling, Tony Becker then sold everything that he had bought earlier, lock stock and barrel. The following day he would return everyone's money to their accounts, plus a certain amount of profit. And then he would close the financial door. And that would leave Woodvale Investments with a proverbial stash of cash, and no one the wiser. Everyone would see a profit, and that kept everyone happy.

A job well done. Nice one Woodvale Investments. And no questions asked.

In truth, Tony Becker was very astute at his job. He was actually a very good investment manager for the bank, but he'd had to be. Because Tony Becker was in fact, not only a compulsive gambler, he was totally addicted.

In fact, Tony Becker's whole life was much of a lie. Sure, his wife had divorced him. But it wasn't through her having any affair, and neither was it about Tony always being at work, or even that they'd been trying for children but had been unsuccessful. The truth was, that his wife, Margaret, couldn't have children, They'd always known that, because Margaret had been for fertility tests after they'd been married for a couple of years and they'd then been told the bad news. Bad news for Margaret, however, not for Tony. He'd never wanted any kids anyway, he'd always considered them a 'damn' nuisance'.

So Margaret had thrown herself into her career as a primary school teacher, where she happily dealt with young children all day long. However, by then Tony had already thrown himself into gambling, something that he would have also happily preferred to do too, all day long.

Just a year or so into their marriage, Tony had discovered the delights of the Casino's of New Jersey. It had all started off with a friend's 'Stag Party', when a dozen or so friends got together and went off to celebrate the ending of 'bachelorhood', before the impending wedding.

They'd decided to go to Atlantic City in New Jersey for a 'long' weekend, a favourite gambling Mecca for all those gullible New Yorkers who still believed that they could quickly become rich by beating 'the odds'.

Atlantic City is approximately one hundred miles from New York. A flight there takes roughly forty-five minutes. By car or by bus it can take two hours. So, the flight was booked and off they all went. They were booked into the 'Tropicana Hotel & Casino', a huge, luxurious palace that was very well situated, close to the Marina and right across from Atlantic City's beautiful beachfront. They'd arrived there at around four o' clock in the afternoon and immediately hit the bar. By eight o' clock they were all fairly smashed. Half of them had wandered off to the casino, the rest had staggered off to find a decent strip club and from there, further entertainment. Tony Becker however, had gone back to his room and gone to sleep. Though everyone in the party knew one another, and although Tony did know the 'groom' fairly well, he was actually only reasonably acquainted with two or three of the others. The rest, he'd never met before in his life. And he was feeling slightly left out. And the alcohol hadn't helped either. Tony wasn't a particularly strong drinker and he'd watched and then become slightly irritated as these 'long term' buddies continued with the backslapping and the nonstop. '...do you remember when..?'

And so, he'd sloped off to bed, and he wasn't missed. He knew that.

The one other problem was the money. The other guys all seemed to be noticeably 'well-off" and were running up huge tabs at the bar and were then tipping the waitresses with what seemed to Tony to be 'wads' of cash. And then there was talk about 'splashing the cash' in the casino, or throwing money at the some strippers, and then whatever. It was all a bit too much for Tony. He'd just taken on a huge mortgage on their first home and he was still finding his feet at the bank. It was early days for him back then and he was still on a very average wage and was not yet earning those hard earned, but promised bonuses.

Tony had slept until about one in the morning. And then he woke up with a slightly thick head and a very dry mouth, and along with that, he was hungry. After a glass of water, he thought things over. He was going to have to be careful with his cash. There were another two days to go, and he didn't want to embarrass himself in front of the other by having to admit that he'd run out of money.

And then a thought suddenly struck him. Downstairs in the Casino, the food and drink was free, he knew that. Everything in the Casino was complimentary, as long as you gambled. Hey, maybe he could get away with it. Well, he didn't have to gamble, did he? The Casino would be busy, it always was, and surely they wouldn't have people in there, just walking around and checking whether or not you were actually gambling at any particular moment. And anyway, his excuse could be that he couldn't eat and drink and gamble all at the same time. Tony thought about it for a moment. And then he decided to give it a try.

He splashed some water in his face, ran a comb through his hair and spruced himself up a bit. And then he left his room and headed for the lift. A few minutes later he was downstairs in the huge reception area.

The Tropicana Hotel complex was designed to a 'Cuban' sort of theme. All bright pastel colours and exotic hanging plants, with an assortment of small palm trees and other various types of foliage, all in hand painted terracotta pots, and all immaculate and purposefully placed. Tony looked up at the mock wooden 'rustic' signs which gave the guests directions to hotel's different amenities. He walked straight through the reception area, then past the restaurants and the bars as he headed in the direction of the Casino.

Finally, he figured out just where it was and in due course he walked through a large arched doorway and into the Tropicana's huge Casino. Tony gazed around. It was vast, and it was busy, very busy.

And so he decided to walk around, just to get his bearings.

He saw lines and lines of slot machines, that people were seemingly feeding with coins as fast as they could. And then he walked around the 'tables'. All seemed to be busy, with folk playing blackjack and roulette. And then he heard people laughing and shouting and he headed in that direction, finally arriving at the 'Craps' tables. Somebody was obviously winning at one of the tables because the crowd there were going wild. Tony looked at some of the other tables and he noticed a couple of the guys from his party. One was watching the gambling and another had his arm around a blonde girl's waist. All of them were drinking and laughing and looked pretty drunk. Tony left them to it and he walked back past the roulette tables. He stopped there for a short while and watched the play. Then he looked around again and walked away. Finally, he spotted something. At the far end of the Casino he saw people sitting and eating.

It was the Hotel buffet, thankfully, and so he made his way there straightaway. And there it was, huge amounts of displayed food, hot and cold. You just took a plate and helped yourself, and Tony did just that. He filled a plate with hot sliced beef with fries and beans. It was piled high, and more than he could eat really, but what the hell. Everyone else seemed to be doing the same. He picked up a knife and fork and found himself an empty table and then began to eat.

'Champagne, sir?' somebody suddenly asked.

And Tony quickly looked up, to see a waitress standing at the side of him. She was carrying a tray full of filled, fluted glasses, obviously Champagne.

'Would you like some Champagne, sir?' the smiling waitress asked him again.

'Oh yeah...yes please,' he replied, as he thought to himself '...and why not?'

The waitress, her badge read 'Fiona', picked up a glass and then placed it efficiently on the table in front of him, and smiled.

'Thank you, cheers' said Tony.

The waitress, Fiona, smiled.

'Thank you,' said Tony, again.

Fiona just continued to smile.

And the Tony realized. He needed to tip her.

'Oh, sorry,' he said, and he stood up and pulled out of his pocket a fairly slim wad of notes, which Fiona also regrettably noticed. He peeled off two dollar bills and put them onto her tray, on top of the fifty dollar and the one hundred dollar notes that already lay there, along with an assortment of the Casino's gambling chips.

Fiona held her smile. 'Why, thank you, sir,' she said to Tony, in a rather clipped tone. And as she walked away, so did her smile. She shook her head, but there you go. Her job was all about keeping the customers happy, and accumulating her tips. Some guys, in the past had tipped her five hundred dollars when they'd been successful and won.

Others, like Tony, didn't. Yes, it was all about accumulation. Just keep smiling, girl.

Tony finished off most of his food, and then the champagne, and then he sat back and quietly belched. It actually wasn't bad, dinner and a glass of champagne for two bucks, nice one.

And after a futher few minutes of contemplation, he decided to have a look around, as well as keeping his eye out for another waitress. He wandered back over to the slots, where he eventually found another of the smiling waitresses, who this time was carrying a tray full of white wine. He helped himself a glass of wine and then again 'treated' the waitress to another two dollar tip.

The waitress then walked away in a similar fashion to 'Fiona'.

After the good food, the champagne and the wine, Tony was actually feeling a lot better. And as he stood there and watched the players on the slots, he thought to himself...'why not?'

So he wandered off to find the cashier's booth where he changed a twenty dollar note into chips. He put the chips into his pocket and headed back to the slots. On the way there he came across the same waitress again and he stopped her for another glass of wine. And although he'd already tipped her before, he decided to give her another couple of bucks. He was generous that way.

He made his way back to the slots and stood there for a while, sipping his drink. And then in front of him, an elderly lady stood up, she picked up her bag and just walked away, and she didn't look happy. Tony had actually noticed her before when he'd first entered the Casino. She was wearing a slightly worn fur coat, which seemed quite strange, since it was already quite warm in there. Tony looked at the empty seat and thought, 'what the hell, she must have put a fair amount of money in there, and it might just pay up?' and so he took her place. He pulled a chip out of his pocket and pushed it into the slot and pulled the handle. Then he watched as the three wheels spun round and then came to an abrupt stop, only to display three different kinds of fruit. He sighed, and pulled another chip out of his pocket, put it into the slot and as he took another sip of his wine, he again pulled the handle. Then suddenly, there was a bit of a commotion behind him. Somebody had accidentally collided with Tony's favourite wine waitress and her tray full of drinks had gone flying. Worse than that, so had her tips. And as she dropped to her knees, whilst attempting to recover her hard earned tips, a large man just stood there in front of her, trying to apologize. Then there was another sound, and Tony Becker immediately realized that the sound was coming from his own slot machine. He turned back quickly, as a steady flow of chips began to drop into the machine's collection tray. He looked up, and on the display it read 'three bars'. Tony couldn't believe it, he'd just won the machines jackpot. And he watched with glee, as the tray in front of him filled up with two hundred dollars worth of chips. A woman sitting at the machine adjacent to him looked over and said 'Nice one.' And nice one indeed. Tony couldn't believe his luck.

From there, he then put thirty dollars back into the machine before becoming slightly disenchanted. Guessing that the old lady in the fur coat must have previously 'fed' the machine, he certainly wasn't prepared to do the same. And so he gathered up his winnings and decided to go for a wander around. He grabbed another glass of wine again from the same waitress and this time he tipped her with five dollars worth of chips.

What the hell, he'd won.

Tony wandered over to the roulette table. He stood back and watched the people there playing. He didn't really know the rules of roulette, other than if the ball that was bouncing around in the spinning wheel, landed on the number you'd picked, you obviously won.

He looked on, fascinated, as people placed their chips all over the table and he quickly understood how things worked. You didn't just have to place your money directly on the number on any square, you could also place your money on the lines between two adjoining numbers, and so with two numbers you had doubled your chances of winning, but obviously you then lowered your winnings as a result, if there was a result. The same thing happened if you put your money on the corner of a square, then you had the chance of winning on any of the four adjoining numbers, but with an even lower return.

After twenty minutes and another glass of wine, Tony decided to take the plunge. He approached the table, sat down, and reached over and placed four chips on the lines between four separate numbers, giving him the odds of eight possible wins. The croupier called 'no more bets' and spun the wheel, and to Tony's delight, one of his numbers came up and he got a return on his money. Not a lot, but it 'was' a return. He carried on like this for the next half dozen spins of the wheel and won twice. He was doing okay. And then as he watched and his confidence grew, he saw that the people who were putting stacks of chips on the table, as opposed to his single chips, well they won more money. What a surprise. So Tony started to put two chips on his numbers. He was still splitting every bet, with chips placed on lines between the numbers, but on the second spin of the wheel he won again, and this time he got the higher return. Now this was really good. And before long, Tony was putting half a dozen chips on each of his bets, and when he won, which he did, he suddenly realized that he was accumulating a fairly decent profit. And after an hour he had a reasonable amount of chips stacked in front of him.

And then, fate came into play.

A short blonde lady arrived at the table, she was quite attractive and was obviously a little drunk. She also had very ample breasts and was wearing a fairly low cut black dress. There were no seats left around the table, and one 'true' gentleman actually offered her his seat.

But the blonde just laughed quite loudly. Yes, she'd had a drink and was quite talkative.

'Don't mind me boys,' she remarked, 'if I can win some money, I'll be out of your hair and back to the bar,' and she laughed again.

For a moment, most of the men around the table, including the croupier, almost forgot about the gambling as they all gazed at her quite magnificent breasts. It's a man thing, of course.

However, as the game continued, and every time the blonde leant over to place a bet on the roulette table, the men opposite her struggled to concentrate. The croupier too, was definitely having problems, as he tried to keep one eye on the chips and the other on the blonde's cleavage.

After about three or four more uneventful games, and in a moment of sheer irritation, Tony decided to put a large stack of chips on the line between 14 red and 15 black, it was as the croupier was just beginning to call 'no more bets.' And at that same moment, the blonde decided to place the same bet. She had to struggle as she leant over the table, and the men there stared in disbelief as her breasts nearly fell out of her dress. And at the last moment as she placed her bet, she fell slightly forwards and in doing so she accidentally pushed Tony's chips off the line and into the square...'15 black'.

As he spun the wheel, the croupier was still eying the blonde's cleavage, and then he blinked as he rolled the ball around the wheel. He didn't see what had just happened. And as the wheel spun, Tony glanced down at his bet, and then he suddenly realized that his chips had been moved, and then he also realized how. And for a brief moment he considered complaining, and then, no, he didn't. What was the use? And he sat back and sighed, he'd been stupid putting all that money on the one bet. There would be other games, and he promised himself to keep an eye on things more closely in the future. And then it suddenly struck him that he had already made his mind up, and that he would have to visit the Casino again. He found it all quite exiting.

'Black 15'...the croupier suddenly called out, and the blonde 'whooped' at her own success. But Tony just sat there, spellbound. And now it was Tony Becker's turn to blink. He couldn't believe it. And then he could. It had all been a simple mistake. The croupier then looked down at the table, trying to make sense of who should be paid their winnings before the rest of the chips on the table were scooped away, to be added to the Casino's already vast profits.

The croupier did the maths, then picked up several stacks of chips and pushed them in Tony's direction. And suddenly, to his amazement, Tony Becker had won over a thousand dollars.

159

The croupier handed the blonde her winnings, who then decided that she needed to go back to the bar. After all, she'd come here to find some 'well off' guy, and not to gamble her money away. She wanted somebody who was interested in her figure, and not the figures spinning around on a roulette wheel.

'I'll see you later, boys,' she laughed, as she rather unsteadily meandered away.

But Tony Becker was going nowhere. And he also had a change of strategy. He began to place five bets with five decent stacks of chips on certain numbers around the table. He had five particular numbers and he stuck to them, bet after bet. His theory being that at some point his numbers would have to come up. It was the law of averages, surely. And it worked.

The gods were smiling down on Tony Becker that night, because he won, and he continued to win. And it got to a point where the other people around the table were starting to follow Tony's example and they were beginning to use his numbers too. The croupier was suddenly not a happy man.

And then his luck stopped. Tony had by then, over six thousand dollars in chips in front of him, he was staggered. But then the table turned and he'd stopped winning. And after gambling away almost a thousand dollars he'd realized it, and Tony Becker was nobody's fool. He gathered up his chips and left the roulette table and then made his way back to the cashier's booth to turn those same chips back into real money. He'd won five and a half thousand dollars, it was unbelievable.

And he was just about to leave and go back up to his room with his winnings, when something in his head ticked.

'What the hell' he thought to himself. And he turned around to the cashier and gave her five hundred dollars, which she then changed back into chips. Tony looked around the Casino, and then he took another glass of wine off another waitress, this time he gave her a twenty buck tip. And then he headed for the blackjack tables.

Tony Becker used the same strategy as before. He stood there for twenty five minutes, watching the players and the dealer as he began to understand the game.

160

Finally, he sat himself down at the table. And he won. He'd won over three thousand dollars before his luck again began to turn. But this time he realized it, and he threw in his hand and left the table. After a trip to the cashier's booth to exchange his chips into cash, he made his way back to his room. Once there, he threw all the money onto his bed and began to count it.

Over eight thousand dollars, he couldn't believe it. And with that, he lay on his bed on top of all of that delicious money. It felt so wonderful.

For the next two days, Tony Becker continued to gamble. He would meet up with the 'gang' every morning over breakfast in the hotel's dining room. Most of them had bad hangovers and couldn't remember half of what they'd been up to, so Tony just went along with it all and everyone just took it for granted that he'd been with one group or the other.

He'd have a few drinks in the afternoon with them all, and then he'd wander off to the Casino, and he did the same thing again, every evening. He had a few drinks with them, and then when he felt that the time was right, he would just disappear, and nobody was any the wiser.

At one point they dragged him off to Caesars Casino for a change, but even there he managed to accumulate over five hundred dollars.

During that weekend Tony Becker learned to win, and he also learned how to lose. But somehow, that didn't seem to worry him. For Tony it was all about the 'thrill' of the chase.

After the weekend, they all finally flew back home, a weary crowd. But Tony Becker arrived home with ten thousand dollars in his pocket. It was something that he would keep a secret. Especially from his wife.

However, life then changed somewhat, for Tony Becker. Atlantic City wasn't that far away. From where he actually lived, it was about an hour or so by car. And he started to disappear back there, sometimes at night, sometimes on the weekend. And when his wife started to complain, he got himself the apartment in the city, due to the 'pressure' at work, along with the everyday commuting problems. But gambling quickly became Tony's accepted habit, and once he'd finished work of an evening, he

161

began to regularly jump on the train or a bus and head back to Atlantic City.

After a night's gambling, he would more often than not travel back to the city and back to his apartment. But sometimes, especially if he'd won, he'd book a room and stay over, and then get up early in the morning to get back to work.

However, gambling is like a swinging pendulum. And it's a lot easier to lose than it is to win. The Casinos have it all worked out. It's called the 'Odds'.

Simply put, it's all down to the maths.

However, Tony Becker didn't get that. And like all addictions, the gambling took hold of him and it wouldn't let go, which then caused Tony to spiral into debt. At times, he'd borrowed money off some quite unsavoury people, who also wouldn't let go. And it had only been through his success at his job, along with Woodvale Investments, that he'd been able to pay off some of the more substantial amounts of his debts.

The 'crunch' at home finally came when his wife, Margaret, discovered a bank statement for one of Tony's 'secret' little bank accounts and then found out that he was vastly overdrawn. So she then went through all and every bit of paperwork in the house, most of which Tony had rather stupidly just left in his desk, and she discovered another several overdrawn accounts. And then she found their mortgage statements for their house. They'd taken out a 'favourable interest rate mortgage' through the bank at First Global. Most of its employees did, it was very advantageous. But when Margaret looked through the figures, and to her absolute dismay, she realized that Tony had only been paying off the 'interest' on their mortgage. And in fact, they still owed as much on their home as on the day they'd moved in.

Margaret Becker had always known that her husband was a gambler, but not to what extent. But now this? In the past they'd had countless arguments over his gambling. He was always heading over to Atlantic City. And at one point Margaret Becker had actually thought that her husband must be seeing another woman and she'd hired a private detective, to have him followed. But after several attempts, her detective could only report that her husband had spent all and every night at the Casinos, just

162

sitting at the tables and gambling. In fact, the private detective was glad to see the back of the job. He'd never been so bored.

So when Tony Becker had finally arrived home, his wife how shown him all the statements and demanded to know the truth. From there they'd had a huge row, which ended in Tony packing his bags and leaving.

His parting words to his long suffering wife were...

'You want to live here...you pay for it.'

And with that, he'd moved into his apartment in the City.

However, today, Tony Becker had bought and just sold a huge amount of 'Cantor and Fitzsimons' stock, and First Global stock too.

And by using other people's money he'd also made himself a lot of money. And he needed it. A considerable amount of the money now in 'Woodvale Investments' would have to be used to pay off an impending gambling debt. Never mind, he would be back and fluid again.

Though, as he'd sat there at his desk, congratulating himself on his own success, a thought did run through Tony's head. Today, he'd used several millions of dollars of other people's money, which he'd put through Woodvale Investments. And he would pay them back, and with a profit. But suddenly, something occurred to him. If things went wrong, and went badly wrong, he could do exactly the same thing again. But this time he wouldn't invest the money. No, he would keep it. Keep it in Woodvale Investments, and then he'd run. He'd disappear.

Chapter 7

The next morning, when Adam Tyler awoke, he felt both apprehensive and slightly nervous. Today was going to be a big day. It was the day of the meeting. He would meet the heads and the principal staff of Cantor Fitzsimons, and with a bit of luck he might even get the chance to speak to the legendary Berni Speegle too. But whatever, Adam had done his homework, and for him it was the beginning of a new relationship with this company.

Yesterday's financial upset was in truth, Norman Roth's problem. But Adam knew the score, they were all accountable.

Adam got himself ready for work and then met up with Paul Maynard as they made their way to the Trade Center and to the offices of the First Global Bank.

The elevator shot them both up to the 93rd floor. They always did this, and then Adam would take the stairs down to his own offices, down on the 92nd. As they got out of the lift, they bumped into Reza, along with Tony Becker. By then, everyone had already heard the news about Cantor Fitzsimons moving over to First Global.

'So, Adam,' said Paul Maynard, 'Big day today, for you. Good luck with your meeting, pal.'

Adam thanked him.

'Yes,' said Reza, 'Good luck, mate.'

Tony Becker smiled and nodded.

Good luck or no luck. It didn't matter to him, he didn't give a damn.

Once in his own office, Adam Tyler once again began to run through his presentation. He basically knew it off by heart, but he was leaving nothing to chance, nothing at all.

At nine of clock he rang Norman Roth. The meeting with Cantor Fitzsimons was scheduled for ten o' clock. And even though their offices were not yet fully fitted out, the decision had still been made that they should all meet up on the 95th floor.

164

Norman Roth picked up the phone...'Yes...Hello' he asked immediately.

'Hi Norman, its Adam, can I nip in and see you?'

'Yes, come over now, okay.'

Two minutes later, and he was sitting in Norman Roth's office.

'You ready for this?" Norman Roth asked him.

"Yes,' Adam replied. 'The only thing I need to know now is how do things stand with Cantor Fitzsimons, not just the directors, more the management and the staff that I'll be talking to. '

Norman Roth shook his head.

'No problems there. Cantor Fitzsimons keep their finances and their creative people as separate entities altogether. Only the directors know what happened yesterday, it's not a problem. Obviously, they quite openly discuss budgets and projections and turnover with their managers, but the inner finances, such as loans, etc, are for the discretion of the directors only. And really, that's how it should be. And it works".

'That's okay then, Adam replied, 'because I want this meeting to be positive and I want to get us all off to a good start. And that won't happen if there are any unanswered questions hanging in the air.'

'Absolutely, and I agree with you, Adam", Norman Roth continued. 'It is the best way forward, and I believe that everyone up there is quite enthusiastic.'

Norman Roth looked at his watch.

'It's ten past nine. The meetings scheduled for ten. We'll both go up together. Apparently everythings still unfinished up there but it doesn't matter. It'll be like us being there right from the start, sort of thing.'

Adam agreed. They discussed another few minor issues and then Adam went back to his own office to quickly check through his papers once more.

At a quarter to ten, Norman Roth and Adam Tyler took the elevator up to the 95th floor and walked into the 'soon to be', brand new headquarters of Cantor Fitzsimons.

It was a large unfinished room, and quite full of people. Brand new desks had been pushed together in a long line to give a 'boardroom' effect. On the desks there were bottles of water and shiny new glasses, and there were notepads and folders, along with an assortment of pencils and pens. Adam glanced at the seating arrangements and judged there to be around thirty people there. Most of them were over in the corner where there were two long tables, set out with coffee and assorted sandwiches.

Norman Roth straight away introduced Adam to the two directors, they were Alan Pynchon and David Angelou, and then, of course, to Berni Speegle. They were stood together and had been in some sort of discussion, but immediately welcomed Norman Roth with open arms. They all shook hands and then Berni Speegle congratulated Norman on a job 'well done'. They all spoke for several minutes and then Adam mentioned that he wanted to go over and meet some of the managers, and with that, he tactfully excused himself so that Norman Roth could speak to them privately. Norman Roth nodded, as Adam left them to it.

Adam then made his way across the room and grabbed a cup of coffee off one of the tables, though he wasn't in the least bit hungry. He noticed that behind the tables there were three or four cases of wine, along with a couple of large cardboard boxes, full of wine glasses. And that made Adam smile. So this was some sort of celebration after all. Now all he had to do was talk to everyone and make it all work.

He began to mingle, it was a good way of making first contact with the people who he would hopefully be working with, and he wanted to get to know their characters and their different attitudes to all of this, as a first step forwards. He introduced himself to five or six different managers, and from there he was introduced to others. Things seemed to be going okay.

And then somebody tapped him on the shoulder.

'Adam..?'

Adam broke off his conversation and turned around.

And then he almost gasped in shock. She just stood there, right in front of him.

It was Miss Joanne Berkley, his first love.

Adam couldn't believe his eyes, and for a moment he just stared at her. What 'on earth' was she doing here? He just looked at her in amazement.

'Hello Adam,' she said, and she smiled at him.

Adam continued to stare at her. It was Joanne. She looked exactly the same. Same hair, same smile, nothing had changed. It was a though the last six years had never happened.

But for Adam, things had happened, things had changed. And he remembered their last meeting, when they parted and he'd walked out of the pub. And for a moment he frowned.

'Are...are you okay, Adam?'

He suddenly recovered his composure and gave her his best smile.

'Joanne...I don't believe it,' he said to her, and with that he reached over and hugged her. And in that moment he took in a breath and realized that her perfume was exactly the same too. And with it came all the memories. Good and bad.

Joanne looked up at him.

'I don't believe it either, Adam.' And then she laughed. 'Are you here with the bank?'

'Yes, I am. I'm working alongside Norman Roth, he's over there, he's my boss.'

Joanne glanced across the room for a second.

'I thought you'd disappeared to Spain or somewhere. That's what I heard anyway.'

'Yes,' Adam replied, 'I was based in Barcelona, I did three years there with the Santander Bank. It was different. But what about you, how come you're here in New York, and here at Cantor Fitzsimons? I thought you were in Australia 'living the life' on Bondi Beach or something.'

Joanne raised her eyes. 'Well that didn't go exactly as planned. After twelve months I had to come home.'

'Oh, really,' he replied, expecting to hear more, but Joanne changed the subject.

'So, how come your here now with First Global?' she asked him.

Adam just shrugged his shoulders.

'I just needed a change,' he said. And that was all he said too.

167

There was a fraction of silence as they both looked at one another.

And then. 'So why are you here today?' Joanne asked. 'I take it your something to do with our new project'.

Adam smiled. 'Yes I am. Actually it's me who's putting all of this together. It's been my project. It was handed to me and I need to make it work. This is very important for Cantor Fitzsimons, and for the bank too.'

Joanne nodded, 'Yes, I know. It's a whole new venture.'

'And what do you do, Joanne?'

'I'm one of the heads of the design team. It will be our department who picks and chooses what works and what doesn't work, and if it's going to be viable or not.'

'And of course, just how much it's all going to cost.' said Adam.

'Well, yes. I suppose so,' Joanne replied, and suddenly she was slightly unsure of herself.

But Adam just laughed.

'And this is exactly what I'm here for,' he said to her, 'this is what today is all about...'

He was about to continue, but at that moment, Norman Roth called for attention, and asked if everyone could take their seats as the meeting was about to begin.

Everybody sunddenly began to move towards the line of desks, and Adam and Joanne just looked at one another.

'Okay then, he said to her, 'I'd better go and make a start.'

'I'll catch you later.' Joanne said quickly.

'Yes, yes okay,' Adam replied. And with that, he quickly turned around and made his way over to Norman Roth.

Joanne watched him as he walked away. She had her memories too.

Everyone finally found a seat. Berni Speegle and the other two directors moved to the back of the room and sat down near the tables with the food and the coffee. They were there to observe, not interfere.

Norman Roth stood up and introduced himself and then gave a brief statement on how the First Global Bank were extremely happy to have Cantor Fitzsimons as a customer and were looking forward to everyone working together. From there, he then introduced Adam.

'Adam Tyler is my right hand man and he has also become the man that I depend on. Adam will be the link between Cantor Fitzsimons and the First Global Bank. He will be here to liaise and advise. This is what we do here at First Global, we aid and assist.'

Adam stood up and looked down at the two rows of people in front of him, all expectant, and maybe slightly apprehensive; they were a freshly formed team of personnel who needed both guidance and gusto. These were talented people. But Adam already knew that, he'd made it his priority to find out as much as he could about some of the staff there, and he'd done his homework. He already knew the backgrounds of about half the people sitting there. The others he would have to find out about. Joanne Berkley, for one, was someone who'd managed to slip under his 'radar'.

And that threw him somewhat. As he looked down the table he could see her looking at him, almost expectantly. Meeting her again had thrown him slightly, more than slightly, but he was here for a different reason. He had to concentrate on the job in hand.

So as he stood there, he introduced himself to everyone, and then he began to speak.

'Hello everyone, and good morning, I'm Adam Tyler.'

From there, Adam laid out his plans for the future of Cantor Fitzsimons. He told them how the bank was going to be involved as a working partner and not just as an institution that sat back and pulled the financial strings and held the financial handcuffs.

He talked about a positive future and about the exiting times ahead for everyone. In fact, he exuded enthusiasm. He made it sound like fun, because he meant it. When people really enjoyed their work, they gave a hundred percent in return, he knew that. He'd done it in Barcelona and he could do it here in New York. In fact, he'd already accomplished this with his own team, two floors below. He had a strong team of people there who backed him to the hilt.

After half an hour, he turned the meeting into a 'question and answer' stage. It was interesting to listen to other people's views and their different ideas. Very cleverly, Adam Tyler was already 'team building', and there was a buzz around the room.

This continued for the next forty minutes or so, and then Adam brought the meeting to a conclusion.

His final words to everyone, 'Okay everybody, let's go and have a glass of wine.'

There was applause. Everything was good. It had all gone very well.

Norman Roth came over to him, he was grinning.

'Great speech, pal. Absolutely fantastic.' And he patted Adam's arm.

'Yeah, I think it went well,' Adam replied.

'It was great, you nailed it,' said Roth. 'Come on, we'll go and talk to Berni Speegle and the others,' and so they went over to speak to the three waiting directors.

There were handshakes all round, and everyone seemed pleased.

'That was an excellent presentation, Mr Tyler,' said Berni Speegle. The other director's agreed straightaway.

"I think you're in the wrong job, Mr Tyler,' Director Alan Pynchon chirped in.

They all laughed, but with somewhat of a glint in his eye, Berni Speegle continued.

'You know, if you ever want a change off profession. We'd love to have you onboard with us.'

And with that, he winked across at Norman Roth.

But Roth was having none of it. He good naturedly put his arm around Adam's shoulder and declared, 'You're gonna have to share him, boys.' And with that said, they all laughed.

They spoke for the next fifteen minutes and then Adam once again bowed out. He needed to speak to the other staff personally. And he did, he spoke to several of them both individually and others in formed groups. Everything was going well, everyone was enthusiastic. But more than that, Adam knew that he had gained their respect and the possibilities of friendships, and with that, the start of a strong working relationship.

Eventually of course, he spoke to Joanne. Part of him wanted to, part of him didn't.

He'd had two loves in his life, and he'd been badly let down by both. Very badly. And it had hurt him. He was trying his best to forget Dominique Cassens, but she was always there, somewhere at the back of his mind, still his addiction.

In fact, he'd never looked at another woman since he'd arrived in New York. Adam had simply thrown himself into his work. He loved this job.

The First Global Bank was now his mistress. She consumed all of his thoughts, and his time.

'Brilliant speech, Adam,' Joanne said to him, 'absolutely fantastic.'

'Thanks.' he quickly replied, 'I wanted to get us all off to a positive start.'

'Well, I think you certainly managed that.' And she smiled.

'Yes well, I want us all to be going in the same direction, onwards and upwards. I want us to hit the ground running; we're building a team here. This new publication it's going to be big and its going to be a success, it has to be.'

'Wow, well you've certainly got everyone buzzing, you really have. Everybody's raring to go, I've spoken to a few people. We're all on a roll with this".

Adam smiled. 'Good,' he said to her. 'That's what I wanted to hear.'

Joanne looked at him for a moment.

'So, I suppose we're going to be working together then?' and she gave him a quizzical smile.

'Err, yes. I suppose we are.' And for a moment he felt slightly awkward.

'That'll be nice,' she said.

'Err, yes,' he said again, 'it will.' And then with an almost nervous movement he checked his watch.

'Oh, right, well I'd better go and speak to the rest of the people here, I need to have spoken to everyone.'

Joanne blinked for a moment.

'Oh, okay then. Yes of course.'

But in truth she was slightly taken aback. She had just been rebuffed, not impolitely, but there it was.

'Okay, I'll see you,' said Adam. And for the second time that day he turned around and walked away. Miss Joanne Berkley watched him go. This was all very curious, and somehow, she felt a little bit hurt.

The very next day, and Adam was involved from the word go. The offices at Cantor Fitzsimons were being fitted out with everything. Desks, computers, design and photographic equipment, in fact, the whole works. Everything had already been placed on order, and the different supply companies were all proving to be very efficient.

Eventually, and after speaking to several people, Adam found Joanne Berkley's office. He'd had to enquire. She was in office number 106, however the names and job titles had not yet been put on any of the doors yet, so there was still a certain amount of confusion. Everything was hustle and bustle, a sort of organized chaos.

Adam tapped on the door.

'Yes?' he heard her voice, and with that he opened the door and put his head around the doorway.

'Everything okay, are you settling in?"

Joanne was sitting at her new desk. There were papers and sketches and copies of photographs roughly spread-eagled about. She looked up at him and her eyes widened and she smiled.

'Good morning,' she grinned.

'Good morning,' he replied, 'and how's everything going?'

Joanne stood up.

'Well it's been a bit chaotic, but we expected that. I'm getting there, I just need to sort everything out and get things filed in the right place, and then we can get going. I've a meeting this afternoon so I need to sort this paperwork out.'

'Oh, okay, I'll leave you to it. You're busy.'

'No, no,' Joanne replied quickly, 'please, come in.'

Adam stepped into her office.

'I've got a meeting this afternoon too, it's all go.'

'Yes,' said Joanne, 'we're all working around the contactors, but once they've installed everything and finished we can get on with things...'

She was about to continue when there was at tap on the half opened door.

Joanne glanced over Adam's shoulder to acknowledge someone.

'Oh hi, Katy...err...come in,' she said suddenly.

Adam turned around as a young woman walked rather breathlessly into the office.

'Hi Joanne,' she said...I've just flown in, I've come straight here but I'm a bit lost. Do you know which office is mine? Somebody told me that it's along here somewhere but all the doors are still just numbered.'

'Yes,' Joanne replied, 'you're three doors up. Your office is at number 109.

The young lady shrugged. She was carrying a small suitcase in one hand and a briefcase in the other.

'How's your mother?' Joanne then asked her.

'Oh, I think she's going to be alright. A bit of a scare really, but my dad's looking after her.'

And with that, the young lady suddenly turned to Adam, it was as though he'd been an afterthought, and she gave him a slight but mannerly smile.

'Oh, hello,' she said.

Joanne then intervened.

'Adam, this is Katy Ritsos.'

Adam looked at her. Miss Ritsos had shoulder length dark brown hair. She was around thirty something and wore a pair of black, thick framed glasses that exuded a 'professional' look. There was something of the Mediterranean about her. She was neither beautiful nor plain. 'Pretty', would have been a nearer description.

Adam took a stab at it.

'Spanish?' he asked her, rather clumsily.

'I beg your pardon?' she replied.

'Spanish?' he asked again, 'your name, is it Spanish?'

She looked at him quite sternly.

'I'm Greek,' she replied. And that was it, nothing more.

Joanne again intervened.

'Err, Katy. This is Adam Tyler. He's the manager at the First Global Bank. Adam is the person who is going to liaise our joint operation here. He will be overseeing everything.'

It was a form of explanation of course. Katy needed to know who Adam actually was, because things seemed to have got off to a rather awkward start.

Katy Ritsos eyes widened slightly.

'Oh right,' she replied, and with that she introduced herself. 'I'm Katy Ritsos, I'm one of the head financial accountants.' And with that said, they shook hands.

Adam frowned for a moment.

'Ah yes, Miss Ritsos. Actually, I had you on my list. I should have spoken to you yesterday at our meeting, but obviously I missed you?' It was almost a question.

'Yes you did, obviously,' she replied, 'but I've been away for a few days. I had to fly out to Pasadena. My mothers had a slight stroke and I had to be there.'

'Oh, well I hope she's going to be okay?' Adam asked. It was generally good manners to say something.

Katy Ritsos just nodded.

'Thank you,' she replied.

'To tell you the truth, I need to speak to you,' Adam continued, 'I need to bring you up to speed and let you know what's happening, and how we're going to handle things.'

Katy Ritsos glanced down at her watch.

'Well I've got a lot to do Mr Tyler,' she replied. 'If you want to speak to me, you'd better come along to my office right now.'

It was almost an order. And with that said, she grabbed her bags and walked quickly out of the office.

Joanne took a deep breath. She was used to Katy Ritsos' rather brash manner.

Adam watched Miss Ritsos leave the office and then he turned back to Joanne. His eyes widened and he held out his arms and shrugged.

'Good god, She's a 'bit of a one.'

Joanne Berkley burst out laughing.

'Ah well, that's our Katy. She's rather a one off.'

'You're not kidding. She reminds me of my old schoolteacher.'

Joanne giggled.

'I'd better go,' he said to her, and he shook his head. But then Joanne called after him.

'Do you fancy lunch sometime, we could have a catch up?'

'Yes, okay,' he replied, and he smiled as he left.

Joanne Berkley just stood there and watched him go. Maybe...just maybe.

Australia had not gone well for Joanne Berkely.

She'd left Winchester University before finishing her Degree because of a lucrative job offer, and had flown off to Sidney in Australia to work for 'Delany Advertising', a very successful Australian company.

She'd arrived at Sydney's Kingsford Smith Airport full of hope and enthusiasm. She was met there with open arms by Steve Hansford, an old boyfriend from an old relationship. They'd parted company in the past on fairly good terms, it was Joanne who had to go off to University.

It had been agreed that Joanne would stay at Steve's house until she got herself settled, and then at some point she would then find a place of her own.

So no pressure, and no problems, or so it seemed.

However, Steve Hansford had slightly other ideas, and rather different intentions. Having the very beautiful Miss Joanne Berkely back there in his house, could also mean that she could be back in his arms, and back in his bed.

The first three months had been mayhem. Joanne had been straightaway involved with a major advertising campaign, which promoted the launch of a brand new range of hair care products, a Japanese backed Australian venture. Everything had been a success, and three months quickly turned into six months. They were heady days, her job was exiting and there were a lot of new people in her life. And as her social circle expanded, Joanne's life seemed to revolve around endless lunches, bars and restaurants and a nonstop roll of barbeques, the great Australian habit. And involved in most of all this was Steve Hansford. He'd invited Joanne into his wide circle of friends, of course he had. And in fact, a lot of his friends actually did think that they were a couple, and to a point, hopefully so did Steve. But on two or three

175

different occasions, Steve had heard Joanne laugh as she'd informed different friends that there was nothing 'at all' going on between them, and that she and Steve were actually 'just good friends', and that was all.

And that had hurt him.

But when word got around that the beautiful Miss Joanne Berkeley was in fact single, and available, some of Steve's male friends began to take an interest. And that not only hurt Steve, it made him quite desperate. And he had to take several of his so-called 'mates' to one side and tell them to 'back off', and in no uncertain terms.

And that was it. Jealousy had suddenly become the 'name of the game'.

And then the inevitable happened. Steve took her to a new restaurant that had been highly recommended. It had been a Friday night, the end of the week, and Joanne had been working hard, it had been an extremely busy week for her.

It was just the two of them, and that was nothing new, in fact, for Joanne it was a welcome change, she was feeling quite jaded and a simple meal out with a friend was nice, and comfortable. But the night became fuelled by alcohol. Beers, to 'chill out', then cocktails, followed by a few bottles of Australia's most excellent wine, and after finishing off their meal with some 'good' brandy, they were more than a little intoxicated and giddily carried on drinking 'shots'. They both drunkenly fell into the taxi that took them home, and once they were there Steve produced a bottle of tequila and some lemons and salt. By the time they were half way through the bottle, Joanne was completely out of it. And with that done, Steve walked her into his bedroom and put her in his bed. Then he stripped her naked and climbed in bed with her.

Technically it was rape. Joanne awoke the next morning with her legs splayed, a terrible hangover, and with Steve Hansford lying on top of her. She was horrified.

As she began to wriggle from under him, a slowly smiling Steve awoke and he started to kiss her. Then he began to call her 'darling' or something ridiculous and then he wanted the obvious to continue. Joanne had pushed him away and jumped out of bed, grabbing up her discarded clothes to hide her embarrassment.

Steve was shocked. He thought that they'd sealed the deal. And then he too became embarrassed. And then he became angry.

A row ensued and the accusations flew. His excuse being 'don't you remember', but of course Joanne didn't. And then the 'old' obvious...'well, you were up for it.' But Joanne hadn't been up for it, certainly not in her mind anyway. And then Steve continued to ask her just 'what' her problem was, and that after all, they'd slept together before, back in the day, and actually, it was nothing that they hadn't done before.'

Joanne was horrified. Steve hurled abuse at her as she packed her bags and then left. She then moved in with a girl friend for the next two weeks before moving into a rented apartment in the city centre.

However, work became difficult. Working for the same company was not ideal. They both handled the situation by completely ignoring one another. This remoteness was quickly noticed by others. Rumours began, fuelled of course by Steve, who had then hinted that Joanne had a drug problem and that because she'd been dealing with some very undesirable people, he'd had to ask her to leave. Word got around, and suddenly the lunch invites stopped, and so did the barbeques. But worst of all, Steve, very cleverly gained access to her computer. Suddenly he knew her timetable and he knew her work schedule. Very clever indeed, and when Joanne had a scheduled meeting with some important new clients, a large perfume company, the night before the meeting and after work hours when most of the staff had left and gone home, Steve had got into Joanne's computer and had deleted all of her reports and her artwork. Unfortunately, this was work which Joanne had mistakenly not bothered to back up, because she'd been so busy. It had been a disaster. She'd arrived at the intended meeting, red-faced and looking apparently clueless, which she was. The new clients were totally unimpressed, the meeting had been a complete waste of time and was cancelled. Then the contract was put on hold.

Her bosses at Delany Advertising weren't impressed either. And then it was hinted that Joanne apparently had a drugs problem and that she and Steve Hansford had a falling out over it. The bosses at Delany then called Steve in for an informal 'chat'. Steve was well thought of within the company and had been with them for a number of years, a very loyal employee. Once there, and in front of the heads of the company, Steve did a complete hatchet job on Joanne, it was all to be confidential of course. He told them that he'd known Joanne years ago, back in the UK, and that was why he'd recommended her. However, she'd changed. He'd offered her free accommodation until she'd found her own place, but living with her had become a nightmare and eventually he'd had to ask her to leave. It was because of the drink and the drugs. In truth, he'd tried to help her, and in fact, half of the ideas and the work that she'd seemingly put into her first big advertising campaign, the launch of the so successful new hair care products, were actually his.

He'd tried his best.

His bosses were totally sympathetic, after all, Steve Hansford was a 'top bloke'.

Joanne was called into their office and was then informed that they would have to 'let her go.'

They would of course supply her with an excellent reference, as long as she didn't make a fuss, and also that she left immediately.

Joanne was devastated. There was nowhere else for her to go.

In the end she packed her bags, along with her reference, and flew back to England. She then went back to University to finish her degree. From there she went to work for a good Advertising company that was based in London. Her reference from Delany Advertising helped enormously, in fact, it clinched her the job. During the interview, Joanne described her time in Australia as 'work experience'. And it had been, without doubt.

After a couple of very successful years in London, and she'd worked hard, very hard, she got the opportunity to go and work for the legendary American advertising agency, Cantor Fitzsimons. She'd jumped at the chance, and had been with the company for nearly two years, two very successful years where she'd again worked incredibly hard and with it, to her true ability. Joanne Berkeley was without doubt a talent, and that talent had been acknowledged and she'd been promoted...and so, onwards and upwards.

Joanne Berkeley was a force, and she was driven and she'd become a true asset to the company.

It was during her time back at University that Joanne began to remember her happier times with Adam Tyler. She had been very fond of him. On reflection, she'd been more than a little bit stupid and she'd realized that. Adam was a really great guy, he had a lot of promise and a great future. He would be successful, obviously, and along with that, if she'd stayed by his side, there would always have been a good life and a great lifestyle. Yes, Adam Tyler would have looked after her, always. She knew that. And he loved her, and she knew that too.

And so, once she'd started to work in London, Joanne had tried to contact him, she knew that Adam worked at 'some bank' or other. But finally, she was told that he'd gone off to Spain, somewhere. And that was it. Would she ever see him again, probably not?

And now this, and suddenly he was back, and back in her life...possibly.

And so it started, again.

For the next two weeks it was nothing but meetings and lunches, it was a very busy time.

Adam introduced Joanne to Reza, along with Tony Becker. Joanne already knew Paul Maynard of course, from those heady days back in University, when she, Adam and Paul had all been chums. But Paul remembered the end of their relationship and took a determined decision not to comment or get involved in any way. It was safer, easier and less complicated. Adam Tyler was his own man, the decisions were his.

Reza Mastoor took an immediate shine to Joanne. She was blonde and beautiful, much like his own American wife. He continually joked out loud that 'if only he'd met her first...'

Joanne had just laughed. But Reza had taken Adam to one side on a couple of occasions and again jokingly told Adam to get 'his act together' and ask her out, and whatever.

However, Adam had never discussed his past relationship with Joanne, with either Reza or Tony Becker, though they did suspect that there was some sort of past history between them, it was rather obvious, especially from Joanne, who always sat closely next to Adam whenever they all did lunch together. But

Adam had all the excuses, always. He was always too busy, and then there was always the old advice, 'don't mix business with pleasure' as a good motto. Reza just shook his head and told Adam that he must be mad, deluded or blind.

Tony Becker however, took a slightly different stance. Sure, he was very sociable towards Joanne, and they both spoke and joined in on the conversations with the others. However, Joanne Berkeley was simply just not his type. In between his gambling and work, Tony Becker had very little time for any woman in his life. He did however have one little partiality, and that was his liking for the dark skinned, and he had a definite fondness for the Puerto Rican and the Mexican women. Tony Becker had his own apartment in the city, and through his connections at the Casinos, he'd been given contacts to those certain agencies that supplied just the type of women that he desired. In fact, they supplied women for all tastes, for a price, of course.

Two weeks of nonstop mayhem. But the five of them lunched whenever possible and after work, and whenever possible, they sometimes managed to have a drink together, especially on the Fridays. And it was fun, good fun, and Joanne was enjoying herself, and so was Adam. Everything seemed to be going well, and so Joanne decided not to push things. She would let nature take its course and see what happened. She'd watched and listened as Reza Mastoor continually joked about everyone, especially Tony Becker and his ridiculous moustache. It was no wonder that Becker's wife had cheated on him. Joanne found Tony Becker slightly distant and certainly not the world's finest conversationalist. They were a strange mix of friends, but it did all seem to work.

But Joanne also realized that Adam Tyler was now a slightly changed character. No longer the love sick youth of their University days, Adam was now much more confident, more mature, and comfortably in control of his self. In effect, the boy was now the man.

And Joanne Berkeley liked that. She liked it a lot.

On occasion, just the two of them would go for a drink after work, but as yet Adam had never invited her out for an actual evening meal, which would of course become a date, and from there, who knew? And it was while they were out together on one of these early evenings that they began to talk more earnestly. The wine helped.

'You've changed, Adam. Do you know that?' Joanne had asked him.

Adam laughed. 'Really, do you think so?'

'Yes I do. You've become all older, and wiser.'

And they both laughed at that statement.

'So now I'm an old man am I..?'

And Joanne giggled as she touched his arm.

'You know what I mean,' and she pouted cheekily at him.

Their conversation continued like this, as they recollected their past, especially when back at University. However, Joanne had begun to notice something slightly mysterious about Adam.

It was whenever she'd asked him about his time in Barcelona, she noticed that he subtly changed the subject. And it was his habit to answer a question with another question, and very cleverly. And then she realized that she knew absolutely nothing about his time in Spain, other that he'd lived in Barcelona and that he'd worked for the Santander Bank there.

A woman's curiosity is a never ending peculiarity, and so on that particular evening, Joanne decided to take the plunge. After all, they were good friends, more than just good friends, really.

So she looked at him, her head slightly tilted and somewhat inquisitive.

'Can I ask you something, Adam?'

He looked at her. 'Of course you can.'

'Go on then, tell me', she said, 'what happened to you in Barcelona?'

Adam just stared at her for a moment, almost expressionless.

'Nothing,' he replied. 'Why do you ask?'

And with that, Joanne Berkeley realized that she'd hit a nerve.

'Well, you never really talk about it, she continued, 'you may not realize it, but whenever I ask you anything about Barcelona, you immediatly change the subject.'

'There's nothing to talk about,' he replied. 'I just worked there for a few years and then I decided that it was time for a change. A job opportunity came up here in New York with First Global and I just grabbed the chance. And it's been great here, really great. I'm enjoying every minute of it.'

But he spoke too defensively, and Joanne immediately recognized the tone in his voice. She'd known Adam Tyler for far too long for false justifications, and she knew an excuse when she heard one. And all of a sudden, Joanne realized that something had gone wrong. It was obviously not his career. Otherwise he would have never been offered the chance to work at the prestigious First Global Bank, they only employed the best, actually, the best of the best. So it was something else, it was his personal life.

And so, out of the blue, she asked him.

'Did you have any girlfriends in Barcelona?'

Adam blinked. For a split second he didn't speak, but his expression said everything.

'No,' he said quietly. 'No girlfriends...I was too busy.'

And those few words said it all. Joanne knew it was a lie, and he suddenly looked so sad, it was almost a moment of despair.

Joanne immediately changed the subject, she had to.

'Well never mind,' she said, 'you've got half of us women in New York loving you now.' And she laughed and punched his arm gently, which invoked him to laugh too, if only from embarrassment.

Joanne then changed the topic of conversation, and she spoke about her early days, when she first joined Cantor Fitzsimons. She went on to tell him some humorous story which made Adam laugh and the mood quickly changed.

But at the back of her mind, Joanne Berkley realized something. Somewhere back in Barcelona, there had been another woman in Adam's life, and she had hurt him, and she had hurt him badly.

Back at Cantor Fitzsimons, things were going 'almost' extremely well. Adam Tyler was working alongside the team and the ideas and the whole production of the new and highly prominent glossy magazine were beginning to come together well. Very well in fact, except for one seemingly small hiccup. And that hiccup was without doubt, Miss Katy Ritsos.

182

They had not got off to the best of starts. On the morning when they'd first met in Joanne Berkley's office, Miss Ritsos had almost given him his starting orders.

Her words, 'If you want to speak to me, you'd better come along to my office now, Mr Tyler', had slightly thrown him. The woman simply didn't seem to understand his position. He was the manager at First Global, First Global, who was actually financing this whole project.

And it was Adam Tyler who would be overseeing everything. But this woman just didn't seem to get it. On that first morning when he had followed her into her new office, they both sat down and Miss Ritsos had said to him, 'What do you actually want to speak to me about, Mr Tyler? As I told you earlier, I am extremely busy today.'

Adam began to speak, and he was about to repeat the same speech that he'd given to the rest of the Cantor Fitzsimons staff on the previous day, and fair enough. But just as he began, Katy Ritsos suddenly opened her briefcase and began to pull some of her files and put them into the different drawers of her brand new desk. This more than slightly irritated Adam. In fact, he was getting rather annoyed with what he considered her bad manners and rudeness. He stopped talking and just sat there in silence.

Katy Ritsos looked up.

'What's wrong?" she asked.

'Are you going to listen to what I have to say, or are you going to continue with these silly games?'

She looked across at him and frowned slightly.

'Mr Tyler, I am quite capable of doing two things at once, it's what we women are good at.'

And before Adam could utter another word, she simply raised her arms.

'Okay, okay Mr Tyler, you have my full attention.' And with that said, she sat back in her chair and folded her arms and then stared directly at him.

Strangely, Adam found this to be even more disconcerting.

Anyway, he started once again.

His first words, 'I need to bring you up to speed and let you know what's happening, and how we're going to handle things,' brought a raised eyebrow from her, but he continued.

At the end of his rather passionate and very enthusiastic speech, Katy Ritsos had just looked at him.

'So that's how 'you' think things are going to be run?' she said.

Adam didn't know whether that statement was a question or a threat.

'Err, well yes,' he replied, and then, 'And everyone else seems to be in agreement...' and his words trailed away.

But Miss Katy Ritsos continued to speak.

'Yes well, half of them are clueless, Mr Tyler. They're like sheep. Its all 'Arty' stuff and glamour, and glossy photos and chitchat. But it's the advertising and the subsequent sales of this magazine that will make everything work. And that's what I'm here for. Do you understand?'

Adam did, or he thought he did.

'I do know that,' he quickly replied. 'However, we all have to work together as a team...'

Katy Ritsos cut him off immediately.

'Yes, and they'll 'all' run away with your chequebook, Mr Tyler. I know these people, they do not understand finance and how everything actually works. Leave me to work out the finance, and then I'll discuss it with you and let you know what money we need, and where and when.'

Adam couldn't believe what he was hearing, this young woman was trying to cut him out 'of the loop' and go against all of his plans.

He was about to remonstrate with her and had actually managed to say the word, 'But'...when she interrupted him again.

'Mr Tyler, you're from the world of banking, and I'm from the world of publishing. I have the experience and I have the knowledge.'

Adam stood up, he'd heard enough, and this was getting them nowhere, and so he delivered his parting words.

'Miss Ritsos, you're going to have to learn another way, believe me.'

And with that, he turned and left her office.

And so it began. It became a battle of wills. They argued about ever single financial decision.

One day, when at lunch with the usual friends, including Joanne. Adam remarked on how 'the only thing he and Miss Ritsos hadn't discussed was the cost of the toilet paper.'

Joanne burst out laughing.

'I can believe it,' she said, 'Katy drives everyone mad. We all try our best to avoid her.'

'If only I could,' Adam replied. 'Every time I have to go up to her office at 109, my heart sinks.'

Joanne laughed again.

'Why don't you have her come down to your office, maybe it's a sort of 'territorial' thing?' and she giggled. 'Get her on home ground, Adam.'

'I've tried that,' he replied, 'but she always says she's far too busy. The woman's a bloody nightmare. Are all Greek women like her, if they are, it must be a bloody dreadful place?'

Everyone around the table laughed, and then Reza Mastoor turned to Tony Becker.

'She sounds like the perfect woman for you, Tony. She's a miserable bastard too.'

They all laughed out loud, everyone except Becker.

'Piss off, Reza,' he replied, and he shook his head as he continued to eat his lunch.

At the end of the week, it was on the Friday afternoon, Norman Roth gave Adam a call.

'Could you nip up and see me, Adam?' he asked.

I'm on my way,' Adam replied. And within a couple of minutes, he was in Norman Roth's office. He sat himself down at the desk, facing Mr Roth.

Norman Roth tapped the top of his expensive desk with his very expensive pen.

'I've found a trace to our leak here at the bank,' he said.

Adam looked at him for a moment.

'You mean over the selling of the Cantor Fitzsimons stock, the insider trading thing?'

'Yes, I think so,' Roth replied.

'So go on, tell me,' Adam asked.

'Well,' Roth replied, 'I've called in a few old favours and also spoken to a few contacts, and we've found a name.'

'Who is it?' Adam asked. It had always concerned him that he could have been implicated in this, but for the life of him he couldn't think of who it could have been. In fact, he'd always considered that it must have been someone from Cantor Fitzsimons, because no one, except Norman Roth and himself had known anything about the merger. But Norman Roth had always stated explicitly that only the three directors there knew what was happening.

'And it's not a 'who', well not a person,' said Roth, 'It's actually a company.'

'Really?' said Adam.

'Money always leaves a trail, Adam. Especially big money. And a source of mine, who has links to the banking system in the Cayman Islands, finally came up with something.'

Adam whistled. 'The Caymans...wow! I thought the money that ended up there was totally untraceable.'

'It is, usually. But my contact there is also a very well connected man.'

Adam, quite wisely decided not to ask.

'Anyway,' Norman Roth continued, 'we've come up with a name. The company's called 'Woodvale Investments' and they hold an account at the Fidelity Trust National Bank in the Cayman Islands. It's a private account in a private off-shore bank, and so we are at somewhat of a loss. We can't go anywhere near it, we can't touch it and we can't source it. It's just a name on an account. We can't find out who owns it or how much cash the account holds. The account may actually be empty, and whoever owns Woodvale Investments could have transferred the money to some other bank anywhere in the world, and probably has. The money could be in Switzerland, it could even be in Hong Kong. Who knows?'

As Adam Tyler sat there listening to all of this information his mind was beginning to stir.

There was something in the name 'Woodvale' that was misplaced inside his brain.

'And there we have it,' continued Norman Roth. 'It's a bit of a dead end. I spoke to my contact and sort of 'hinted' that there could be a considerable financial benefit to the manager of 'Fidelity Trust', if he could give us any further information, but

186

that all came to a dead end. The manager there, who is already quite a wealthy man, was having none of it. My contact informs me that a lot of laundered private money ends up in the Fidelity Trust Bank and that it involves some very bad and powerful people. And if for one moment, the word got out that the manager there couldn't keep his mouth shut, well, who knows?'

Adam caught the gist of what Norman Roth was implying.

'So it's a dead end then?'

'It is,' Norman Roth replied. 'Though I'll keep pushing it, you never know. But somehow, I think there's a leak here at the bank, and this could just be the tip of the iceberg, who knows?

But if it is, it could cause a financial scandal that could rock this bank. After all, we're in a position of trust here.'

It was time for Adam to say something.

'I've got to tell you, the name 'Woodvale' rings a bell somewhere. But I don't know if it's Woodvale Investments. I can't remember. But I have a feeling that I've seen the name somewhere.' Adam then shrugged, 'It could be something as simple as a road name, or even some shop that I've walked past. I don't remember, but I just have a feeling that I've read it or seen it somewhere, that's all. Maybe it's just me being stupid, it may be nothing at all.'

Norman Roth looked at him for a moment.

'Well, I've checked the names of all the bank employees who work anywhere for First Global, and we don't have anybody called Woodvale, so that rules that out.'

Both men sat in silence for a moment, their meeting was at an end. Adam stood up to leave.

'I'll keep you posted if anything comes up,' said Roth, 'and vice versa.'

'Yes,' Adam replied, 'and vice versa.' And with that, he left.

That same Friday evening, after work, Adam, Paul, Reza and Tony met up for their usual drink at 'The Trinity' bar and restaurant on Broadway. Joanne couldn't make it on that particular night, she was busy. And as they sat there at a table, enjoying their first drink and discussing the week and the weekend, Adam suddenly made a remark.

'Hey, while we're all here, can I ask you something? Does anyone know anything at all about a company called 'Woodvale Investments?'

Everyone around the table sort of looked at one another.

'Never heard of them,' said Paul Maynard, and he looked across at the others.

'Who are they?' Reza asked.

'They're just a firm that Norman Roth wants me to look into, that's all.'

Tony Becker just shook his head. 'I've dealt with a wide range of investment companies but I've never heard of them, either.'

'No, I just thought I'd ask, that's all,' said Adam. And for him, the subject was over.

However, Reza Mastoor, as usual, had to have the last word.

'Well if that Norman Roth wants to find out about them, there must be something going on. That Roth's a tricky bastard. I wouldn't trust him as far as I could throw him.'

'Unfortunately, I have to, Reza,' quipped Adam, 'he's my boss, remember?'

They all seemed to chuckle and then they ordered another round of drinks.

Everyone sat there talking, except for Tony Becker. He was pretending to listen to the banter, but he wasn't. Tony Becker was actually in deep thought. Norman Roth was onto him. If they knew about Woodvale Investment, then they must have found out about his account in the Cayman Islands at Fidelity Trust. Tony Becker's stomach muscles tightened. Even though Woodvale was a private account in a private bank, just how safe was it? Tony had always thought that Woodvale Investments was invisible, and that so was his account. But now, suddenly, it was not. Roth had somehow found it. And what next? Because Reza Mastoor had been right. Norman Roth was indeed, one tricky bastard.

Tony Becker knew that he would have to form some sort of escape plan. Because if they ever came looking for him, he would have to run.

The four of them continued to talk, and drink. And then a discussion began about where they should eat. Should they stay

188

at 'The Trinity', after all, the food was very good there, great steaks with huge portions of fries, or should they meander elsewhere. But at that moment, Reza announced that he wouldn't be joining them. It was Friday of course, and he had to catch the train home and get back to his wife and kids.

They asked him to take a later train but Reza was adamant.

'Hey, I've spent most of this week here at the apartment. I need to go home, and anyway, I've not seen my kids all week.'

The rest of them couldn't argue with that, his ethics were right, obviously. But Reza just had to leave them with his usual parting shot.

'And while you sad clowns are still staggering from bar to bar tonight, I'll be tucked up in bed with my very beautiful 'wifey', so 'adios amigos', he chirped, and then as usual, he laughed loudly at his own joke.

As he walked away, he heard one of them call out some derogatory remark, but he chose to ignore it. He was going home. But as he made his way to the train station he had other things on his mind too. It was Tony Becker. When Adam Tyler had asked them about Woodvale Investments, Tony Becker had denied any knowledge of the company. But that was a lie. And Reza Mastoor knew it. Something wasn't quite right, and Reza decided that he was going to have to look into it. Reza knew that Tony Becker had dealings with Woodvale Investments.

Reza knew a lot of things really...about everybody.

Chapter 8

Reza Mastoor was not an Egyptian.

And neither was that his true name. It was all a lie. Everything was a lie.

His real name was Reza Hasan al-Mastoor, and he was born in Saudi Arabia.

In fact, Reza Mastoor had only ever been to Egypt twice in his whole life, and that included a two hour delay for an emergency stopover at Cairo Airport whilst someone was taken off the plane due to a heart attack.

His route to America had been long and difficult, but it had been planned from the outset, by his father, Jabra Hasan al-Mastoor.

Jabra Hasan al-Mastoor had two sons, he had only two children. The eldest son was Khalil, and the youngest, Reza.

Jabra Hasan al-Mastoor had a hatred of the West, in particular, the United States of America.

And in his eyes, for a very good reason. But in truth, his hatred should have been guided against one person and not a country and not the western world either. And if truth be known, the people who contributed to the flame of his hatred and his misery were actually a lot closer to home.

It had been over twenty years ago, and back in the late seventies, when Jabra Hasan al-Mastoor was living a relatively peaceful but industrious life in the city of Dhahran in Eastern Saudi Arabia. He was in those days, obviously a younger but happier man. Married to his young wife, Samira, their two sons. Khalil, the eldest boy, was thirteen years old at the time, and Reza, the younger, was just eleven.

Jabra Hasan al-Mastoor worked as a teacher at a local school, where his specialized subject was mathematics. His salary, though not huge, was adequate, and his job and his position did give him some standing within the local community. In fact, he was also quite involved within the local Mosque, where he was held in quite high esteem. And Jabra Hasan al-Mastoor, who was quite a religious man, could also count on the Imam there, the highly revered, 'Abdullah Abu Billah', as one of his closest friends.

A close friend, and also his religious advisor.

To boost their income, Jabra's wife, Samira, worked as a typist at 'Aramco Oil', which was an American-Saudi Oil company, a jointly owned and very successful venture, formed between the two countries, and which had in time turned out to become highly lucrative. The company itself was huge and involved millions of barrels of crude oil which were then turned into millions of American dollars.

Jabra and Samira Hasan al Mastoor actually lived quite a westernized lifestyle. Samira wore western clothes, especially for work, where it was deemed more acceptable alongside her American and other similarly dressed Arab work colleagues. In fact, at the time the head covering garment known as the 'Hijab', had become rather unfashionable for the younger generation, and Samira only wore it when travelling to and from work, as a sign of respect to her husband.

Samira worked in the offices at Armaco, a job she loved. She was popular there, and the money was quite good too, for a woman. In the mornings Samira would drop young Khalil and Reza off at her mother's house, which was just down the road from their own house, and her mother would in turn make sure that the boys got off to school in time. All was well.

And then Samira was offered a promotion. It was a bit of a surprise for her really, up till then Samira had worked in the main office along with several other girls and she'd just got on with her work. But apparently her efficiency had been duly noticed and she was offered a job as a personal secretary to one of the production analysts. He was Winston Geller, an American who had been formerly trained as an accountant back in the United States before getting into the 'oil business'.

Winston Geller had been with the company for around six years, and although he hated the country, the heat and the people, along with the flies and the food, he did enjoy the very generous salary that he was being paid. However, Winston Geller, who was fast approaching his fifties, had of late become rather bored.

Life somehow seemed to be passing him by. And living in this hell hole of a country wasn't helping either. Over the years he'd had several secretaries, all had been American of course, and most of them had been plain, or overweight, or just plain ugly, but at least they'd been efficient. However, after a time, and usually once they'd also accumulated enough money in their bank accounts, they too had abandoned Saudi Arabia and scuttled off back home to the USA, their bank account intact. But his last secretary, a Miss Janet Lacey from North Carolina, had been a slightly different cup of tea. Unlike his past secretaries, Miss Lacey was actually quite attractive. And Winston Geller had taken an immediate shine to her. The only problem with Janet Lacey was that essentially, she wasn't very good at her job.

Winston Geller was soon to realize this slight problem when he discovered that any of the reports that his now 'new' secretary typed up for him, came back full of typing errors and misspellings. Along with that, her use of punctuation was a complete mystery to him.

In the end, Winston sat her down in his office one afternoon to ask her 'what the hell was going on?' And at that point, Miss Janet Lacey had immediately burst into tears.

Now, had Janet Lacey been plain, or overweight or ugly, Winston Geller would have probably taken a different tack. But she wasn't was she? And so Winston had apologized and asked her to dry her tears. After a short conversation, Miss Lacey admitted to him that her typing skills were 'self-taught' and in truth, she'd lied about most of everything during the interview which had got her the job in the first place. And back in those days of 'heady inefficiency' within a lot of very large companies, the references that she'd promised to send to the company simply never arrived, and of course, nobody ever bothered to ask why?

Truth be known, Janet Lacey was rather naive in some areas, but quite clever in others.

Clever, in the fact that she got herself the job in the first place, a job which promised a decent salary and some foreign travel. And clever in the knowledge that she knew she was pretty, and that by shedding a few tears and putting on a show of honesty, she could possibly wrap her new boss around her pretty little finger. But she was also naive, because there is always a balance. And a favour given, often demanded a favour in return.

And so they formed a little pact, a little alliance, in which Winston Geller suddenly became not only her boss, but also her friend. And he offered to possibly 'overlook' some of her discrepancies, along with the offer of 'showing her' just how everything was done, or should be done.

And that was it, well it was for Janet Lacey anyway. She'd walked out of Winston Geller's office on that afternoon, inwardly smiling to herself. Yes, she'd sorted that little problem out. And now she could carry one working with the same low expectations. And anyway, she had no intentions of being there forever. In fact, twelve months should probably do it.

But as she was walking out of his office that afternoon, Winston Geller was eying Miss Janet Lacey's rather shapely legs and her nicely firmed bottom, and he suddenly felt an urge.

Winston Geller had been on his own for far too long and he really missed some female company. But suddenly, things were looking up, and suddenly there were possibilities.

Janet Lacey was such a lovely, friendly sort of girl. And well, a favour did deserve a favour.

The next two weeks became quite taxing.

Every time Janet Lacey came into his office, Winston Geller somehow managed to touch her. Be it a hand on her shoulder or a slight brush of the arm, but somehow he managed it.

And Janet plainly didn't seem to bother, which Geller found quite promising. Truth be known, she thought that he was just being friendly, and ever the naive, she began to look upon Winston Geller as a sort of 'uncle' type of figure, who really did care about her well being. This was actually the furthest thing from Winston Geller's mind. The only thing he cared about was getting his sweaty hands onto her firm young body. Things nearly came unstuck when in desperation, he asked Janet if she would like to go for something to eat after work, but the silly girl didn't understand just where he was coming from, and genuinely thought that he meant for them to just grab something from the company's canteen, And she told him quite truthfully, that by the end of the day she'd had enough of work and she just wanted to go home, but thank you anyway.

Winston Geller was confused, and frustrated. This entire 'touchy' thing was beginning to get to him.

And then, in what could be called 'a moment of madness', he very pleasantly asked her to stay behind for an hour after work. He wanted to show her a new format that the company now required when typing up his reports. It was all a lie of course, and he knew that Janet wouldn't know any different, whatever the format. Janet, who was always ready to please, agreed. After all, as Mr Geller had put it...'it was for her benefit.'

Back in those days most people used electronic typewriters, and so shortly after five o' clock that same evening, Janet unplugged her machine, it was quite a lightweight affair, and she carried it through into her boss's office and placed it on his desk. For Janet it wasn't a problem, they'd always enjoyed a very casual relationship and they both got on very well.

Little did she know?

There was the usual banter between them, a joke and some office tittle-tattle. And then Winston Geller sat her down in his chair in front of the typewriter and then 'found' some bogus report or other. Janet turned on the typewriter. Winston Geller was already turned on. He'd been planning this all day.

He then stood behind her and leant over her shoulder as she loaded the paper into her typewriter. He could smell her perfume, mixed with her own odour from the heat of the day, and he found it intoxicating. He then outlined the new format for his report and how he wanted it set out. Actually, it was just larger gaps between the paragraphs, but Janet as ever, didn't see the simplicity in this.

She was about half way down the page when Winston Geller slowly ran his hands under her armpits and then he grasped her breasts. In his mind, he thought that she would stop typing and then possibly moan with pleasure, and then she would lean back and let him carry on, and then god only knows what.

However, that was never going to happen, definitely not.

As soon as she felt his hands on her, Janet Lacey screamed. And then she jumped up from the chair and spun around to face him. And in that instant, naive or not, Janet suddenly realized what that was going on, or was about to go on. And Janet was not having it, in any way, shape or form. She also immediately realized that all this 'so-called' friendship and his caring attitude towards her had all been aimed at getting into her panties.

'What the hell do you think your doing?' she shouted at him.

However, Geller's reply, 'Come on Janet, don't be so damn soft,' didn't do him any favours either. She raised her hand and then slapped him mightily across his face. A strong girl, she left a nice line of red finger marks across his left cheek. And with that, Janet Lacey stormed out of his office. She went through to her own office and picked up her handbag, and then she marched out of the building, never to return. Two days later, and she was on a plane back to the USA and then onwards, back to North Carolina.

A lesson learned for Winston Geller? Unfortunately not. And the chain of events that would arise from his actions that day would eventually have consequences far and wide.

And instead of learning his lesson, or learning anything at all really, the only thing that Winston Geller would learn from that experience was how to become cleverer, and more determined.

From there, Winston Geller was suddenly looking at the women who worked for 'Aramco' through totally different eyes. Basically, there were women who worked there who he would like to have sex with, and then there were others who he certainly didn't. His experience with Janet Lacey had also led him down another path. The American women working there were far too liberated, and as he'd learned, they could be somewhat antagonistic when cornered, No, what he needed was a more submissive type of woman. Someone who he could dominate, and someone who would also keep quiet about it. And with that thought in mind, his attentions turned to the Arab women who worked there for Aramco Oil.

And then, bingo, he stumbled upon the very lovely, Mrs Samira Hasan al-Mastoor.

It wasn't hard really. With the loss of Miss Lacy, the personnel department at Aramco would have to find him a replacement, no doubt somebody would be offered the job over in the United States, once again. However, all of this would take a certain amount of time and so Geller had asked if he could use one of the girls from the central office from time to time, and only when need be. He was told that it 'wouldn't be a problem'. And from there, Winston Geller suddenly had free reign. During the next couple of weeks he'd wandered in and out of the central office to ask one or two of the different girls there if they could type him up some report or other. Always just a small task, he was clever not to make waves or become a nuisance. And then he spotted Samira. She was without doubt very beautiful, and stood head and shoulders above the rest of the girls there in the office. In fact, Geller was quite smitten. Samira had those striking aquiline Arab features, along with the most beautiful dark brown hair. But Geller was clever, he didn't make a fuss. And whenever he needed a bit of typing doing, he slowly but surely went to her. And she was very pleasant about it too, always accepting his requests with a smile, and what a smile. He was actually quite taken with her, and the more he saw her, the more he liked her. And the more he liked, the more he wanted.

And then the sexual fantasies began to run through Geller's mind. Winston Geller was becoming a dangerous man, in fact, Winston Geller was fast becoming a sexual predator.

But he had a plan, and with it a different approach. He wouldn't be fooled again or refused.

Because Winston Geller knew the Arab ways.

And so, Samira was offered the job as Winston Geller's personal secretary. And it was indeed a promotion. Geller had approached personnel and informed them that he had found a very 'satisfactory' replacement secretary that he thought would fit the position, therefore saving everybody's time in having to recruit someone all the way from the USA. It would save a lot of time, money and effort, and that he thought that this 'local' girl would be quite adequate for his needs, in fact, she was very good. And if there were any problems he would soon sort it out. Yes he would. Personnel of course agreed, it was obviously one problem less and yet another problem solved.

On hearing that she'd been offered this promotion, Samira had gone home that evening to tell her husband, Jabra, the news. She would of course have to ask her husband's permission first. The job may take up a bit more of her time, and Samira was a good Arab wife and mother, and her family and her husband must always come first.

However, she needn't have worried. In fact the news was taken as a celebration. Along with the promotion to this now prestigious position, there was a great increase in salary, it almost doubled. And in truth, Jabra was very proud of his wife. Actually, he had always been proud of her. She was a beautiful woman and she was the wonderful mother who had borne him his two sons. He had always respected his wife, because he loved her.

And now this, and now his wife was not just some mere typist in an office with a host of others. No, now she had a position, and along with it a very good salary.

And when Jabra went to the Mosque later that evening, he spoke to his Imam and friend,

Abdullah Abu Billah, about Samira's promotion. Imam Abu Billah was pleased for Jabra and his family, and he blessed them for their good fortune.

Along with his blessing, Imam Abu Billah also commented that 'the more money that they could get out of those 'American devils', the better. It was God's way.'

Two days later, and Samira moved into her new office and became accustomed to her new surroundings. She also had to get used to working on her own, and at first she felt quite isolated, lonely even. But she started a routine and kept herself busy, and she also discovered a freedom, in that at any time she wanted to, she could go back down to the main office and have a chat with the girls there who were her good friends.

She also discovered that her new boss was quite pleasant. He was friendly enough and very civil, and any of the problems that she had encountered, he would soon put right. And to her surprise, the job itself didn't seem too taxing, either. In fact, it was a lot easier than being down there in the main office, typing nonstop all day long. It seemed that in working for Mr Geller, all she had to do was sort out his timetable everyday and type up any of his personal reports. Yes, life seemed good.

And so, two or more weeks passed by, and Samira had got herself into a comfortable routine.

And then, on the Monday morning and at the start of the week, Mr Geller dropped the news. Apparently he would have to spend most of his time that week down at the plant, some emergency had arisen and he would have a rather heavy workload. However, he would need any of his reports typing up immediately, they would need to be submitted the very next day, and therefore he would require her to stay at the office for an extra hour or so after work, when he would get back from the plant with his paperwork. Mr Geller knew that this was a bit of an imposition, however as recompense, he told Samira that since he probably wouldn't be there most of the week, she could come into work later in the day, why not somewhere around lunchtime?

Samira felt that she couldn't refuse. She would have to discuss it with her husband of course, but she didn't think that it would be a problem. So she basically agreed, and anyway, it would give her more time in the mornings and she could see the boys off to school herself for a change. So yes, okay, it wouldn't be a problem.

And it wasn't. Jabra realized that his wife now had greater responsibilities, and yes, she would obviously be able to spend more time in the morning with the boys.

So all went well, and for the rest of the week Winston Geller would arrive back at the office after work with pages of scribbled reports for her to type up. She didn't understand what was written of course, but that wasn't her job. All she had to do was copy them to type.

But Winston Geller hadn't been to the plant, he hadn't been anywhere near it. In fact, he'd spent most of his week back at his apartment watching TV, along with the odd pornographic Arabic video that he'd managed to acquire, and that did nothing more than fuel his obsession. During the day he would sit and write another bogus report for Samira to type up, most of it was utter gibberish, but she wasn't to know that was she?

And then late on the Friday afternoon he rang Samira at his office. He apologized profusely to her, but he'd had another job to go to and he'd got stuck in the traffic. And though he would definitely arrive, he would be slightly delayed. Once again he apologized, but he was on his way and would be there as soon as possible. Samira understood and she told him that she would wait for him.

Back in his apartment, that really pleased Winston Geller, and with that done, he poured himself a glass of whiskey.

He waited for another hour and a half and drank another full glass of whiskey, and then he got into his car and headed off to work. He arrived at Aramco head office around half an hour later, by then it was almost six o' clock and most of the staff had left for the weekend, in fact the whole place was almost deserted.

Winston Geller parked his car and entered the building through the main doors and then he skipped up the steps, he needed to look as though he'd been in a hurry. He walked quickly into the office, to find Samira sitting there, waiting for him. And he liked that. She smiled of course, what else could she do, she certainly couldn't complain. And he liked that too.

She was compliant, of course she was.

He apologized, naturally, and then he began to chat to Samira whilst he 'got his breath back'.

He made a joke or two, and then he asked her how her family were getting along. All friendly banter, and the ever compliant Samira, who was still smiling continued to talk to him. But in truth, Geller wasn't listening to a word she was saying. As she now moved around the office he was admiring the line of her body and her very, very beautiful face.

Samira approached his desk and she said to him quite innocently, 'What do you want me to do, Mr Geller?'

Those words, were like a catalyst to him.

He reached over and slid his arm around her waist and pulled her towards him. She was shocked, and he'd caught her off balance and she almost fell into his arms. And with that he pinned her against the desk. Before she could even utter a word he kissed her on her mouth. And then she smelt the whiskey. She tried to push him away but suddenly his hand was on her breast. She broke away from the unwanted kiss and shouted 'No', but he wasn't listening. And Winston Geller had also stopped talking, there was nothing he wanted to say to her anymore because he

199

was past talking now. He grabbed hold of her blouse and ripped it open and he stared at his prize, her beautiful breasts. He pulled her bra down as she struggled, but he had her, and then he had his hands on her open breasts and she was pinned against his desk. He was too strong for her. He went to kiss her again, but in panic and in fear and anger at what was happening to her, she shot her head forwards and managed to get his nose between her teeth, and she bit, she bit hard. Winston Geller howled with pain and his grip on her slackened, but she wouldn't let go and he was now in excruciating agony. For a moment, she thought she had a chance. And then Geller punched her fully in the stomach. Samira just keeled forwards and Geller was then free, and very, very angry. He began to repeatedly hit her in the face and with his third punch he knocked her out and she collapsed backwards onto the desk.

Geller stared down at her, he was incensed. But now she was his to do whatever he wanted.

More than his prize, she was now his gift.

His mind began to go into overload at the thought of it. There was no turning back now, he knew that. He quickly ripped off her blouse and her bra, and then he grabbed at her skirt and pulled it from her, along with the rest of her underwear until she was completely naked. He looked down at her. In his mind, she was like a piece of meat. And then he took hold of her and rolled her onto her stomach and then he splayed her legs. And with that done, he stepped out of his own pants and took hold of himself and then entered her from behind.

After several minutes of intended pleasure, Winston Geller found that he couldn't satisfy himself. Samira was still unconscious; there was no movement from her, and with it, no real fulfilment for him. She was in fact, still just a piece of meat. He stopped what he was doing and pulled away. Then he took hold of her and rolled her over, and he lifted her off the desk and onto the carpeted floor. Then he got on top of her and entered her again and got himself comfortable, and then he began to slap her face. After several attempts, Samira finally regained some sort of consciousness and she blinked as she began to recover her senses. And at that moment Winston Geller took hold of her buttocks and resumed his unwanted sexual intercourse.

In shock and in pain, Samira realized what was happening to her and she started to scream. But Geller didn't care, because he knew that there was nobody there to hear her. And then in a last attempt to fight back, Samira reached up and grabbed hold of his cheeks and then attempted to scratch his eyes out. Geller again screamed in agony, and he had to stop once again because he had to grab hold of her arms. He was now furious, and he was livid at what was happening and that everything was going wrong, because of this fucking stupid woman. And then he went berserk. He started to smash Samira's face with his fists and he felt her nose break as he knocked her unconscious again. But that wasn't enough. He stood up, and then he looked down at her, she no longer looked so pretty with her smashed and bloodied face. Just a piece of meat, that's all she'd ever been. And his temper and all his frustrations took hold of him and he started to kick her repeatedly in the face and then in her stomach and her chest, until he heard a rib break. Finally he stood back, breathless.

And then he looked down at her, she was dead.

There was blood everywhere. He stopped for a moment, trying to get his breath back. And as he stood there, breathing heavily, the enormity of everything that had just happened and the appalling reality of it all suddenly struck him.. He had just raped and murdered a woman, an Arab woman, and a woman who had a family. And suddenly he began to panic.

It shouldn't have happened like this, no, this wasn't what he'd planned. Winston Geller had every intention of raping his secretary that evening, of that there was no doubt. But once he'd finished, it was also his intention to sit her down and explain things to her, sensibly.

Firstly, he was her boss, and she was also a married woman. And what would happen if her husband found out? There would be a great disruption in her household. Because yes, Winston Geller knew the Arab way.

And from there he would have blackmailed her into having sex with him whenever he wanted. If of course she wanted to keep her reputation, along with her job.

It was all going to be that simple, but not now, no. And Winston Geller suddenly realized that he had committed the wrong crime in the wrong country. And also, that he was an American.

He stood up and rapidly dressed himself. After quickly looking around, he switched off the lights and left the office. He almost ran down the steps and got to his car, and then he drove back to his apartment. He took a quick shower to get himself cleaned up and he changed his clothes, and then he threw some bits and bats into a small suitcase and grabbed his passport. He locked up his apartment and then got back into his car and drove straight to the airport. When he got there he dumped the car in a busy car park and headed for the main terminal. He was by then becoming increasingly desperate. He made enquiries at several different desks, but there were no flights back to anywhere in the USA for another twelve hours. And then he got lucky. Air France had a flight leaving for Paris in less than an hour. That would do. Anywhere would do, anywhere except here.

He bought himself a seat on the plane, he paid for it immediately and then headed for the appropriate gate. Fifty very long minutes later, he breathed a sigh of relief as the aeroplane took to the air. He'd escaped. He would fly to Paris, and from there he'd get another flight back home to America, thank god. Once there he would have to change a few things, his bank account and probably his name. Just in case the police did ever come looking for him.

As Winston Geller's flight was just about to take off, the cleaner entered his office back at Aramco Oil in Dhahran. As she switched on the lights she looked around, and then she stared down in horror. Lying there on the floor was a woman, and there was blood everywhere.

Then suddenly, the woman gasped and then she moaned in agony. For a moment, the cleaner just stood there in shock, and then in panic she looked around to find a phone.

She rang security and screamed for help. Security immediately rang for an ambulance, and then they rang for the police.

Both the ambulance and the police arrived within minutes of one another. Samira was immediately put onto a stretcher and lifted into the back of the ambulance. She was taken at high speed to the local hospital. Unfortunately, back in those days, the local hospital was little more than a glorified clinic, with hardly any amenities. And the local doctor there took one look at Samira and knew that he was out of his depth. He had Samira put back into the ambulance and instructed them to drive as fast as they could to the main hospital at Riyadh, the nation's capital. With lights flashing and the siren blaring, the ambulance driver managed to achieve the four hour trip in less than three, and in doing so he probably saved her life.

Back in Dhahran the police were busy making enquiries. They finally got hold of the phone number of someone who worked in personnel, and after they explained what had happened and in which office they'd found the injured woman, they quickly came to the conclusion that the woman could only be Samira Hasan al-Mastoor, who was Winston Geller's secretary.

Another police car was dispatched to a given address, and half an hour later a policeman knocked on Jabra Hasan al-Mastoor's front door. After discovering that Jabra's wife had not yet returned home from work, the policeman informed him of what had happened, and that his wife had been taken to the main hospital in Riyadh.

Jabrah immediately rang his mother-in-law, and told her to come over at once and to look after the boys. Then he got into his car and set off to Riyadh. When he arrived at the hospital he was straight away taken to Samira's room. He couldn't believe what he saw there. His beautiful wife had most of her head bandaged, but the rest of her face was purple and black and unbelievably swollen. She was almost unrecognizable to him. The doctor then took Jabra to one side and informed him that Samira had been raped and very badly beaten.

The news put Jabra into a state of shock. How could this have possibly happened?

The doctor there had no further information but recommended that Jabra should speak to the local police, back in Dhahran.

Jabra Hasan al-Mastoor sat at his wife's bedside for the next twelve hours. He was heartbroken. He truly loved and respected his dear wife.

Eventually, he was told that it would be better to keep her sedated for the next two or three days. It would help her to recover and it would also help her to contain the shock of her ordeal. Jabra went back home, the hospital would phone him when she regained consciousness or if there was any change in her condition. And yes, he should phone them every day for an update.

Jabra finally arrived back home in Dhahran at around midday. He spoke to his mother-in-law about what had happened, but he purposefully didn't mention that Samira had also been raped. Jabra asked her to stay at the house to look after the boys. From there he went to the local police station where he was taken to a room and spoken to by an Inspector Mohamed Choukri. The inspector told him the case details up to the present time. Samira's attacker had apparently been her boss, Winston Geller. The police had been to Mr Geller's apartment but he'd evidently fled. From there, they had obviously checked with the airport and with customs and immigration, and it seemed that Mr Geller had managed to get himself onto an Air France flight to Paris on the previous evening. Inspector Choukri then informed Jabra Hasan al-Mastoor that their investigations would be 'on going'.

So that was it, his wife's attacker had been her American boss.

.

From there, Jabra then went to the Mosque to speak with his personal friend and his mentor, Imam Abu Billah.

Imam Abu Billah was shocked when he was informed about the events, and he immediately ushered his friend into his private rooms. They both sat there as Jabra recounted to his Imam exactly what had happened. And then he told Abu Billah about the rape. He had to.

After a short prayer and a blessing, both of them sat there in silence for a moment of reflection. And then Imam Abu Billah spoke to his friend.

'This is a terrible act, my brother,' he said.

Jabra just sat there with his head bowed.

'Not only that,' Abu Billah continued. 'This will bring disgrace to your family.'

Jabra Hasan al-Mastoor slowly looked up at his Imam. This was something that he already knew, and something that he'd thought about as he'd driven all the way back from the hospital in Riyadh. And now, he was looking for guidance.

There was another short period of silence as Abu Billah carefully considered his next words

'Can I speak to you with openness, my brother?' he then asked.

Jabra looked directly at Abu Billah.

'Of course you can. You are my Imam. And you are my friend.'

Abu Billah nodded.

'Your wife, Samira. She recently got a promotion at work. Is that correct?

'Yes...yes she did,' Jabra replied.

'Can you tell me how she got this promotion, brother?'

Jabra shrugged. 'I don't really know. Up until then she just worked in the main office with all the other girls. Apparently her boss, this man, 'Geller', thought that she was a very hard worker. She has always been very conscientious.'

Abu Billah dismissed those last few words, and he continued.

'So out of an office full of girls, this man suddenly decides to choose your wife?'

Jabra just nodded, he didn't really understand the direction of the conversation.

'And your wife, was she happy with her promotion?'

'Yes, she was very happy. We both were.'

Abu Billah once again dismissed those last words. And he sat there for a moment, in deep thought.

'Do not take this as a criticism, my brother. But as you know, I am a traditionalist, and I do know that you younger generation, do like to follow the western fashions. But your wife, she doesn't wear the traditional 'Hijab'?

'She does whenever she leaves the house, Imam,' Jabra replied, in his wife's defence.

'But she does not wear it once she gets to work?'

'No,' Jabra again replied, 'none of the girls there do.' Again he spoke in her defence.

Abu Billah was again silent in thought.

'Your wife Samira. I do appreciate that she is a very beautiful woman. I do understand that.'

For a brief moment, Jabra thought about his wife's smashed and broken face as she lay there in the hospital bed. It was something that he would never forget.

But Abu Billah continued. 'And the American, maybe he chose her for her beauty, above her brains?

Jabra was sullen. 'I do not know,' he replied.

Abu Billah continued.

'But your wife, she must have been very pleasant to the American, surely. If she had not been, he would not have chosen her, obviously.'

Jabra just sat there. There was no answer.

'So we have your wife at work, with her beautiful looks and her beautiful hair, which she must be aware of. And she doesn't wear the Hijab, and she's suddenly being pleasant to this American. And then he gives her a promotion, simply because she's very pleasant and beautiful, and possibly accommodating?'

Jabra looked at Abu Billah.

'I don't understand, Imam,' he said.

Abu Billah shrugged.

'No man will ever truly understand a woman, my brother. They are a creature that will always work towards their own ends, always. But let me put this to you. Your beautiful wife was given a promotion because the American was possibly lusting after her. Those people are like dogs, they have no respect for our women, as we now realize. See what he's done to her?

And there is your wife, smiling and being pleasant with him, and actually in the eyes of God, she was flirting with this man. She may not have realized it, a lot of women don't, but it's in their nature to try to be alluring to men. And this American, what does he get from all of this? Not just a secretary, he could have chosen from any of those girls who work there to be his secretary. No, no my brother. He saw the promise, and he would want the reward. Your wife must have done 'something' for him to have chosen her above the others.'

Jabra just sat there, as he listened carefully to his friend and mentor.

206

'And this week,' Abu Billah continued, 'you say that your wife stayed behind at work. She had to work late in order to help this man?'

Abu Billah almost scoffed. 'Believe me, my brother. All is not what it seems. Why would she stay late, when she had a family at home to attend to? Was she paid any extra money for her time?'

'No, I don't think so,' Jabra replied.

Imam Abu Billah raised his arms and shrugged.

'There is more to this than meets the eye, my brother, believe me. They could have been having an affair. The American would want his reward, obviously, and something must have been going on, because look what's happened. Maybe she wanted to end the affair, or maybe the American wanted her to run off with him and she refused. I do know that she would never have left her children. Maybe that's it, and then everything backfired and it led to this?'

Abu Billah's very appeasing words and his logical reasoning spun around in Jabra's fragile mind. Yes, there must be something. These things don't just happen. Abu Billah was his Iman, and his friend, and his mentor. He must be right.

Abu Billah said another prayer, and then both men sat in silence for a while, for another period of reflection.

And finally, Abu Billah turned to Jabra.

'You do understand the dishonour that's been laid upon you. You're family's good name and your children's name has been shamed.'

Jabra Hasan al-Mastoor did understand, and he slowly nodded.

'You do realize that when the truth comes out about your wife's behaviour, the people will want her to be stoned to death? And it will happen, my brother, believe me.'

Jabra closed his eyes, and once again he slowly nodded.

And then Abu Billah put his hand on Jabra's shoulder, in an almost fatherly way.

'Your family name will forever be disgraced, and you my brother, you too will be disgraced as 'the man who couldn't keep hold of his own woman.' You realize how people will talk. They will sneer at you behind your back. You will lose the respect of your friends and you will also lose those friends. And then of course, your children. One must think of them too, and their futures.

My friend, the fault of all of this is the American. They are a terrible people. Their greed is unfathomable. They steal our lands, our oil, and now your wife. They are the enemy. Remember that, always remember that.'

Abu Billah was very plausible, and for Jabra,, his friend was telling him the truth.

He rubbed his eyes, he was now becoming distressed.

'What am I going to do, Imam,' he asked?

And there it was. Finally, the words that Imam Abu Billah had been waiting for.

'We will do God's will,' he replied. 'And you my brother, must be strong.'

Both men sat for the next half an hour in deep discussion, and then Abu Billah sent Jabra home.

Now left on his own, the Imam Abu Billah inwardly congratulated himself. After this, he would convert Jabra Hasan al-Mastoor into his growing band of believers.

Iman Abu Billah had one mission in his life. He would protect Islam from the growing powers of the West. And he saw the American presence in his country and their alliance with the fawning Saudi Royal family as an insult. It was his intention to fight back, and in his mind he was making the plans for something that he would later call, 'a Jihad'...a Holy War. And from there they would drive the Americans from his homeland and punish the West for all of its evils. It was a growing plan. And at some point in the distant future, he would meet a visionary young man with whom he would share the same ideals and principals.

That young man was Osama bin Laden.

Jabra Hasan al-Mastoor went back home to his family with Imam Abu Billah's instructions firmly embedded in his mind.

At the end of the week he drove back to the hospital in Riyadh to pick up his wife, Samira, who was now recovering and would be allowed to go home. She was able to walk, but with difficulty, and though she had a broken nose and ribs, she would in time recover. Her face however was still badly bruised and swollen.

Jabra had arrived at the hospital at around seven o' clock in the evening. He'd had a busy day at the school, but he'd driven straight there. Once there he made one phone call to his mother-in-law back at home in Dhahran.

Samira was put in a wheelchair, and Jabra slowly pushed his wife out of the hospital, he lifted her into the car, and then they set of back to Dhahran, a four hour drive. The last rays of the day's sun shone down on them as they drove away. On the way home they spoke very little, neither of them wanted to talk about the attack and so Samira asked about the boys. But she wasn't well and everything was an effort.

They were about an hour away from Dhahran, it was now dark and on the road that they were travelling along, the lighting was very sparse. In fact, there was very little traffic at all and Jabra had to concentrate on his driving.

Hen suddenly, he cursed. 'Oh damn, no.'

Samira turned to him.

'What is it, husband. What's wrong?'

Jabra pulled the car over to the side of the road.

'I think we've got a puncture in the front wheel, the cars not steering right.'

He sat there for a moment.

'I hope the spare tyre's ok. I haven't checked it.'

And with that, he got out of the car and looked at the front tyre, he shook his head in frustration and then he went around to the back of the car and opened the boot. He had to move some sheeting to get to the spare wheel and also find the torch that he always carried there for emergencies such as this. He rolled the spare wheel around to the front of the car, it was okay, it was still fully inflated. Then he went back to the boot for his torch and to find the car's jack and a wheel wrench. He switched on the torch and laid it on the ground for some illumination, which was not very efficient. And then he attempted to get the jack into position.

Samira watched as her husband struggled and she heard him curse. She tapped on the window, and he looked up.

'Can I help, husband?' she asked.

Jabra looked at her for a moment.

'Could you manage to hold the torch for me, I can't see what I'm doing.'

'I'll try my best,' Samira replied, 'could you help me out of the car?'

Jabra opened the door and lifted her out of the car and onto the ground. She knelt there and Jabra picked up his torch and handed it to her.

'Please, just shine the light there on the jack, Samira.'

And at once he could see what he was doing and he placed the jack in the correct position. Then he stood up and went to get the wheel wrench.

Samira just knelt there, she was weary with the effort, when suddenly she felt Jabra's hand on her shoulder.

'My wife, you have brought shame to our family. You know what must be done.'

For a moment, Samira didn't understand, and she was just about to speak when she felt his grip tighten. And then suddenly, she realized.

'Go to God with my blessing,' he said to her. But at that moment, Samira's only thoughts were for her precious children.

And with that, Jabra raised the steel wheel wrench and clubbed his wife to death.

Jabra Hasan al-Mastoor wrapped his dead wife's body in the sheeting that he'd previously stored in the boot of his car. He wrapped the body tightly as he'd been instructed, and then he carried it to the boot of his car, on top of the spare wheel that he'd never had to use. There had never been a puncture of course. Everything had been planned.

He then prostrated himself by the side of the car and prayed.

Jabra Hasan al-Mastoor drove back to Dhahran, and straight to the Mosque there, where he was met by Imam Abu Billah, who was waiting for him. The two men then carried Samira's body into the Mosque.

Jabra then drove home where his family and closest friends were waiting in mourning. Jabra had rung his mother-in-law from the hospital in Riyadh and told her that Samira had died due to 'complications'. Family, and their friends were to be informed as to what had happened. He would bring his wife's body home and take it straight to the Mosque. The funeral would be the next day, as was the tradition.

The two boys were inconsolable.

The funeral was quickly over, and Jabra had the sympathy of the community and of everyone who knew that his wife had been killed by an American. Rape was never discussed.

Jabra Hasan al-Mastoor had to rebuild a life without his wife, Samira, he would never remarry. It had been his Imam's recommendation.

Eventually, Jabra had to sit down with his two young sons and explain to them how their mother had been killed by an American.

The boys handled the upset quite differently.

Khalil, the elder, became silent, there were no tears. He shut his grief away, and eventually that grief would turn to anger. Reza, the youngest and the baby of the family just cried, he was completely devastated.

As the years passed by, the hatred within the family towards America grew like a festering sore. Even more so with Jabra and his eldest son, Khalil.

Jabra Hasan al-Mastoor soon became a member of Abu Billah's inner circle, a trusted convert.

At eighteen years old, and after two successful years at a local college, Khalil Hasan al Mastoor was sent to Riyadh's very prestigious King Abdulaziz University, where he studied Computer Science. Khalil, like his father, had an aptitude for figures, in fact he was quite brilliant, and driven.

Two years later, Reza was sent to America as an Egyptian born, International student with a false passport and false papers. There would never be a trail. He was enrolled into the Massachusetts Institute of Technology, the legendary 'MIT' of America, where he was educated in Economics, Business Studies and Finance.

Yes, everything had been planned.

Reza finally left MIT with distinctions, and was immediately snapped up by the First Global Bank. He would be based in New York where, and after several years and more, he would eventually work his way into the Investment Department.

However, in his early days at the bank he worked in Finance and Loans.

And at one time he was asked to go to see a business customer who was experiencing some difficulty and required a refinancing loan. Another thankless task really. Reza was sent to see the customer and have a look at the business and examine the books, and then assess the feasibility as to whether the bank should hand over a lump of cash which it could ultimately lose.

And so, on a dull and rainy Tuesday morning, Reza arrived at the Northern area of New York in a District known as the 'Yonkers'. From there, he finally found the business premises he was looking for, it was near the junction of Wells Avenue and River Street.

A large and slightly aging building, 'Jeffersons Family Fabrics (established 1933)' was akin to something from the past, hence the year in the company name. It was a five story building which was quite large actually, and the ground floor seemed to be used as a shop premises.

Reza walked into the shop, which caused a doorbell to ring. And then he stood around for several minutes waiting for someone to appear. As he stood there he looked around the fairly large shop which seemed to be piled high with enumerable rolls of fabric, large and small and thick and thin. In fact, it was difficult to know whether it was a shop, a showroom or a warehouse.

Eventually, a man arrived from nowhere. He was around sixty years old, and as he spotted Reza he called out, 'Good morning, sir. And how can we help you?'

'Well,' thought Reza, 'good old fashioned service...it goes with the shop.'

The man wore thin wired glasses, along with a light blue shirt and a subdued red tie.

'Mr Jefferson?' Reza asked.

The man paused for a moment at the mention of his name.

'Err, yes,' he replied.

Reza reached out to shake Mr Jefferson's hand.

'Hello Mr Jefferson, I'm Reza Mastoor. I'm from the First Global Bank. I have an appointment to see you today.'

They shook hands, and there was a look of acknowledgement on the man's face as he suddenly realized that Reza wasn't a customer.

'Ah, you're from the bank I wasn't expecting you so early,' he replied. 'You see we set a date with the bank but not a particular time. But I'm always here you see, so any old time wouldn't be a problem for me.'

Reza smiled, 'Well I'm here now, Mr Jefferson.'

'Bob...please, call me Bob, err...Reza, isn't it?'

Reza again smiled, 'Yes Bob, it's Reza.'

'Well Reza. I think we need your help. I'll just lock the door and then we can go upstairs to my office and talk.

And with those words, 'I think we need your help', Reza realized that he was actually dealing with an honest man here, instead of the usual type who thought that they could 'pull the wool' over the bank's eyes.

They went upstairs to a similarly aging office where they both sat down.

'Want some coffee, Reza?' Bob Jefferson asked.

'Umm, no thanks...Bob. I'll have some later if that's okay. But first of all, can we have a chat and see what this is about. You've apparently applied for a refinancing loan?'

Bob Jefferson sighed.

'Okay Reza, let me put my cards on the table here, and let me tell you a bit about the company history,' and with that, Bob Jefferson rearranged his glasses.

'My grandfather opened this store back in 1933, and my father took the store over from him, and eventually it was handed down to me. We have a lot of history here and in the past the store was always busy and was quite profitable. We had some very good years here, and in the past we made a decent amount of money. However, and as you're probably aware, Reza, times have changed. We used to have a steady flow of shoppers walking past our doors, but these days there aren't so many. And you can't park around here anymore either. Customers used to be able to park up right outside the store and wander in and out and buy material and then load it into their cars and drive away. But not now, there are parking restrictions all around here now. And don't get me wrong, we have a hell of a lot a traffic passing the place, but unfortunately, none of them can stop. And now everyone seems to go to the shopping Malls. It's all out of town shopping these days, people can park freely and just wander about.'

Bob Jefferson then went on to talk about the drop in their turnover, and the overheads of running the place and the long serving staff that they'd had to let go.

After half an hour's discussion, it didn't paint a pretty picture.

Reza sat there and listened intently. He liked this man. And above all, he admired his honesty. At no point were there any lies or attempted trickery. Unlike a lot of others that he'd had to deal with.

Finally, Reza spoke.

'Okay Bob, so I understand your predicament, I really do. But tell me, what do you actually need the refinancing loan for?'

Bob Jefferson sat back in his chair.

'Well. There's a piece of land at the side of the store that we've found out we can buy. It's fairly sizeable and it would make a really good car park. I was thinking that if we had a car park, well then, people could stop and come into the store and look around to their hearts content. It would be just like the old days.'

'Okay,' said Reza, though in truth he wasn't quite sure.

On hearing the word, 'Okay', Bob Jefferson suddenly became quite positive.

'Hey, are you ready for some coffee now?' he asked.

'Yes,' Reza replied, 'that would be good.'

Bob Jefferson picked up the phone and pressed a button. There was a 'click' on the other end.

'Hi Suzy. I've got the guy from the bank here with me. Could you bring some coffee down for us, please honey?'

Someone on the end of the line said, 'Okay'. And with that, Bob Jefferson replaced the phone.

He looked across at Reza.

'That's my daughter Suzy, she works here too. Her mother died three years ago, so it's just me and her now.'

Reza nodded, he understood what was being said.

214

'Okay then Bob, I'm going to need three years accounts. And probably a stock list too. We'll need to know the amount of stock you hold, everything's looked upon as an asset you see, And then we'll have to look at your overheads, wages, utilities, and whatever rents you pay, obviously.

Bob Jefferson gave a low whistle.

'Err...the stock list may be a bit of a problem, Reza. You see, we have another three floors, two of them are jammed full of fabrics, and the top floor is where we do our own work, a bit of design and we have a small weaving loom up there too, plus another load of different fabrics.'

Reza took a deep breath, this could turn out to take a lot longer than he thought.

But Bob Jefferson just smiled.

'Hey, at least there's one problem you don't have to worry about. We don't have to pay any rent. We own the building lock, stock and barrel. Always have, my grandfather saw to that.'

And he laughed, as at that moment the office door swung open and Suzy Jefferson walked in holding a tray, on it was a jug of coffee, two cups, and some cream and sugar.

And at that moment, any thoughts about sets of accounts and a stock list went completely out of Reza Mastoor's head.

Suzy Jefferson was as American as 'Apple Pie'. At around five and a half foot tall, with strawberry blonde hair and a smile that made you feel that little bit 'happier'. She was the prettiest thing that Reza Mastoor had ever seen in his life. And for a moment he could only stare.

Suzy came into the office, bubbling with life and she started talking from the word go.

'Hey dad, here's your coffee. Oh hello, you must be the guy from the bank. Where should I put the coffee, I'll put it here on your desk. Do you want me to pour? Do you take cream and sugar Mister...?'

'Reza'...said Reza.

'Oh hello Mr Reeza, do you want cream or sugar, or do you want to help yourself?'

'No...I'm Reza,'

'Yes, I know...'

'No, really, I'm Reza, Reza Mastoor.'

Her eyes widened and she laughed.

'Oh, I see,' she replied. And with that, Suzy Jefferson put the tray of coffee down on the desk, and then she turned to him.

'Hi, I'm Suzy...Suzy Jefferson.' And she shook Reza's hand.

Bob Jefferson interrupted.

'Suzy works upstairs, she does some of the design work and also works with Vincent on the weaving loom.'

'Vincent?' Reza asked.

'Oh yes, Vincent,' Bob Jefferson replied, 'He's been with us for years, well he's officially retired but he comes in two or three afternoons a week, or whenever we need him really. He's sort of Italian, 'Vincent Pasalino'. His family were apparently weavers back in Italy at some point, anyway he comes in part time, he's like one of the family really".

'Yes,' said Suzy, 'over the years he's shown me how to use the loom. He's brilliant.'

'Yes,' Bob Jefferson continued, and if any special orders come in, Suzy can handle the work now, along with the design work. She's brilliant too.' And Bob Jefferson looked up at his daughter and smiled.

Suzy Jefferson just laughed at the compliment.

'Okay then. I'll leave you to it. I'm busy.' And with that, she almost skipped out of the room, which then left Reza a little bit flustered.

'She's like a whirlwind,' said her father.

'Yes, she certainly is,' Reza replied.

Reza collected the books and took them back to the bank to examine. It was a start.

The next day he returned. There were other areas of the business he needed to look at. But that was an excuse really. The real area of the business that he wanted to see was Miss Suzy Jefferson. And being there gave him a chance to speak to her. And they did, they became quite good friends. And towards the end of the week, and after a couple of more visits, Reza spoke to her about the amount of stock they had and really, that it all needed to be accounted for. This was going to be a rather long and tenuous task. And then Reza came up with an idea.

'I'll tell you what,' he'd said to her. 'I'm obviously tied up with the bank during the week, but if you want, I can come over on Saturday morning and over the weekend we can tackle the job then. I need the figures and this is probably the easiest way to do it'.

And so that's what happened.

He and Suzy got together on the Saturday, while her father ran the store downstairs. It was a mammoth task but they had a lot of fun doing it. At lunch time they sat on rolls of fabric and ate sandwiches and drank coffee and laughed, and then they continued and worked till late.

In the evening they sat on the rolls of fabric and ate pizza from the local pizzeria and they were still laughing. Something was going on, and Reza returned early the next day, a Sunday, and they continued. But during that day they formed some sort of bond, which blossomed into a romance. And Reza, he was smitten.

Another week passed by, and Reza had been at the store almost every day and had meticulously checked through just about everything. In the evenings he and Suzy would eat somewhere, or sometimes they would just sit in the closed store and talk until late, and then finally, to make love.

The following Sunday, Reza organized an informal meeting at the store. He needed to speak to them both.

The three of them sat there together in the first floor office as Reza broke the bad news.

'I have to now speak to you professionally, and not as a friend,' and at that point he glanced at Suzy. She just nodded back at him, she understood how all of this placed him.

Reza then turned to Bob Jefferson.

'The bank will not consider your loan. The figures simply don't add up.'

Bob Jefferson sat back in his chair and sighed. Another door, and his hopes, had just closed.

Reza continued. 'You see, your venture to buy the land next door is looked upon as just too risky and nothings guaranteed. Buying the land doesn't necessarily mean that you will increase your trade. I know there's no magic formula, but that's how the bank looks at it. And in truth, I personally have to advise you against the purchase. If the bank had offered you the loan, then they would have put a charge on this building as a guarantee, and if you failed to make the repayments, and looking at your present trading position you would definitely fail, then the bank would step in and take this building off you. You would lose everything, and I mean everything, and I'm speaking to you as a friend here, and not just somebody from the bank.'

Bob Jefferson just sat there. But then he slowly nodded his head'

'Thank you son,' he replied. 'I do understand your advice, and I appreciate it.' And with that, he turned to his daughter.

'Well love,' he said to her, 'it looks like we're stuck.'

Suzy looked at her dad, and there was a knowing silence between them.

But suddenly, Reza spoke.

'Actually, maybe not.'

Suzy and her father looked at him.

Reza moved in his chair.

'I've, well, sort of been looking at your business. And I have an idea, well the start of an idea, and it won't cost you a lot of money really'.

They both looked at him.

Reza took a deep breath.

'Okay. Well, times are changing. You've said that yourself, Bob. People are shopping in the Malls now, so that they can park and load up their cars easily. And the way I look at it is that the old traditional way of main street shopping is changing. Not just changing, it's already changed. Sure, you'll always have your local grocery store and deli, and the food outlets. But these are regular and minor purchases. Your business just isn't like that. So I've looked at the alternatives. The first of course, is moving into one of the Malls. But that is hellishly expensive. That's why basically, you only find the large chains of businesses in those Malls. They're the only ones who can afford it. Plus the fact, that to fund that move, you would have to sell this place, but then you would need warehousing for your stock, so that would be another cost, and I think that the one would outdo the other. And still no guarantees as to what trading figures you could actually achieve. So basically that's still a no-no.'

'So what's the alternative, Reza?' Bob asked.

'Okay, so we've got to move with the times, we do understand that. And for me, the future is on the internet and on the computer. The internet is going to be the new storefront, believe me. The internet is far reaching, and I really do think that it's going change the way that people purchase things in the future. And in time, I think that the internet will even have a lasting effect on the way people shop at the Malls.'

Bob Jefferson suddenly looked exasperated.

'Hey Reza, I don't know anything about the Internet, not a damn thing. I wouldn't even know where to start,'

But Suzy interrupted him.

'No dad, but I do. Listen, I understand the internet, and I understand internet shopping. I've even bought stuff online myself. I bought my last pair of trainers off the internet and they were mailed to me here, directly to the store. And they were a lot cheaper than the Mall. But I've never considered that we could sell our stuff on the internet too, but Reza's right, we need to listen to him, dad.'

Bob Jefferson looked at his daughter, and then at Reza.

'Okay then son, what's your plan, tell me how it works.'

'Well, look at it this way, Bob. At the moment you have one store on one road, one storefront and basically one window, just on this one road. With the internet, we set up what's known as a website. And your website would basically display everything that you have for sale in this shop. And on that website there are different web pages that you can click on to look at your different products. Really, it like a mail order catalogue, but with the internet, you browse through the different pages on your computer and pick out whatever you like. And then you buy it and it gets delivered by a courier service, directly to your home. The thing is, a website is really a shop front, and instead of having one shop front on one road, you would have millions of shop fronts, in fact, you would be in the home of every single person who owns a computer, and I'm not just talking about here in New York State, Bob, I'm talking about nationwide, I'm talking about the whole of America. That's how you could run this business.

'And how would I get paid?' Bob asked.

'That's the beauty of it,' Reza continued. 'You get paid by a debit or by credit card over the internet. And the money goes immediately into your bank account before you've even taken the fabric off the shelf.'

Bob Jefferson actually laughed.

'It all sounds too good to be true. But how much would all of this cost to set up?'

It was Reza's turn to laugh. He turned to Suzy.

'So you've got a computer?'

She smiled back at him.

'Of course I have, and its basically brand new. I only got it earlier this year, it's all up to date.'

Reza then turned back to her father.

'In that case, Bob, you're half way there.'

And then he looked at Suzy.

'Can you make us some coffee, love, I could really do with some right now. And then I'll tell you both my plan'.

Bob Jefferson smiled to himself. He'd heard the word 'love', and he'd also seen the closeness grow between them both. He knew what was going on.

Ten minutes later, Suzy arrived back in the office with the coffee.

Their conversation then continued.

'Okay,' said Reza, 'I've looked at several online retailers and they're all doing okay. In fact, we already have two or three of them who are with our bank, and I've checked them out and they're making good money. Actually, I've been onto a couple of them already and asked them about setting something up. And one company, and the owner who I've dealt with before, has put me onto a website designer friend of his who'll design an actual website for us and help us to set it all up. The owner of company also owes me a favour, and so his web designer will basically do it for free.'

And with that, Reza winked knowingly at Bob Jefferson.

Suzy looked at him, sort of strangely.

'Reza Mastoor, you've had this whole damn thing planned from the start.'

Reza just shrugged and then he laughed.

'The thing is, I've been looking closely at your business, and your actually 'cash rich'.

Bob Jefferson looked at him. 'I don't understand you?' he said.

'Well, it's like this. First of all, you own this place, lock stock and barrel. You also own your own home, I know you have a decent house over in Rochelle. And though it isn't part of the business, you own it outright and it is an asset. But more than that, I've been going through you're stock, you have an incredible amount of stock here over these five floors. Suzy and I have tried to catalogue as much of it as we could, but I've done a rough estimate according to market prices and you're currently holding well over three quarters of a million dollars worth of stock, and that's a very conservative estimate. In truth, it's probably a lot more.'

Suzy and her father looked at one another, they couldn't believe what they were hearing.

An amazed Bob Jefferson then said, 'Well, I suppose we've always carried a lot of stock. In this business you have too, you need the variety. It's always been one of our selling points.'

'So there you go then,' said Reza. 'You already have the goods, and you have Suzy to make up any of the different 'one off' designs, and you already have the weaving loom here to produce them. And you have the computer, and soon you'll have a website and will be ready to trade.'

Reza smiled, almost apologetically.

'And another thing. We need to re-brand you. I'm sorry folks, but 'Jefferson's Family Fabrics', along with 'established 1933' just won't do anymore. I have a new name for the company.

Bob Jefferson just laughed and threw his hands up in the air.

'Go on then son, it's your show. And damn the family history. What's the name?'

'Jefferson-Jefferson...Designer Fabrics'

Suzy Jefferson smiled,

'I like that Reza, I really do. It sounds so modern.'

And then she looked at him.

'How long have you had all this planned?'

He smiled back at her.

'Since the moment I met you,' he said.

221

Six months later they married. They bought a nice house over in New Haven. And twelve months after that their first son was born, Robert.

The transition within the business was a success from the word go really. And in the end the downstairs store was closed completely and was used for further storage. From there, they had to employ more staff once again, to help with the busy work load. All was well.

Two years later, a second son was born, Andrew. And it struck Reza that his sons had been born two years apart, just the same as him and his brother, Khalil.

But everything was a lie.

Reza had told Suzy, and her father, and everyone else for that matter, that he was Egyptian.

And along with that, he gave the story that his parents were both dead and that he'd been an only child who'd been brought up by an elderly uncle. Not a happy childhood, and a period of his life that he was reticent to talk about. And because of that, everyone respected his wishes and as a result it was never mentioned. Therefore, the likelihood of trips to Egypt to see any 'family' over there, would never happen.

But Reza did speak to his family, his family in Saudi Arabia. But only ever to his father, and usually around once a month. Strangely, he'd actually never spoken to his brother, Khalil, for years, in fact, never since Reza had gone off to America to study. In the early days he had asked his father about Khalil, but his father had told him that Khalil had other important plans. And so Reza learned very quickly, not to ask.

However, it hadn't ended there. Once Reza Mastoor was comfortably installed at the First Global Bank, Jabra Hasan al-Mastoor had his son open several different bank accounts for him under several different assumed names. Those accounts could be accessed from anywhere in the world via the online banking system. And from there it was quite simple to transfer money in and out of those accounts, money that could always be easily accessed, and money that would be utilized for a later date.

222

And then one day, Reza received a phone call from his father, which was very unusual, in fact, it was almost unknown. Reza always carried a second mobile phone, which was on a simple 'top up' contract to a name unknown and was therefore virtually untraceable. But in the past it had always been up to Reza to contact his father, And now this. Reza was quite surprised, it was something that he would have never expected. There was never any love, or even friendship, between him and his father. That had all been lost years ago after the death of Reza's mother. Because from that day on, he'd lost his father too, Jabra Hasan al-Mastoor had long ago become distant from his children. In fact, for Reza, even his brother had become distant, and it had become a cold, loveless existence for a child who had just lost his loving mother.

Jabra Hasan al-Mastoor may not have loved his children, however, he did demand absolute respect from them. And all of his conversations with Reza were simply nothing more than a series of orders and commands. And as always, at the end of every conversation that took place between them, his father would finish with the same words.

'Remember, it was the Americans who took your mother from us.'

And so with that in mind, Reza had never dared to tell his father that he was actually married an American, and also that he now had two sons by her.

But on that day, when Jabra Hasan al-Mastoor rang his son, he involved Reza into in a far deeper plot.

Khalil Hasan al-Mastoor, Reza's elder brother, had lived a rather more complex life.

His father, Jabra, had always communicated far more openly with his eldest son. And after the death of his wife, Jabra had taken it upon himself to pass on the teachings of Imam Abu Billah directly to Khalil, so that the boy would know the truth of everything through God's eyes. And that also included his deep hatred for America and the West.

Jabra Hasan al-Mastoor would repeatedly scorn America as the 'Great Satan'. A country run by the Jew and the country that

223

had funded those Jews who had invaded Palestine and stolen its lands. And had then dared to call itself the 'Nation of Israel'.

When Khalil was fifteen, Jabra introduced him to the Imam. And from there, Abu Billah took the young Khalil under his wing and he also took it upon himself to indoctrinate the boy.

By the time Khalil was sixteen and starting college, a greater part of his life had already been planned out. Khalil had a great aptitude for figures, it was a natural talent, and a talent that would be used. From college, Khalid was sent on to University in Riyadh. He would study Computer Science there. Computers were the future. And computers would be the tools that would help the likes of Imam Abu Billah succeed in a Holy War...a Jihad.

At University, Khalil Hasan al-Mastoor turned out to be a remarkable student. He lived for computers. And whilst in his third and final year there, he came up with an idea for a computer programme that would eventually prove his brilliance. It actually took him a few years to perfect, along with a certain amount of trials. But Khalil never gave up on his project, and in the end it worked. And finally, to make the programme work properly, all they needed was a conduit. And that conduit would turn out to be his younger brother, Reza.

Khalil had named his programme, the 'Tayir Saghir', which essentially meant 'little bird'.

And its concept was quite brilliant. If his computeer programme was downloaded into the right computer, and by that, it had to be a computer that belonged to someone who had access to the banking world, then his 'little bird' could go to work. And through that programme, it would have secret access to any account, in any bank, in any country, all over the world.

And it was a random access, there was no pattern to it at all. And like a little bird, flitting from tree to tree, and branch to branch, searching for food, so the 'Tayir Saghir', would do exactly the same.

It fed off random bank accounts from anywhere all over the world, but with one exception.

It would never touch Muslim-based money. And the beauty of the 'Tayir Saghir', that little bird, was that it would only steal one quarter of a percent of the amount of money in any one bank account. So if it flew into someone's bank account which contained a hundred dollars, it would just pinch twenty five cents, an amount hardly noticeable, and then it would fly away. Similarly, if it was lucky enough to come across a bank account with a million dollars, the little bird would fly away with two and a half thousand dollars. Which would be an annoyance, but it's hardly going to put a hole in the million, and in reality, a million dollar account was still somewhat of a rarity. But for the average man in the street with a bank balance of around a thousand dollars, the little bird would just pinch two and a half dollars. And for most people, what's a couple of bucks? It was hardly worth the trouble. And the same thing would happen all over the world, from America to Russia, and the whole of Europe in between. And the other cleverness was that the little bird never returned. It never went back to steal from the same bank account. As soon as the programme had accessed the money it closed the trail down immediately, and it never returned again to a possible trap. The secret was to not overdo things or let the programme run away with itself. That was the way to get noticed, and if it got noticed, then other computer experts, like Khalil, would be called in to find it and eventually close the 'little bird' down. Better to have a steady but constant flow of money coming in, daily and monthly, and year after year.

And so by this system of 'little thefts', there was never an outcry, and no ripples in the pond.

However, the 'little bird' had to have a nest. The money had to go somewhere, but it could not be sent directly back to Saudi Arabia, or any other Muslim country for that matter. Because if found out, it could lead to bigger things, suspicions would be aroused and the CIA, with all its clever meddling could get involved.

And that was how Reza Mastoor became implicated in it all.

His father had contacted Reza and told him to expect a CD through the post. And from there, Jabra Hasan al-Mastoor read out the written instructions that his eldest son, Khalil, had

225

dictated to him. Reza was to download the programme onto his own computer at work, and that would be it. The programme would simply become undetectable on Reza's computer, like a virus in hiding. But then it would go to work, and it would be untraceable. But this is where Reza's position in the bank came into play. All of the stolen money could only go into just one of his father's bogus bank accounts. And it would be up to Reza to split that money up into the other several false accounts. Because if that one single bank account suddenly became huge, it may flag up on the bank's own main computer which was set up to stop any money laundering operations. And so from there, whenever any of those several accounts contained a certain amount of funds, Reza would simply notify his father and then the money would be withdrawn, leaving the bank account reasonably empty. Once again, no fuss, and again, no ripples in the pond.

Reza Mastoor wasn't entirely happy about the situation. But what else could he do? These were his father's orders and he had to obey, he just had to.

But for Reza, there was another, bigger moral problem. And it was that Reza Mastoor absolutely loved and adored his wife and his children, of that there was no doubt. They were his life. He'd found the chance to find love and happiness again, and it was the first feeling of love that he'd experienced since losing his darling mother when he was just a child. It had always felt as though a part of his life had been missing, and now he had it back, and he had it all. Reza loved his life, and he loved the American way and the success that he and his American family had achieved.

And because of that, Reza Mastoor had promised himself one thing. If his father had ever demanded that he go back to Saudi Arabia, would he go? No he would not.

And so, Reza would continue to lead his double life. And everything was a lie.

It was a lie to his father in Saudi Arabia. It was a lie to his wife and his family, and it was even a lie to his closest friends at work. Nobody, and nobody at all, knew the truth about Reza

Hasan al-Mastoor. And no one person would ever really know the true Reza Mastoor.

Reza also had a somewhat unethical view in respect to his job as an investment manager.

And to keep himself in front of the rest, he would one way or another, try to glean information from any of his other work colleagues, and even his closest friends.

Ever the jovial character that he was, Reza would continually wander around the office talking to the other managers there, and his favourite trick was to lean over their shoulders and take a quick glance at their computer screens to see whatever that particular manager was dealing and trading in. He would eternally keep his eye open, and if someone disappeared to the toilet or for a coffee, Reza would quickly saunter over to their desk and take a quick look at whatever they'd been doing. And all of this kept him in the loop. It was quite easy really, and Reza had got it all off to a fine art. Doing this sort of thing was a shortcut to success, and it also stopped him having to do a lot of the tedious investment 'footwork'. He would leave that to the others. His other little trick was to have the odd lunch with the right people or even better, the 'drink after work'. It was surprising what people would tell you once they'd relaxed and had a glass or two of the 'good' wine that Reza always paid for. But that wasn't a problem, because Reza Mastoor had always made very good bonuses.

But where he did overstep the mark, was when he hacked into his two best friend's computers. His victims, were of course, Paul Maynard and Tony Becker. And it had been quite easy really. He'd simply stayed behind after work.

Reza knew that Paul and Tony were very good at their job, both of them were so totally committed, and clever. And so one evening when he was left alone in the office, Reza simply began to rummage through Paul's desk. He opened the various drawers to look for any clues as to a password, a password that would give him access to Paul Maynard's computer. He was looking for anything, names, or places, or anything at all significant. But he couldn't find anything, not even an odd scrap of paper. And then by a stroke of luck, he picked up one of Paul Maynard's old diaries, just an old and slightly dog-eared book with a list of past appointments in it that Paul had attended. And then he considered it strange, why would he keep this book. Reza casually flipped through the pages, there was nothing but lists of names and dates and times, nothing more. Until Reza got to the last page, and there written on the inside flap of the book, there was a number...78349287. It could have been a phone number, but somehow the digits didn't fit. So Reza leant down and turned on Paul's computer. It immediately flickered into life and the same screen that was on every other bank employee's computer came up. It asked for a name and password. So he typed in 'Paul Maynard' and then he entered the number as the password. And suddenly, 'Bingo'. Paul Maynard's computer burst into life.

Reza had immediately turned off the computer and he wrote down the numbers. Then he went around to his own computer and turned it on, and on his own screen he then entered Paul's name and the same password. And suddenly, once again he was given access to Paul Maynard's account. Reza just couldn't believe that it could be so simple.

The following week he did the same thing to get into Tony Becker's working account. Again in the empty office, and after work, Reza had gone through Tony's desk, but this time he found nothing. There were odd bits of names written down, but they all seemed to relate to racehorses. Reza already knew that Tony was an avid gambler. But he turned Tony's computer on anyway, and then he typed 'Tony Becker' in on the screen and tried several of those various names as passwords to see if any of them would work. But no, nothing at all.

Reza sat there for a few minutes, he was trying to think of something. And then, rather casually, he typed 'gamble', but no, that didn't work either. Then he tried 'Roulette', but no. And then 'Dice' and then 'Cards' and nothing came up, and then, he just typed in 'Blackjack', and suddenly, he was in. It had been 'Blackjack', and Reza almost laughed at Tony Becker's simplicity. Reza never even checked it with his own computer, he knew he could now access Tony Becker's account. And from there, Reza's life became a whole lot easier. He would simply log into their accounts and follow their trades.

But on that Friday night, as Reza made his way home after leaving Paul, Tony and Adam at the 'Trinity' Restaurant, Reza began to wonder just what was going on ? Adam Tyler had asked them about 'Woodvale Investments', and Tony Becker had categorically stated that he'd never heard of them. But that was a lie and Reza knew it, because Reza had logged onto Tony's computer and he'd watched with some fascination, as Tony had bought huge amounts of Cantor Fitzsimons stock, principally for Woodvale Investments. In fact, Reza had jumped on the bandwagon himself, as he realized that his friend was obviously onto something good. And of course, Reza also had to deny any knowledge of Woodvale, since it might have aroused Tony Becker's suspicions.

So as he stood at the station awaiting the train that would finally get him home, Reza Mastoor realized that he would have to keep his eye on Tony Becker. Something was definitely amiss.

And for Reza, somewhere in all of this, there could be a profit.

Chapter 9

The following Monday morning, and everyone had returned to work after the weekend, and the world of finance began to turn once more in an effort to shape our lives.

It was back to business as usual.

And at First Global, when lunchtime finally came around, it had been agreed that Adam, Paul, and Tony and Reza would meet up and go down to the Esplanade and find somewhere different for lunch. It would be nice to have a change.

But at the last minute, Tony Becker shied off, with the excuse that he was quite busy at the moment and that he would have to give it a miss.

Reza Mastoor took note. And when they arrived back from lunch, Tony Becker was still there at his desk, working intently in front of his computer screen.

That evening, Reza stayed late. And once the office was quieter, he switched off his own computer, and then gave it a couple of minutes before switching it back on again and logging on as Tony Becker. Once again the computer opened up Tony Becker's working account.

From there he clicked on 'search' and then typed in 'Woodvale Investments'...and nothing.

So he typed in just 'Woodvale', and again nothing. From there he typed in several different derivates of the name, Woodvale, but again nothing. The office was almost empty now, so Reza went off to get himself a coffee, just to waste some time. When he got back, everyone had left. And so Reza went over to Tony Becker's desk and turned on Tony's own computer and logged in. He then sat there for the next half an hour, and nowhere on Tony Becker's own computer, was there anything at all referring to Woodvale or Woodvale Investments.

Tony Becker had wiped his computer clean.

Reza sat there for a moment. 'What the hell was going on?'

The next day, the four of them did meet up for lunch. Once again they went down to the Esplanade, there were several bars and restaurants down there that were worth checking out.

After half an hour of the usual conversations, and the food and the drinks had arrived, Reza suddenly brought up the subject.

'Hey Adam. Did you ever get any joy on that company that you were looking for, what was it called again, 'Watford', something or other?'

Adam stopped eating for a second.

'Woodvale,' he said through a mouthful of burger, 'Woodvale Investments.'

'Oh right,' Reza replied, 'Woodvale.' Did anything turn up?'

Adam shook his head as he picked up his burger again.

'No, nothing, I think Norman Roth's on with it.'

Paul looked up at them both, 'Strange it can't be found?' he added.

Adam Tyler just shrugged, he didn't know anything more. He'd not spoken to Norman Roth since their previous meeting.

But out of the corner of his eye, Reza had been watching Tony Becker. And all the way through their conversation about Woodvale, Tony Becker had just continued to stare down at his food in silence and continue to eat. And Reza smiled to himself, it was proof enough.

Coincidence is a funny old thing. Do coincidences happen for a reason, or is it purely a matter of good luck versus bad luck? Who knows..?

On the Wednesday morning, Adam Tyler overslept. For some reason he'd either forgotten to set his alarm, or the battery wasn't working properly, or whatever. But the first thing he knew about it was when his mobile phone started to ring and it was Paul Maynard.

'Hey buddy,' he asked, 'where are you? I'm at Katz's getting some breakfast.'

Adam immediately looked at his wristwatch, and then he groaned.

'Oh hell...is that the time? Oh Jesus, Paul, I've overslept,' and then he had to make an immediate decision.

'Listen Paul, you go in, I'll have to have a quick shower and get ready and then I'll grab a cab, okay.'

'Okay,' said Paul, 'I'll probably see you at lunch,'

'Yeah, okay,' Adam replied, 'I'll catch you later.' And with that he clicked off his phone and dashed off to the bathroom.

Twenty minutes later, and he was showered and changed, and he rang for a cab as he poured himself a cup of coffee.

It is estimated that there are, give or take, around 14,000 taxis drivers in New York.

Yellow Taxicab drivers, that is. And obviously, not all of them operate at the same time.

Some drivers will work only through the day, and others only work in the evenings and then through the night, and some will do a different shift pattern altogether. Whatever the hours, and whatever hours suited the driver.

And it was on that particular Wednesday morning, when a 'coincidence' suddenly came into play.

Adam had just begun to drink his coffee when he heard a car sound its horn. The sound came from the front of the apartments and Adam realized that it must be his taxi. He took one last swig of his coffee, and then he grabbed his bag and left to go to work. He skipped down the apartment steps, he couldn't be bothered to wait for the lift, and then he made his way outside to where a yellow taxicab was parked up, ready and waiting for him.

Adam walked quickly over to the cab and jumped into the back seat.

'Hi buddy,' he said to the driver, 'could you take me to the World Trade Center, please, the North Tower.'

But the taxi driver just looked through his mirror grinned at him.

'Hey there buddy,' he said, 'and how are you doing?' And with that, he started the car.

Adam thought that the driver was just being friendly, in a New York sort of way.

'Yeah, yeah, I'm okay,' he replied.

The driver then shook his head and laughed.

'Yeah, you are now.' And with that, they set off.

Adam sat in the back of the taxicab, and he considered the driver's comment a bit strange. What did he mean by 'Yeah...you are now?' Was he missing something here in the conversation?

Adam smiled somewhat quizzically, but he had to ask, and pleasantly.

'What do you mean...'I am now'?

The taxi driver just laughed.

'Hey, the last time I saw you, man, you were smashed. Your friend was bad, but you, you were completely out of it,' and he laughed again out loud, 'Man, you were totally smashed.'

Adam sat there. He didn't understand.

'So, you've brought me home before?' he asked.

'Yeah, you and your friend.'

For the life of him, Adam couldn't remember what the driver was telling him, or even remember coming home so drunk. Paul had never mentioned anything about it. In fact, he and Paul had never actually ever been that drunk.

Adam grinned at the driver, a bit naively.

'Was that a while ago? He was trying to remember his nights out over the past several months. Maybe he'd forgotten one of his nights out, but even so, he couldn't remember being that drunk, or could he?

'No,' said the taxi driver, 'it was only the other week, don't you remember?'

Adam continued to grin, and he shook his head. But he still didn't understand.

'No, I don't remember a bloody thing,' he replied.

The taxi driver laughed, 'Yeah, it was about two or three weeks ago.'

Adam sat there trying to remember what had happened just 'two or three weeks ago'.

'What night was it, can you remember?'

The driver tapped his steering wheel as he thought about it.

'Hey, yeah, it would be a Friday night. Yeah, it was a Friday, it was my last night. I don't work weekends, I have my kids. I'm divorced'.

And suddenly, out of the blue, Adam remembered.

It was the night that he'd got drunk with Tony Becker. But not just drunk, he was 'out of his head drunk'. And apparently he'd staggered off somewhere and left Tony in some bar.

But who the hell was the man who'd brought him home then?

Again, Adam didn't understand.

'And you say somebody brought me home?'

'Yeah,' said the driver, 'Strange looking guy, sort of tall, ginger hair and a stupid moustache.'

Adam just sat there. He couldn't believe it. It had to be Tony Becker.

And then he asked, 'Did he just drop me off?'

'No,' said the driver,' he carried you inside. He paid me up and then he helped you up to your apartment. I sat there and watched you go inside, to make sure you were both okay. Don't you remember anything, man?'

But Adam just gave a false laugh.

'No,' he replied, 'I don't remember a damn thing.'

The traffic that morning was quite heavy, and the taxi got stuck in a jam much of the way there. But as he sat in the back of the cab, Adam tried to mull things over in his head.

If Tony Becker had brought him back home to his apartment, why had he lied? And why had he said that Adam had 'just disappeared', when clearly he hadn't. Again, he didn't understand. And he tried to work the dates back to that particular day. What had happened?

He, Tony and Reza had gone out for a drink, yes, but Paul wasn't there, he'd been ill. And then Reza had left them to it and they'd gotten really drunk. And then Adam had been rough for two days. He was still not fully recovered when he'd gone into work on the Monday. Yes, it was the week of the Cantor Fitzsimons merger and he'd struggled to finish off his reports. He'd had to work late at home the Monday night to finish those reports and get them printed off. Yes, printed off, along with the rest of his reports, all those reports, all there in his apartment....

And then suddenly, Adam Tyler had the strangest of thoughts. It was almost embarrassing really, almost impossible. But it was possible.

A scenario suddenly went through Adams mind. Tony Becker had taken Adam home, and somehow he must have got Adam back into the apartment. But that wouldn't be hard, Adam's keys would be in his pocket. And Tony Becker must have been in Adam's apartment while Adam was unconscious on the settee. Adam's mind was racing now. Would Tony have gone though Adam's papers? But why would he, and what good would it do him?

Tony Becker didn't have anything to do with Woodvale Investments.

And then, and suddenly, it all happened. He remembered. Adam remembered, he finally, finally remembered where he'd seen the name 'Woodvale Investments. Oh dear god, no.

He'd seen the name 'Woodvale Investments' on Tony Becker's computer, it had been on the Monday morning when he's gone to ask Tony about what had happened on their 'Friday night out'.

And then Adam remembered last Friday, when the four of them had gone for a drink after work, and he'd asked if any of them knew anything about 'Woodvale Investments'.

And Tony Becker had said that ' he'd never heard of them.'

But Becker had lied. Tony Becker dealt with Woodvale Investments, he knew all about them.

'Oh my god, no....but oh my god, yes.' It was Becker.

It was Becker who'd been the insider trader, and it was Becker who had nearly floored the merger at Cantor Fitzsimons.

Yes Becker it was you. Damn you.

They finally arrived at the North Tower and Adam paid the driver, and also with a decent tip, and then thanked him, for everything really.

The driver smiled.

"Hey, take care buddy,' he said, and then he drove away.

Fourteen thousand taxi drivers in New York City. A coincidence, indeed it was.

Adam quickly made his way upstairs and took the elevator up to the 92nd floor. He went straight into his office and threw his bag onto his desk and immediately picked up the phone and rang Norman Roth's office.

Roth's secretary answered.

'I need to see Mr Roth, straightaway,' he almost demanded.

The secretary was a bit taken aback by his tone, but she recognized Adam's voice.

'Is that you Mr Tyler?'

'Err, yes, yes it is, and I need to speak to Mr Roth in his office, please.'

'Mr Roth is out of office, Mr Tyler. I'm sorry, but he won't be back in until this afternoon.'

'What time can I see him?' Adam asked.

Norman Roth's secretary checked her boss's appointments.

'He'll be free at three o' clock, Mr Tyler. Would that be okay?'

At three o' clock, Adam Tyler walked into Norman Roth's office and sat himself down.

Norman Roth looked at him.

'What's up?' he asked. There had been no particular reason for them to meet up, any minor business was usually done over the phone. And the appointment itself had given no explanation as to what this was all about. In fact, Norman Roth was slightly worried that Adam could be about to resign. Rising talent was always in demand and was also regularly head hunted. But no, not today.

'I know who it is.' Adam almost blurted it out. 'I know who it is, the insider trader and the link to Woodvale Investments. I'm almost sure I know who it is.'

Norman Roth just stared at him.

'Who is it, Adam?' he asked slowly.

'It's one of the Investment managers upstairs. It's Tony Becker.'

Roth looked at Adam for a moment.

'I know him,' he replied.

'So do I,' said Adam, 'We're supposed to be friends.'

'So go on. Roth asked, 'What do you know?'

And with that, Adam Tyler told him everything, the whole story.

An hour later, they were both wiser men.

When Adam had told Norman Roth how drunk he'd been on that Friday night and that it had taken him two days to fully recover, Roth had hinted at the possibility that Adam could have been drugged. And that explained a lot to Adam, because he had no recollection at all about that night, except what Tony Becker had told him. And that was obviously a lie, it all was.

'Okay,' said Norman Roth. 'This is how we'll handle it. I'll speak to Tony Becker tomorrow, I'll have him in here and I'll speak to him and see what he has to say. I'm going to have to get clever with this one. But for now, I want to keep you out of this Adam, totally. I don't want any animosity and I don't want you to get involved, at all. Do you understand?'

Adam agreed, though at that moment he felt like going upstairs and dragging Tony Becker across the office floor.

'No,' said Roth. 'I'll have to speak to him first, and we'll take it from there, slowly but surely. You see, we have no real evidence other than that of a taxi driver and some unnamed bank account in the Cayman Islands that we can't trace. And I can't link them together, it would just look ridiculous.'

'But I saw 'Woodvale Investments' on his computer,' Adam exclaimed angrily.

'Yes, I know you did, Adam. But that would just be your word against his. And also, that would immediately implicate you. No, I'll play it another way. I'll give him a nudge so that he knows that we're onto him, and hopefully he may panic and slip up. But nothing's going to happen overnight. And actually, it's better if you just stand back and observe, just keep your eyes and ears open. Something just may come up'.

The next day, Thursday, Norman Roth rang Tony Becker and asked him to nip down to his office.

'What's it about?' asked Becker.

'Oh, I just need a quick chat, that's all.'

'Well, I am quite busy at the moment,' said Becker.

'It won't take long,' Norman Roth replied, 'I'll just pass you over to my secretary.'

By the time Tony Becker put the phone down, his mind was beginning to race.

Lunchtime didn't happen.

Adam, for one, wasn't in the mood for sitting at any table with Becker. He still didn't know if he could contain his temper and knew that he would be in danger of saying something. It would only take one word. And he'd promised Norman Roth.

So in the morning on their way to work, Adam, somewhat casually, told Paul that he wouldn't be there for lunch, and that for the next week or so he may not be around so much because he had a very heavy workload upstairs at Cantor Fitzsimons. Paul completely understood, he knew Adam had a lot on at the moment.

So come lunchtime, Reza left his desk and wandered over to Tony Becker.

'Hey buddy, you up for lunch?' he asked.

But Tony Becker had not long ago had the phone call from Norman Roth's office and now he had other things on his mind.

'Err...not today Reza,' he said, 'I'm really quite busy, I've got a hell of a lot on today.'

Which Reza found quite strange, because Reza had been coming in to work early ever morning for the last few days, and before anyone else was in the office, and he'd been logging onto Tony Becker's computer every morning, as he had done again this morning, and Tony Becker hadn't seemed to be any busier than usual.

So Reza ambled back to Paul Maynard's desk.

'Hey Paul, you and Adam ready for some lunch?'

Paul Maynard looked up over the top of his computer screen.

'Adam's not doing lunch today. He's busy.'

'Oh bloody hell,' Reza replied, 'Tony's not coming either. He's got a lot on too.'

And with that, Reza looked at Paul.

'Okay buddy, so it's just me and you then.'

But Paul just opened the top drawer of his desk and took out a brown paper parcel, which he waved in front of Reza.

238

'Pastrami salad sandwich,' he said, 'from Katz's'. And then he grinned.

Reza just shook his head and walked out of the office. He would have to eat alone. Oh well, there was a McDonalds just down the road.

Paul Maynard smiled as he watched him go. He wasn't in the mood for Reza Mastoor today, or on any other day really.

At two o' clock, Tony Becker went downstairs to Norman Roth's office. He sat waiting in the reception area for several minutes, before Mr Roth's secretary finally showed him through. As he entered the office, Norman Roth was speaking to someone on the telephone. He turned to Tony Becker and gestured to him to take a seat. And then he continued with his phone call.

It was all a power play, all a ploy to make Tony Becker feel slightly uncomfortable. And to a point, it was working.

Tony Becker sat down and gave a slightly agitated cough. He would have to keep his wits about him. He had an idea what this was about, but he'd already given it some thought.

Eventually, Norman Roth finished his phone call and then he turned to Tony.

'Ah Tony,' he said, 'thank you for coming down, I know you must be busy.'

And Norman Roth let those words hang there, as though he required a reply, and he waited for one.

'Yes I am,' Tony replied, 'I've got a lot on at the moment.'

'Oh good,' said Roth, and that was all he said, as he then leant over and began to glance through some random papers.

Tony Becker found all this slightly frustrating.

'What do you actually want to see me for, Mr Roth?' he asked, 'you never said.'

Norman Roth glanced over at him. It was rather a brusque question. He put the papers down.

'Okay,' he said. 'It appears that we have a security issue here within the bank, Tony.'

Tony Becker said nothing.

'Yes, apparently we've had a case of illegal insider trading here at the bank, which has caused a confidentiality issue within the bank and with one of its business clients. It's been a bit of a problem really, and highly embarrassing. And the 'powers that be' seem to think that the source of the problem comes from upstairs, from the investment division. In fact, they assure me it is.'

This threw Tony Becker somewhat. Who were the 'powers that be', and what could they possibly know. Tony knew that he'd covered all his tracks.

'How do they know that?' he asked.

'Oh well, it seems that everything's sort of 'monitored',' said Norman Roth casually. 'It's a security thing apparently.'

'I wasn't aware of that,' said Becker.

Norman Roth just smiled at him.

'No, neither did I, Tony. We live and learn.'

'So what's this got to do with me?' Becker asked.

'I just wondered if you'd noticed anything, or heard or seen anything that may raise any suspicions.'

'Why would I?'

'Well, there could be possible links.'

'What links? What do you mean?'

'Woodvale Investments.' Norman Roth replied.

And there it was, the words that Tony Becker had been waiting for. And now his defence plan could come into action. He was ready.'

Who are 'Woodvale Investments?'

'You tell me. Tony?'

'I don't understand.'

Apparently, it seems that you have traded with Woodvale Investments in the past, in fact, you may still be trading with them, but we need to know all about them, we need to know who they are. Because Woodvale Investments are behind all of this.'

Tony Becker looked at Roth. Was this a bluff, or did they really know what had been going on with Woodvale. But how could they? He was slightly unsure now.

'I've never heard of any 'Woodvale Investments.'

'Apparently you have.'

Tony Becker was slightly annoyed with that allegation, it insinuated that he was lying, and he was also becoming a little agitated.

'So I'm lying then?' he said.

Tony wasn't happy with the direction this interview was now taking. And so he decided that it was time for him to take a stance.

Norman Roth just shrugged. But Tony Becker continued.

'I've just told you that I don't know anything about any 'Woodvale Investments'.

'Apparently you do.'

Tony Becker was becoming somewhat exasperated with all this. He decided to call Norman Roth's bluff. It was a gamble, but gambling was nothing new to Tony Becker, was it?

'Show me then,' he said, 'show me 'where' and 'when' I've supposedly dealt with this firm. Where's your evidence?'

'Well, I'll have to access the files of course,' Roth replied, 'But I'm assured that they have all confirmation we need.'

'Confirmation for what?'

Norman Roth leant forward on his desk, it was almost a threat.

'To find out who exactly is behind all of this, Tony.'

And there it was. Yes, that was a threat. And Tony Becker suddenly lost his temper.

'I'm not having this,' he said abruptly. 'This is some kind of witch-hunt. You've dragged me in here and you start accusing me of illegal activities and some kind of insider dealings. I've been with this bank for nearly ten years now and I've never put a foot wrong.I've worked damn hard, and now you're accusing me of this?'

Norman Roth looked at Becker, and he knew he'd pressed the right button.

'Tony, Tony...calm down. We're not accusing you of anything.'

But Tony Becker angrily tapped the top of Norman Roth's expensive desk.

'Oh yeah. So why me?' he asked. 'Why me then? I don't see you interviewing anybody else over this, just because you think you can connect me to this 'Woodvale'.

But Norman Roth just smiled.

'It's alphabetical order,' he said.

Tony Becker just stared back at him.

'What?

'Alphabetical order, Tony'

'What are you on about? Becker asked again.

Norman Roth just continued to smile.

'It's simple. We have no A's upstairs, Tony. You're B...B for Becker.'

And that simple statement stopped Tony Becker's argument about the injustice of it all. He just sat there, feeling very frustrated.

'We shall of course be interviewing everyone else, in their turn,' said Norman Roth, 'and there are no accusations here, Tony. We haven't accused you of anything. We're just looking for any information and we're following up any link we can find into 'Woodvale, and obviously your name must have come up, that's all.'

'I've already told you...'

But Norman Roth interrupted him.

'Don't worry about it Tony, we'll sort it all out, really we will.'

And suddenly, Roth took a different line. He would now become friendly, and personal, and become Tony's confidant. But he was about stick the knife in, just to let Tony Becker know exactly 'what' he knew.

'It's just a process we have to go through, Tony,' he said pleasantly, 'I know it's difficult, and between you and me, I wish somebody else could do it, but unfortunately it's been handed down to me. But really, I would like you to keep an eye open for me, just in case you come across anything at all. And if you do, if you see or hear anything at all that raises your suspicions, please come and tell me. It will all be treated in total confidence, obviously'.

It was all becoming chummy now. And Tony Becker just sat there and nodded, and he began to breathe a little more easily.

Once again, Norman Roth leant forwards, now in a sort of conspiratorial way.

'To tell you the truth, Tony,' he said, 'we do have a link. And it's something that could blow all of this wide open.'

'What's that?' Becker suddenly asked.

And Norman Roth slid out the 'knife'.

'We've found an account, linked directly to 'Woodvale'. It's in the Cayman Islands. It's with the Fidelity Trust National Bank over there. We even have the account number. But at the moment

242

we can't find the name that's behind it all. But we will. Believe me.'

Tony Becker went rigid in his seat. This was his darkest secret. How the hell had they found out about it? But he had to try to remain calm, he felt the panic well up inside him but he couldn't let it show.

'I thought the Cayman's banking system was pretty unassailable,' he said.

'Yeah, it pretty well is. But there's ways and means.'

'Is there?' Becker asked. This was the first he knew about it.

'Oh yes. First Global has a lot of clout. We'll get the law involved, and then possibly a politician or two, someone at the top that'll lean on them. After all, banks talk to banks, we have to, and anyway, Fidelity Trust won't want the publicity. I mean, we all know that they handle illegal money. They just don't want to be seen to be handling it. It may take a while, but we'll get there. And basically, all of this is actually money laundering, and that is illegal. And whoever's behind it will be going to prison for a long, long time.'

There was a moment's silence, as those words just hung in the air.

And then Norman Roth looked at his watch.

'Hell, is that the time. Okay, Tony, our chats over, I've got another appointment.'

Tony Becker sat there, he was still hearing the word 'prison'.

'Tony...' Roth said again.

'Oh yes, right,' Tony Becker suddenly replied. And with that, he stood up.

Norman Roth leant over his desk and then firmly shook Tony Becker's hand.

'Thanks Tony,' he said, in his friendliest manner.

And so, with that, Tony went to leave the office.

But just as he was walking through the door, Norman Roth called after him.

'Oh, Tony'

Tony Becker suddenly stopped, and he turned around.

Norman Roth just smiled back at him.

'Keep in touch,' he said.

Tony Becker almost sprinted back to his desk. He had to think. He really did have to think. These bastards were on to him. And how 'on earth' had they found out about his Cayman Island account at Fidelity Trust. He couldn't believe it. But now he had to get his head together, because if they found out that it was his account and that he was the person behind 'Woodvale', they would come looking for him and then he was going to end up behind bars. Anyone involved in financial fraud and money laundering was always dealt a very hard prison sentence. He had to think up a plan, he had to. Maybe it was time for him to run.

Norman Roth had watched, as Tony Becker walked out of his office.

He'd planted the seeds of fear. There were never any 'powers that be' and there was no 'secret monitoring' either. That was all down to Roth himself, and it was all a bluff. But Roth knew that Becker was implicated. He trusted Adam Tyler's explanation explicitly. And Adam Tyler was right. Tony Becker's body language had said it all really. Tony Becker had been very uncomfortable, especially when Roth had come up with the hidden Cayman Island account. Yes, Tony Becker's face had said it all.

Norman Roth picked up his phone and he made a call.

On the Saturday, when the bank was closed, he would have his own team of specialists come in and technically take Tony Becker's computer apart. If there was anything on it that was even vaguely associated to 'Woodvale Investments', then they would find it.

The next day, Friday, Becker was the first into the office, even before Reza Mastoor.

He'd been awake for most of the night, but finally, he'd come to a decision.

At nine o' clock, he went into action.

Tony Becker would spend the whole of the day seemingly buying stock. He utilised, and borrowed, and this time actually stole from companies and from people's trusted bank accounts, in fact he stole money from every source that he had currently available. And every single pilfered dollar that he stole was immediately transferred to Woodvale Investments.

There would be no lunch that day for Tony Becker, obviously. And when he saw Reza Mastoor meandering over in his direction, he immediately closed down his computer's screen. Reza asked him about lunch but Tony had quickly dismissed him, rather rudely actually.

But whilst doing so, Reza had practised his old trick of glancing over Tony's shoulder to see what he was doing. But the screen was switched off, and that was a first, in the past Tony had never thought to turn off his screen. And that made Reza wonder. Reza again lunched alone. It seemed that Paul Maynard had gone back to a life of pastrami salad.

When Reza returned from lunch, Tony Becker was still working. So Reza sat himself down at his own desk and quietly logged onto Tony Becker's computer. He looked on in amazement. He couldn't believe the activity. What the hell was going on?

At just after three o' clock in the afternoon, Tony Becker stopped stealing other people's money. He stopped stealing, he stopped trading, he stopped everything. And then he transferred nearly eight million dollars over to his account at the Fidelity Trust National Bank in the Cayman Islands. From there, he wiped his computer's hard drive completely clean.

He had the software to do it. And after fifteen minutes, that software had erased absolutely everything. There wasn't even a full stop left on there. It was as though everything had simply vanished into thin air.

With that done, Tony Becker put a few personal items into his briefcase and then he stood up to leave. It was four o'clock, and he walked quickly out of the office.

He would never return, ever.

Reza Mastoor watched Tony Becker go, and for once he didn't make a comment. He just watched Tony walk out of the door.

Reza gave it about ten minutes, just to make sure that Tony wasn't coming back, and then he logged onto Tony's computer.

245

There was nothing. Nothing at all. All that came up was a completely blank white screen. Reza tried to manoeuvre the mouse to try to navigate to a site. But there wasn't even a mouse on there, not even a pointer. He pressed several different buttons and again, there was absolutely nothing. It was dead.

Reza sat back in amazement. What was going on? And what on earth was Tony Becker up to?

At that moment, Tony Becker was actually sitting in the back of the taxi that was taking him back to his apartment. The taxi would then wait for him as Tony went up to his apartment and picked up the two suitcases that he'd packed the night before. And then from there, the driver would take him on to J F Kennedy International Airport. Tony Becker was booked on the nine o' clock flight to the Cayman Islands. It was booked one way only.

At six o'clock that same evening, Adam sat back in his office chair. He rubbed his eyes. It had been a hard day. It had been a hard week. He was in the middle of things with Cantor Fitzsimons, the budget was going through the roof and it was beginning to spiral out of control, and Adam knew that it was up to him to try to put a lid on things. After all, he was supposed to be running their finances. And then there was Katy 'bloody' Ritsos. All they ever seemed to do was argue over the figures and it was beginning to wear Adam down. And what was even worse was that he had the nagging feeling that Miss Katy Ritsos could have actually been right when she'd told him that 'these people will run away with your cheque book.' Because in all honesty, they were.

And all the upset over everything with Tony Becker hadn't helped either. Adam's brain felt like it was in two places. Two very hard places.

He skipped through some papers that he'd just printed off. They were for Katy Ritsos to inspect and sign. So no doubt he would have to go through another series of painful arguments with her before he could get her to put pen to paper.

He sat back. He needed a drink and some company, and he suddenly wondered what Joanne was up to. He'd not seen her for most of the week. And then he began to think about her. Good old Joanne, she was a bit special to him, still. And a thought then struck him, he could go upstairs and see if she wanted to go for a drink, he could do with some female company and a bit of fun. And then from nowhere, his mind suddenly switched back to Dominique Cassens and their time together in Barcelona. And then suddenly, he was annoyed with himself. Why couldn't he get this woman out of his damn mind? And so he made a quick and possibly rash decision, It was more in temper really. He slid the papers into a large envelope, grabbed his jacket and then walked out of his office. He was going to go upstairs and take Joanne out. And if they got drunk and ended up in bed, so what. Maybe it's what he should have done all along, after all, he wasn't blind.

So he skipped up the stairs, and while he was up there he would drop the papers off on Katy Ritsos's desk.

He walked down the corridor, there in front of him was Joanne's office at 106. He took a deep breath. Was he going to do this? Yes...yes he was, and what the hell.

Full of expectation, he knocked on the door and opened it. He always did, he and Joanne had no secrets, really. But when he opened the door, the office was in darkness. It was empty, and his heart sunk. 'Oh damn' he thought to himself. Joanne had gone home, or wherever. He stood there for a moment, feeling disappointed. Maybe he should have rung her first, and then again, maybe he should have rung her earlier. And then he toyed with the idea of ringing her anyway, and suddenly his spirits lifted slightly. He could go and get a quick drink somewhere and then he'd ring her and see where she was. And then the thought struck him that if she was back at her apartment he might get an invite, and that made him smile. He knew that she still felt something for him, she was always touching his arm and putting her arm around him, all of those little touchy things that lets a man know when a woman's comfortable with him. And whenever he arrived, her eyes always seemed to light up. Okay then, so that was the plan.

He would just drop the papers off in Katy Ritsos's office and be on his merry way.

Dear god, he needed a drink.

He made his way to 109, and without really thinking, he just opened the door and walked straight in there. And then he stopped. The office was in partial darkness, dimly lit, there were only a couple of lights on over the desk. And sitting there at the desk and on her own, was Miss Katy Ritsos.

And Miss Katy Ritsos was crying, and she was drinking.

Adam just stood there as Katy Ritsos looked up at him. And then she recognised that it was Adam and she rubbed her eyes.

'Oh Christ,' she said to him, 'you're the last person I need to see.'

She was sitting there with a glass in front of her, which was half filled with some pale brown liquor. And at the side of it was an opened bottle of spirit with some foreign label on it.

'Are you okay?' Adam asked her. A rather stupid question really, because she obviously was not.

'Yeah, yeah, I'm okay. Don't worry about it,' she quickly replied.

He stood there for a moment.

'It's just that I've brought you some papers, they'll need checking and signing,' and then he felt like a bit of a callous fool. There was obviously something wrong with her, and here was he talking 'shop'.

Katy Ritsos just shrugged.

'Put them on the desk, I'll sort them out.' And then she took another sip from her glass.

Adam did as he was bid, and he was just about to leave, but something inside made him stop. He couldn't just leave her like this. And anyway, this could have something to do with her work, and somehow Adam felt vaguely responsible.

'Is there anything I can do, Katy?' he asked.

But she just shook her head, and then she wiped away a slow tear. She didn't say anything.

Adam took a deep breath, and he thought that he'd better go. And he turned to the door to leave. But then he suddenly stopped and turned around again.

'You got another glass?' he said to her.

Katy Ritsos looked up at him.

'Christ,' she said, 'I'm not going to get rid of you am I?'

248

And then she sighed and opened a drawer and took out a glass. She slid it across the desk towards him.

'Here,' she said to him, 'knock yourself out,' and with that, she pushed the bottle in the same direction.

Adam sat down on the chair opposite her and he took the bottle and poured some of the liquor into his glass.'

'What is this stuff?' he asked her.

'Greek Brandy.'

'Is it any good?'

'Taste it,' she replied.

He did, and it tasted alright.

'Hey, this is good,' he said to her.

'It's the best, it's Metaxa for god's sake. It's Greek brandy. Of course it's good.'

Adam considered himself told. He certainly wasn't going to argue.

So they sat there in silence, just savouring their drinks, not a word said.

Katy Ritsos swallowed her drink and then reached for the bottle and poured herself another shot. She looked across at Adam.

'Top up?'

He slid his glass back towards her and she did the honours, and it sort of broke the moment.

He sat back in his chair and looked at her.

'So come on then, what's wrong?'

She looked at him.

'You don't have to do this, believe me,' she said to him.

'I know that,' he replied. 'So what's wrong?'

She shook her head, 'God you're a pain in the backside.'

But Adam just smiled, 'Yes, I know I am,' he said.

Katy Ritsos sighed. 'It's my mother, she's had another stroke.'

Adam looked at her, he could see the strain in her eyes.

'I'm so sorry, Katy,' he said, 'I really am.'

She looked up and managed a slight smile.

'Thanks,' she said. And then she looked at him again. 'I really mean it, thanks, Adam.'

'Hey,' he said to her, 'it must be tough. How is she?'

'Not bad really, I suppose. She's had another slight stroke, and my dad's looking after her. But he's not in the best of health either, and I worry. And I keep wondering if I should just pack everything up here and move back home. It's just that I've worked so hard at this job and, well you know what I mean.'

'I do,' said Adam. 'And what does your father say? Have you spoken to him?'

'Oh yes. He's having none of it of course. He's told me to stick with my career.' And then she sort of laughed. 'He's told me that if I come home he won't let me in the house. They're Greek, they're all crazy,'

Adam looked at her. 'You don't have to tell me about that,' he said.

She looked at him. And then she took another sip of her brandy.

'Oh yeah, I bet you'd be glad to see the back of me, really.'

Adam looked back at her, and he thought about it for a moment.'

'Do you know something, Katy, I actually wouldn't. I know we have arguments all the time, but in truth, half of what you say is right. And I'm actually having to learn that the hard way'.

She looked at him and suddenly laughed, and then she raised her arms in mock derision.

'Hallelujah, the Englishman, he finally admits he's wrong. There 'must' be a god.'

It was Adam's turn to laugh. 'Okay, okay,' he said, 'I'll give you that one.'

And so their conversation started, and they sat there for the next two hours, they discussed family, they discussed everything really. And at the end of it all, Adam realized that he could have possibly misjudged Miss Katy Ritsos. She was actually a very strong and independent woman who'd had to fight her way to the top of her own personal tree.

And then she looked up at the clock on the wall, it was past eight thirty and they'd drank all the brandy.

'Oh hell,' she said, 'look at the time. I need to get home, I've got an early morning flight to catch tomorrow to Pasadena. I'm going back home for two or three days to see my parents.'

And then she suddenly realized something.

'Hey, you need me to sign these papers. Do you want to sign them now and get them out of the way?'

Adam looked at her in amazement.

'Hey, hey Miss Ritsos. Don't you be going soft on me here. You could be signing anything.'

She shrugged, but then she smiled. 'Yes, you're right. I must be losing my mind. I blame the brandy.'

'There's no rush,' he said to her. When are you actually back here in the office?

'Oh...I fly back Monday night. I'll be back in here on Tuesday morning.'

'Okay then,' he said, 'we'll sort it all out next week.' And then he glanced at his watch.

'Hey it's getting late. I'll ring a cab and drop you off first, okay.'

Roughly half an hour later, the taxi they were in stopped outside Katy's block of apartments, she lived just outside Greenwich Village.

'Will you be okay,' he asked her, 'do you want me to walk you in?'

'No, no I'll be alright,' she replied, And then she looked at him.

'Thank you, Adam,' she said to him. 'You've got me through a rough night, I mean it, thank you,'

'It's not been a problem, Katy, it hasn't. I've enjoyed talking to you tonight.'

She got out of the taxi and said goodnight.

'Have a safe journey,' he replied. And then the taxi drove him home.

On the Saturday morning, Norman Roth's two technical experts were let into the bank's offices. They went over to Tony Becker's computer and switched it on. It didn't take them long to figure out what had happened, after all, they were experts. The computer had been wiped totally clean, there was nothing on the hard drive at all. They would file a report and sent it off to Norman Roth's office on the Monday morning.

Although actually, it was all too late.

When Monday morning finally arrived, Tony Becker didn't. But in truth, hardly anyone noticed that he wasn't even in the office. Tony Becker was that sort of guy. But Reza noticed. He mentioned it to Paul Maynard, but Paul just shrugged, non-committal as usual. Reza then quietly logged on to Tony's computer, but he was one again presented with just a blank screen.

Reza was slightly concerned. It was all a bit of a mystery.

Lunchtime loomed ever closer, and Paul Maynard just knew that Reza would start to pester him again. So he picked up the phone and rang Adam's office.

'Hi pal,' he said, as Adam answered. 'Listen, I know this morning you said that you'd probably have to miss lunch, but you've got to help me out here. Tony's not turned in and Reza's beginning to hover. I can't handle lunch with him on my own, I'm likely to throttle the annoying little bastard.'

Adam burst out laughing. It wasn't like Paul to be so overtly outspoken.

'How come Tony Becker's not in?' he asked casually.

'Don't know,' Paul replied, 'he's just not turned in.'

On hearing this, Adam gave a sigh of relief. Yes, in that case he'd go to lunch with them. It would actually make a nice change. He was getting sick of eating in his office, alone.

And he'd not heard anything from Norman Roth either. Apparently Roth was over in Los Angeles for a few days on business.

The three of them met up. They went down to the Esplanade again, apparently some new 'designer' burger place had just opened there and Reza had heard about it and wanted to try it out. So obviously, they had to go. In the end, and after looking through the restaurant's extensive menu, Adam and Paul plumped for two of their everyday, normal burgers with fries. The very enthusiastic waiter was suddenly less than enthused. Reza ordered something that was laced with coriander and paprika, along with a fancy salad.

As they sat there waiting for their food, Reza made an announcement.

'Okay guys, what are you doing tomorrow, anything or nothing?'

'Why?' asked Paul Maynard, rather hesitantly.

Reza laughed, 'Because, my friends, it's my birthday.'

Adam saw the look on Paul's face, and he had to stop himself from laughing.

'Is it really?' said Adam, in mock surprise.

'Yes it is,' said Reza. 'And I want us all to go out and have a nice lunch somewhere, actually I've already found a place. And then after work, we can all go out for a drink. Adam, you must invite Joanne too. And Paul, no surprises please, unless of course you want to buy a cake. That would be nice.

'In your dreams,' said Paul.

Tony Becker had been in the Cayman Islands for just two days.

The Caymans themselves actually consist of three islands, Grand Cayman being the largest. Tony had booked himself into the prestigious 'Cayman Club' in George Town for a week, but he might decide to stay longer. And if things went according to plan, he would rent himself an apartment somewhere, and stay for as long as it suited him. After all, there were worse places to have to live in luxury.

And now it was Monday. And Tony Becker was on his way to the Fidelity Trust National Bank. His funds were now safely deposited there. But maybe not for long, and so Tony Becker had a plan.

When Becker had first 'invented' Woodvale Investments, he decided that he may need a 'safety valve', just in case anything went wrong. And that 'safety valve' was the bogus account that he had set up for himself at First Global. It was easy enough of course, for him.

The account was opened under the name, 'Tony Decker'. Tony thought that was quite humorous, and clever. The names 'Becker' and 'Decker' might only be a couple of letters apart. But in the world of computers, it was a million miles.

Then he'd deposited five thousand dollars into the account, just to keep it 'fluid',

And now he was going to transfer seven of his eight million dollars back into his bogus account at First Global in New York, to his account registered to 'Tony Decker'.

And if Norman Roth and his cronies every obtained the legal power to open the Woodvale Investment account, here in the Caymans, they would only get their hands on the remainder of his money. And there would be even less there, if Tony decided to stay here long term.

Yes, while Norman Roth was searching the Cayman Islands for Woodvale's missing cash, it would all be back there in New York, right under Norman Roth's smart-arsed, stupid nose.

And that one thought alone, made Tony Becker smile.

Back in New York, and with Tony Becker's timely absence. Adam had asked Paul and Reza if they felt like having a drink after work. They did, and it was organized. So they all met up later at a place called 'The Brew House Bar', it was one of their local haunts, and Joanne joined them. She sat herself down next to Adam of course.

'I actually nipped into your office on Friday night,' he said to her, 'at about six o'clock. I was going to take you for a drink but you'd already left. But anyway, I had to deliver some papers to Katy Ritsos, so I ended up talking to her.

'Oh right,' said Joanne, 'yes, I finished early. I was tired. I went home and had a shower and a glass of wine and had an early night.'

Reza looked over at her. 'That's the first sign of old age, Joanne,' he interrupted, and then he again laughed at his own joke.

But actually, Joanne had been out on a date. She hadn't stayed in.

It had only been a casual sort of thing, some guy she'd met at the gym. They went out for a meal, but unfortunately for Joanne, he seemed to be more interested in his own body than in hers, and all he did all evening was talk about his own fitness regime. At the end of the night, he'd put her in a taxi and sent her home.

'And could he see her again?'

'Of course he could'...not.

It had been a date though, and the reason why..?

Because she couldn't just wait around for Adam Tyler forevermore, or could she?

At the mention of Katy Ritsos's name, Joanne laughed.

'How did you go on with Katy then, another hour of aggravation?'

Adam smiled, and he thought about Katy Ritsos for a moment. But he didn't say anything.

The all drank a bit too much. Adam ended up with his arm around Joanne, as usual. And at the end of the evening he and Joanne shared a taxi together and he took her home. In the back of the taxi they continued to laugh at each other's silly comments.

'I'm really drunk,' she said to him, 'really, really drunk, I need to sleep it off.'

And when they reached her apartment she got out of the cab laughing, and then she waved him goodnight. The taxi waited, just to make sure she got into her apartment building safely.

In the front of the cab, the taxi driver had been listening to their conversations, and he was quite surprised that Adam wasn't following her in there. He knew he would have.

'I'll tell you something, man,' he said to Adam. 'She is one beautiful lady,' he remarked.

Adam watched her go. 'Yes, she certainly is,' he replied. And he smiled.

Adam watched Joanne disappear into her apartment block.

Yes, she was beautiful, and she was absolutely stunning. And now he had a decision to make.

When he'd arrived back to his own apartment, Reza Mastoor had been getting ready to go to bed. And it was as he was emptying his pockets of his money and his keys and his mobile phones that he noticed that there was a message on the phone that he used when he spoke to his father. He looked at it and he frowned. It was a simple text message, but explicit...

'...Do not go into work tomorrow...Repeat...Do not go into work tomorrow...There will be a problem.'

Reza read the message twice. And then he went sick to the pit of his stomach.

Oh dear god, they'd been caught. Someone must have finally discovered the 'little bird' programme, or maybe they'd found all the false bank accounts and with it all the money that was flitting in and out and finally making its way back to Saudi Arabia, and to an unknown source.

What was he going to do?

Reza sat on the edge of his bed and he ran his hand over his head. What was going to happen? Would the bank have him arrested? Would the police roll up tomorrow and drag him off, or would it be something a bit more subtle? Surely the bank wouldn't want all that bad publicity, would they, or wouldn't they? He didn't know.

And then it struck him that actually, he didn't have the full facts. He needed to speak to his father to find out just what was going on. So he picked up the phone that he used for that one purpose, and he made the international phone call, and he listened as it began to ring.

But there was no answer. He rang again, but there was still no answer, and then again several times during the night, but there was nothing, no reply, not even a text.

Reza Mastoor was stressed. He'd hardly slept, and he kept reading his father's warning.

'...Do not go into work tomorrow...Repeat...Do not go into work tomorrow...

There will be a problem...'

Reza lay there in bed. He was going to go to prison, he knew he was. And then his thoughts returned to Suzy...and his kids.

The next morning, Tuesday, Adam and Paul made their way to work together, as usual.

And on that particular morning, they didn't have to stop at Katz's Deli because they were having a birthday lunch for Reza Mastoor.

And Paul Maynard was not a happy man.

'All this fuss about that jumped up bloody idiot,' he remarked. 'He always has to be the centre of attention. You know what he's like.'

Adam wasn't entirely happy either. There was every chance of him having to finally meet up with Tony Becker today, and he

256

wasn't looking forward to that. But he'd had to think it over. He could have course, just not turned up for the lunchtime celebrations, he could have feigned some excuse. But Adam realized that at some point they would all have to meet up, and so he might as well get it over with. He'd also promised Norman Roth not to do or say anything, and with that thought in his head, he wondered when Roth would be returning from Los Angeles.

However, at that moment, Adam Tyler had far more important things on his mind.

They arrived early, it was just approaching eight fifteen. And as they walked towards their building, Adam turned to Paul.

'You go in,' he said to Paul, 'I've just got a quick errand to do.'

'Okay,' Paul replied. 'I'll see you at 'the lunch.' And he raised his eyebrows.

Adam laughed.

And as Paul made his way into work, Adam turned and walked off in the opposite direction. He quickly made his way over to Liberty Street, to 'Yasmine's Flowers', a well known New York florist. Once inside he bought a dozen beautiful red roses, which were expertly put together as a bouquet by the young lady who worked there. They looked stunning.

Adam then made his way into work.

Reza Mastoor sat in his apartment in his underwear. He was drinking yet another cup of coffee as he half heartedly watched the TV. He'd been drinking coffee for most of the night really, along with trying to contact his father, but still to no avail. He looked at his watch, it was nearly eight thirty. He should have been in work. He should be there, doing his job.

And now this. And he cursed his father for ever implicating him in all of this deceit. He was going to lose everything and he could end up in prison. And once again he thought about Suzy and the kids. He'd been thinking about them for most of the night.

Then suddenly, his phone rang. and Reza spun around. But damn it, it was the wrong phone.

It was his own phone, the phone that he used every day. He picked it up. Would it be work? Would it be the bank wanting to have a word with him?

And so he turned down the TV before he spoke.

'Hello?' he said.

'Surprise..!!'...a voice shouted down the line, and then...'Happy Birthday.!!'...and then he heard his children's voices, 'Happy Birthday, Daddy, Happy Birthday..!'

It was Suzy and the kids.

Reza laughed. 'Hi there,' he said. 'Yes, happy birthday to me.'

'Where are you?' she asked. 'We're waiting for you.'

Reza stopped for a moment, and he stopped laughing.

'What do you mean?'

'We're here, we're waiting for you. Where are you?'

'I don't understand?' Reza was confused.

'It's all organized, Reza. We're here waiting for you. Have you not spoken to your boss?'

'Suzy...where are you?'

'We're here at the bank. Well, not 'at' the bank. We're upstairs at the restaurant, we're at the 'Windows on the World' restaurant. Me and the kids. We've organized a birthday breakfast for you. It's all been organized with your boss. You don't have to work today. We're all going to have the day out in the city to celebrate, and then we can all stay at the apartment tonight. Have you not spoken to your boss, Reza?'

Reza was flabbergasted. This was without doubt, the last thing he needed. And suddenly, he had to think quickly. He had to think of something, very quickly.

He falsely laughed down the phone.

'You're not going to believe this, but I'm still at the apartment, I'm just leaving actually. I've overslept, Suzy, I was out with 'the gang' last night.'

'Oh Reza,' she said down the phone, 'you're hopeless.'

'Don't worry,' he said to her, 'I'm on my way right now,'

Another lie.

Reza put down the phone and he hurried into the bathroom for a quick shower. Hopefully the warm water would make his brain start to work.

He stood under the shower for five minutes, trying to find some respite under the warm spray. He would have to meet up with Suzy and the kids. But he couldn't go into the office, he would give that a wide berth. He'd meet up with Suzy and the kids in the restaurant and hopefully they'd get through the breakfast without any interruptions, and then he'd get them out of there and into the city for the day. Whatever was going to happen, he would have to face it tomorrow.'

The 'Windows on the World' was the world renowned restaurant on the 107th floor at the top of the North Tower of the World Trade Center. From there, there were spectacular views over Manhattan and the Statue of Liberty and all the way down to the Hudson River.

Reza's children absolutely loved it there.

Adam Tyler made his way back to work. But he wasn't going into his own office. Not yet.

He got into the elevator and pressed the button for the 95th floor. In less than a minute, he was there. He got out of the lift and walked down the corridor. There in front of him was Joanne's office, number 106. He inwardly smiled, and then he shrugged. She was a lovely girl, she was beautiful, and a beautiful friend. But he'd made a decision. And with that, he turned right and made his way down the corridor to Katy Ritsos's office, and once there, he tapped lightly on the door.

'Come in,' Katy called out.

Adam opened the door and walked in, He stood there, his case in one hand, the bouquet of red roses in the other. And Katy just stood there too, as she stared at him.

'I need to talk to you,' he said to her.

She looked at him. 'Yes?' she said quietly.

'I want to take you out, Katy,' he said, 'I want us to have a relationship, and I want us to make something of it...and really make something of it.'

And there it was, he'd said it all. Just two short sentences.

Katy walked straight over to him. She'd been thinking about him all weekend.

She looked up at him before she spoke, and then...'I thought you'd never ask.'

And with that, he leant forward to kiss her.

It was 8-46 in the morning, on the Tuesday of the eleventh of September, and the year 2001.

And as Adam Tyler leant forward to kiss Miss Katy Ritsos for the very first time, and with it all the promise of a future, there was an explosion that they would never even hear.

At that moment, the hijacked Boeing767, American Airlines Flight11, smashed into the side of the North Tower of the World Trade Centre, between the floors 93 to 99.

Being on the 95th floor, the offices of Cantor Fitzsimons were engulfed in the fireball caused by the explosion. Adam Tyler, Katy Ritsos, Joanne Berkeley, along with the whole of the Cantor Fitzsimons staff who were working there that day, were all killed instantly.

Two floors down, Paul Maynard, along with everyone else who was working there at the First Global Bank were also killed.

For all of them, it was over.

Reza Mastoor was just coming out of the bathroom, he was rubbing his wet hair with a towel when he glanced up at the TV. Something had happened. And then he looked on in absolute horror. He almost ran to the TV to turn up the sound. There'd been a terrible accident. Somehow, a plane had flown into the North Tower of the World Trade Centre. How on earth had it happened? And then Reza's phone began to ring.

He snatched it up immediately. It was Suzy.

'Reza,' she screamed. 'Something's happened, there's been an explosion. There's smoke everywhere, and the lifts have stopped working. I think we're stuck up here. I don't know what's happening, I don't know what to do, and everyone's panicking.'

'Suzy, Suzy...there's been an accident, a planes hit the side of the building. Just stay where you are and wait for the fire people. Listen to me. I'm on my way. Look after the boys. I'm on my way right now.'

Reza threw his clothes on, and then he ran out of the building and to flag down a cab.

One stopped almost immediately, and Reza flung himself into the back.

'World Trade Centre, as quick as you can, buddy, I'll pay you double.'

The driver sped away. 'You know there's been a bad accident down there,' he said, 'a plane's hit the building.'

'Yeah, yeah, I know,' said Reza, 'my families down there.'

The driver glanced at Reza through his mirror and he saw the expression. And suddenly, he tried to get past the slowing traffic a little bit faster.

And then, within just a couple a minutes, an announcement was made to the driver through his radio.

The driver just uttered the words, 'Oh my god,' and again, he looked back at Reza through his mirror.

'What's wrong, what's happened?' Reza asked him.

'Another plane...another plane has flown into the South Tower.'

There was a moments silence before the driver spoke again.

'This...this it isn't an accident. It's an attack. Someone's attacking the World Trade Centre.'

And with those words, Reza Mastoor felt like he'd been hit by a hammer. He just sat there in the back of the cab, fear, panic and stunned with the realization that he knew what all of this was about. Yes he did. And in his mind, all he could think of was his father's warning.

'...Do not go into work tomorrow...There will be a problem.'

The traffic was quickly becoming a nightmare as the City rolled to a complete standstill and the junctions slowly became gridlocked. Reza sat there in dismay as he saw what was happening around him, and in the end, his taxicab came to a complete stop. They'd been travelling for over half an hour, but were still a long way out. In the far distance, plumes of smoke that were obviously coming from the burning towers could be seen against the clear blue sky.

Suddenly the driver turned around to face Reza.

'Hey man, I'm really sorry, but I think I'm wasting your time here. I just can't see us making it to the Trade Center, all the traffic's against us.'

Reza had already realized what he was being told, he felt paralysed with fear. But those words from the driver instilled something in him. He got straight out of the cab and stuffed a wad of money into the driver's hand, and then he set off running. He had to get himself over there, he had too.

And then his phone rang again. And Reza stopped running. He pulled the phone out of his pocket, it had to be Suzy, it had to be.

'Hello.!!' he shouted down the phone.

The reply was...'Daddy.!'

It was Robert...it was his son.

'Robert. Where's your mum?' Reza shouted.

'Daddy...she's collapsed, Andrew has too. It's all the smoke, we can't breathe, Daddy.'

And then his son started to cough.

Reza wanted to scream.

'Robert'..he shouted down the phone again...'Robert'. But all he could hear was his son coughing violently. And then there was nothing, nothing at all.

'Robert,' he shouted frantically. But the line had gone silent.

Reza began to run, and as he ran he cried in desperation. And it took him nearly half an hour, but Reza could now see the Towers in the near distance. They were both burning furiously. He was exhausted, but he had to keep going. And then from nowhere he heard a sound. A deep rumbling that seemed to vibrate in the air. And as he looked up, he watched in horror as the South Tower suddenly collapsed into huge clouds of rubble and dust. Reza simply couldn't believe what he was seeing. This was impossible. It just couldn't be happening.

He began to run again. But he was going against the tide of people who were running in the opposite direction. On and on he tried to push his way through, but in the end the police stopped him. He tried to remonstrate with them and then he started to fight with one officer. And then, suddenly, there was another grinding rumble, and Reza watched the North Tower collapse right in front of his eyes. There were clouds of dust everywhere, it was blinding, no one could see. And at that moment, Reza just slowly sank to his knees and crumbled to the floor. His darling wife, and his beautiful, beautiful children. They were all dead.

He sat there on the pavement for over an hour. His head in his hands and covered in the grey black dust. He was lost.

Everything was lost. Everyone was lost. His family, his friends, they were all lost to him. If only he'd known.

But there were things that Reza would never know, and neither would his father.

Jabra Hasan al-Mastoor would never know that because of his involvement and his failure to fully inform his son, he had actually caused the deaths of his own two grandsons.

And Reza...'Reza Hasan al-Mastoor', would never know that his brother, Khalil, had been one of the terrorists that had hijacked the plane that flew into the North Tower, and in doing so had killed his brother's wife and his own two nephews.

And for Reza, he'd lost everyone he'd ever loved, his mother, his brother, and his wife and his children. And all in the name of a religion.

And on that terrible day, another three thousand lives were also lost. Three thousand innocent lives and three thousand good and honest, and hard working people.

And for what, nothing would ever be resolved.

And like the ripples in a pond, those deaths would go on to affect many thousands of other lives, all of those families, and those friends, all who were left behind and forever wondering. Why..?

Reza Mastoor would go on to have a complete nervous breakdown. His life would never be the same again.

And a year later, the police broke into his house over in New Haven. Reza Mastoor was dead. He'd never really recovered from the breakdown and he'd hung himself.

Chapter 10

Six months later.

Tony Becker was living a pretty good lifestyle. He had plenty of money in the bank, well in two banks actually. And really, he thanked his lucky stars for the decision that he'd had to make. In retrospect, if Tony had stayed where he was at First Global and had tried to 'weather the storm', he would now be dead, there was no doubt about it. He would have been in the office with Paul Maynard and Reza Mastoor, along with the rest of the clowns who worked there and he would have burned to death.

Ah well, there you go. He'd never really liked any of them anyway, and let's face it, none of them really liked him either.

And really, everything had worked out pretty well for him. And although he wasn't absolutely sure, he could only assume that back in the USA, everyone must now think that he was dead. Even his stupid ex-wife must have thought that Tony had died, along with everyone else who worked for the First Global Bank in the North Tower.

So here he was, now invisible, or 'persona non grata', as he liked to think of himself.

And his lifestyle had changed too. Once he'd settled in Grand Cayman, he'd rented a decent house, just on the outskirts of George Town, and all very private. And that suited Tony too, living in George Town made it easier for him to reach the Casino's. And though he wasn't a total beach lover, Tony had gone out and bought himself an unassuming but rather 'cool' motor bike, for the days that he fancied dipping his toes into the warm waters of the Caribbean Sea.

Yes, it was all very low key, and he liked that. Plus, along with this change of lifestyle, he'd also had a change to his own personal style. Gone was the unkempt hairstyle and the silly moustache. After being in Grand Cayman for two or three weeks and observing some rather smart people, he'd looked at himself in the mirror and had finally come to the conclusion that he looked like an idiot. So he'd wandered around George Town until he found a stylish looking 'designer' hair salon, where he put his faith and his head, in the very capable hands of a very attractive girl called 'Samantha'.

When she'd enquired, he'd just told her to do 'whatever she wanted'.

Anything would look better than the way he looked right now. Samantha agreed, and then she'd worked a miracle. She shaved off his moustache and had then given Tony a very sharp razored haircut. Tony had been amazed, in fact he'd had trouble even recognizing himself.

And now he went back to the salon every two weeks to 'maintain his style', and he now called Samantha...'Sam'.

Gone too were the dowdy clothes. Along with his new motorbike, Tony had also decided to become 'cool.' And now, during the day he wandered around in smart Bermuda shorts along with 'not to bright' Hawaiian shirts, with good sandals and classic Ray Bans. If he was perusing the bars in George Town in the evenings he would wear some light linen suit with an open shirt. And if he went to the Casinos, he would wear a sharper suit altogether. Somehow it gave him more respect, and he liked it when people called him 'sir' or 'Mr Becker'. Especially when it was one of the dark haired, dark skinned women that made him tick. They may have been high class prostitutes, but what the hell.

Yeah, life was pretty good.

And in his mind, he'd considered that he could easily live this lifestyle, possibly indefinitely.

Maybe...maybe not. Tony Becker's only problem would be repetition, and then boredom.

Because somewhere deep inside him, was the need to do something with all of his millions, yes, those millions of dollars that were safely sitting in his bank account at the First Global Bank.

Tony Becker had always had a yearning to build his own 'little empire'. He wanted the prestige of it all, or maybe was it just greed? But at the moment, everything was good...

So what the hell.

However, life has the habit of tripping you up sometimes, and just when you least expect it.

One afternoon, Tony Becker had been wandering around George Town, visiting his usual watering holes. There was a good selection of bars there and Tony liked to meander from one to another and talk to the different people drinking there, in fact, he'd got himself quite a decent little social life going on. And for the first time in his life, people seemed to like him. He was almost on the verge of being 'popular'.

It was Tony's habit to ride his motor bike into town and park it around the back of his favourite bar, 'The Green Dog', down on the Harbour Road. The owner of the bar, 'Ronny' didn't have a problem with that. After all, during a normal week, Tony Becker put more than enough coin through Ronny's till. And Tony could park his bike there all year long if he liked. Ronny was on a roll.

Tony would always have his first drink, or two, at the Green Dog. It was great bar which faced directly onto the main Harbour Road, and there was always a great mix of people either in the bar or walking past it, and that was always good for easy conversations. From there he would have an 'hour or two' around the other bars, but he would always end up back at the Green Dog. He liked it there, and he liked Ronny too. He was a pretty decent guy.

So on that particular day, it was about four o' clock in the afternoon, and Tony had already done the rounds. And he had returned once more and was now sitting comfortably in the Green Dog. He was facing the road and watching the ladies walk by. It was nice, and Tony had been chatting to several of the regulars, including Ronny, who was there working behind the bar that afternoon.

Tony Becker ordered himself another bottle of beer, and then he took off his sunglasses and rubbed his eyes. As he sat there he watched the passing traffic, which was slowly starting to build as people finished their working day and began to make their way home. And just like Tony, to probably have a cold bottle of beer once they got there. It was the Caribbean way. Tony liked to do this, because occasionally some car would slow to a halt, and then somebody that he knew would exchange a few friendly words.

Yes it was the Caribbean way, and all very laid back, and Tony liked that.

266

It made him feel good that he 'knew' people.

And so he sat there as the passing traffic slowed, and as he glanced down the line of cars, he spotted a huge black Mercedes-Benz limousine in the queue. It was probably on its way from the airport where it had picked up some VIP or other. Maybe it was somebody famous, maybe even a film star or some Pop singer. They got all types here in the Caymans, it was a favourite haunt for the rich and the famous, and the unscrupulous.

Tony looked at the car, he was always interested to see if some celebrity had arrived. The car moved up a couple of spaces, and then stopped. And then it moved up another space and stopped exactly opposite the Green Dog Bar. Tony looked to see who was in the car, there was a man sitting in the back, and he was on his own. And for a moment Tony looked at the man and he did somehow recognize the man's profile. Tony thought that it must be some actor or other, and he tried to place him. But he was having difficulty. And then the man slowly turned to look across at the bar. And he stared directly at Tony.

And Tony Becker went rigid.

Because the man sitting in the back of the limousine, was Norman Roth.

They both looked at one another for only a matter of seconds, and then the limousine moved off again. But Tony Becker just sat there in a state of disbelief. He just couldn't understand it.

Norman Roth, surely he was dead, or should be dead. Was he not in his office when 9/11 hit the building? Norman Roth was his nemesis. And Tony Becker suddenly panicked, the limousine had moved on, but Tony could still see it and at any moment he expected the rear door to open and Norman Roth to emerge and come looking for him.

Tony grabbed up his sunglasses and he turned to Ronny.

'Hey Ronny, if anyone comes in here looking for me, you don't know me, okay?' he said, rather desperately. And along with that he passed several large bills over the bar.

Ronny just nodded appreciatively. He'd seen it all before, of course he had.

Tony walked quickly around to the back of the bar and immediately started his motor bike and then he rode straight home. Norman Roth must have come to find him. He must know.

And now Tony needed to think. Tony needed a plan.

Norman Roth had been sitting in the back of the limousine. He'd landed in Grand Cayman an hour ago, because he was attending a Banker's Convention that was being held there this year at the luxurious Ritz-Carlton Hotel complex. In the past, the same convention had always been held in New York, with its obvious connections to Wall Street. But this year it was deemed inappropriate, due to the disaster that had left the city reeling and broken.

The terrorist attack on 9/11 had severely damaged First Global. A lot of its talent had worked at the New York office.

And since then, well firstly they'd had to relocate, and then Roth had spent most of the last six months trying to recruit personnel of a similar standard as those who'd died, but it had been hard. The well-oiled machine had been truly broken.

And now this convention. It was a time to rebuild and a time to rebuild confidence. Norman Roth had been asked to speak at the convention, and on the flight over there he'd been putting the finishing touches to his speech. The theme being that there should be more integration between the banks and that there should be a greater sharing of information, all for the good of everyone. His speech of course was also a little sideswipe at the Cayman Island's own banking system, which was one of the main culprits.

And as Roth was being driven from the airport and to his hotel, he'd sat there in deep thought, he kept running things through his mind and was trying to put everything in place.

Yes, it had been a difficult time.

And then his limousine had slowed down as it got stuck in the traffic. Norman Roth shook his head. As usual, he couldn't do a damn thing about it. And as he sat there, he'd glanced out of the window. There was a man sitting there at a bar, looking directly at him. The man was staring intently, almost strangely, it was a bit disconcerting really. And after a couple of seconds, Norman Roth had looked away as the limousine had set off once more. But for some reason, Roth still held the man's face in his mind. It was all a bit strange. Did he know the man, no? No he didn't.

But there was just something about him. Roth then dismissed it, and then he thought about the theme of his speech again. There would obviously be 'invited guests' from the Cayman Island's many banks, who would also be attending the convention. He wondered if any of them would take any notice of his speech, probably not. It wouldn't be in there interest, would it? And one of the main reasons for his speech, was over his past frustrations in dealing with the Cayman Islands banking system, and in particular with the Fidelity Trust National Bank.

His quest to find out about the infamous 'Woodvale Investments' account had hit a brick wall. There was no way that they were going to divulge any information about the person behind it.

And then, Norman Roth froze. He couldn't believe it. It couldn't be, it simply couldn't be.

The man back there at the bar who was staring back at him, it was a different haircut, and he'd shaved, but Norman Roth remembered that face. It was without doubt, Tony Becker.

Roth shouted to his driver, 'Stop here.' And then he grabbed the door handle and jumped out of the car and he ran back to the bar where he'd just seen Becker. But Tony Becker had gone. He'd disappeared. Norman Roth desperately looked around, but no, Becker had vanished.

He turned to the bartender.'

'Hey, there was guy here, just a minute ago. Do you know where he went?

The barman just shrugged, vaguely.

'Do you know anything about him?' asked Roth. 'Do you know where he lives?

But the barman just looked at him.

'Hey pal, we get loads in here.'

And that was it.

Norman Roth went back to his limousine, which was now holding up the traffic. And the people in the cars stuck behind it were becoming more than slightly annoyed. Roth got back into the car and they sped away.

But Norman Roth just sat there, stunned. 'My god...'

He'd always assumed that Tony Becker had been killed, along with the rest of the First Global Bank staff. Roth himself had been in Los Angeles on the day of the attack, and he'd always accepted just how lucky he'd been. But now this...Becker. And so Becker obviously hadn't been there on the day. And then Norman Roth thought back to the last time he'd actually spoken to Tony Becker, it had been on the Thursday before the attack.

So what had happened?

And then Norman Roth shook his head as he suddenly figured it out. He'd been right, and Adam Tyler had been right. It 'had' been Tony Becker who was behind the 'Woodvale' scandal. And after that meeting with him, Becker must have decided to run. And where did he run to? Well, the Cayman Islands of course, because that was where his money was.

Norman Roth sat back in the seat of his air-conditioned vehicle. He took a deep breath, and then he sighed. And what could he do about it? Actually, nothing. He couldn't find Becker, and Becker had probably changed his identity anyway. And if he went to the local police they wouldn't want to know, or even get involved. And as for the Fidelity Trust National Bank, well, forget it. No, there wasn't a damn thing he could do. Other than relate the tale to one or two of his old banking associates, once he was back in the USA.

Norman Roth may not have been able to do a 'damn' thing. But Tony Becker wasn't to know that, was he?

He'd gone straight back home that afternoon and had spent most of the rest of the day, pacing the house. By midnight, he'd made a plan. He would run, again.

After all this, he wasn't going to go prison.

The next morning he made several phone calls. An hour later, he got on his motor bike and went over to the Fidelity Trust National Bank. Whilst there he withdrew ten thousand dollars in cash from his account, then he transferred the remaining money over to his First Global account in New York. Then he went back home and rang the taxi that would take him, along with his two suitcases, to the airport.

From there, he would then get on an aeroplane bound for Southern Spain, to Malaga.

Several hours later, Tony Becker stepped out of the plane and into the bright Spanish sunshine. He smiled to himself. He'd just managed to swap one sunny destination for another. He walked through the airport after clearing customs and then he hailed a taxi.

'Where too, signor?' asked the driver.

'Take me to Marbella,' Tony Becker replied.

Five months later, and Tony Becker considered himself safe, more than safe really.

And Tony had continued with his lifestyle. Marbella was full of clubs and bars and good Casinos, and those dark haired Spanish women that he really did like.

Tony was living in a Penthouse apartment on the outskirts of town, just between Marbella and the resort of Puerto Banus. It suited Tony, because Puerto Banus was also a very stylish town, and just like himself, it was full of millionaires.

Along with that, Tony had bought himself a Porsche, and he was generally looked upon as someone who was 'sharp with money'. Something that he'd enthusiastically promoted, and from there, and mainly because of that, he'd made a good circle of acquaintances who liked to call 'his friends'.

And it was in talking to these 'friends' that Tony had become interested in the property market. Everyone there seemed to be in on it, and they were all making a fortune, apparently.

After all, the property market along the whole of Spain's southern coast was on the rise as half of Europe seemed to want a piece of the sun.

Yes, Tony was interested. And after all, he was sitting on all of that money which was doing nothing, absolutely nothing at all. And along with that, this could finally be his chance of building that 'little empire' that he'd always dreamt about. And if all went to plan, the empire might not be all that little either. And suddenly, Tony Becker had aspirations of becoming a property developer. He'd spoken to several different people for advice, and had subtly let it be known that although he was 'cash rich', he was nobody's fool either.

And then one of his 'friends', a man called Luis Vega, who owned a chain of Estate Agents along the coast, mentioned that he knew just the man who Tony should speak to.

Luis Vega knew someone who had made a fortune through property. In fact, Luis Vega had sold a lot of those properties for him, and had made some 'seriously' good money.

Tony was quite interested, and so Luis organized an introduction.

Three days later, at five o'clock in the afternoon, Tony Becker was sitting at Sinatra's Bar in

Puerto Banus, he was drinking a Martini as he once again glanced at his watch.

At that moment, a silver grey Ferrari pulled up across from the bar and a man got out. Smartly dressed in a pale blue suit and in his early thirties, he looked over at Tony and nodded. Tony acknowledged him. And then the man walked around his car and he opened the passenger door. Out of the car stepped a woman, she was absolutely beautiful. She had the darkest brown shoulder length hair and the most exquisite features. Tony just stared at her as they both walked towards him. The woman was wearing a dark blue dress which hugged her stunning figure. He was totally entranced.

'Is it Mr Becker...Mr Tony Becker?' the man asked, and then he smiled.

'Yes...yes it is,' Tony replied, and they immediately both shook hands.

'Hi,' he said. My name is Carlos Villena...and this is my sister, Dominique...'

The End.

9 798673 238431